The Revised Life
of
Ellie Sweet

Other novels by Stephanie Morrill

THE REINVENTION OF SKYLAR HOYT

Me, Just Different
Out with the In Crowd
So Over It

The Revised Life of Ellie Sweet

STEPHANIE MORRILL

PLAYLIST

Young Adult

FICTION

The Revised Life of Ellie Sweet
© 2013 Stephanie Morrill

Cover designer: Angela Llamas

The author is represented by MacGregor Literary Inc. of Hillsboro, OR.

ISBN: 978-0-9887594-3-5

This book is a work of fiction. Names, characters, places, and incidents are the product of the author's imagination or are used fictitiously. Any resemblance to actual events, locales, or persons, living or dead, is coincidental.

For Roseanna White.
Simply put, Ellie would not have survived without you. Thank for fighting for her, even when I felt too tired to carry on, for answering my constant grammar questions, and of course, for buying that red briefcase.

Chapter 1

I'm ninety-nine percent sure the only reason I'm interested in Palmer Davis is because I know without a doubt I could never have him.

"Ellie?"

I turn from the doorway—the one Palmer stands in with Diego Ortiz—and face Lucy. "Sorry, what'd you say?"

She blinks her beautiful eyes at me, as if unable to comprehend what might have drawn my attention away from her. Lucy's accustomed to being the most captivating person in the room. "Were you able to solve number four?" She glances around the Algebra classroom, searching for Ms. Purdon, I assume.

I flip my binder to the Algebra section, unclip the homework I completed two days ago, and offer the sheet to Lucy.

She snatches it from me. "You're an angel." And she gets to work copying.

Come test time she'll be screwed, but Lucy's not the type to anticipate consequences. That's more my thing. One of the many reasons why I've been labeled *boring*.

I steal another glance at Palmer, who's digging through his backpack, still blocking the doorway. And my ability to think clearly. I look away before he catches me watching.

When the new school year arrived, so did he. Kentucky born and raised, he has a charming southern drawl I've only heard in movies. We don't get many southerners here in the California valley.

Palmer and I have had exactly two conversations. They went like this:

Palmer: Where's Lucy?
Me: Bathroom.
Palmer: Oh.
Conversation number two:

Palmer: Where's Lucy?

Me: Dentist appointment.

Palmer: Ah.

It's embarrassing how many times I've relived these. Especially because Palmer Davis isn't my type at all. Not that—being only sixteen—I've had much time to develop my type, but I know he's not it. Palmer's the kind of alpha-male hero you might be drawn to in a novel, but someone you should have the smarts to avoid in real life. He's too good looking, too smooth, too funny. I'm more into the quiet, slightly nerdy guys. Who, if they took off their glasses and unbuttoned their shirt, could possibly be Superman.

Lucy turns in her seat. With her pencil, she gives my homework an impatient tap. "Seven or a nine?"

I lean to inspect. "Seven."

"For being such a brainy chick, you sure have lousy handwriting."

"Next time I'll write clearer so it'll be easier for you to shamelessly copy."

Lucy laughs and brushes away eraser dust. "Would you?"

A loud male voice breaks into our conversation. "Wait—what'd you say, Ellie Sweet?"

I turn and look into the dark eyes of Chase Cervantes. How long has he been sitting there? And why is he looking at me with that shocked expression? Surely he of all people won't judge me for letting Lucy copy. "What, Chase?"

Even with his smirk, the hard line of his jaw sends a ripple of fear through me. "Did you just say you have a crush on Palmer Davis?"

I think my heart just stopped beating.

What on earth made him say that? Please God, tell me it only *seemed* loud. Tell me no one else heard.

But the eruption of giggles that fills the classroom is evidence otherwise.

"What are you talking about?" I intend to snap this at Chase, but my voice sounds as weak and wobbly as my knees. What would make him say such a thing? "Lucy and I were just talking about math." My voice trembles. Everyone's looking at me. Everyone.

"Yeah." Chase throws his ratty sneakers up on his desk. "As in you, plus Palmer, equals love."

I shoot Lucy a look of desperation—please validate my story!—but her head is thrown back with laughter, her expensively straightened teeth gleaming. Some best friend.

I glance at Palmer, a heart-stopping vision even under the fluorescent lights. He's still in the doorway, but he's no longer oblivious to me. Instead, it seems he's looking at me—really looking at me—for the first time.

I shrink in my chair as every flaw I'm sure he sees flits through my mind—my pale skin, my glasses, my T-shirt that reads FUTURE LIBRARIAN.

A normal guy in this situation would duck his head and mutter an unintelligible response. But Palmer isn't normal. He swaggers across the classroom, all eyes on him. Just the way he likes.

I turn away and bury my burning face into my math book. Now would be a really good time for the rapture.

In my peripherals, I see faces turn my way as Palmer slides into the empty desk behind me. He leans forward, close enough that his breathing stirs my hair and spikes my heart rate. "Hey, Sweet. Or, should I say, sweet*heart*?"

More giggling. Someone even does one of those stupid, "Woo-woo," things. Someone who I would like to personally strangle. Where is Ms. Purdon, and why isn't she here in the classroom where she belongs?

I turn halfway over my shoulder. "Palmer, I *don't* have a crush on you. I don't know why he said that." I send Chase a withering glare, but he merely chuckles and faces forward. Maddening.

Palmer clutches a hand to his heart. "Oh, sweetheart, that's painful."

Why can't he just shut up and let this blow over? Why does he have to inflame Chase's weird joke and make the humiliation worse? I flash Lucy another look, but she's looking past me, grinning at Palmer as if this whole thing is just *so funny*.

But I've known Lucy my whole life, and I see the shadow in her smile. I can practically read her thoughts. Normally Palmer sits in front of *her*. Normally he teases *her*.

As Ms. Purdon strolls through the door—about a minute too late in my opinion—the snickering fades. I mentally draft the email I'll write to Bronte once I get home. *You think you miss high school? Just wait until you hear what happened to me today . . .*

I already know how she'll respond—"use it." That's always what Bronte tells me when I talk about Lucy and my other brain-dead "friends." She tells me, "Good writers take their emotional hurts and weave them into stories."

It seems Chase Cervantes is trying to give me plenty of inspiration.

I cut him a nasty look, but he's busy listening to Ms. Purdon. Or at least pretending to do so.

I should focus too. I copy the equation Ms. Purdon has written out on the board.

There's a tap on my shoulder. I bristle, but ignore him.

Palmer inches close to my ear. "Sweetheart, can you explain this to me later? I don't understand a word she's sayin'."

"Shh," I hiss, keeping my gaze trained up front.

Someone snickers. Palmer? Diego?

Nope. It's that evil Chase Cervantes, who I will hunt down and kill when this class is over. I don't care that he towers over me, has two big brothers in jail, and has the reputation of being a thug himself. He will pay for this. Every villain in every novel I pen will have shades of Chase Cervantes.

Palmer leans close and inhales deeply. "You smell good. Like sugar and spice and everything nice."

Diego and Chase are both laughing now.

An emotion I've never experienced twists within me. It's akin to humiliation, only more. Deeper. As if I can actually feel the scars of this moment being carved on my heart.

I inhale slowly, hoping I can make the tears dissolve with sheer willpower. *I can use this*, I repeat to myself. I imagine myself sitting at my computer, my manuscript open, my fingers a blur of motion over the keyboard. *I can use this.*

Ms. Purdon turns from the board and arches her eyebrows at the silly, obnoxious children seated by me. "Something you'd like to share with us, boys?"

How will I later describe the color of red my face surely is? Poppy? Cinnabar? Cardinal?

"No thanks, ma'am." Palmer's drawl is even more pronounced, and I bet he's offering her his southern-gent smile.

But at least he decides to keep his mouth shut for the rest of the lesson.

When Ms. Purdon grants us the last ten minutes of class time to work on homework, I feel another tap on my shoulder. "Can I borrow your calculator, sweetheart?"

Lucy's giggle sounds forced as she turns in her seat to catch Palmer's eye. "Oh, Palmer, leave poor Ellie alone."

I hold my calculator over my shoulder. "Only if you stop calling me sweetheart."

"Of course." He snatches it from my grasp. "Whatever you want, darlin'."

Lucy's laugh is airy, and she flips her sheet of dark hair over her shoulder as she turns back to her homework.

I face him then, mind full of retorts. His gray eyes are alight with mischief, challenging me. As I'm debating between insults or a plea to shut up, Palmer flashes me That Smile, effectively wiping my brain of all intelligent thought.

I do an about-face before he notices my eyes have turned into throbbing cartoon hearts.

Fortunately, this is our last class together today. Which means when Palmer returns my calculator with a wink and a, "Thanks, sweetheart," it'll be the last I suffer.

What isn't so fortunate is that Chase hightails it out of the room before I have the opportunity to slap that smirk off his face.

Lucy's giggle still has an edge to it. "Well, that was a crazy class. I mean, what's the deal with Chase just pulling out of nowhere that you have a thing for Palmer? He must be trying to get tight with us."

I shrug and swing my backpack over my shoulder.

"But what a random thing to come up with." Lucy wraps a strand of chestnut hair around a finger as we head for English class. "I mean, why would he try to embarrass Palmer like that?"

Ouch—it'd be *embarrassing* for me to have a crush on him?

Lucy, oblivious as always, rushes on. "It obviously didn't work. Palmer is, like, impossible to throw off. He's so quick."

"Mm-hmm."

She appears to realize our conversation is one-sided. "Something wrong, El?"

I shift my backpack. "I just don't want to talk about this anymore."

Her eyes broadcast that she's floored by my reaction. "But *why?*"

"Why *would* I want to talk about it? That was . . ." The fresh wounds on my heart pulse. "It was beyond humiliating."

"Ellie, *Palmer Davis* just spent an entire class period calling you sweetheart. Any other girl in this school would kill to be you right now. *I* would kill to be you right now."

Except he was joking and we all know it. He sits by Lucy because he wants to. He sits by me to make everyone laugh.

Lucy loops her arm through mine, like best friends do on TV. With how long we've known each other, it shouldn't make me squirm inside. "*Do* you like him?"

There's that jealous edge in her voice again. What would she do if I told her the truth? I can picture her, Bianca, and Marie giggling about it over mochas. *She actually thinks she has a chance with Palmer Davis. Can you believe her?*

No, this is a secret I'm taking to the grave. It's just a little crush, anyway. It'll vanish soon. I'll make sure of it. "He's cute, I guess, but he's not exactly my type of guy."

Lucy snorts her real laugh and pulls me tighter. "Ellie Sweet, you're baffling. If you have eyes, he's your type."

Ahead of us, far enough that I'm sure he hasn't heard our conversation, I spot Palmer veering toward a classroom. Lucy notices too and waves. Palmer winks at her, but doesn't spare even a glance my direction.

Though I roll my eyes at Lucy's giggles, my chest burns with jealousy. Yep, I need to get a grip on this silly crush of mine. With a best friend like Lucy, glossy and flirtatious, I'll never be anything more than the girl on the sidelines.

The sidewalk is cluttered with clumps of Redwood High students headed for their cars, but Chase walks alone. How unfortunate for him.

I weave through the chattering cliques, a Chase-seeking missile. "Chase!" I yell when I'm close enough to catch him if he bolts.

But Chase appears to have no desire to dash.

He turns, his expression half-bored, half-amused. "Ellie Sweet." Did he just imitate Palmer's drawl?

He's broad-shouldered, solid-chested, and a good half-foot taller than me. Even now, when he seems to be somewhat entertained, the hard planes of his face remain.

In his shadow, I realize I'm glaring at him as openly as I would my brother. That's probably a bad idea, considering Chase's reputation, but I can't seem to soften. "What *was* that today?"

He blinks slow and stupid. "What?"

Seriously? He's going to pretend he doesn't know what I'm talking about? Swell. "You know what."

"I do?"

"What you said in class." I glance at the students streaming around us, but none have familiar faces. Good. "About me liking Palmer."

"That bothered you?"

My fists clench and unclench, as if there's a chance of me taking a swing at him. "You concocting a vicious lie and using it to gain attention? Yeah, that bothered me."

Chase turns his shoulder to me. "I don't know what 'concocting' means, but I get the general idea."

Chase resumes walking, and I trot along behind him. "Feel free to apologize at any time."

"Okay."

I think I actually growl. I'm a yappy terrier nipping at the heels of a dog big enough to crush me with a mere swipe of a paw. But I can't back off. "Tell me why you did it."

We've apparently arrived at his car. Something old with a logo I don't recognize. Chase gives me a wave—a kind that seems to mean "goodbye and good riddance"—and tosses his backpack into the backseat.

I plant my hands on my hips. "This isn't the end of this discussion, you know."

He shrugs. "Later, Ellie." Then he shuts himself inside the car, fires up the engine, and abandons me and my outrage here on the sidewalk.

"Was that Chase?"

I startle at Lucy's voice. She's standing there in her blue and white cheer outfit, hair done up in a long, perky ponytail. "Where'd you come from? Why aren't you at practice?"

"Cancelled—don't get me started. Were you just *yelling* at Chase? He could kill you with his bare hands, El."

I cross my arms over my chest and glare at Chase's car, idling at a red light. "I have to know why he said what he did."

"He's a guy. Who knows why he does anything? Just let it go before you get hurt." Lucy shudders. "He's a Cervantes, after all."

The reminder makes my insides shiver. "He wouldn't hurt me *here*. In daylight."

"But don't tempt him, okay?" She takes several prancing steps down the sidewalk, toward where she typically parks her car. "And who cares why he said it? You know what they say, El—any attention is good attention."

"No, that's *press*. Any press is good press."

She shrugs, waves, and bounces down the sidewalk.

Figures. Judging by how Lucy lives her life these days, she believes her false cliché. Lucy's yet to meet attention she doesn't like.

I, on the other hand, would be content to spend the rest of my days tucked behind my computer, dreaming up other worlds.

Chase revs his engine when the light turns green. Did he just wave to me as he sped off?

I watch his car fade from sight. Yes, I definitely prefer the worlds I create. I like it better when everyone plays by my rules.

Chapter 2

At home, I'm greeted by silence and my brother James's larger-than-life headshot. When Lucy comes over—or when she used to, anyway—she always sighs and blows his senior portrait a kiss. Even unnaturally close, James is perfect.

Framed beside him is the artwork from my dad's first children's book—*James*. Yes, that's right. My brother is the inspiration for James, the mischievous cow children know and love. Dad's been working on an addition to the series for a couple months now. I asked him if cow-James was ever going to get a little sister.

He had pursed his mouth as he thought. "I don't know if another sibling really fits into James's story."

Super. Thanks, Dad.

When the time comes to take my senior pictures, I've requested Mom and Dad don't waste their money. The last thing we need in this house is my goofy face plastered next to James's. So far Mom and Dad don't seem to be listening. But that's nothing new.

I go through my usual coming-home routine—drop my backpack on the floor and head for the kitchen. Mom keeps us well-stocked with what she deems "appropriate" after-school snacks. Fresh fruit, granola bars, hummus and veggie sticks. She even keeps juice boxes in the fridge, like I'm still eight.

Some days I consider digging into the ice cream instead. Or raiding the bottom shelf of the cabinet, reserved for cookies, chips, and other yummy things. But I'm a rule-follower. I grab a chilled carton of "Apple berry" and a granola bar.

I heave my backpack over my shoulder and navigate the hall to the only bedroom I've ever lived in. And it shows. The gingham ribbon that ties back my curtains matched my crib set, and the pink, wooden letters on the wall spell out the name they've never called me—Gabrielle.

I gaze at my laptop, itching to open my manuscript, to transport myself to medieval Italy, to rewrite my day as Lady Gabrielle would have handled it. She would have known how to put Chase in his place, how to laugh it off with Palmer.

I should really do homework first . . .

As I reach for my laptop, my eye catches on the gleaming red convertible pulling into Lucy's driveway—Bianca. Marie rides shotgun, finger-combing her auburn hair.

I should look away, I know, but I can't. Instead I move closer to the window.

Bianca presses the horn, a succinct *Beep!* which brings Lucy out of her house. Lucy's changed again, into a skirt that's too short for the school code. My guess is they're going for coffee in hopes of picking up boys from the community college.

Lucy's been my best friend all my life, but the four of us were total BFFs in elementary and junior high. It wasn't until last year, when we were sophomores, and they slid into the world of party dresses and strange boys buying them drinks, that things began to change. When they realized it wasn't exactly my brand of fun, invitations to hang out with them outside of school happened less and less.

Not that I blame them. Or even mind, since it was rather annoying to say no all the time.

But I like coffee. And my bedroom window overlooks the front yard. They aren't even slightly worried about me noticing and getting my feelings hurt?

Lucy stops next to the car, and her dark hair falls in a sheet down her back. Totally unfair. Even with expensive shampoos, leave-in conditioners, and a flattening iron, my hair won't do that. It won't do anything but fuzz. Which is why, as much as possible, I keep it trapped in an intentionally messy knot.

I cock my head at the scene unfolding across the street. The way Lucy has her hands on her hips, I'd guess she's arguing with them. She still does the toddler thing when she doesn't get her way—the chin juts out, her voice gets high and wobbly. While I've never actually seen it happen, I suspect she isn't above lying on the floor and screaming at the top of her lungs.

Lucy stomps a foot as she presses her cell phone to her ear. She appears to be giving Bianca and Marie quite a lecture. Weird. Bianca and Marie basically worship Lucy. The only thing the three of them ever disagree on is—

In my back pocket, my phone vibrates.

I leap out of sight, as if it's a crime to look out my bedroom window. "Hey, Lucy."

"Ellie! Hi! What are you up to?"

"Just homework."

"Oh, okay. Bianca, Marie, and I are going for a coffee. Wanna come?"

A yes sits on the end of my tongue. I could escape homework for a few hours, and maybe Bianca or Marie could help connect the dots on Chase's weirdo actions today.

But as my mouth opens to say, "Sure!" I peek around the curtain and see Bianca's face twisted into something ugly as she glares at Lucy. It would be that horrible for me to come, huh?

"I wish I could, but I have so much to do." I hope the hurt that edges my voice sounds more like regret on Lucy's end.

"Well, if you change your mind, you know where to find us. Bye!"

Lucy slides into the backseat of the car, her mouth wide with a smile, and Bianca roars off as if she's escaping something dreadful.

I turn my back to the window, eyes hot with anger and bottled-up tears.

Why am I so upset? This is nothing new. And I don't need them like I once thought I did, not now that I have medieval Italy to escape to.

I power up my laptop and pull it near. The blinking cursor feels like a warm greeting from an old friend. I read the words of my last scene, close my eyes, and brush my fingertips over the keys.

Gabrielle saw Ladies Lucia, Maria, and Bianca loitering in the square. No doubt they hoped the prince might take notice of them. How pathetic they all were, trying to gain favor with a man of no substance.

But she would have to talk to them, she supposed. Only a few minutes, and then she could steal away to be with Rafe and his mischievous gray eyes all afternoon . . .

Mom spoons green beans onto my plate like I'm three years old. "How was school?" Her every-night question.

"Good." My every-night answer.

Dad takes the green beans from Mom. "Learn anything interesting?"

His question varies. Other potentials are, "What are you guys doing in English class?" and "Did anyone offer you drugs or cigarettes today?"

"Nope."

Dad winks at me. "Another waste of a day, huh El?"

My neck tingles where Palmer's breath tickled it. "Pretty much."

"James called today." Mom punctuates this with a sigh. They've covered me and can move on to talking about the kid they actually like. "He sounds so happy in D.C. If he didn't, I couldn't stand him being so far away."

"I knew he'd do well." Dad pops a bite of baked chicken into his mouth. "He has the personality to get along in a big city."

According to my parents, James has the personality for everything. While I'd die before admitting it, I agree. Somehow James manages to float to the top of circumstances and situations, regardless of where he starts.

A trait that didn't get passed on to his little sis.

The conversation turns to my dad's work day. He's a pharmaceutical rep by day, children's book author by night. Even with how successful the James series has been, money from writing is apparently too inconsistent to depend upon.

"Oh, Ellie." Dad turns to me. "After I stopped in on some of my doctors, I went over to Visalia Coffee Company for a little pick-me-up. I saw your friends there."

Fortunately I just took a bite of bread. It'd be rude to answer with food in my mouth. By the time I swallow, I can say in an unaffected voice, "Yeah, they like that place."

Dad spears several green beans with his fork. "Did you not feel like going?"

"Too much homework."

Mom grins at Dad. "That's our girl."

I attempt a smile, then poke at my chicken. You'd think I'd be used to the gnawing guilt by now. Since Lucy and them stopped inviting me out, I've been lying about how much I need to study. Math is really the only subject where I work for my A. The rest comes naturally, as if all the information I learn in school has already been logged in my brain, and my teachers are simply recalling it.

No way am I going to tell my parents what I'm really doing during the hours I'm shut up in my room. I haven't even told Aunt Karen, and I tell her everything. Even about my crush on Palmer.

Writing began as an outlet for all those thoughts and feelings buzzing around my head. The ones nobody wanted to hear about but somehow needed to be expressed. And keeping a journal just seemed so boring when I had the option of making stuff up. So about a year ago I started taking the idiotic things Lucy, Bianca, and Marie said and put them in the mouths of Lucia, Bianca, and Maria, ladies of noble birth living in Italy circa 1410. Ladies who work hard to corrupt the reputation of Lady Gabrielle Moretti, a marked favorite of the prince, but she's far too smart and witty for them to ever get the best of her.

Yes. A total fairy tale. But way more fun than documenting my real life.

"Studying" provides a good cover for what little time I now spend with people who used to mean everything to me. For the Friday nights when my parents notice Bianca and Marie's cars parked in Lucy's driveway, and they wonder why I'm not there too.

And I can't deny that on those nights, writing feels like some form of payback. For not getting invited, for rolling their eyes when they think I can't see, and for whispering about me when they imagine I can't hear. Writing is my own sweet, silent revenge.

Chapter 3

"Hey, Kelly."

Why do I look up? Kelly isn't my name.

But I guessed right. Palmer leans against the tree I'm reading under and hooks his thumbs in the pocket of his shorts. The others— Diego, Troy, Bianca, and Marie—snicker.

"What?" I snap, provoked by their laughter. Although, now that I think about it, I'm annoyed with myself for *not* being annoyed with Palmer. He's been hanging out with us for over a month and doesn't realize it's *Ellie*?

The wind tousles his hair as if he's starring in some kind of dream boyfriend ad. "You know where Lucy is?"

"Nope." I look away so I can focus on things like, you know, *breathing*. What's the deal with this guy? It's got to be more than the cute-factor. I've talked to a number of cute guys in my life and not one of them has had this effect on me.

With our normal exchange about Lucy's location complete, I assume Palmer will turn back to the others and resume discussions about video games and college football. That's what he normally does during our time in the Quad before school.

Instead, he crouches beside me. "You got big weekend plans?"

My mouth is dry and the witty part of my brain barren. Which never happens to Lady Gabrielle.

The school's warning bell rings.

I stuff the novel I'm reading into my backpack. "Not really."

"Hmm. Well—"

"Davis, let's go." Diego sounds bored. Or stoned. It's hard to know with him.

Palmer grins at me, his gray eyes sparkling. "See you in bio, sweetheart."

Then he straightens and saunters away. I avert my gaze, not wanting to get caught watching, but I'm not fast enough. Bianca and Marie eye me suspiciously.

"Is there something . . . ?" Bianca trails off and exchanges a look with Marie.

I linger, despite needing to leave about five minutes ago to make it to class on time. Stupid interesting book, delaying me. "You'll have to give me more than that."

Marie rubs a strand of auburn hair between her fingers. "He called you sweetheart. He asked about your weekend plans . . ."

"It's a joke, you guys." I force myself to roll my eyes, to sound lighthearted. "He started doing it in Algebra yesterday. I don't even remember why."

"Oh!" Bianca's face lights. "Lucy told us about Chase. That's just crazy."

Marie nods and says in a sage voice, "I think Chase clearly has it bad for Lucy."

I blink a few times at Marie. What about the events of yesterday involved Lucy? But who knows how the story was told to them over coffee. Lucy has a knack for twisting details in a way that makes her the star.

But before I respond, Bianca and Marie mosey away, absorbed in a new conversation—colored mascaras, trashy or fun? They don't say bye.

In some ways they look just like the girls I used to traipse all over the playground with, our arms linked. Bianca's freckled nose and blond waves. The way Marie's eyes turn to crescents when she laughs. In third grade, had someone told me we would end up like this—Lucy no-showing without any of us knowing why, Bianca and Marie flat-out ignoring me—I would have called them crazy and returned to my game of four-square. I couldn't imagine the world without the four of us linked together. But recently those links feel more like shackles.

❦ ❦ ❦

Through World History and Spanish, the knots in my stomach are nearly painful. What did Palmer mean by his question about my weekend plans, followed by "See you in bio"? Were these merely casual questions and comments, or—

Don't go there, Ellie. STAY AWAY.

Here are three unavoidable pieces of evidence against Palmer being on the verge of asking me out:

1. He's been flirting with Lucy since he stepped foot on campus.
2. He can't remember that my name is *Ellie*, not Kelly.
3. I spent all first period casting sidelong glances his way.

Judging by the "See you in bio," Palmer doesn't even know we have World History together.

I repeat these three points to myself for two class periods, but still race from Spanish to Biology. No big surprise, I'm the first one here. I take my normal seat up front and fuss with my binder in an attempt to appear busy.

When Palmer and Diego enter the classroom, I know without turning around. Their conversation about a prank Palmer pulled on his older brother is loud and filled with lots of, "Dude, nuh-uh!" I peek over my shoulder as they slide into seats in the back row. Palmer doesn't even glance my way.

Despite the unavoidable evidence I had forced myself to brood over, my heart deflates like the clichéd balloon stuck with a pin. Or a knife. Or a battle axe.

Stupid Palmer for flirting with anything female within sight.

Stupid me for letting this crush happen.

I force my attention back to my binder and . . . whatever it is I'm doing. I've rearranged the subject dividers in alpha order rather than sequential. Which makes no sense.

As I rearrange my rearrangement, I glimpse over my shoulder. They're still in the back row. Palmer still isn't looking at me.

I organize a couple more binder sections. Wait, did Palmer just say my name? I give another sly glance. No. Apparently not.

When Mr. Hunt walks into the classroom, I use him as an excuse to eye Palmer in my peripherals.

"Do you have any idea"—the voice is husky and warm in my ear—"how obvious that is?"

I whirl to find Chase Cervantes close, too close, to my face. His coffee-colored eyes mock me.

When did he get here? And why's he sitting next to me?

I turn away, my nose in the air. "I don't know what you're talking about."

Chase chuckles and leans so his chair balances on its back two legs. "Sure you don't, El."

"*Don't* call me El."

Ellie's fine, but I *hate* El. I mean, seriously. El is a letter, not a name.

I love my real name, Gabrielle, but no one ever calls me that. Not even my parents when I'm in trouble. Even then I'm "Ellie Jane Sweet."

Mom regularly tells the story (apparently she doesn't get that it's insulting) of how she always wanted a little girl named Gabrielle. Before I was born, they had an entire roomful of linens monogrammed with my name, but unfortunately I—and this is a direct quote—"didn't look right." But since they'd already run up the credit cards with personalized towels and baby blankets, they chose to keep the stuff and call me Ellie.

Because every kid needs a permanent reminder that they've fallen short of their parents' expectations.

"Yeah, you aren't really an 'El,' are you?" Chase gives me a long, evaluating look that I do my best to ignore. "Or an Ellie either. It's too . . . something."

I sear him with a glare. "Are you done with your analysis?"

Chase barks a laugh. I'm apparently amusing him. "You popular chicks. You're mean."

Is he for real? Lucy, Bianca, and Marie—*they're* the popular chicks. "I'm hardly popular. They just put up with me. Everybody knows that."

"Do they?"

"I'm not like them, and you know it."

He flicks the end of a pencil, sends it spinning. "I don't know you at all, really."

But that's not true. He knew something about me that I hadn't shared with anyone except my aunt. And he'd turned my embarrassing secret into a theatrical prank to get attention for himself.

"Well, from what I know about you, I'd say that's just fine with me." I hope my glare is as cold as my voice. "I want you to tell me why you pulled that stunt in Algebra yesterday."

Chase doesn't seem to notice I'm doing my best to intimidate him. He just sits there and blinks at me with those worldly eyes of his.

My teeth grind together. "Why'd you do it?"

Chase shrugs, lazy-like. "Why not?"

"Because you embarrassed me. Because it's not true."

He snorts.

"I want an apology," I say through a locked jaw.

"No way."

No way? Who says that to someone? I study Chase for the first time in . . . ever. With the hard planes of his face, the old-for-my-age gleam of his eyes, it wouldn't surprise me if every bit of gossip I've heard about him is true. That he was driving the car the night his big brothers robbed the convenience store. That he broke Jose Paredes's arm last semester because he gave his last cigarette to someone else. That he paid Nina Huerta to have an abortion.

There's no threatening a guy like that. "You're a real jerk, you know?"

Chase shrugs again. "If you say so."

Why am I still talking to him? I face forward, anxious for the bell to ring and Mr. Hunt to begin class. Maybe then I'll be able to get my mind off Chase. What's his deal? Even if I do have it bad for Palmer, what does it matter to him? Why humiliate me in front of our entire Algebra class?

I'll probably never understand. I should stop trying to figure it out and just apply Bronte's advice—"use it." If he were a character in my novel, what motivations would I assign him? Maybe some bad blood between the families. Or vague mommy issues. Mommy issues are always a safe bet. Or maybe the Chase character (Ciro? Carlo?) wouldn't actually be trying to bring down Lady Gabrielle, but instead has a vendetta against Rafe . . .

When I recognize Chase's throaty chuckle, I realize I've done it again, looked back at Palmer. Who still hasn't seemed to notice me.

I grab my textbook and start flipping pages. "Shut up."

The closest thing to an admission anyone will drag out of me.

At lunch, when Lucy's still a mysterious no-show, I sequester myself to a quiet, sunny spot on campus and sprawl out on the brittle grass. Lots of people think the valley is ugly in the dry season, but I love it like this, hot and golden. The warmth of the ground soaks through my clothes and into my skin, like being wrapped in an embrace.

Normally, I suffer through lunch with Lucy and the others, but lunch with the seven of them is . . . well, let's just say, I'm not going to miss anything. The daily conversations are the same, just the restaurant changes. Lucy talks about style trends or a trashy article she just read in *Jane* or *Cosmo*. Bianca tugs at her size-four pants and gripes about how "fat" she's getting. Marie gabs incessantly about a guy at UCLA she chats with on-line. Diego, Palmer, and Troy talk about tricked-out cars, violent movies, or music any smart girl knows to be offended by.

But today I don't have to put up with them. I press in my earbuds, munch on a tasteless sandwich I snagged from the cafeteria, and open my laptop to resume revisions of *Invisibly Yours*.

I finished the first draft a couple months ago, then spent about six weeks revising it before I allowed my writing friend, Bronte, to read it. After I clicked send, I was so nervous I could barely eat. Fortunately, despite having three kids under age six, Bronte reads fast. And she liked it. I had a private celebratory feast when I saw her glowing email.

But one of her big hang-ups with the manuscript was that Prince Domenico seemed flat to her. I've been reading through the manuscript, looking for places to "add dimensions" as she called it, but it's hard. Prince Domenico isn't *the* guy, even though that was my original intent. He wound up getting overshadowed by someone new to town. Go figure, right? When Rafe burst onto the page, Prince Domenico became an antagonist of sorts.

I smirk at one of the prince's lines I've always liked. *"Lady Gabrielle, you may ask all the questions you like, but eventually you must resolve to content yourself with not knowing the whole truth."*

Funny. It almost sounds like something Chase might say. Well, if Chase had the education of a medieval Italian prince.

Hmm. Chase. *That* might be helpful . . . He *has* been something of an antagonist in my life recently. I may have just found some dimensions.

Lost in medieval Italy and indie rock, my thirty-five minutes evaporate.

What a dream it'd be to spend every lunch period this way. No one gasping at how many calories are in a bag of Cheetos. Or reciting song lyrics so dirty I'd be embarrassed just *thinking* those thoughts, much less setting them to a beat and sending them out in the world.

I guess I *could* do this every day, but it'd hurt Lucy. For all her faults, she's the only one who still tries to include me in the group, as if she thinks the four of us girls are every bit as tight as we were in grade school. If someday she no longer cares who I hang with, fine. But for now I'll stick it out.

$$\mathscr{G}\mathscr{G}\mathscr{G}$$

"You didn't eat with us."

The simple sentence of Palmer's, spoken from the desk behind me, sends my heart into a flurry of activity. I don't turn around or even pause punching numbers into my calculator. "I was busy."

"Studying?"

"Yep."

Palmer doesn't respond, but my ears are attuned to every noise he makes—the whisper of flipping textbook pages, the scratch of his pencil against paper. Now that I think about it, he hasn't uttered a word since the start of class. Nearly forty minutes ago.

When I turn, he looks at me through his lashes. "Yes, sweetheart?"

"Where's Diego?"

"I don't know, actually. After lunch, he went to his car for a smoke but never came back." A slow grin spreads across his face. "Why, you gotta thing for him?"

I love how words sound so different coming out of his mouth— Whyy, you gotta thang for 'im?"

I roll my eyes. "Yeah, stoners. Those are the types of guys I go for."

"You're more into southern gents, right?" He winks.

I face forward without answering. Palmer would twist any response into meaning I have some desperate crush on him like every other girl in this school. Instead of what I really have, a fleeting sense of attraction that will disappear any day now.

"So . . . what's the deal with Lucy?" Palmer's tone has shifted from teasing to casual curiosity. Fake, I'm guessing.

"How do you mean?" If I can judge accurately, I do a darn good job keeping my rampant jealousy hidden.

"Is she interested in me?"

"What is this? Middle school?"

His chuckle is low and warm. "You're her best friend. I thought you might have some inside info for me. Did yesterday make her jealous? All the attention I gave you?"

I hope he doesn't notice how I stiffen. "Was that the plan?"

"Sweetheart, I don't need excuses to flirt with cute girls."

Cute. He called me cute! I hate what this does to my heart rate. He doesn't even care what kind of effect he has on me, does he? I'm expendable, a pathway to Lucy.

He needs to be taken down a few pegs. He needs to fall in love with some girl who's completely indifferent to him. Who can't remember if his name is Palmer or Parker. That would teach him.

Unfortunately, it won't be Lucy. How can Palmer not know she'll do back flips when she finds out he likes her?

I erase a wrong answer on my paper. "You'll just have to ask her out and see how it goes."

"Thanks a lot." Palmer rolls his eyes—I can tell even without looking at him. "Real helpful, sweetheart."

"Stop calling me that," I grumble.

He either doesn't hear or doesn't care. When the bell sounds, Palmer hitches his bag onto his shoulder and calls, "Later, sweetheart!" for all of Redwood High to hear.

He swaggered down the street as if he owned it. As if he was Prince Domenico. "Lady Gabrielle, I don't need excuses to flirt with beautiful ladies."

Gabrielle rolled her eyes. What was this guy's name again? Raphael? Raffiano? "Kindly step out of my way, sir."

Sir—like he deserved such a courtesy.

I pause and consider the inserted lines. Hopefully they're a good start toward "punching up" the scene, like Bronte advised.

I'm trying to make my first three chapters perfect. Well, I'm trying to do that with the whole book, but apparently the first three chapters are all a literary agent will originally want to see, so that's the priority.

The thought of a literary agent looking at *Invisibly Yours* sends a shiver of nerves through me. Especially when I think of what will likely follow them reading it—a rejection letter.

But if I want to be published, there's no other way.

The dream of publication has burned for a year now. That's when I opened the fresh Word document and typed, CHAPTER ONE. That was the moment I first envisioned the book on store shelves. Cover out, of course, because you never like to think of your baby being relegated to showing only its spine. I saw the title, big and glossy, my name at the bottom. Gabrielle Jane Sweet. Or maybe just Gabrielle Sweet.

In the beginning, the words flowed as steady and strong as a faucet. And there was no turning it off. Sometimes, I was afraid to. Afraid it would never come back on. Those were the nights I stayed up until 3 or so.

And as words flowed, that image of my story being a real book on a real shelf in a real store blazed stronger.

So I got curious and Googled "fiction writing," which led me to the Association of Fiction Writers, or AFW. For a hundred bucks, I could become a member and have 2,000 writing friends. I could have access to multi-published, best-selling authors. I could take on-line classes and post my writing questions on forums.

When I first joined, I barely ever left my room. My time was spent reading archived classes and studying the forums. First I studied my primary interest—getting published. And that's when I realized I wasn't even close.

I didn't know what a query letter was. Or what genre I wrote. Or how to summarize my book in a page, a paragraph, or much less a single sentence.

And when I read through an agent's list of top ten mistakes they saw in newbie manuscripts, I didn't understand half of them. The other five, I'd already made.

Panic set in. Every sentence I wrote became a chore, my mind full of dos and don'ts. Don't write passively. Do use nouns and verbs. Show emotions, don't tell.

I turned to the forums for help. "I just joined," I wrote. "I thought I was ready for publication, only to discover I still have so much to learn. Now that I know, every word I write feels like torture. I can't seem to shut off the voice telling me I'm doing everything wrong, that I'm just going to have to go back and fix it all."

It spurred a whole thread of conversation on the forum, but Bronte was the first to email me privately.

"Every writer has been where you are," she began. "For me, the trick has been to allow myself to write awful first drafts. I don't have to have the perfect word yet, or the zippiest line possible. I just need to get the general idea down and trust the editing process. Yes, it's overwhelming to think about writing 100k words. But you don't have to do that right now. All you have to do is write the next sentence. Best of luck to you, Gabrielle."

She was the first to call me Gabrielle since whatever substitute teacher I had last, and it instantly endeared me to her.

Bronte ran a blog of daily writing tips, tricks, and prompts. At first, I borderline cyber stalked her. I checked the blog multiple times each day and read all the archives. She wasn't published yet, but she had a contract. Her first book was slated to come out in 18 months, and I was determined to be mentored by her. Even though her time was stretched with writing and raising three kids, she agreed.

I soaked up everything she told me. I learned to write active sentences. I slashed my adjectives and adverbs. I hunted down useless words—that, felt, was, as—and showed no mercy.

The faucet eased back on. At first it was a trickle, but then I became better at shutting off the voices, the voices that whispered things like "What makes you think you're good enough? What makes you think you've got anything of value to say?"

And now, as I steel myself for sending *Invisibly Yours* out into the world of literary agents and contest judges, the voices are back with new taunts. "Do you know how impossible it is to find an agent? Do you know that publishers are making cuts? Do you know how many others are dying to do this professionally? You're only sixteen!"

I bow my head and press my fingertips into the tender spot on my neck. One of my headaches is coming on. They're not severe like migraines, but stress always brings on a dull ache. "Go away," I murmur, as if a headache can be sweet talked. "I have a book to get published."

The doorbell rings.

I sigh. Gabrielle and Rafe will have to wait.

The doorbell rings three more times before I make it to the front door. It has to be Lucy. She's the only one I know who's self-absorbed enough to think every teensy-tiny thing going on in her life deserves the urgency of everyone around her.

Well, let me rephrase. She's the only one who feels that way and chooses to talk to *me*.

But as soon as I fling open the door, I swallow the saucy remark waiting on my tongue.

Lucy's wearing ratty gray sweatpants and a T-shirt she often sleeps in. Her sleek hair hangs limp and oily. There isn't a speck of makeup on her face—that hasn't happened since seventh grade—and the dark rings under her swollen eyes make it clear she's broken inside.

"Lucy . . ."

She collapses against me, sobs shaking her narrow frame. "My parents are getting divorced. And I'm moving to San Diego."

Jan and Stephen Shears have had problems for as long as I can remember. While my parents tend to be strangely polite when they interact with each other, the Shears constantly pick. They say they're joking, and they laugh at each other's digs, but even as a kid I recognized what the jokes were—a thin veil for their eroding relationship.

So as Lucy unloads the entire tale—how her parents sat her and her little sister down last night and gave them the, "Mommy and

Daddy will always care about each other, but . . ." speech—I'm not surprised.

What does surprise me is the entire family moving to San Diego.

"A job opened up for Dad down there." Lucy's voice is small and childlike. She keeps tugging at her hair, which explains the oily sheen. "Mom's always wanted to move further south, and they want to share custody as much as possible, so . . . to San Diego we go."

"I'm so sorry," I say for maybe the hundredth time. There are no good words for situations like these. Nothing that sounds as fresh and sincere as I'd like.

"How can I leave everything?" Lucy presses her hands to her face and breaks down again.

I rub her back and do my best to turn off the tightening in my throat. The last thing Lucy needs is me crying too. "It's good that you'll still have your family. Your parents will at least be in the same town."

Lucy uncovers her face. "My entire life is here. My friends . . ."

It's getting harder to blink away the burning of my eyes. There's something contagious about tears. "I know."

"Moving during high school? This just sucks. Everybody in San Diego will already have their group of friends, and I won't fit in at all."

Something Lucy's never worried about. The rest of us stress about fitting in with her.

"Maybe you'll finally learn to surf. You always wanted to do that."

"Surfing would be cool, I guess." She bites her lower lip and looks up at me, eyes brimming with tears. "What will I do without you, El? I'll miss you so much."

She flings her arms around me and squeezes so tight I can't take a full breath.

Our friendship has been nothing but nostalgia since last year when Lucy's boobs came in and mine didn't. (Still waiting on those, actually.)

But my cheeks are wet with tears as well. I've never known life without Lucy. The first day of kindergarten we bounced into the classroom together, wearing matching shirts so everyone would know we were best friends. And while she starts over in San Diego, I'll be starting over as well.

I clutch her closer, and find myself crying just as hard as she does while I consider how there's no way Bianca and Marie will put up with my nerdy ways once Lucy isn't around to insist they be nice to me. While it's been a long time since I've enjoyed hanging out with them, Lucy, Bianca, and Marie are the only friends I've ever had. And learning that my place in the group has an expiration date on it sends a shudder through me.

Yet in my head is Bronte's voice offering me a cold brand of comfort regarding my murky future. "Use it, Gabrielle."

Whatever pain, hurt feelings, and solitude might come my way with Lucy's departure, I'll always have that—I can use it.

Chapter 4

"You're so lucky," Bianca says as we discuss Lucy's move ad nauseum the next day. "I would kill to get out of this town."

Palmer pops a nacho in his mouth. "What's so bad about Visalia?"

"There are way better places to live. The day after graduation, I'm moving to San Francisco."

I fight off an eye roll. Bianca can twist any conversation into being about her. Even Lucy's move.

Lucy picks at her tacos. Usually her appetite is horse-like, but not today. "Leaving is the last thing I want to do."

A rare silence settles over our table. All around us, conversations buzz. Most here at Taco Bell are Redwood students, and you can tell the lunch period will be ending soon. Students shovel in their Value Meals while playing catch-up with friends. Drinks are left untouched—those can be sucked down on the walk back.

Chase sits on the other side of the restaurant, sharing a booth with Jose, Grant, and this week's group of sleazy girlfriends. When he glances my way, I avert my eyes, burning with embarrassment. But why? Is it a crime to notice my surroundings?

"So." Palmer's voice draws my thoughts back to the table. "Two months."

He says it like it's a death-sentence. And for his and Lucy's budding romance, I suppose it is. What a shame.

I wince. How petty of me. I'm no better than Bianca.

Lucy sighs. "Yep. Two months."

Troy flicks an oily scrap of lettuce at Diego, who laughs. I roll my eyes at Lucy, and she responds with a wan smile.

"We'll just make the most of the time you have left." Marie has on her peppy cheerleader smile. "And it's so easy to stay in touch. Cody and I are so close, even though we've never actually met. Ooh, maybe I can meet him 'IRL' when I come see you. How close is San Diego to L.A.?"

"I don't know." Lucy pushes away her tacos. "I don't know anything about San Diego. I don't know any*one* in San Diego. Who will I eat lunch with? Who will I shop with? And how will I get around? It's a *big* city, and . . ." Lucy shakes her head, as if too overwhelmed to continue.

Palmer takes one of Lucy's hands between his. It stirs the pot of jealousy inside me, the one that's simmered since we were kids and I noticed strangers never called me beautiful or enchanting like they did her.

"Look, Lucy. Being new is scary, but it doesn't have to be horrible. I've only lived here a couple months, and already I've got friends, and"—Palmer's hesitation seems rehearsed to me—"I've got you . . ."

"Palmer, I'm barely here for another two months." Lucy lowers her gaze to her lap, and her long lashes whisper against her cheeks.

Palmer grins. "So we'll enjoy 'em."

I turn away as Lucy's face blooms with a smile.

❀❀❀

Bronte sighs. "I just hate to see you waste your time and money on a writing contest, is all. I'm not saying it's a totally useless experience . . . but it's a fairly useless experience."

I press my finger to my ear to block out the traffic noise below while I cross the bridge to the other side of campus. "But lots of people on the AFW forums had good things to say about the Great Debut. And they just posted this morning that one of the final round judges for the young adult category is Abbie Ross with Blue Door Press! Can you imagine . . . ?"

Even with the roar of traffic, the hesitation in Bronte's silence is clear. "I understand the draw to the Great Debut, I do. But there are so many people who enter that AFW has to scrape the barrel for first round judges. Which means you might have some old fuddy-duddy writer who's never read a single young adult book and doesn't appreciate your lovely, young voice. Therefore they give you low marks, bad advice, and you pay forty dollars for the privilege."

I skirt around a group of dawdling freshman boys. "Well . . ."

"Trust me on this, Gabrielle. You're much better off investing your time in finding a literary agent than entering some stupid contest."

But Abbie Ross's name dangles in front of me like a carrot. "I just think as soon as an agent hears my age, they'll dismiss me."

"They don't *ask* your age." Bronte's words are edged with impatience. "Rose has never once asked me mine."

"Okay. Well, I guess it won't hurt to at least send out a couple query letters."

"If you really want to enter the Great Debut, I'll support you. I just happen to think it's a waste of time and money. But your book's great. If you get a first round judge with any intelligence, you might final."

I loiter outside the classroom door. "I've gotta go. School's starting."

Bronte laughs. "Well, if you say *that* to an agent . . ."

I force myself to laugh too, then hang up and find a desk. I had been *so* excited that morning when AFW announced who the final round judges were. Abbie Ross has edited some of my favorite YA novels, and I had just thought . . .

But I'm sure Bronte's right. I mean, what are the odds that I'll actually be one of five finalists? Hundreds enter, I'm sure.

"I heard Lucy's moving."

I startle at Chase's greeting. Have we always had this class together?

His backpack falls to the ground with a thud. "You deaf?"

I glare at Chase. "Yeah, she's moving."

"You doing okay?"

His question makes me blink. Am *I* doing okay? No one's thought to ask me. Not even my parents. All they'd talked about was the shame of Jan and Stephen splitting, of the growing divorce rate.

"You're not much for conversation, are you?"

From sweet to obnoxious in thirty seconds or less. "What's your deal, Chase? We've been in school together for ten years, and you've talked to me more this week than those years combined."

Chase ducks his head and pulls a notebook from his backpack. "Maybe I'm curious about you."

I snort. What about me provokes curiosity?

His dark gaze pierces me. "That so hard to believe?"

His face is more of a man's than a boy's. And combined with his reputation, he's the type of guy dads fear most. Why's he talking to a goody-two-shoes like me?

"What do you want to know?" Compared to Chase's, my voice sounds delicate and airy.

He opens his mouth, but before he can speak, I hear:

"Mornin', sweetheart." I turn as Palmer plops into the vacant seat beside me. He seems unaware that I'm already involved in a conversation. "You comin' next week?"

Half my brain is still engaged with curiosity over what Chase was about to say. What's Palmer talking about? "Coming to what?"

"Homecoming. Wouldn't be the same without you." He punctuates this with a wink.

Does he even know he's flirting, or is it just something that happens when he's awake?

"I can't. I'm busy." I'm mindful of Chase's perked ears, even though he's angled himself away from us.

Palmer gives me a look. "You're always busy."

He's noticed? "My brother's coming home for fall break. I think my parents have some special dinner planned." Though according to my parents, every dinner with James is special.

"What about after your fancy dinner? Marie's throwing a party."

"No thanks."

Is there something wrong with me that I would rather be in my room writing than at a party? Because the other students here can't get enough of the whole booze-and-abuse lifestyle. A lot of them even party on Thursday nights too.

Palmer's mouth curls into a teasing smile. "Is it because you're afraid to be in the same room with me now that I'm with Lucy? Afraid you can't control yourself?"

My gaze skitters to Chase. Is he still listening, or is he as focused on his sketching as he seems?

I laugh wryly. "That's it."

"Don't worry, sweetheart. Still a special place in my heart for you. Hey, your tag's sticking out."

He returns the tag of my shirt to its rightful place. The simple action raises goose bumps on my arms, which I hide beneath the desk.

Please God, don't let Palmer or Chase notice. And cure me of this stupid crush before I get hurt any worse.

I'm rushing away from World History when I hear a familiar, "Sweetheart!" behind me.

Palmer jogs down the sidewalk, sandy curls flopping, making him even more boyish. Several around us laugh, a few point and whisper, but most carry on like they don't even notice.

"Why can't you call me Ellie like a normal person?" I ask once he catches up.

He flashes a smile. "Now, where's the fun in that?"

I continue on my way. "I gotta go. Spanish is on main campus."

Redwood High is seriously old. Like, my grandparents went here. Since the city built up around the school and there was no room to expand, they built a massive bridge over Giddings Street and stuck classes at what used to be Sierra Vista Elementary. Even with nine minutes between periods, it's nearly impossible to move from campus to campus without being late. Especially when you're being held up.

Palmer trots alongside me. "I think you should be careful with Chase."

I don't even know how to begin to respond to that. It's not like I'm seeking Chase out or trying to befriend him or anything.

Palmer blinks a couple times. "I mean Chase Cervantes."

"Yeah, I know," I say with a laugh. "I was trying to figure out if you're being serious."

Palmer grips my arm and pulls me out of the stream of students, over by a drooping oak tree. "I'm completely serious." And he looks it. "His brothers are in jail. Do you know that?"

I'm having trouble thinking clearly with his hand clutching my elbow. "Everybody knows."

"I think you should be cautious."

As if I know how to be anything but. "I didn't ask your opinion, Palmer."

I turn to keep walking, but Palmer makes another grab for my arm and holds me there. "Wait."

"I'm gonna be late for Spanish. Can we at least walk and talk?"

"No, I meet Lucy here." He releases my arm, as if he's decided I won't go anywhere without his permission. "Look, I'm serious about Chase."

"I don't know where you're getting your information, but there's nothing going on with me and Chase, okay?" I hug my textbook to my chest, feeling an odd sense of vulnerability. "And even if there was, it'd be none of your business."

"Oh come on, sweetheart. I'm your friend, aren't I?"

"You can't even remember my name." I press my eyes closed. Gosh, that sounded bitter.

"Gabrielle Jane Sweet." The humor has vanished from his voice. "But everyone calls you Ellie."

When I look up at him, my heart swells like in that old *How the Grinch Stole Christmas* movie. How tall is Palmer? Six foot? I'm five-eight, and he's got a few inches on me. What does he see as he watches me through those gray eyes of his? Does he notice I'm not like Lucy, Bianca, and Marie? And does he consider that a pro or a con?

Before I can think of a response, I hear the *ksh-ksh* of a camera shutter. I turn to find Lucy grinning at us, her SLR still poised for the shot.

I adjust my Tina Fey style glasses. I really should stop being lazy and pop my contacts in every once in a while. But I got on a roll last night editing *Invisibly Yours*, and stayed up into the single digit hours. "You're supposed to tell people before you take their picture."

Lucy rolls her eyes. "Not when it's for your 'candid' photography assignment."

Palmer tosses his arm around her shoulders. "How you doin', beautiful?"

"Good." She lowers her camera and frowns at me. "Isn't your Spanish class on main campus?"

"Right, yeah." I back up several steps, taking in one last glimpse of their perfection as a reminder of why I need to expedite the getting-over-Palmer process. "See you, guys."

Palmer salutes me. "See you, sweetheart."

Behind me, I hear Lucy snap the lens cap on her camera. "Why do you keep doing that? She thinks it's annoying."

I slow my steps to hear his response. "She knows I'm just playin'."

"You're making an idiot of yourself. She already thinks you're obnoxious. You don't need to add to it . . ."

Their voices fade before Palmer responds. Drat.

I trot toward the bridge, but my mind is still back by the oak tree. Is Palmer hurt by what Lucy said about me thinking he's obnoxious? Well, if so, he deserves it. He's been flirting without a moment's thought of how it might impact me.

"You're gonna be late for Spanish."

Chase Cervantes's words pull me away from the conversation I just overheard. He's leaning against the base of the bridge's looming staircase, as if waiting for someone.

I slow my steps. "How do you know what class I have next?"

"Because I'm stalking you."

"That's what it's starting to feel like."

Chase doesn't seem fazed by my accusation. Or really, his accusation. As I ascend the metal steps, I feel him fall in behind me. Had he been waiting for *me*?

When we're on the bridge and I've regulated my breathing, I turn to him. "Seriously. What's the deal? How *do* you know what class I have next?"

His laugh is gruff. "Typical. Lost in your own Ellie world. Can't be bothered with things like who all is in your Spanish class." His voice goes high and breathy as he imitates me. "Oh, there are other people on the planet besides Palmer Davis?"

Okay, that's uncalled for.

I stop and glower. Chase comes to a lazy stop too, and other late students skirt around us.

One guy—a freshman, I think—sneers at me. "Great place to have a conversation."

Chase fixes him with a ferocious look. The freshman ducks his head and scuttles down the staircase to Vista.

"What's your problem?" I plant my hands on my hips and half-yell over the traffic below. "This week, I can't seem to take a step without tripping over you. Without you critiquing my every move or making up ludicrous lies and blabbing them to our entire Algebra class."

Chase smirks. I suppose at the "ludicrous lies" part.

"I'm serious." I stomp my foot for emphasis, but the sound gets lost among the whooshes of speeding cars. "Tell me what's going on."

Chase's smirk vanishes, and he's back to his normal facial expression—indifferent with a touch of scary. "I want to take you to homecoming."

Did I hear that right? Who would ask somebody to homecoming up on the bridge? He must be messing with me. Or maybe he's joined a gang and this is part of the hazing.

The wind whips my bangs into my face, and I brush them away. "Are you serious?"

"Wouldn't that be a strange thing to joke about?"

I narrow my eyes. "Everything about you seems strange."

Chase arches his thick, black eyebrows. "Considering the guys you normally spend time with, that's fine by me."

I bite my lip, but the smile pops up anyway. "Good point."

I resume walking, and Chase shortens his stride in order to fall in beside me. How can he be serious about homecoming? I can't really picture Chase in a suit and tie. Or coordinating the corsage with my dress. Or meeting my parents.

And those things aside, how can he think I'd go with him after what happened this week?

When we're back on main campus and the rush of traffic is behind us, Chase stuffs his hands in his pockets. "So, what do you say? About homecoming?"

I study Chase as best I can while we walk. "You really embarrassed me on Monday."

The corner of his mouth twitches. "What's actually embarrassing is that you like that guy. And I think *that's* why you're so angry."

"Oh really? Because I'm pretty sure I'm angry with you for saying what you did to the entire class."

Chase shrugs as if this is a moot point.

Well, it's a pretty big deal to me.

"What made you do it? Lucy and I were talking about homework, and you were sitting close enough to know that."

Chase shrugs again, his mouth pressed into a straight line.

"I'll go to homecoming with you if you tell me why." The offer pops out before I can think it through.

The look Chase gives me is stern, almost fatherly. "I only want you to go with me if you *want* to."

Why do I feel such a bite of rejection? I don't even want to go with him. "Then I guess we're not going together."

"Guess not." He saunters past me into our Spanish class as if nothing out of the ordinary just happened.

Chapter 5

Just before clicking the button and opening *Invisibly Yours*, my finger hesitates. This is always the hardest part of the process for me—untangling Gabrielle from all the Ellieness of my day, dressing myself in the skin of a heroine.

I replay my day through the filter of Gabrielle's eyes. How would she have responded to Chase's invitation to homecoming? Other than, "no," of course. Somehow Gabrielle would weasel the mysteries of Chase right out of him . . .

I rewind my mind to even earlier, when Palmer called me by my full name—Gabrielle Jane Sweet. I focus on the clench of my heart, the warmth that filled me. How would I put it on the page?

Like soaking up sunshine on the first warm day of spring.

Or like being complimented for a trait you hadn't recognized in yourself.

I'm meditating on the particular color of Palmer's eyes—steel? smoke? granite?—when I hear the familiar "ping" on my computer.

I smile at Bronte's screen name—BronteWrites. "Get to work," it says.

> SWEETGIRL: Trying. I'm still searching for the right adjective for Rafe's eyes.
> BRONTEWRITES: Perfectionist.
> SWEETGIRL: Isn't that what you taught me? Agents and editors are looking for reasons to say no—don't give them any.
> BRONTEWRITES: I don't think you'll be rejected because *you* don't feel you've picked the right descriptor.

I'm typing a response when Bronte posts again:

BRONTEWRITES: Ugh! Munchkin #2 just woke up wailing. Gotta go.

I sigh and close out the window. It's probably for the best. I can get so caught up in talking about writing with Bronte that I don't get any actual writing done.

Back to picking an adjective. I close my eyes and conjure up Palmer's image.

For research purposes, of course.

While Palmer's eyes are more of a steel, I choose "smoky" for Rafe. It has a sound of mystery to it, which seems good for a hero like him.

Ping.

BRONTEWRITES: Sorry about that. Typing one handed, but wanted you to know—Reese Literary just added a new agent. Her name is Emma Miller, and she's looking for clients who write YA!

I know it's cliché, but butterflies fill my stomach.

Reese is my dream agency. Their client list reads like a list of my favorite authors. The thought of seeing my name amidst theirs . . .

Snap out of it, Gabrielle.

SWEETGIRL: My query letter isn't ready.
BRONTEWRITES: Then get it ready.

With Bronte, everything is so black and white.

BRONTEWRITES: I know you're nervous, Gabrielle. But you can't spend the rest of your life revising *Invisibly Yours* and entering it in contests with brainless judges. Gotta take the plunge sometime.

I'm still trying to figure out a response when my computer pings again:

BRONTEWRITES: Spit-up everywhere! Yuck! GTG.

Just as well. I don't know how to explain to her that I'm full up on rejection at the moment. There's no hope for querying without rejection. And writing . . . well, it's my safe-haven. It's a rejection-free zone. A place where I'm in complete control.

But eventually, to achieve my dream of being published, I'll have to give that up.

Since Chase's little announcement in our Algebra class on Monday, I've looked forward to this moment—Friday after the final bell. This has been the longest week of my life.

"Ellie!"

If the voice behind me hadn't called for "Ellie," I'd have thought for sure . . .

I turn, and yep, there's Palmer. The sunlight makes his hair gleam blond as he jogs toward me.

He grins when he catches up. "How'd you do on the Algebra test?"

"That's what you ran to ask me?"

"Not exactly. I was walking alone and saw you up here, so thought I'd join you. Don't mind, do ya?"

Yes and no. Stupid confused brain.

"So." Palmer matches my stride. "I wanted to say I'm sorry for bugging you with the whole 'sweetheart' thing. I was just foolin' around."

Hopefully Palmer will assume any redness in my face is merely the effects of the blazing afternoon sun and my heavy backpack. "It's not a big deal."

"I wasn't serious about any of it."

I glance at him, but avert my gaze when I find him already looking at me. "Yeah, I know."

And, truly, I knew it all along. But the acknowledgment still makes my heart squeeze.

"I think Lucy's a little jealous, so I'll start calling you by your name now."

"Good idea."

"You like Ellie or Gabrielle best? Gabrielle Jane? Ellie J.? Miss Sweet? Sometimes the girls call you El—"

"*Not* El."

His mouth quirks into an amused smile. "Okay. Not El."

After a beat of silence, Palmer launches into how he feels he did on the Algebra test, then he effortlessly segues into Ms. Purdon's voice making him crazy.

Conversation appears to come easily to him, a skill I long for. That's one reason I like writing so much better than speaking, the ability to edit.

Oh, if only you could edit real life. I'd edit those stupid words right out of Chase's mouth . . .

"You okay?" Palmer's question awakens me to the fact that he's continued to talk, and I have no idea what about. "Usually my Ms. Purdon impression kills."

"Sorry. I'm distracted, I guess."

"By my charm, right?"

Is flirting, like, a reflex of his?

I turn away, unwilling to engage. "Do you know why Chase did what he did?"

Palmer hesitates. "What do you mean?"

How's it possible the events of sixth period on Monday are permanently etched in my brain, yet Palmer's clueless?

"I mean why he made up that thing about me liking you." My face flushes. Why did I bring this up? "It just doesn't make sense."

Palmer laughs loud. "You playin' around, Ellie? Everybody knows Chase Cervantes is crazy about you."

"Shh!" I glance around us, but none of the other students are in hearing range. "Don't say that kind of stuff."

"True stuff? I don't need to keep my voice down. *Everybody* knows. Within my first week here, I knew." Palmer doesn't seem to be kidding.

"But . . ." I shake my head. "No. That's just weird. Before Monday, Chase and I had barely ever talked."

Palmer hitches his backpack higher on his shoulder. "Don't know what to tell you. Maybe he was afraid to talk to you?"

Afraid? Chase? Yesterday, with just a flick of his gaze, he sent that freshman scrambling away from us. "I don't think Chase is afraid of anything."

"All guys are afraid of *something*. My best guess is he wanted to talk to you, and this was a way to do it."

"But why this week? And why like that?"

"Dunno. Maybe he saw something on Monday that scared him worse than the idea of talking to you."

"It's not like I'm some terrifying person. And I'd have been nicer about it if he hadn't embarrassed me in front of everybody."

"The idea of having a crush on me is embarrassing?" Palmer clutches his chest. "Oh, it hurts . . ."

I laugh and slow to a stop as we reach my Accord. "You know what I mean."

"I do, El." He shoots me an apologetic look. "Ellie. Sorry."

"I prefer Gabrielle, actually."

Okay, where did that come from? I mean, it's true, but why bother? With Palmer of all people?

He smiles, crooked and endearing. "Gabrielle."

I hadn't noticed last time he used my full name, but it sounds different with his accent. Like I'm not my boring self but someone fun and exciting. Like I'm Gabrielle Moretti and he's Rafe Grayson.

This line of thought is trouble. I've gotta get out of here.

I look at him, goodbye on the tip of my tongue, when I realize his eyelashes are bronze. I never noticed before. Oh. Probably because I've never stood this close to him. Why *are* we standing so close? How did this happen? And why can't I look away?

His eyes are silver in the sunlight, and my image reflects in his pupils. My heart pounds with almost painful intensity. I sag against my car, and the heat it's collected from the sun seeps through my shorts.

My movement does the trick. Palmer mutters something that sounds like, "Gotta go." He jogs down the sidewalk, leaving me dizzy and queasy, like when you walk into one of those perfume stores and your senses overwhelm.

Climbing into my car, I run the last few minutes through my head. Was it minutes or only seconds? I can't be sure. Funny how those types of moments seem suspended from time, like they're too big to be contained. And that's what just happened, right? We had a moment.

I'm not sure of it until the next Monday.

Palmer doesn't call me sweetheart or Ellie or Gabrielle. He doesn't call me anything. He doesn't smile or wave or nod. And when he's trying to figure out where Lucy is, he asks everybody but me.

Without a doubt, whatever connection passed between us on the street, Palmer felt it just as intensely.

Chapter 6

Long before I was born, maybe even long before James graced Mom and Dad with his presence, we've had dinner at Grandmom and Granddad's on Thursday nights.

I'm aware some people have warm, fuzzy grandparents who think they're perfection walking around on two legs. I somewhat remember my dad's parents being like this, but I was eight when they died. My mom's parents are . . . well, what's the opposite of warm and fuzzy? Cold and prickly?

Granddad hardly ever speaks, and Grandmom mostly complains about politicians (all crooks) and how this whole state is whooshing down the "commode."

I hate Thursday nights. The only perk is seeing Aunt Karen. She's in her thirties and embodies everything I want to be when I grow up. Except I'll live in Honolulu, Istanbul, Barcelona, or somewhere else that's fabulous. And I'll be a writer, not a hotel manager.

"How are things going with"—Karen suggestively wiggles her well-defined eyebrows—"you know."

Palmer. While I tell my aunt almost everything, I had already decided on the way over that I wouldn't tell her about our "moment" nearly a week ago. For one thing, I'm sure I would sound totally stupid trying to describe it. "So, yeah, then we just kinda looked at each other, and it was really intense for some reason . . . and then it ended and now he won't talk to me."

But even if there was an intelligent explanation for it, that moment feels private. Like writing, it belongs to me, and I'm not ready to reveal it to anyone in my real life.

I pluck at the frayed hem of my jeans. "Nothing new."

"Crazy boy." Karen takes a swig of her water. "Doesn't know what he's missing."

I roll my eyes. "Yeah, yeah."

"Karen?" Grandmom calls from the kitchen in her scratchy voice. "Fetch the tablecloth from the closet. The fall one with the orange and brown leaves?"

Karen wrinkles her nose, then abandons me in the living room. Across the room, Granddad is absorbed in the nightly news. He has the television cranked even louder than I play my music.

After a few seconds' deliberation, I migrate into the kitchen. Dad's leaning against the counter, staying out of the way as best he can. When I stand beside him, he hangs his arm across my shoulders, dad-style.

My mom peeks at the chili she's been stirring. "Mom, I think this is ready."

"Take it to the table, Allison."

"Do you think it'd be better to serve from over here? Then we wouldn't drip chili on your good tablecloth."

It's strange, watching Mom morph into a daughter every Thursday night between 5:30 and 7:30. Outside these walls, she's an executive accountant. She has a commanding presence and speaks with authority. But in Grandmom's kitchen, everything's always, "Do you think . . . ?" and, "Would it be better if . . . ?"

Karen swishes into the room with fall linens that are unintentionally retro, a wedding gift probably. She hums as she spreads the cloth across the round table. How's it possible that Karen, so light and joyful, came from two people like Grandmom and Granddad?

Though tonight she seems extra light and joyful. Did she meet a guy? I'll have to ask her next time we're alone.

After Granddad prays for our food, Grandmom asks, "What time does James's flight come in?"

"Nine-ten," Mom and Dad say. They smile at each other.

"Shame he couldn't get a flight earlier in the day. Would've been nice having him here for dinner."

"You'll get to see him, Mom. Don't worry. Why don't you and Dad come over tomorrow night for dinner?"

Karen grins. "Am I invited to this shindig too, or . . . ?"

Mom gives her an exasperated look. "You're welcome anytime. You know that."

"I still don't understand why he thought he needed to go to Georgetown." Grandmom munches on a saltine. "Useless, if you ask me."

Karen and I exchange a smile at the resurrection of an old, tired subject. Grandmom appears to be against a college experience beyond California state schools. She says anything else puffs up young people and gives them unrealistic expectations. I think it's just that she doesn't like change in any form. It's a miracle, really, that she ever got married and had kids.

Dad dabs his mouth with a floral napkin. "James really likes it there, and I think it's good for him. Chili's great, Nancy."

Had my mom said it, Grandmom would have pressed the argument. Instead she just says, "Thank you, Stu."

"Well." Karen clears her throat and beams at everyone. "I have an announcement."

I pause buttering my corn muffin. From the spark of interest in Grandmom's eyes, my guess is she's thinking exactly what I am—Karen's finally found someone. According to Karen, Grandmom's considered her an old maid since twenty-five. When Grandmom was young, I doubt many single thirty-seven-year-old women went on to get married.

"I'm moving to Phoenix."

What . . . ?

Grandmom's spoon drops from her hand and lands with a splat in her chili bowl. She doesn't seem to notice the greasy red flecks now decorating the tablecloth.

Karen's leaving? But . . . that's impossible. She never even told me she wanted to move. I mean, I knew she didn't *love* the valley or anything, but . . .

"That's . . . amazing, Karen." Mom sounds as stunned as I feel. "What's in Phoenix, exactly?"

"Scottsdale, actually. I've taken a position at The Phoenician. I'll be the director of convention services." She glances at me. There's an apology in her eyes.

I turn away as anger brews in my gut. Karen is the closest thing to a friend that I have. I'll have no ally on Thursday nights. No one to hang out with when I have writer's block or just can't stand being alone anymore.

Granddad's wrinkles deepen with his frown. "But at the Radisson, you're the manager of the whole property."

Karen nods, her dark bangs falling into her eyes with the movement. She brushes them away. "I realize it sounds like a demotion, but The Phoenician is a five-diamond hotel. My résumé at the Radisson doesn't exactly wow a property like that."

"I don't understand why you'd give up everything you have here." Grandmom's voice is shrill, and I shrink in my chair. As a kid, that tone usually led to a "swat on the behind" that made my butt feel like it was on fire. "You have a steady job, and all your family's here. The kids at church look up to you, and Pastor David needs you to run the youth program."

The youth program is me and twin brothers who go to Tulare Union. They're more interested in gaming than anything else. Including, apparently, showering.

Karen's smile is the same I've seen her use with ruffled hotel guests. "I've lived here my entire life, Mom. I'm ready for a change."

Which I get . . . but couldn't she have told me that sooner? Given me a bit of warning?

"You can't go to Phoenix," Grandmom sputters. "You just can't!"

It's jarring for Grandmom's words to echo my thoughts.

"Mom, maybe we should be more supportive of Karen. I'm sure it'll be tough for her to leave everything here." My mom gives Karen a look that clearly says *Agree with me, or live to regret it.*

Karen bobs her head. "Of course it will be." She glances at me again and bites her lip.

"What if you run out of gas on the side of the road? What if you get sick? What if you have to go to the hospital? You won't know anyone."

"I understand you're worried. But it's not unusual for people to leave their hometown. Most do it long before I am."

Grandmom grunts at this. "I don't understand your generation's obsession with moving. I was born and raised here. Why would I bother moving to a new place when everybody I know is here? What kind of living is it away from your friends and family? What's so great out there that we don't have right here in Visalia?"

"Mom—"

"I think y'all are running from something. From commitment. Honoring your word. Like telling Pastor David you'll take care of the youth program and then hanging him out to dry."

"I've been in charge of the youth program for five years now. I'm hardly hanging Dave out to dry."

Grandmom mutters something and stabs at her chili with her spoon.

Dad glances across the table at Mom and me—stunned silent— and takes conversation upon himself. "So, when do you move?"

Karen sucks in a breath and puts on a smile. "Three weeks."

Three weeks?

"Three weeks!" Grandmom drops her spoon again. "You'll never be ready in three weeks! Why, you don't know the first thing about moving. You have to sell your house before you can buy a place down there. And somehow you have to get all your stuff down to Phoenix. Three weeks! That's the most absurd thing I've ever heard."

Karen's smile never wavers, but her voice is tight. "I'll manage, Mom. Don't worry about it."

I duck my head, attempting to hold in tears. The only person who really knows and understands me is leaving in *three* weeks. If only she would pack me up and take me with her.

Well . . . is that so crazy?

She wouldn't have to worry about me at all, I'd make sure of it. I could even cook for her. Karen hates cooking.

So, yeah, I don't know *how* to cook, but I can figure it out. Can't be that hard.

I look across the table and find Karen watching me, awaiting my reaction. I smile at her. "Congratulations on the job. Sounds great."

Karen stops biting her lip and smiles. For real. "Thanks, Ellie."

"I think starting over like that would be awesome."

Grandmom snorts. "Fiddlesticks."

Mom glances at her mom, then says, "I bet you'd feel differently if we yanked you out of school and plopped you in a strange city."

Try me, Mom.

"Move me someplace cool like Phoenix, and I think I'd be okay with it. In fact, you have a spare room in your new place, Karen? Want a roommate?"

Karen grins.

Dad winks at me. "Yeah. Want a teenager?"

"Do you have any idea how hot it is in Phoenix?" Grandmom says to no one in particular. "It's the desert!"

I dig into my chili with renewed vigor. "Have you found a place yet?" I'm picturing a downtown loft with the walls painted something funky and urban, like lime green.

"Not quite yet, but there's lots of places for rent in Scottsdale—"

"That's the most absurd thing you've said so far." Grandmom stirs her chili with vigor. "You're too old for renting!"

"It's not my long-term plan, certainly. I anticipate having an apartment for the first year while I get a feel for the area. And hopefully I'm promoted before too long and will be able to afford something fairly close to work."

"The good thing about renting is that when you hate it, you won't be locked into anything." Grandmom raps her spoon on the edge of her bowl. "Millie Vespa lived in Phoenix for a year. She had to buy everything dust-colored because it all got covered with dust anyway."

Granddad raises his bowl to his mouth and slurps up the last drops of chili. Um, gross.

"It's an unnatural place to live." Grandmom pushes a corn muffin into her mouth. "That's all I'm saying."

"I think Phoenix would be great." I flash another smile at Karen. In three weeks, I could be done with this place. Three!

After classes, I would go hang at the hotel with Karen. I'll put on my bathing suit and sunglasses, then lounge by the pool and write. Maybe I'll get a job at the hotel too, so I can meet all kinds of exotic people and get plenty of fresh ideas. Karen's move to Phoenix could be the best thing that ever happened to me.

Karen rolls her eyes. "Oh, Ellie."

"'Oh, Ellie?' What does that mean? It's not such an absurd idea."

"You don't think your parents would miss you at all?"

"I think they'd be fine with it. They've adjusted okay to James leaving, and they don't like me nearly as much."

Karen gives me a look. "You're being ridiculous. And James went away to college. It's different."

"In a couple years, I'll be doing that too. What's the big deal if I leave now instead?"

Karen glances at the door to Grandmom and Granddad's, as if she can see the four of them inside sipping weak coffee. "To your parents, it'll matter. Trust me."

"I promise I won't get into any trouble." Desperation bleeds into my voice, but I don't care. "You'll hardly know I'm there."

Karen sighs and leans against the post. "It's not about that. Honestly, I think you'd be a lot of fun to live with. I just don't think it's in your best interest."

"My best interest? Do you have any idea what high school's like these days? I'm basically the only person not spiking my morning coffee." Tears prick my eyes. "I have no real friends at school. And when you move, I'll have no one at all."

Karen pulls me close. She's crying too. "I'll miss you the most." As if that should somehow make this better.

I squint through bleary eyes and select a bowl from the kitchen cabinet.

"I hear there's a mass exodus out of Visalia."

Hand over my heart, I turn and find James grinning at me from the kitchen table. His hair is rumpled from sleep and his T-shirt has creases from being stuffed in a suitcase.

When his flight got delayed until eleven, I elected to stay home and catch up on the sleep writing had cost me. I instead clicked around on the AFW Great Debut's contest site and tried my hand at writing the one-page summary of my book that the contest requires. I had barely dozed off when they rolled in the driveway after midnight.

"Why are you awake already?" I pull a box of Mommy-approved cereal off the shelf and join him at the table. "I thought college students slept until noon at the earliest."

James shrugs and sips his coffee. "My internal clock is all messed up. I spent all day yesterday on a plane, and my body doesn't know if I'm on the east coast or the west."

"The west."

He rolls his eyes, then goes back to reading the *Visalia Times Delta*.

I pour my milk, then watch my brother for a bit. Six weeks isn't a terribly long time, I suppose, yet I feel a definite this-isn't-normal tension in the air. "Since when do you read the newspaper?"

James gives me a condescending look. "I'm a poly-sci major, sis." He flips the page. "Not that this feature on the new landscaping at the mall holds much interest to me."

I poke at my cereal. "So Mom and Dad told you about Karen?"

"I think it's awesome." James crunches into his toast, then finishes his thought despite his mouth being full. "I've always wanted a reason to go to Phoenix."

"I tried to convince her to take me along, but no luck."

James chuckles. "Oh, come on, El. I'm sure it seems pretty bleak with Lucy moving too, but you'll be fine. You've still got Ditz One and Ditz Two to keep you company."

"What a huge relief."

He grins. A plus about having James around is he doesn't look at me like I've sprouted a second head when I use sarcasm.

James folds his paper and shoves it aside. "So. Who are you going with tomorrow night?"

I stare as he takes a bite of toast, chews, and swallows. What on earth is he talking about? "What do you mean?"

"Tomorrow. Who are you going with?"

"I heard you fine. I don't know what you're asking."

"Isn't homecoming tomorrow?"

He's talking about homecoming? He didn't think that merited clarification?

Well, I refuse to feel shame as I inform him, "I'm not going."

James's eyes widen. "You're not going?"

It can't be *that* shocking, can it? I doubt my acting skills would win me any Oscars. Surely my parents and James realize I'm not a girl who's likely to be voted Homecoming Queen.

"No, I'm not."

"You don't have to go with a guy, you know."

"That's not the problem. I just don't want to go."

"But why not?"

"Dances aren't really my thing." I stuff a bite of cereal in my mouth.

"Since when? You went last year. With . . ." James snaps his fingers a couple times. "Why can't I think of his name? The principal's son . . ."

"Troy."

Troy's girlfriend had broken up with him the morning of the dance, and since I didn't have a date (shocking, I know) everyone thought it'd be perfect if we went together. He'd been buzzed when he picked me up and flat-out drunk by the time we arrived. An enchanting evening. Especially the part where I got to scrub vomit off my dress.

"Right. Troy. Who's he taking this year?"

I set my coffee cup down with more force than intended. "Is it some crime to skip a dance? I think they're stupid, and I don't want to go."

James holds up his hands, as if surrendering. "Fine, don't go. But as your older, wiser brother, I'll point out you only get to do high school once."

"One too many times, I say."

I dump the remainder of my cereal in the sink and stalk back to my bedroom to finish my coffee in peace.

Chapter 7

"You doing anything for Halloween?"

I lower my book and squint in the bright sun. Chase looms over me, an impressive silhouette.

"Most people start conversations with hello. Maybe you should give it a try." I shift my weight against my backpack. It's hard, lumpy, and only slightly more comfortable than lying flat on the ground.

"Hello." With his face obscured by shadows I can't know for sure, but it sounds like he's smiling.

I bite back a smile of my own. "Hello."

Ever since Palmer enlightened me about how "everybody" knows Chase is "crazy" about me, I haven't known how to act. Fortunately Chase hasn't initiated conversation since asking me to homecoming two weeks ago.

Chase settles onto the grass a couple feet away. "You know, I don't think anybody actually says hello anymore."

"My grandparents do."

Chase gives an exaggerated look around. "No entourage today?"

Over the last couple weeks, since Lucy announced her impending move, I've begun the process of separating myself from the group. Once Lucy's gone, it's inevitable that I will be too. Therefore, why endure lunch with them five days a week?

I reopen my book. "I gave them the day off."

"Gotcha." Chase plucks at his shoelace for a moment. "You and Palmer are acting weird around each other."

Even bathed in sunshine, a chill runs through me. "Are we?"

"You're not talking as much as you used to."

I shrug. "I hadn't noticed."

"Sure you hadn't." Chase leans back on his palms and crosses his long legs. "Wanna know what I think?"

"Is it that I'm interested in my book and want to keep reading? 'Cause if so, you're right."

"I think it's obvious he likes you." This statement doesn't help my concentration. "Probably thanks to me."

A laugh bursts from me. "Thanks to *you*?"

"Yeah. I think my announcement made him notice you."

"Yeah, and once he did, he started dating *Lucy*." Please say Chase didn't pick up on my obvious bitterness . . .

Chase shrugs. "I still say he likes you."

I try to ignore the way my heart launches into jumping jacks in my chest. Time to turn the table on this conversation.

"I think you guys would get along well." I close my book, then settle against my backpack and shut my eyes. I don't want to look at him when I say this. "He's as absurd as you are, because he says the same thing as you."

"That he likes you?"

"No. He says the same thing, but he says it about you."

"You mean he thinks *I* like you?" Chase sounds amused.

He's supposed to be uncomfortable, and *I'm* supposed to be amused. "Mm-hmm."

"Well, here he comes now."

I crack open my eyes and spot the whole crew crossing the Quad. Watching them move as a group always reminds me of those schools of fish, how they move together fluidly and decidedly, yet no one really seems to be leading. What does it look like when I'm walking with them? Do I look like some tag-along little sister?

Palmer's saying something to Troy, a grin on his face. For the first time today, we make eye contact. He frowns.

I snort. "Oh, yeah. That's a look of love if I ever saw one."

Chase fixes me with a look of his own that I can't decipher. "You're real dense, you know that?"

The bell sounds, and he offers me a hand up that I ignore.

I brush dried grass off my jeans. "You know, you never have anything nice to say about me. I wonder why you talk to me at all."

"So I can copy off you in math. Maybe World History too."

"Why not? Lucy already does. What's one more?"

Before I can stop him, Chase throws my backpack over his shoulder.

"You don't need to carry that." I practically have to jog to keep up with his long strides. "You'll hurt your back carrying both our bags."

"I can manage."

I glance around, feeling like everyone must be wondering why Chase is carrying my backpack. But no one seems to notice.

After a minute of walking in silence, I say, "You said something about Halloween."

"Oh, right. My buddy, Grant—you know Grant?"

I nod.

"He's having a big party Saturday. I assume you're busy with your *friends*"—he mocks the word—"but I thought maybe you'd want to come."

I bite my lip, searching for the right answer. "You must need a lot of help with math."

Chase grins at me. "You've no idea."

I must have never seen him smile before because I would remember this. He's got deep dimples that give him a boyish look, and one of his front teeth has a slight chip in it. The effect is so endearing, my stomach does a weird flip.

What's that about?

I look away, hot embarrassment creeping up the back of my neck as if there's a chance Chase can hear me thinking about how cute he is, and slow to a stop. Chase stops with me.

"The thing is . . ." I struggle for the right words. Have I ever told the truth about this? "The thing is, I'm not really into the whole drinking, partying, illegal substances scene."

He's not smiling anymore, just watching me.

I go for the whole enchilada. "I'm a Christian."

No expression. "Really."

"Yep."

"Like a real Christian? Father, Son, Holy Spirit, all that stuff."

"That's right."

"Wow. I didn't know they existed anymore. Round here, I mean. I thought they all lived in Nebraska and Iowa. Places like that."

I think of my little Baptist church, the one my parents grew up in. The congregation shrinks with every death. "We exist."

Chase gives me an appraising look. "So this goody-goody thing of yours . . . it's real. It's who you are."

I resume walking, and Chase falls in step. He seems to be making an effort to match my pace. "Basically."

"You don't party?"

I shake my head.

"Never?"

"Never."

"You're missing out."

I've experienced Lucy the morning after—bloodshot eyes and breath that could kill. "I really don't feel like I am."

Chase exhales sharply, his version of laughing. He looks me over again. "You confuse me, girl."

I think of two and a half weeks ago, when he blurted out my secret to the entire Algebra class. "It's mutual."

"Okay. So, no partying, but we could still hang out sometime. We can . . . I don't know. What do you do for fun?"

"Read."

He rolls his eyes. "Well, we're not doing *that*. How about coffee? You drink coffee, or is that too hard core for you, Saint Ellie?"

"Well, plain coffee's fine. But you get into the long ones you can't pronounce . . . I don't know how Jesus feels about those." I smile at my own joke, feeling a strange combination of free and self-conscious over Chase knowing I'm a Christian.

Chase's dimples pop again once he realizes I'm joking, and it does strange things to my pulse.

I look away, hoping he won't notice my burning cheeks. "Actually, I just can't drink anything too caffeinated at night or I'll be up until, like, four a.m. Learned that the hard way when Lucy and I went for Americanos after dinner one time, and the barista was flirting with her, so he kept bringing us free drinks"—*Stop talking! He doesn't care!*—"and I couldn't sleep."

"No nighttime coffee runs. Got it." We reach the Algebra classroom, but instead of going in, he holds open the door. "Go ahead."

"Oh." The only guy who's ever held the door for me is my dad. "Thanks."

Lucy waves me over to where we normally sit with Palmer and Diego. When I meet Palmer's eye, he looks away from me. It's been this way ever since our "moment," or whatever it was, by my car.

Chase dumps my backpack at my feet. "Later."

And by the time I say, "See ya," he's moving toward an empty desk.

"We missed you at lunch, El," Lucy says brightly as I sit in front of her. "Did you finish your homework?"

It takes me a second to remember "homework" had been my excuse for hanging around campus during lunch. "Yeah."

Palmer flicks a pen and sends it spinning across his desk. "Chase help you?"

Wow, a sentence. "No."

Lucy blinks at him, then looks at me, clearly confused. "Were you hanging out with Chase?"

"No. Of course not."

She shakes her head, confused but apparently willing to let it go. "Whatever. Anyway. You know what we decided over lunch? We're going to Bianca's lake house tomorrow after school. We're gonna build a bonfire and have all kinds of crazy fun. You have to come."

"I can't. I have—"

"Homework," she finishes with a roll of her eyes. "I knew you'd say that, but I'm not taking no for an answer. December's gonna be here before you know it, and I've hardly seen you recently. We're driving up tomorrow after school and staying overnight."

It feels good to not have to lie: "My parents would never let me do an overnight with boys."

Bummer. Really.

Lucy winks. "You leave that to me."

❦❦❦

Is that . . . ?

Yeah, I think it is. Palmer's leaning against my car, arms crossed over his chest, face set in a rare serious expression. He's barely talked to me—barely *acknowledged* me—since our weird, electric moment. Now he's seeking me out?

"What's going on?"

My question awakens him from a trance. His look is sharp and appraising. "You tell me."

"Okay . . . I don't know what that means."

"Are you and Chase like . . . ?"

"Like . . . ?"

"Like dating?"

Is he serious? "We're not 'like dating.' We're barely 'like talking.'"

His mouth twitches, a flicker of a smile. "It's your life and all, but . . ."

I roll my eyes as I dig for my car keys in my backpack. "Finish your sentences, okay? That's annoying."

"He just doesn't seem like the best guy for you to be hanging around. You're a nice girl, Gabrielle. And guys like Chase . . . they're bad news for nice girls."

My insides tingle when he calls me Gabrielle, but I brush him aside and throw my bag in the passenger's seat. "I can handle him, okay?"

"Maybe you think that now, but sometimes you think you've got a situation under control, and then . . ."

I shut the door and look at him. "Then what?"

He swallows and looks away. "And then you discover you don't."

"I knew Chase Cervantes when he wore overalls to school. I can handle him."

Palmer nods, his handsome face still averted. My crush isn't just about his good looks. His features sound ordinary enough when I assign words to them—sandy curls, gray eyes, strong jawline. There's something else about him. Some quality that draws me.

I look at my flip-flops, hoping to curb my coveting. It was one thing to feel this way before he was with Lucy, but now he's my best friend's boyfriend.

"You should come this weekend." Palmer's words pull my gaze back up.

I shrug. "No thanks."

"Not much of a party girl, are you?"

I wonder what he'd say if I told him what I told Chase earlier. "I prefer to avoid throwing up whenever possible."

"You don't have to drink if you don't want."

"It's not much fun sitting around watching everybody else get sick. Been there, done that."

"You wouldn't be watching *me* get sick. I never get sick when I drink."

"What esteem that must win you."

Palmer's eyes light with his smile. "I like talking to you. You always say things in a way I wouldn't think to." His gaze catches on something beyond me. "Well, gotta go. See ya."

He turns and rushes away.

As I climb in my car, I cast a casual glance down the sidewalk. Yep. That's what I thought.

Bianca, Marie, and Troy are headed this way. They're probably headed to Bianca's car; they live in the same neighborhood and often carpool. Lucy and I used to, but now she has cheerleading practice after school.

The trio doesn't notice me as they pass. I'm invisible.

Though not to Palmer. To Palmer, I'm just embarrassing.

I'm not sure which hurts worse.

Chapter 8

Dear Ms. Miller

My fingers hover over the keyboard and I stare at the blank space beneath the words.

My name is Gabrielle Sweet, and I'm seeking representation for my young adult novel.

Yawn.

I delete the sentence and click back over to the Reese Literary website, even though I've read their guidelines and suggestions for querying about a hundred times now.

I try again.

Everyone knows Lady Gabrielle Moretti is destined to be the next princess. Prince Domenico has done everything to mark her as his except offer her his hand in marriage, but—

It sounds so stupid when I boil it down like that. My finger itches for the delete key.

Bronte tells me writing my query letter is as simple as writing back cover copy. But what makes good back cover copy?

I peruse my bookshelf, withdrawing several recent additions to my collection. They were books I found on one of those tables at Barnes and Noble, ones that I hadn't heard of but intrigued me. I search for a common element in the descriptions.

Hmm. Reading sounds like a lot more fun than writing my query letter.

I sink onto my bed and open one of the novels. Really, it's research. I can see how they boiled down the plot into a simple paragraph.

And, okay, maybe I'm procrastinating.

I decide I don't care and curl up on my bed with the novel.

I've noticed, since I started studying writing, that it's hard to lose myself in reading. Every element has become something to study. Like with this book, I'm fascinated by how I like this main character even though I'm not sure I should. How did the author do that? Is there something—

"Honey, I just got off the phone with Jan. For what earthly reason are you not going away with your girlfriends this weekend?"

I blink at my mother standing in my doorway, pencil skirt still on but high heels gathered under her arm. Are non-readers totally clueless about how obnoxious it is to be engrossed in your book only to find someone suddenly talking to you?

I take a few seconds to process. She just talked to Lucy's mom, who must be under the impression that only Lucy, Bianca, and Marie are spending the night up at the lake.

"Homework."

Mom sighs and leans against the doorframe. "Ellie, I love how seriously you take your studies, but come on. Your best friend is going through such a rough season right now. Doesn't she deserve some quality time with you?"

I chew on the inside of my lower lip. If I tell her the real reason I don't want to go—the drinking, the smoking, and total weirdness of boy-girl sleeping arrangements—not only will I be tattling on Lucy, but my odds for surviving high school will plummet.

My mom will tell Jan, and Jan will not only ban Lucy from going, she'll tell the other moms too. And I'll spend the next two years fishing my stuff—my backpack, car keys, cell phone—out of the creek that runs through campus. With Troy's dad being the principal, somehow I doubt they'd get in trouble for harassing me.

"There's a bio lab due on Monday." It's scary how quickly I can come up with excuses these days. "I'm supposed to meet with my group Saturday morning."

Mom frowns. "Halloween?"

"Yep."

"They can't meet that afternoon? Or on Sunday?"

"I seriously doubt—"

"Call them. Somehow I bet early Saturday morning isn't their first pick of times."

My heart thumps an ominous beat in my chest. Now what?

Mom settles on the edge of my bed and places a hand on my knee. "School's important, Ellie. Your father and I really appreciate all your hard work. I know your grades don't come easy to you. But friendships—especially like yours and Lucy's—are important too. I'd like to see you devote a little more time to your friends and a little less to school. The occasional B won't kill you."

Wonder how Mom would feel about her pep talk if she knew she was pushing me into a boy-girl slumber party.

I lower my gaze to my book, my brain buzzing as I search for a way out. I can't see one. Somehow, I've been backed into a corner. I have to go.

I swallow. "I'll call my bio group and see . . ."

Mom smiles and pats my leg. "Thank you, Ellie. I don't want you having any regrets on things you missed in high school."

What's with James and my mom? Why do they think they're experts on what I'll feel I missed out on? They don't get that my fate has been sealed in regards to high school—I'm invisible, and there's no changing that.

As I cross the Quad the following morning, toward the oak tree where we normally gather, Lucy greets me with a mischievous smile. "Didn't I tell you your parents wouldn't be a problem?"

Palmer's eyes widen. "You're in?"

The others give me a cursory glance, then return to their conversations.

I laid awake a long time last night trying to get myself out of this. I've always thought of myself as an intelligent person, but it's getting me nothing at the moment. I can't come up with a single way to escape this unscathed.

I sigh. "Yeah. I'm coming."

Lucy squeals. "We're gonna have the best time!"

I attempt dampening my smile, but I can't help it. It's nice to be wanted. "It's just one night. It's not a big deal."

If only I could convince myself of that. They all think it's harmless fun, but if something goes wrong this weekend, it'll be me— the non-stoned, non-drunk girl—who's responsible for fixing it.

But they've partied hard plenty of other times and always survived. There's no reason why tonight will be any different.

"Here."

A Starbucks cup materializes in front of me. The hand holding it is big and the color of cinnamon.

I look up and blink at Chase. "Uh . . . thank you."

He nods—curt—then strides away.

My friends gape at him. Especially the girls.

Lucy's mouth is an O. "Ellie! You and Chase?"

"We're not dating."

But my words are drowned out by Bianca. "When did this happen?" She grabs my arm and the coffee sloshes inside the confines of its cup.

Marie jostles my other arm. "I heard his brothers are up for parole soon. Is that true?"

"We're not dating." I can only imagine how red my face is. "It's just . . ." I look at the cup. He brought me coffee. A guy brought me coffee. "It's just coffee."

Palmer laughs. "Ellie, don't hold out on us. He's bringing you coffee, you *know* he has a crush on you, why pretend like—"

"Chase has a crush on *Ellie*?" This from Lucy, Bianca, and Marie.

Um, ouch.

Palmer looks at them like they're stupid. "How do you not know this?"

Lucy shifts her gaze from me to Palmer, back to me. "How long has this been going on?"

"Nothing's going on," I say as Palmer says, "A long time."

I glare at him. Why does he insist on making my embarrassing moments worse?

He rolls his eyes. "*Everybody* knows, Ellie." He glances at the girls. "Except your friends, apparently."

Bianca throws her arms in the air. "This is crazy! Chase and Ellie? I don't believe it."

Again—ouch. Does it not occur to these people that I have feelings? Maybe I don't spend our lunch periods going into great detail about every riveting thought I've had so far that day, but it doesn't mean I'm numb inside.

"It's true." Diego speaks up from the grass. His eyes are slits and his voice mellow like we're all around a campfire or something. "Chase and Ellie."

Palmer glances at me. "That *he* likes *her*."

The warning bell sounds—two minutes until first period. I throw my backpack over my shoulder and hurry away.

"Wait!" Lucy, Bianca, and Marie trot after me.

"Give us the scoop." Marie dances alongside the sidewalk. "What kind of kisser is he? Bad boys make the best kissers."

"I think I resent that," Palmer says from behind us, but no one's paying attention to him.

"There's no 'scoop.'" I hitch my backpack higher. "Palmer claims 'everybody knows' Chase has a thing for me, but I've never heard it before."

"Me neither." Lucy.

"Same here." Marie.

"I thought he liked Lucy." Bianca.

It's not like I expected anything different, but at least Lucy could have said I'm not so unlikeable. Isn't your best friend supposed to convince you that the only reason every guy in the school hasn't asked you out is because they're intimidated by your awesomeness?

I sip at my coffee. An Americano. Strong, smooth, and the perfect drinking temperature.

Lucy bumps me with her hip. "How's the coffee? He know just how you like it?"

Marie giggles, but Bianca makes a face. "I think it's creepy. His brothers are in *jail*. You don't want to accept drinks from some weirdo like that."

"He's not a weirdo." Why's my tone so sharp? "Your brother got arrested for drunk and disorderly conduct. Should we hold that against *you*?"

Bianca's eyes narrow. "Whatever, Ellie. Enjoy your coffee and whatever else he put in there." She splits off from us, down the hall toward her class.

I should probably feel bad. That wasn't a very nice thing to say.

Marie jogs after her. "Bianca! Wait for me!"

Lucy doesn't seem to notice their hostile exit. Instead, her face draws into a sincere pout. "I can't believe you didn't tell me you've got your first boyfriend."

"He's not my boyfriend."

"Well, your first crush, then."

"I don't have a crush on Chase. I don't have a crush on anyone."

Lucy sighs. "You're so stubborn."

She's silent until we've hoofed it over the bridge.

"You think this is why he did that thing in Algebra class?" Lucy asks between huffs of breath. "Where he said you had a thing for Palmer?"

Palmer leans into the conversation. "That's what I think."

"I've asked Chase. He won't tell me."

Lucy grins wickedly. "You make him tell you. You use your womanly vials."

"Wiles." Why am I blushing? What am I, ten years old? "And I wouldn't know the first thing about how to do that."

Lucy laughs and bounds down the sidewalk. "See you at lunch, Ellie! Enjoy the coffee!"

As Palmer and I walk toward World History, I feel him smirking at me.

"I don't want to talk about it," I say when he opens his mouth. "It's just a cup of coffee. I don't know why everyone's freaking out."

Palmer snorts. "Yeah, ya do. You just don't want to admit it."

I choose not to respond. Whatever I say, he'll twist my words. We're almost to the classroom anyway, and then I'll be done with him until bio.

But Palmer follows me to the front of the class and takes the seat next to me. He notices me watching him. "Oh, sorry. Is this seat for Chase?" There's a gleam in his eye.

I glance at Chase, who's slouched over a notebook in the back corner of the class, his earbuds in. He's oblivious to me.

I pull my World History notebook from my backpack and face forward. Part of me wants to chuck the coffee, just to shut Palmer up. But Chase bought it for me. And it's not like the Cervanteses are rolling in money.

Besides, I like coffee.

I take a drink and ignore Palmer's chuckle.

⚜ ⚜ ⚜

As I head back to the bridge, Chase materializes beside me. His hands are crammed in his pockets, and he's quiet as we make the 56-step climb.

He remains silent once we're on the bridge as well. Is he waiting for me to say something, to acknowledge him?

"Thanks for the coffee," I say over the rush of traffic below our feet.

"You already thanked me."

"I did?"

"When I handed it to you."

I frown. "That didn't really count. I was too surprised to say a good thank you."

"Sounded fine to me."

He slides in behind me as we head down the stairs.

As we move away from the crush of students at the bridge, Chase clears his throat. "I know you don't want to go to the party tomorrow night, but what are you doing tomorrow morning? Like for breakfast?"

There's a tremor in his voice, slight but undeniably there. Impossible. I'm a five-foot-eight beanpole of a bookworm, and I'm making *Chase* nervous?

The realization presses on something tender and bruised in my heart—Chase likes me. He's nervous, but he's asking me out anyway. Because he likes me.

"Well . . ." But that's the only word I'm capable of getting out. Well, what? I'll still be at Shaver Lake tomorrow, so I can't. Unless I somehow get out of going to Shaver.

Somehow I think my mom would frown upon me giving up a "girl's night" for a date. Especially one with Chase Cervantes. Though if she knew what tonight would really be like, she'd probably change her tune.

There's still time to tell her . . . but of course that means social suicide. They'd see it as tattling to mommy, and they'd never forgive me. My days of hanging around the group would certainly be over.

But, so what?

So what if they no longer like me? What exactly am I afraid of? My popularity—if it can even be called that—already has an expiration date. Why am I letting myself get sucked into this stupid, dangerous night away?

Chase and I have arrived at Spanish class, but I linger outside the door. "I have a question."

"You can't answer mine first?" The strain in his voice makes me ache.

"I think it affects my answer."

Chase wears a cautious expression. "Okay, fine. What?"

"If something were to happen to me and my friends . . . Like if they weren't my friends anymore . . . Or say they were suddenly really mad at me . . ." Gosh, why can't I get the words out?

"You know, none of those were actually questions." He's teasing, probably trying to relax me.

I bite my lip, mutter, "Never mind," and rush into class.

It's such a silly thing to request of him, to stand by me when things go awry after I get honest with my mom about tonight's sleepover. Chase and I are barely even friends. And if it weren't for stupid Palmer filling my head with ideas about Chase having a long-standing crush on me, I would never think to ask.

I yank my textbook from my backpack and set about finding the page number marked on the board. Chase wordlessly takes the desk beside me. He's probably thinking I'm even weirder than he realized. That my non-answer is a blessing because it means he doesn't have to go to breakfast with a crazy girl.

Well, I don't *need* Chase. I can take care of myself when the fall-out comes. So my stuff might get tossed in the creek on occasion. Maybe they'll spread a rumor or two. None of them have the creativity to do worse, and those are things I can survive.

Things I can "use," Bronte would say. I'm a writer. I should welcome emotional torture.

The bell sounds, and Señora Lopez starts class by pairing us up for riveting conversations about what kinds of objects we might find in various rooms.

Chase turns to me with an expression so intense, so caring, my breath whooshes out of me.

His voice is low and deep. "*Tengo tu espalda.*"

It takes me a few seconds to translate—I got your back.

Tears tickle my eyes. In my stilted Spanish, I say, "*Me parece bien el desayuno.*"

Breakfast seems good to me.

Chapter 9

As I pace the lobby, waiting for Mom to come down, my cell phone buzzes every couple minutes with calls and texts from Lucy. They've loaded up the cars and want to know where I am. I sent Lucy a text saying I'm not coming, but she's still begging me to join them. How long will it take Bianca and Marie to convince Lucy to leave me behind? And whose side will Palmer be on?

Mercifully, my phone is about to die, so it can't go on much longer regardless of how long Lucy decides to text.

Mom breezes through the door, her bob of straight hair swinging in step with her. "Hi, Ellie. Aren't you supposed to be on your way to the lake right now?"

I glance at the receptionist, who's chatting on the phone. "That's why I'm here."

I sit on an overstuffed love seat, taking care to keep my spine straight and my shoulders back, like she's taught me.

Mom sits as well. Her deep frown resembles an expression of Grandmom's. Not that I'd say so.

I swallow. "The thing is, I don't want to go to Shaver. And it's not about homework. It's because the entire group is going."

I can tell by Mom's blank expression she doesn't realize what I mean.

"Like, the boys are going too."

Now I get the reaction I expected—widened eyes, a hand raised to her mouth in an *Oh my* kind of way. "But . . . Jan said it'd just be you girls . . . ?"

"I'm sure that's what the parents were told, but everyone's going. And today, I heard Diego and Troy talking about what of their 'stash' they should bring."

Mom stares at me.

"Drugs, Mom."

"I'm not stupid, honey. I'm just processing." She runs her fingers through her slick, chocolate-colored hair. "And there's no chance Lucy's in the dark on this? That she really does think it's a girls' slumber party?"

I shake my head.

"She always seemed like such a nice girl . . ."

I wipe my slick palms on my jeans. "I know this puts you in a weird position. Sorry about that."

"I'll have to call Jan, won't I?" Mom gazes out the window, as if she can see the trouble this will cause. "Oh, what a mess. Life was so much easier when you girls were little."

"Sorry."

"Don't apologize. I'm sure this wasn't easy for you, telling me."

I huff a humorless laugh. "This is nothing compared to what Monday morning will be."

"Oh, honey." Mom reaches and squeezes my knee. "Maybe it won't be as bad as you think. Maybe, because of your actions, they'll think through the consequences and realize how stupid it'd have been for them to behave in such a way."

Oh yes. I'm sure that's exactly what will happen, Mom.

Even though I'm sure Lucy and everyone left for the lake long ago, going home to an empty house makes me nervous. Instead, I flee to Karen's. The sanctuary I'll soon be losing.

Karen answers the door wearing tattered yoga pants and a bandana in her long waves. "You're a Godsend. I'm trying to organize, but I'm failing miserably."

The sight of half-filled cardboard boxes, of Karen's empty bookshelf, makes my throat tighten. It's really happening. In barely two weeks she'll set off for Scottsdale, off to new and exciting adventures, and I'll be here.

It was bad enough when I thought my only company would be Bianca and Marie. Now I won't even have that.

Karen's been talking, I suddenly realize, since I crossed the threshold.

". . . but there's no way I can list the house until I get all of this taken care of." She flutters a hand at the cluttered living room and kitchen. "The good news is I found an apartment, but of course it's a fraction of the size of my place here. The closet's tiny. It's a good thing they only have one season, because I have to get rid of half my clothes anyway. Want a new wardrobe?"

"Uh, sure."

"Come on."

I follow Karen back to her bedroom. On her bed are stacks of sweaters, some of which have toppled, and mounds of T-shirts and tanks. The floor is littered with shoes, coats, and pajamas.

I poke at a grocery bag overflowing with panty hose. "Panty hose? Really?"

"I'm in the hotel business, give me a break." Karen grasps handfuls of her hair. "Though for the life of me, I can't remember the last time I wore hose . . ."

"Is there a system of any kind here?" I gingerly step around more bags—slips, scarves. "Or did your closet just vomit this all out?"

Her mouth sets in a grim line. "I thought somehow it would be easier with it all out . . ."

I reach for a grocery bag of unidentifiable clothing.

"Ponchos. Tons of them. I thought they would be in for more than one season." Karen's voice is watery. "My mother was right. I can't do this."

"We just need a system, is all. Like a pile for things you're taking, a pile for things you're giving away, and a pile for"—I pluck the bag of panty hose off the floor and chuck it into the hallway— "things you're tossing."

Karen sniffles. "There's just so much."

"We can do this. Come on." I grab for the first sweater I can reach on the bed. "Take pile or giveaway pile?"

Karen wipes at her eyes. "I don't know. Ally gave it to me."

"Well, we don't have a pile for that. Take or giveaway?"

"She'd probably be hurt if she knew I gave it away . . ."

I glance at the unfamiliar periwinkle sweater. "When was the last time you wore this?"

"Hmm . . . well . . ."

The pause lasts too long. "Okay, we're giving it away."

"But Ally—"

"Mom is never going to know." I grab another sweater off the floor. "How about this one?"

After a few minutes, Karen's voice loses its hysterical edge, and she even starts sorting through her shoes.

When we've worked for about half an hour, and you can actually see patches of floor again, I point out that I'm being rather helpful.

Karen arches her eyebrows. "This is true."

"Bet I'd be pretty handy to have around in Phoenix . . ."

Karen rolls her eyes. "Ellie."

"I'll sleep on the couch—I don't care." The desperation in my voice surprises me. "I just *can't* stay here."

"Is something going on?"

I quickly fill her in on the Shaver Lake fiasco, how I narced on my friends. "And that's why you have to take me. I just signed myself up for two years of fishing my stuff out of Mill Creek."

"You know, the valley is supposedly going to have a drought this winter."

I give Karen a look. "This *just* happened. I'm not quite ready to joke."

"Okay, sorry." Karen stretches to hand me a pair of creamy, black leather boots. "Does this make up for it?"

"Absolutely."

She smiles at me, but it's tinged with something. Sadness? Regret? I can't tell. "Ellie, the truth is if I thought moving you to Phoenix would save you from the unique pains of high school, I would totally do it. But I think you'd just be trading these problems for new problems."

I zip my foot into a boot. "Maybe I'm okay with that." I stand in my new shoes. "These are incredible." I take a few steps. "I feel powerful. I am definitely wearing these tomorrow morning."

"What's tomorrow?"

Whoops. "My bio group is meeting?"

Ugh, why did I state it as a question?

Karen snorts. "Yeah, right. You have Secret Date written all over your face, kid."

My face burns, yet I can't seem to stop smiling. "It's not a date. We're just friends." Or something. I'm really not sure what Chase and I are. "Can you be just friends with a boy, do you think?"

She ticks her head from side to side, considering. "Who are we talking about?"

I fiddle with a loose thread. "This guy named Chase. He has kind of a bad reputation, but he's actually a pretty decent guy."

When did I decide that?

Her eyebrows arch, as if she already doubts me. "Does Chase have a last name?"

I swallow. "Cervantes."

Her eyes close. "*Please* tell me you're joking."

"He's really not like his brothers, I swear."

Karen purses her lips and studies my face. "That can go in the giveaway pile," she says after a bit.

I realize I've been kneading a sweater in my hands. "Oh, okay. And this one too?" The sweatshirt is gray and stretched out, with a faded Redwood High Ranger on the front.

"No. That one I'll take with me." She reaches for it, as if not trusting me to put it in the right pile.

It's an XL, far too big for my petite aunt. But I guess she wears it more for coziness than fashion.

Karen draws the sweatshirt to her chest and inhales deeply. "I know better than most, Ellie, that forbidding a teenager from a relationship can cause more lasting damage than just allowing it." The sharpness in her eyes tells me not to question. "Chase is quite possibly a nice guy who got dealt a bad set of cards. If anyone could be a good influence while keeping a level head, I think you've got a shot. Just . . . just be careful."

I swallow. "It's only breakfast."

"Sure it is." Karen returns to the closet, and I hear her pulling more items off a shelf. It isn't until she repeats herself—"Sure it is"— that I realize she doubts me.

At home, I find Mom and Dad in the kitchen. Dad wraps foil around garlic bread while Mom stirs the spaghetti sauce.

I drop my backpack underneath James's senior picture. "Smells good in here."

They snap to attention.

"Where were you?" Mom sounds both irritated and relieved.

"Helping Karen pack."

She snaps off the burner. "And why didn't you have your cell on?"

"The battery must have died. Why? Is something going on?"

Mom looks at my father, who gives her a slight nod. That seems bad. "Well . . . I talked to Jan."

The *bump, bump, bump* of my heartbeat intensifies. "And?"

"I hate having to ask you this, Ellie, but I have to."

"Okay . . ."

Mom leans back against the counter and crosses her arms over her chest. "Are you telling me the truth about this weekend?"

My mouth flaps open. Of all the stupid questions . . . "Of course I'm telling the truth. Why would I make all that up?"

Mom bites her lower lip as she considers me. "I know the news about Lucy's move upset you. But you're not"—she swallows—"angry with her, right? And maybe trying to get her in trouble because of it?"

"What? That's crazy!"

Dad lets the oven door shut with a bang. "There's no need to shout, El. Your mom's just trying to piece together what's going on."

I try to control my volume better. "I'm not angry with Lucy. I just didn't want to get dragged into an overnight with her and her boyfriend, that's all."

Mom reaches for the washcloth and absently wipes the counters. "I called Jan almost immediately after you left my office. The kids had already left, but needless to say, Jan was really worried. She said she'd call Lucy on her cell."

Mom sighs and pushes the cloth away. "And then she called me back five minutes later. In all our years of friendship, I've never heard Jan so angry. According to Jan, Lucy said that you had wanted to hang out just the two of you this weekend. When Lucy instead suggested that all four of you girls do something, you were mad and jealous. So when she invited you up to Shaver with Bianca and Marie, you threatened to get her in trouble unless she backed out of her plans and hung out with just you."

Is it possible for blood to boil? Because something inside me is.

How could Lucy do this? How could she say something so vicious about me? I knew she'd be mad, but I thought on some level she'd understand . . . what? That I wasn't trying to be mean? That she had started it all by manipulating me into coming? What exactly had I thought she would understand?

"Is it true, Ellie?"

I awaken from my thoughts to find Mom watching me with inquisitive eyes. Did I hear Mom correctly? "You're asking me if Lucy's story is true?"

Mom nods. She's biting her lip again.

I turn on my heel and march to my bedroom, trusting the slam of my door to be enough of an answer.

In an instant, Gabrielle knew she'd underestimated Lady Lucia. "We're supposed to be friends." Gabrielle's stomach churned. She could still hear the vicious rumor being spread around the market place. Why would Lucia tell everyone about her relationship

with Rafe? They were only half-truths, yet if this managed to reach the ears of Prince Domenico . . . Gabrielle didn't want to think about it.

"One should not look to the court for friends," Lucia said, her button of a nose in the air. "You know your happiness lies with Rafe, anyway. What need have you for the crown when you have the love of a man like him?"

"Domenico could have him killed." Gabrielle's head ached, and she realized she'd been gritting her teeth.

"I think you've overestimated the Prince's esteem for you." Lucia glided away, as they'd been taught by their governess when they were just tots. Even then, they were being groomed for the crown. Raised as competitors.

Yet Gabrielle knew that Lucia had merely pulled her to the edge of the cliff. Did she possess the stomach for throwing her off?

Chapter 10

Chase refreshes my coffee without my asking. "What I'm surprised about is that *you're* surprised. Of course Lucy was mad. And what else could she do but lie?"

I pull the mug close to me. "Do you think she had the story ready? Just in case?"

Chase shrugs. "Can't say."

As he dumps a packet of sugar in his coffee, I glance around IHOP. I'm praying no one acquainted with my family happens to be here. Chase Cervantes is hardly someone my parents would label as an "acceptable friend."

Of course, when I'm heading out with a friend, it doesn't take me twenty minutes to get dressed. Yeah—twenty. And I can't even pinpoint *why*. Chase sees me every day in my variety of plain tees and broken-in jeans. Why does this morning feel so different? Why did I agonize for five minutes between the brown shirt or the red? Why did I redo the knot in my hair about ten times before deeming it satisfactory?

"You're zoning out."

I blink a few times and find Chase's intense gaze on me. His eyes are the color of coffee and fringed with thick, black lashes.

"I was just thinking about this whole mess I've gotten myself in." That's more-or-less true. "I can't decide if I'm more amused or insulted by Jan lashing out at me. I mean, major ouch that she thinks I'd do something so hateful to Lucy. But talk about denial. Which story is more plausible? That a girl is sneaking away for an overnight with her boyfriend, or that her friend invented the story out of jealousy?"

"She's choosing to see what she wants." Chase dumps creamer in his coffee. "Happens all the time."

"I guess so."

"So Palmer was going too, huh?" His spoon clinks against his mug as he stirs.

My stomach gives a violent twist. "Yep."

How many hours did I lay awake last night dwelling on what was happening at Bianca's cabin? Were Lucy and Palmer sharing a room? A bed? Did they—

"You know it's over for you, right?" Chase taps his spoon on the edge of his mug. *Clink, clink.* "At best, they'll never talk to you again. At worst . . ."

My imagination runs wild with his dangling sentence. Yesterday, I had presumed my former friends lacked the creativity to hurt me, but after Lucy spun such a wild tale, I wonder how grossly I underestimated them.

Chase takes a swig of coffee, but keeps his eyes trained on me. "I'd guess Palmer won't be too happy with you either."

I pick at my nail polish. "Probably not."

Chase studies me long enough that I feel compelled to embellish.

"It's not like I wanted to get them in trouble, but what else could I do?"

"Why didn't you go? It's just a little harmless fun, Ellie. The worst that could happen is you might enjoy yourself."

"A lot could happen." My mind unintentionally ticks off a list of what I've seen since we entered high school and my friends started partying—Bianca sobbing the night after she lost her virginity to some random guy. Lucy and Marie going at it because Marie kissed a guy Lucy liked. "And I think you know that whether you'll say so or not."

"So, if Palmer never talks to you again . . . ?"

That fear has plagued me since yesterday when I made my decision—this is the nail in the coffin for Palmer and me. Although that implies that there was ever a chance for us, which there wasn't.

I push myself to smile. "I'll survive."

❦❦❦

I learn a lot about Chase during breakfast. The first being that he doesn't believe in talking and eating at the same time. From the moment the waitress drops his plate in front of him to the time he swallows the last morsel of french toast, he doesn't say a single word.

Of course, neither do I. I suppose he could conclude the same thing about me.

When he's done eating, however, he doesn't seem to mind answering questions.

His parents are both Mexican. They moved here when his mom was pregnant with his oldest brother, Mark.

"If your parents are from Mexico . . ."

Chase smiles, dimples and everything. "Then that makes me Mexican, yes."

My laugh seems airy. Almost flirtatious. "I was going to ask why you're taking Spanish."

"Well, I'm not exactly fluent. My parents only speak English to us. They often use Spanish with each other—especially if they're fighting—but they wanted us to be full-blooded Americans. No dual language, citizenship, allegiance, nothing."

I frown. "But why didn't you pick another language? I mean, you could always learn Spanish from your parents—"

Chase laughs. "You ever done anything for an easy A, Saint Ellie?"

I blush and poke at my half-eaten pancakes. Something about this morning has my stomach all in knots, and every bite threatens to come back up. I suspect it has something to do with Chase's dimples and long eyelashes.

"What do your parents do?"

"Dad's in landscaping. Mom runs a day care, which is good for her. She loves kids and wanted more, but my Dad's been in and out of jobs for years now, so they couldn't really afford it."

"There are three of you?"

"I have a little brother too. Donnie. He's in sixth grade and completely crazy. Worse than Mark, Francis, and me combined."

Exactly what we need around here. Hopefully he grows up to be like Chase rather than the older two.

Did I really just think that? That I hope he grows up to be like *Chase*? Clearly, I'm losing my mind.

But there's something about being with Chase off-campus that makes it easy to forget his thug reputation. He still seems a bit rough around the edges, but not like the type of guy who would break his friend's arm for giving away his last cigarette. And Nina had some tendencies toward compulsive lying, so it might not have been true, what she told me about him pressuring her to get an abortion.

"You're doing it again." Chase watches me with an . . . amused expression? A hurt expression? Some kind of combination?

"What am I doing?"

"Every five or so minutes you look around the restaurant. Afraid of someone seeing us?"

I grasp my coffee mug and drum my fingernails against the ceramic. "I didn't exactly tell my parents I was meeting you this morning."

Chase smirks. "They probably wouldn't have let you come, huh?"

"No."

"But you came anyway." Chase cocks his head. "Why?"

Good question. "I don't know."

Chase slides his empty mug back and forth between his hands, like a skilled hockey player moving toward the goal. "You and me. You think it could happen?"

I swallow and look out the window at the IHOP parking lot. "I don't know."

"Do you want it to?" His voice is quiet, vulnerable. I can almost forget he got suspended twice last year. Once for having a BB gun in his car on school property, and once for starting a fight.

I glance at him, expecting to find Chase turned away. If I were him, this conversation would mortify me. But his gaze penetrates mine, and it's me who looks away.

I take a drink of cold coffee. "Why do you like me?"

"Why do you think I shouldn't?"

A nervous laugh bubbles up. "It's not that I think that, I—"

"But you do. And I can't figure out why." Chase leans forward, making his thick arms flex. "You're smart, funny, sweet, and beautiful. Why shouldn't I like you?"

That last adjective thrums in my brain. *Beautiful.* There's something unfamiliar going on in my heart, like a volcano erupting. Warmth oozes and spreads throughout me. My parents are the only ones who have ever described me with that word.

Beautiful.

But I need to get control of this, because I simply can't date someone like Chase. I mean, what would we even do together? I force myself to take inventory of the activities I know Chase enjoys that I don't. And how many girls he's probably slept with.

I drag my gaze up to his. This guy is heartbreak waiting to happen. "I don't think I'm your type."

A muscle ticks in Chase's jaw. "Or is it that *I'm* not *your* type?"

He's certainly not stupid.

"We don't have much in common." I turn my attention outside the window, to the yellow-tinged leaves. Anything that is *not* Chase's probing gaze. "I'm not even sure we could be friends, really."

"Why do we need to have anything in common?"

"Shouldn't we have similar interests?"

"Are you having fun this morning?"

"I am, but—"

"What about those people you pretend to be friends with? Would you rather be with them right now?"

"No, but—"

"Then what's the problem?"

I look at him. Who knew Chase was such a quick-thinker?

"You know, Ellie, with what you just did to your old friends, I don't think it's too smart to turn down a new one." There's a softness in his eyes that makes my stomach muscles twist.

"Let's make a deal." Chase spreads his hands flat on the table. "We're friends, but we're friends with . . . an understanding. That we could be more. If you decide."

"If *I* decide?"

"Because I already did."

"Oh. Right."

I take another drink of coffee. Weird images plague my mind— holding hands with Chase. Nightly phone calls with Chase. Kissing Chase.

They're not unpleasant things to think about. Just . . . weird. I've never thought about him in that way before. I had never really thought about him in *any* way until a couple weeks ago.

He looks out the window, and I take the opportunity to study his profile. Palmer claims "everybody knows" that Chase has a thing for me, so how long has this been going on, and why didn't I notice? Chase is a confident guy, so why didn't he just ask me out from the get-go like I've seen guys do with Lucy, Bianca, and Marie? Or is it like—

No, that's impossible.

How can I, even briefly, entertain the idea that Chase might feel about me the way I do Palmer? Unattainable. Someone who it will only hurt to love, who can't possibly return your feelings. Larger than life.

I take another swallow of cold coffee, tears prickling my eyes with the possibility. Have I been unknowingly hurting Chase even a fraction of how much Palmer has been hurting me?

"You're over-thinking this, Ellie." Chase pulls his hands off the table, but I notice a slight tremor before they disappear. "Just talk to me."

"I was thinking about how the friends-with-possibilities thing seems like something that could really hurt you."

He must see that my eyes are misty because his tone softens again. "That's my problem. Not yours."

"As your friend, things that can hurt you are my problem too."

He tries hiding his smile, but the hint of dimples gives him away. "Fine. Have it your way. Friend."

Chapter 11

"How'd your meeting go this morning, Ellie?" Mom asks as I spoon pasta onto my plate.

"Oh . . . fine." When I left that morning to meet Chase, Mom had assumed I was going to meet with bio group, as we'd originally discussed. And I hadn't contradicted her.

"Did you guys get a lot done?"

"Yep."

"What's your project on?"

But the doorbell rings before I can make up an answer. More Trick-or-Treaters. I don't know why Mom insists we eat dinner as a family tonight. She keeps jumping up from the table every two minutes.

Dad pushes his pasta around on his plate, seeming deep in thought.

"How's the book going, Dad?"

He startles at my question. "The book?" He shrugs, which is strange. Normally he brightens at the mention of the James books. "Ron didn't like my Russia idea. I mean, those weren't the words he used, but I could tell."

"Does that happen often?" I poke at my green beans, hoping I don't seem more interested than a regular, non-writer daughter would. "Your agent not liking your ideas?"

"More than I'd like. I tell you, I just don't get it sometimes. Sales keep climbing, yet I don't seem to gain any trust on what will work and what won't. Even though I'm the one doing the school visits, the one talking to the kids."

"What was your idea?"

"I wanted James to spend some time in Russia. Ron thinks it's risky to move the setting off US soil, that parents won't like it. But kids are so curious about the world, you know? This is always a challenge with kids' books. Parents buy them, and parents read them, but the kids have to like them too, so we're always—" Dad gives me a sheepish glance. "Sorry, honey. I'm sure you're not interested in all these details."

"No, I don't mind at all." I force myself to take a bite of pasta so I don't rush into a new line of questioning. "So, how did you find Ron? I was pretty young and don't really remember. Was it out of a book, or—"

Mom stands in the doorway of the dining room, her eyes on me, her face full of concern. "Ellie . . ."

She knows about Chase. Someone must have seen us this morning. What do I do? He's in my bio class; I could claim he's in our group, that the others were late and—

"Lucy's at the door for you."

Oddly, it's a relief. "Oh."

"Should I tell her you're eating . . . ?"

Like I could take another bite with this hanging over me. "Uh, no." I scoot my chair back. "I'll go talk to her."

The sound of my heartbeat echoes in my ears as I walk to the door. I wish Chase were here. The decision to rat out my friends seemed clearer in Spanish class when he looked at me with those big dark eyes and said, "*Tengo tu espalda.*" In order to have my *espalda* now, he needs to be at my *casa.*

I take a deep breath, say a quick prayer for strength, and pull open the door.

Lucy stands there in a black leotard and cat ears, with a shoebox tucked against her hip.

Before we can say anything, a group of boys runs up the walkway. Two Batmen, a Spider-Man, and two mysterious combinations of ripped up T-shirts and fake blood.

"Trick-or-treat!"

I hold out the bucket of candy. One of the Batmen gazes up at Lucy. "Aren't you too old for this?"

She ignores him (would it kill her to smile or something?) and I toss him an extra packet of Skittles.

As the boys dash off to the next house, I step outside and pull the door closed behind me. Neither of us says anything. Instead, she trains a glare on me. The intensity is dulled by her glitter eye shadow and whiskers.

A minute ticks by. Okay. Somebody has to say *something*. "How's it going?"

Lucy stomps a foot. Oh, man. Tantrum time. "What's *wrong* with you?"

"Look, Lucy." I hold up my hands in a preemptive surrender. "I told you I didn't want to go. I hated to get you in trouble, but—"

"But whatever it takes to keep me from spending time with Palmer, right?"

I blink. What? "Lucy, it's not like that. I didn't want to go, plus I really *was* worried about you guys—"

"Do you have any idea what kind of damage you did? Everything was almost cancelled because of you. I already have to fight everyone to invite you to stuff. Nobody likes having you around. *Nobody.*"

My throat clenches so tight, it hurts when I swallow. "Like I said, I didn't mean to get you in trouble, but—"

"Why do you make yourself so difficult to be nice to? We've known each other our entire lives, but I still don't understand you. You'd rather stay home and do homework than have a fun night away with your friends. That's weird, Ellie. That's really weird."

I bite my lip, lost for a rebuttal. What's there to say? She's right, I would. And maybe that does make me weird, difficult, and not fun.

"And what do you have against Palmer? He's a nice guy, Ellie. I know he's not 'your type of guy' or whatever it was you said, but can't you understand he's *my* type? Can't you just be happy for me?"

"It's not like that."

Lucy rolls her eyes. "I see you watching him at school. I know you're just waiting for him to screw up so you can run to me with evidence that he's bad for me."

My face burns. "I'm not out to ruin anything for you two."

"Whatever." She thrusts the shoebox into my hands. "This is all your stuff. I don't want it lying around my room."

I peel back the box top. A clutch of mine she borrowed for homecoming, a pair of my socks—legitimate items to return. Then I unearth a few trinkets I've given her over the years.

"What, are we breaking up?" I hold up a stuffed cat. "Be serious, Lucy. You hardly need to return some prize I won for you at an elementary school carnival."

Lucy crosses her arms over her chest, a display of sharp, defensive angles. "I don't want it anymore."

I roll my eyes and shove the stupid cat back into the box. "Fine. Have it your way. We're no longer friends."

"I'm beginning to wonder"—her gaze flicks up and down me—"if we ever were."

She pivots on the toe of her pointy boot—reminiscent of a step we learned in dance class as springy six-year-olds—and stalks down the walkway.

Is that her official goodbye? Or will I at least get a wave when she's in the car, San Diego bound?

Monday morning, as I ease into a spot along the curb, Palmer's Jeep pulls in behind me.

My heart beats so fast it feels like it's humming in my chest. What will he say to me? Will he be snotty, or does he secretly understand? Maybe he won't say anything. Maybe we'll just exchange a look, and I'll know he sympathizes. Or maybe it'll be a withering glare.

I step out of the car on my unsteady legs, then wait for the verdict as Palmer emerges.

He throws his backpack over his shoulder, glances at me, and heads for campus.

And when I say glances, I mean *glances*. There's no anger. No sympathy. There's no emotion at all.

I think I would prefer him standing here and screaming in my face, like Lucy did Saturday night. At least then I'd know he felt *something*. That I'd meant *something*.

Had I imagined our connection? Was I playing mind tricks on myself when I thought maybe, just maybe, Palmer was jealous about Chase?

Apparently.

I trudge along the sidewalk, Palmer's golden curls floating in front of me. He's probably headed for our usual oak tree. And what should I do? What now? Should I find Chase and his friends? Carve out my own little space in the Quad?

My phone vibrates in my back pocket. It's a text from Karen. YOU'RE COMING TONIGHT, RIGHT?

Tonight is Karen's farewell party. It's hard to believe it's November 2 already. That in a week she'll drive off for Phoenix.

As I type my response—OF COURSE—the date nags at me. Is something else happening today? A test? An essay? My gaze hovers on Palmer's curls. It seems like it has something to do with him . . . His birthday, maybe?

As I pass through the Quad—on my way to nowhere in particular—I glimpse my old group lounging by the oak tree. Palmer hangs his arm around Lucy's shoulder and she beams up at him. As if everything is wonderful. As if it was no big deal that she yelled at me and gave me back all my stuff on Saturday.

I turn away and press on through the Quad, heading for the isolation of the library. Anger flames within me. It's not that I expected them to act any different—if anything, I expected them to act worse. I just . . .

I want them to *want* to hang out with me, to miss me when I'm not there. And they haven't wanted to or missed me for a very long time.

Tears burn my eyes, and I will them away. *Chin up, Ellie. Lady Gabrielle wouldn't cry.*

Lady Gabrielle triggers the significance of today's date—it's the deadline to enter the Great Debut contest.

I don't realize I've stopped walking until someone bumps into me. The girl gives me a nasty look, despite my, "I'm so sorry!"

I glance at the clock on my phone. I have fifteen minutes before class starts, and my laptop is in my bag. I could enter right now. A shiver runs through my core.

Or later. I could always enter later today.

Or not at all. Bronte says it's a waste of money.

I glance over my shoulder to the oak tree where life continues on just fine without me. No, Lady Gabrielle wouldn't cry over this. She'd get even.

And maybe that's what I'm really doing with this writing thing. In my own quiet way, I'm getting even.

In the hush of the library, I draw my laptop out of my bag. Bronte is probably right that the contest is a waste of money, but entering somehow feels like I'm standing up for myself. Like I'm drawing my sword. Only it's more like drawing my pen, I suppose.

Though they say that of the two, the pen is mightier.

Chapter 12

With Rafe gone, Gabrielle's world felt as dreary as the weather had been this last week.

Ugh. No.

I delete the sentence I just typed.

Rafe hadn't been around much recently, putting Gabrielle in a mood as dark as the looming clouds on the horizon.

I cock my head at the screen in consideration. I change "looming" to "threatening" and cut "much." Then I sigh and erase the whole stupid sentence.

My gaze wanders out my bedroom window, to the empty house across the street. The new family should be showing up any day now. Jan told my mom it's a young couple with a baby boy. Jan also told my mom that Lucy is having a tough time adjusting to life in San Diego, and she's encouraged Lucy to get back in touch with me.

It's sad that my mom is the hottest source I have for gossip.

Time for an email break.

There's a green light beside Bronte's name—she's on-line—but I'm trying to wean myself from Bronte. She has plenty going on and doesn't need me running to her with every problem sentence.

Besides. If I tell her I'm working on the sequel to *Invisibly Yours*, she'll ask me if I've sent out query letters to literary agents. I don't know how to explain to her that I don't want to yet.

Soon finalists for the Great Debut contest will be announced, and those of us who didn't final will get our feedback from the judges. Before I start emailing out queries, I want to take a look at the critiques.

But I can't tell Bronte that because I never got around to telling her that I entered back in November . . .

I click back over to my manuscript. The cursor continues its impatient blink, as if taunting me. My mind is locked on the real life Rafe, though. Since the new semester started, we see each other in shared classes and sometimes around school, but we always ignore each other. Or at least he ignores me, and I follow suit.

After I "attempted to ruin" the Shaver Lake sleepover, I expected to pay for it daily. Instead, they've continued to ignore me. No dirty looks. No snarky comments. I'm more invisible now than ever before.

If this is some form of revenge, they're geniuses. Same as with Palmer on that first day back, I hadn't braced myself for how I'd feel if they didn't care at all. It's like Bianca and Marie were so relieved to be rid of me, so grateful Lucy had finally recognized me for the major drag that I am, they were glad to let bygones be bygones and wash their hands of me.

Tears tickle the corners of my eyes. How annoying. Shallow girls like Bianca and Marie and a player like Palmer do not deserve to be cried over.

I rest my fingers on the keyboard once more.

Gabrielle tried to ignore the spot at the market where Rafe had once sold his goods. She had no right to be upset over his vanishing. After all, she had made her decision. And even if she had known it would lead to Rafe's absence, she would make the same choice all over again. Had she turned down Prince Domenico's proposal and he learned of her involvement with Rafe, she might as well have sentenced him to death.

No, this was best for everybody.

January in the California valley is gray and cold. Not miserable, but it's not like So Cal with eighty-degree Christmases. That's how warm it was for Lucy this holiday season. Or so I heard this morning as I crossed over the bridge. Bianca and Marie walked maybe two feet ahead of me, yet seemed completely unaware of my presence.

Chase settles on the bench next to me. "They were out of Coke. I got you Dr Pepper instead. That's okay, right?"

"Yeah. Thanks."

Chase pops a nacho in his mouth. Most days we eat out with his friends, but his mom's daycare business has struggled since Francis and Mark got arrested, so Chase is perpetually short on cash. When his friends go somewhere other than Taco Bell or McDonald's, we make excuses about me needing to help Chase with math. I've racked my brain for ways to get out of eating with his friends altogether, but no luck yet. Harper and Amanda, the current girlfriends, are okay, I guess, but Grant and Jose make me nervous.

"Did you watch last night?"

"No." My Dr Pepper opens with a *pffft*. "I told you I wouldn't."

"I think you should give the show a chance. You might like it."

I make a face. Chase watches this gritty cop show every Wednesday night. He insists I'd like it, but I don't do well with blood. Even the cheesiest slasher movies make me cover my eyes.

"Maybe you could come over next week and watch it. Our TV is so little, I bet it won't bother you at all." Chase shrugs, as if he really doesn't care what my answer is.

I keep my eyes on my sandwich as I mull over how to respond this time. Hanging out with Chase at school is one thing. I'm here anyway, and I can't just isolate myself. But anytime I've put forth effort to see him off-campus, our "just friends" arrangement gets complicated. My heart does weird things. I start thinking about how much I enjoy being with him, and that it might be possible for us to work.

But I know that's not true. Even if I overlook how we have nothing in common, including our basic philosophies about life, the fact remains that my parents would never allow me to date him.

Chase pushes a jalapeno around with a chip and clears his throat. "Actually, isn't your dentist appointment next Wednesday?"

I swear he files away everything I say. I'm guessing he remembers my appointment is at 3:30, leaving me plenty of time to make it over to his house for an 8:00 TV show.

I toy with a loose string on my coat. "Yeah, that's right."

"Hey, you two!" Harper appears out of nowhere, the way evil is prone to do.

Okay, that's being dramatic, but she's been bugging me this week. She's always flirting with Chase. I know how that sounds, but I'm not jealous. It's just not a cool thing to do while she's dating Jose. That's all.

"Get a lot of 'studying' done?" Harper grins and makes quotes with her fingers.

Grant tosses Chase his keys. "Thanks for the car, bro."

"No problem."

"Awful music, though." Jose sits next to Harper, his arm looping around her waist. "What's the deal?"

Chase glances at me, and I blush. He must be listening to something I loaned to him. His music tastes are as raunchy and poisonous as Palmer's. What's with guys these days?

"I think it's sweet he's listening to stuff Ellie likes." Amanda smiles at me, seeming a bit shy. She's even newer to the group than I am. The guys stay the same; it's the girls who rotate.

I can only imagine what my mom would think if she saw me sitting here. Amanda's lip ring, Grant's dragon tattoo, and how all four of them reek of smoke probably wouldn't make her feel like her baby had settled in with the right kids.

Some sort of pimped-out, low-riding truck thumps down the street, and all three guys turn to watch and critique.

"So when are you and Chase gonna, like, make it official?" Harper murmurs to me. "You should totally snatch him up." She looks at Chase with appreciative eyes, and something uncomfortable squirms in my heart.

"We're just friends."

"Please." Harper gives me a look. "We know what goes on when you guys don't come to lunch."

I can't help chuckling. Most of the time I read and Chase keeps his earbuds in. "It's not what you think."

Harper rolls her eyes at Amanda, who shrugs. "Nice girls don't kiss and tell."

Harper raises an over-plucked eyebrow. "How would *you* know?"

"From watching Ellie, of course."

The two of them laugh, and I force one out too, keeping my eyes trained on the grass.

When I look up, my gaze connects with Palmer's. He's cutting across the Quad, flanked by Diego and Troy. I blink a few times, as if to clear away a mirage. Is he really looking at me? Months of nothing but maybe an accidental glance, and now he's *watching* me?

He frowns, as if annoyed that I'm looking at him.

I turn away, my neck hot and heart pounding. Harper's gaze seems expectant, and I realize she had been talking to me. "Sorry, what'd you say?"

Her smile turns sly. "Thinking about Chase?"

"No, just zoning." I glance at Chase, praying he can't hear this conversation. Fortunately the guys have gone into hypothetical mode—they're making lists of what they would do to their cars if money was no object. There's no way he's listening to us.

"What I said was I'm guessing you'll say no, but Amanda's coming over to my place before the party tonight. You wanna come too?"

"Oh. I have dinner with my grandparents on Thursdays, so—"

A shadow slants across the grass, and I look up to find Palmer grinning at me. "Hey, sweetheart. How's it goin'?"

This is real, right? Or am I dreaming this? "Uh, fine. You?"

"Good." Palmer hooks a thumb in his pocket. "You hear from Lucy much?"

We have an audience. I've finally discovered what will pull Chase out of a conversation about fixing up his car.

"Not at all. How about you?"

"Not anymore. We talked once or twice after she moved, but not recently." Palmer shrugs. "Well. See you in class." He sends one more smile my way, then saunters off to where Diego and Troy wait for him.

Hostility radiates from Grant and Jose's glares, as if I somehow did something wrong by talking to Palmer. Chase looks at his shoes.

My pulse thunders in my ears. I force myself to be nonchalant, to stand.

"Well. I guess I'll see you guys in English," I say to Harper and Amanda, who are gazing after Palmer. I swallow and brave eye contact with Chase. "You ready, or should I just meet you there?"

"No, I'm ready." He throws his backpack over his shoulder and leaves the group without a word.

As we walk to Algebra, I expect him to say something about what just happened with Palmer, but instead he's silent.

"Nice day, huh?" My voice is too bright, like I'm trying to make up for doing something wrong. Why am I doing that?

Chase shrugs. The line of his jaw is hard.

Well, fine. If he would rather brood than talk, I'm not going to force conversation out of him.

Palmer is already settled at his desk when we arrive, his book out and pencil moving across the page. Finishing up last night's homework?

But he doesn't look at me, and I try to follow suit.

Our conversation continues to replay in my mind. Why today? This semester we have four classes together, including Photography, where none of his friends or Chase's would be there to witness our conversation. So why talk to me *now*?

The question plagues me even more by the end of Algebra class, because Palmer didn't look at me once in the last fifty-five minutes.

We pass by Karen's still-empty house on our way home from Grandmom and Granddad's that night. All through dinner, Grandmom clucked about what a mistake Karen had made. "I don't know how she's managing this financially," she said for, oh, the thousandth time. "She's paying a mortgage here and renting that ridiculously expensive apartment in Scottsdale. Foolish, foolish girl."

The only way I keep from going crazy is making mental notes for a future book. Without any embellishment, Grandmom would make a swell character.

Even more frustrating than Grandmom's mantra is the gnawing ache in my chest every time I think of Karen in Scottsdale and me here. We talk and text pretty regularly, but on Thursday nights it's tough to push away the feeling that she abandoned me.

My cell phone vibrates, a welcome interruption to my pity party. I push Chase's call into voicemail and shoot off a quick text: CAN'T TALK NOW. PARENTS. CALL YOU IN 10.

But Mom and Dad are up front bickering about James, so they might not notice me making a phone call. James is home on break and Grandmom was ticked tonight when he didn't show for dinner. He instead went out for a friend's birthday. Unless you're strapped to a gurney and bleeding from the head, Grandmom doesn't understand having anything else planned on a Thursday night.

My phone buzzes again—Chase. Can't he read? I push him into voicemail with an irritated jab.

He calls another time before we get home, and then a fourth as I'm racing to my room. "What?" I hiss into the phone as I pull the door closed. "I said I'd call you when I could."

"Hi Ellie!" That's not Chase. Harper, maybe? "Hey, Jose! I got her."

"Hello? Harper?"

Her high-pitched voice fades into the background.

"Ellie?" It's Jose now.

"What's going on?"

"Hey, can you come pick up Chase?" Jose yells into the phone, clearly not 100% sober. "The light-weight already passed out, and we're leaving. This party blows."

Come pick him up? My heart seems to pause, then break into a gallop. "Why can't you just take him with you?"

"You think we want to drag him along with us to our next stop? He's heavy."

It's *Thursday*. No wonder they're all barely passing their classes. "Where are you guys?"

"Stacey Holbrook's. You know where that is?"

Unfortunately, yes. I've been there a couple times to pick up Lucy and company. Good ol', Ellie—the designated driver.

"I'll be there in ten minutes. And don't you dare leave before I get there because there's no way I can—"

"She's coming. Let's go."

"Jose!" But it's quiet on the other end of the line. "Jose Paredes!"

My phone grows cool in my hand, but still I stand there. I just yelled at Jose Pardes. And I'm getting ready to go drag Chase's lifeless body out of a party. My real life is starting to feel as unreal as Lady Gabrielle's.

I give my computer a forlorn glance. So much for my writing time tonight.

I take a couple preparatory breaths, steel myself for the lie I'm about to tell, then snag my Algebra book from my backpack.

In the living room, my parents cuddle on the couch while watching the news. I beam a sunny smile their way. "Hey, Bianca just called. She left her Algebra book at school. Is it okay if I run mine over?"

"Sure, honey." Dad smiles at me. "How nice of you."

Mom yawns. "Don't get caught up gabbing and stay out late like you did last time."

Last time? Oh, right. About a month ago, Chase was leaving work and his car wouldn't start. I picked him up and took him home, but we got to talking in the car, and I didn't get home until midnight.

I doubt Chase will feel chatty tonight. "I won't. I'll be back soon."

I grab my wool coat and head out the door.

My shoulders tighten with every block as I drive to Stacey's. Walking into a raging party by myself seems like a bad idea, but what else can I do? I can't leave Chase there. Though how I'll drag his hulking body to my car, I have no idea. Hopefully someone won't mind playing white knight to my damsel in distress.

Stacey lives in a secluded section of her neighborhood with just her dad, who travels regularly. She's not well-liked—too loud and in-your-face with her opinions—but people tolerate her because they like to party, and she throws bashes at least once a month.

The party appears to be in full swing. My only parking options are about a quarter-mile down the street, which is bad news for Chase. I'll probably wear holes in his jeans pulling him so far.

Despite the open windows, the air in Stacey's house is hazy with cigarette smoke. I squint, searching for Chase. Instead, I spot my old friends front and center. Marie prattles on about something, a smoldering cigarette in one hand, a red plastic cup in the other. Bianca reminds me of a bobble-head with all her nodding, and the guys appear to have some sort of drinking game going on.

I'm about to turn away when I lock gazes with Palmer. His eyes widen, and my feet don't listen when I tell them to move. He's barely looked at me these last couple months, but today we've done the whole staring-and-somehow-unable-to-look-away thing twice.

Chase. I'm here for Chase.

I turn and ask the closest person, some girl I have gym with, "Have you seen Chase Cervantes?"

She shrugs her bony shoulders. "Maybe out back?" Then she strolls away.

At least I have a place to start. I wade through groups of people, my gaze on the back exit. As I slide open the glass door, I'm unable to stop myself from glancing at Palmer. He's still watching me. So not what I need in this already uncomfortable situation. My skin is sticky, and I haven't even started moving Chase yet.

Out back, it's at least easier to breathe. People splash around the heated pool, yelling drunkenly about whose belly flop made a better sound. The last time I was in Stacey's pool was third or fourth grade, for Stacey's birthday. She invited all the girls in our class, and we swam and devoured hot dogs and swam some more. At least two girls puked. I'm guessing there'll be a lot more tonight.

I search the crowd a second and third time. No sign of Chase. I turn back to the house, giving myself an internal pep talk as I consider the possibility of searching bedrooms, and spot him. He's slumped in a sagging, plastic chaise near the door. I must have walked right past him.

I approach slowly, though I'm not sure why. He's definitely out of it.

With his hair falling in his eyes and his face slack, he looks . . . softer. Like a boy.

I knew he partied, and yet seeing him like this awakens something protective within me. How could his stupid friends just leave him here?

"Chase?" On instinct, my hand smooths a lock of hair off Chase's forehead. I've never really touched him before. Maybe a teasing shove or an accidental brushing, but nothing this intentional or serious. "Chase, can you hear me?"

"Sorry, sweetheart. I think he's out cold." Palmer stands behind me, his mouth quirked into a humorless smile.

"Do you think"—I swallow and force out the words—"something's wrong? Should I take him to the hospital?"

"Nah. Looks like he just couldn't quite handle it tonight."

Yikes, I'm still caressing Chase's hair. I yank my hand back to where it belongs, in my own personal space bubble. Good thing Chase isn't awake. Who knows what kind of wrong idea he would've gotten.

"I just can't believe you're putting up with this, Gabrielle."

I blink at Palmer. "With what?"

He nods at Chase. "You know what I mean."

"What should I do? Leave him here like his other friends did?"

Palmer rolls his eyes, but there's a sharpness in his gaze. An anger. "C'mon. It's obvious you two are more than friends."

I have better things to do than debate my relationship status. "I've gotta get him out to my car. You gonna help, or just stand there and argue?"

In a novel, the hero would swoop in, a gallant knight, eager and willing to save the day. But in real life, sometimes you're stuck wrestling guys like Palmer into their role.

Palmer grins. "Guess I could help. Be a gentleman."

"Yeah, give it a try for a change, would you?" I grunt as I attempt to straighten Chase in the lounge. His eyelids flutter, making my heart leap. Maybe I won't have to drag him after all. "Chase?" I plant my hands on either side of his face and wrench it toward me. "Can you hear me? Can you move at all?"

"Ellie . . ." Chase collapses against me, nearly knocking me over with his weight. "You smell so good . . ."

And then he's out again, his breath hot and sour in my face.

Palmer's chuckle prompts a glare from me. "A little help please?"

Palmer eases Chase off me. "Oh, sure. You guys are *just* friends."

I brush grass off my knees. "That horse is dead. You can put down the stick."

He gives me a confused look.

"Never mind. You grab his torso, I'll get his legs."

"Why do I have to get his torso?"

"Because you're supposed to be the man."

Palmer laughs again as he bends his knees. "You know, I forgot how much fun I have with you."

Only my stomach seems capable of moving; it's doing a strange flip-flop reminiscent of last October, when I talked to Palmer on a daily basis.

After a few seconds of me standing there staring, Palmer's eyebrows arch. "Do I have to move him by myself?"

"Oh. Right. No, of course not."

It takes ten minutes of wordless huffing and puffing to haul Chase out to my car. By the time we arrive, there's a dull ache in my arms, the kind I can tell will be worse in the morning.

"Guys like him shouldn't be allowed to pass out," Palmer grumbles as I open the passenger's door. "Wait, aren't we putting him in the back?"

I sag against my car. The idea of scooching him another two feet makes me want to cry. "Why?"

"Because I'd rather ride up front, if you don't mind."

Every nerve in my body cinches as if Palmer pulled an invisible drawstring. He's coming with me? "You don't need to."

But I'm hoping he will. And hoping I don't sound like I hope he will.

"How else would you get Chase out of the car and inside his house?"

Palmer's thoughtfulness makes my insides warm and gooey. "I'm assuming his parents will be home."

"Still. You shouldn't do this alone."

I keep my misty eyes averted. "Okay. Thanks."

Palmer crawls into the back of my car and pulls Chase into the backseat as I push. Then he climbs out the other side as I fumble for the seat belt.

"That's a girlfriend's job."

I grit my teeth but don't bother responding.

Chase's head falls forward a couple times as I wrestle the seat belt across him, then conks against my shoulder when I click the buckle into place. I ease him off me and settle him against the headrest.

"Come on, Ellie." Palmer's voice is so gruff, I turn to verify it's him. "I don't have all night."

Palmer doesn't say anything else until I've veered off Stacey's street. Then he clears his throat. "By the way . . . I'm not mad at you. For the whole Shaver Lake thing."

"Oh." I shift in my seat. "Okay."

"I mean, I don't like that you told, but Lucy shoulda known better than to push you."

"Uh, thanks. Sounds like she kept you guys out of the hot seat, anyway. Which is good. I didn't want to get you in trouble, but . . ." My shrug feels sharp. "I couldn't find another way out."

Palmer nods, his gaze intense. I hold back a squirm. "So, level with me, sweetheart. Why's a goody-goody like you hanging out with him"—he gestures at Chase with his thumb—"and his friends?"

I shrug again. "Chase is my friend, and the rest come as a package deal. I'm not wild about it either."

"Then why put up with it?"

"What should I do? Tell Chase he can't hang out with the guys who've been his best friends since kindergarten?"

"Couldn't you just hang out with him when the others aren't around? I know I wasn't born here like the rest of you, but Harper and Amber don't seem like the best girls for you to be friends with."

"Her name's Amanda, and I can take care of myself. They're no worse than—" I clamp my teeth over my bottom lip. That's not something I should voice.

"No worse than what?"

"Never mind."

"No, you started it. You should finish."

I swallow. "I'm not trying to be mean or anything, but Harper and Amanda are no worse than Marie and Bianca. They're just poorer."

Palmer doesn't answer right away. "Still. When I saw you with them today . . ."

My heart rate spikes. "Yeah?"

"I dunno. It scared me. You're . . ." Palmer scratches at his knee, then his elbow. He's usually Mr. Laid Back, Mr. No Big Deal, but this looks suspiciously like nerves. "There's a reason I call you sweetheart, Gabrielle. Because that's what you are. And guys like Chase and girls like Harper and Amanda, whether they intend to or not, can ruin that."

"And guys like you can't?" The words are out of my mouth before I can think better of them. Why don't I just take out an ad in the school paper saying I have a crush on him?

Palmer turns and looks out his window. "Touché."

When I get home, I need to look up what that phrase means.

A long, agonizing silence drapes over the car. Finally, an uneasy minute later, Palmer says, "You see they had to move up the spring play?"

Uh . . . what? So, we're just done with that line of conversation? Fine. Probably better anyhow. "No, I didn't."

"Yeah. I guess that water leak in December means renovations for the theater. So they're moving the musical back, and they're doing the play in February in . . ." Palmer snaps his fingers. "Why can't I think of the name of it?"

"The Rotary Theater?"

"Yeah. Did you see what it is? *Anne of Green Gables*. Which seems weird considering the musical is *Cabaret*."

I laugh. "I think some parents were mad about that. I suppose it's meant to appease."

"You tryin' out?"

I snort. Nice, Ellie. Very graceful. "I'm not exactly the theater type."

"Too shy?"

"I guess. I'm not into an entire auditorium full of people staring at me."

"Well, they'd be staring at me. Five bucks says I'll be the lead." He follows this with a cheeky grin.

I purse my lips. "No bet."

If anybody understands Palmer's merits to play the lead, it's me.

I turn onto Chase's street and study the houses. I've only been here twice. That time I took him home from work, and then Monday when temperatures dipped unusually low and his car, again, wouldn't start.

I creep along the street, searching for anything familiar. "I *think* this is the place." I slow my car to a crawl and peer at the white house, the sagging front steps. "Yeah, this is it. I remember the porch."

The crumbling driveway crunches beneath my tires. I kill the engine but sit there in the car and stare at the illuminated windows. I've never met Chase's parents, and my heart flutters in my chest.

"Light's on inside." Palmer doesn't seem anxious to move either. "Maybe someone can help us."

Why am I so nervous? I haven't done anything wrong. All I did was drag home their drunk son. "Will you come with me to the door?"

"Of course."

Palmer and I are only halfway up the narrow walk when Mrs. Cervantes bursts through the squeaky screen door. "What is going on?" Her eyes narrow. In the thin light of the porch lamp, she looks older than I expected. And very tired.

"Hi Mrs. Cervantes, my name's Ellie Sweet, and this is Palmer Davis. We're friends of Chase's and—"

"You are Ellie?" Her gaze softens, and her face blooms with a smile. "I have been telling my Chase we need to have you for dinner. As thank you for taking him and Donnie to school." Her words are clear, just a hint of an accent. She looks to my car and she reaches to clutch the doorframe. "Did something happen to Chase? Is he"—she swallows—"is he okay?"

I muster my most soothing tone. "He's fine. We think he just had too much to drink. Some of his friends called me to come pick him up."

"Who?" Her face is hard now. "Who are these so-called friends? Grant? Jose? Whatever silly girls they run around with this week?"

"Yeah." I gesture to the car. "He's in the backseat. We could use some help getting him in the house."

Mrs. Cervantes sighs and pushes open the screen door. "Marco. Donnie. Come out here. It's Chase."

Mr. Cervantes emerges first. He's a hulking man, and it's clear his three oldest sons get their size from him. Donnie, by comparison, is shrimpy. But if my memory can be trusted, Chase didn't get his height until high school.

I start toward the car to help the three guys, but Mrs. Cervantes catches my arm with a no-nonsense grip. "I am so sorry you had to do this." Her eyes are warm and earnest. "You are good girl. I know this from the things Chase tells me about you."

I'm grateful for the bad lighting. She can't see my face burning red.

"Chase is mostly good boy. Not pure trouble like Francis and Mark. But . . ." She shakes her head. "Not pure good either."

"No one is."

She smiles. "I like the changes I see in him since he started dating you. This"—she gestures to Chase being carried past us—"never happens now."

She keeps talking, but my mind is frozen on the word "dating." Why does she think we're dating? Did Chase tell her that? Or has she just assumed so because I'm a girl and Chase is a boy?

Mrs. Cervantes squeezes my arm, then releases. "You want to come for dinner this weekend?"

After a few moments of grappling, I find the appropriate response. "Sure."

"What about Saturday? You free Saturday evening?"

What else can I say? "Uh, yes, I am."

"Good. See you then," Mrs. Cervantes says as Palmer emerges from the house. "Thank you for your help, young man."

Palmer nods, and we silently return to my car. As I back down the driveway, Mrs. Cervantes waves, then disappears through the doorway.

Palmer flips radio stations, all commercials or junky pop music. He pauses on a heavy metal song. "My Pop-Pop would call this noise pollution."

I make a face. "Your Pop-Pop is right."

Palmer's face lights with a smile. It's infectious.

I clear my throat and return my focus to navigating the empty streets.

"So, we've got"—he glances at the dashboard clock—"about ten minutes until we get to Stacey's. Tell me what you've been up to these last couple months."

I laugh. It sounds forced and nervous. "Same ol', same ol'. Studying. Reading."

"Hanging out with your boyfriend . . ."

I sigh. "What makes you think I'm dating him? Is it how I've told you a thousand times that I'm not?"

"I heard his mom."

I reposition my hands on the wheel. "I don't know why she thinks that, but I'm telling the truth. I had no idea how to respond to her."

"How about 'We're not dating'?"

"From my limited experience, that doesn't work." I shoot him a pointed glare, which only makes him laugh.

"Sounds like you've been a good influence on him."

I chuckle. "Oh yeah. That's what tonight proves."

"Still. I'm sure you're a dream girl for Mrs. Cervantes. Better than Harper or Amanda, anyway." Palmer watches me; I can see it in my peripherals. "What do you think about bein' a dream girl, Gabrielle?"

I've had enough of this.

At a red light, I punch the brake with a bit too much force and give Palmer a square look. "Why do you care?"

"What?" He seems thrown off by me doing something other than protesting.

"You keep harassing me about Chase, but what does it matter to you? You and I aren't friends. We're not anything."

Palmer studies me for a moment, then bursts out laughing. "Are you always this serious? You can't take a little teasing?"

The laughing rattles me, but I don't look away. "I know how these things work. You'll make an innocent joke, someone will overhear, and then it'll get around the whole school that Chase and I are dating. And we're not."

"Your light's green."

I step on the gas, heart still pounding. Is this really just Palmer teasing me, or is something else going on here?

"I don't understand why you're so sensitive about the Chase issue. Unless . . ." Palmer's lips curl, and there's an "Aha!" look in his eye. "I bet that's it. You've got your eye on someone else, don't you, sweetheart? You want to make sure he knows you're available."

I keep my gaze on the road. "You're being ridiculous."

Palmer shakes his head. "No, I think I'm right on this. Lucky guy."

I don't trust myself to respond. Instead I focus on driving, on achieving perfect 10 and 2. Because Palmer flirts for sport. Or out of reflex. I know better than to take any of it to heart.

Minutes later, I pull alongside Stacey's house, where the partying seems to have intensified. "Thanks again for your help."

Palmer unfastens his seat belt and pops open his door. "Sure thing. See you tomorrow."

I glance at the house party. "Will I?"

"Without a doubt. Have a good night, Gabrielle Sweet." Palmer ducks back inside the car, his eyes sparkling with mischief. "And Chase is right about one thing—you *do* smell good. Although, I was the first one to point that out."

I could die a happy death right now.

Chapter 13

I hang around the Quad waiting for Chase, though I'm sure I wait in vain.

Palmer's here, as promised. He sits on a bench, hunkered over something that looks like homework. He's the only one here from his group—not uncommon for a Friday morning before the first bell.

Should I go sit with him?

No. That's definitely a very bad idea born out of exhaustion and hormones.

I stayed awake half the night reliving his parting words: *You do smell good.*

I finally got up around 2:00 and reworked my query letter a dozen times, only to trash it at 4 and fall into bed. Now I'm exhausted, and it's all for nothing. On both fronts. Neither Palmer nor an agent, especially one at Reese Literary, would ever take serious notice of me.

The warning bell startles me out of my thoughts. I wince as I hoist my bag over my shoulder and trudge to Vista for Photography.

I settle into my usual seat and rub at my shoulder muscles, stiff from last night's work out.

Maybe Chase sent me a text message? I reach for my phone. Palmer said Chase had just overdone it, but maybe I should've taken him to the hospital. Maybe—

I blink at Palmer as he slides into the desk beside mine. What's he doing? He never sits in the front.

But if Palmer realizes he's just sat beside me (and how could he not?) he doesn't show it. His gaze is on Mr. Dolcer, who's fussing with the PowerPoint on his computer. It'll be another day of him waxing on about the history of the camera, great photographers of the decades, and so on. I think Mr. Dolcer is in denial of the conveniences of digital cameras. Seems to me, it'd be more beneficial to teach us how to take "good enough" pictures and fudge them into looking great with Photoshop. Instead, we're being taught how to develop rolls of film, expose prints, and a variety of other techniques we'll never use as people of the modern world.

"This class is the worst, isn't it?" Palmer's mouth is close to my ear. "When I signed up for it, I thought we might actually take a picture now and then."

All I can do is blink at him. What's going on? Nothing—not even eye contact—since Halloween. But in the last twenty-four hours, he's gone out of his way to talk to me during lunch, played my knight in shining armor by helping me drag Chase's drunk butt home, and sat by me in class.

Up front, Mr. Dolcer clears his throat. "Everyone, take your seats. Let's get going."

Palmer draws back from me, and I turn my stunned gaze from him to my teacher. I'm dimly aware of class going on around me—the PowerPoint presentation advances, Mr. Dolcer's monotone voice drones—but I can't make myself care. I try a few times, even jot a few notes, but my mind isn't on photography.

I must be going crazy. Obviously my storytelling abilities have advanced beyond Gabrielle and Rafe, because I'm now crafting a story in which Palmer is showing interest in me.

I'm jarred from my contemplations by the sound of desks scuffling against the linoleum. Uh . . . what's going on? I've clearly missed a vital piece of information. Around me, students scoot their desks, chatting as they partner up.

A desk butts against mine.

My gaze connects with a pair of mischievous gray eyes. Palmer's smile hangs slightly crooked. "Hey, sweetheart."

If only there were an invention that kept me from blushing. Like a button I could push or something. I duck my head. "Hi."

Two packets of paper drop onto our desks, then Mr. Dolcer moves on.

I reach for one. "What's this?"

"You weren't paying attention?"

"No."

"*You* weren't paying attention?"

"I zoned out."

Palmer offers a *tsk, tsk.* "Maybe you've been a good influence on Chase, but sounds like he's been a bad influence on you."

I don't answer, just skim the page. "Is this a project or something?"

"It's our photo assignments for the semester, partner."

"Partner?"

"Yep." Palmer gestures between the two of us. "Partner."

I swallow reflexively and scan the first page. *Here are some goals for you and your darkroom partner to keep in mind . . .*

Uh . . . darkroom partner? I'm not just blushing now, I'm sweating. I cannot—can*not*—handle being alone in a darkroom with this guy. Aren't there school policies against boy/girl darkroom situations?

"We're supposed to build portfolios based on these descriptions. So the first one is nature, the second—"

"I can read just fine, thank you very much."

Palmer chuckles. "Sorry. *You're* the one who zoned out."

I ignore him, scanning the sheet. Finally, I find what I'm looking for. We're only in the darkroom once every two weeks. I can handle fifty-six minutes every two weeks, right?

I breathe a sigh of relief, then look up to find Palmer holding my pencil bag. He has a box of brackets in one hand and gives it a brief shake.

"Hey! Didn't your mother ever teach you not to go through a lady's bag?" I snatch for it, but Palmer tilts his chair backward, moving out of reach.

He holds up my mini-stapler. "You have everything."

"I like to be prepared, now give that back."

"You do a lot of emergency stapling? Have a lot of projects that require a hundred brackets?" Palmer withdraws my Wite-Out pen. He frowns and brings his chair's front legs back to the ground. "What's this?"

"Wite-Out."

He shakes it several times. "I've never seen one like this. How does it work?"

"You just press down and pull. It's like a tape, kind of."

He tips his head and studies me like a curious puppy. And much like a puppy, he's hard to resist, hard to act indifferent toward. Regardless of how indifferent I wish to be.

Palmer tries to make the tape work on his page but doesn't press down hard enough. "It's broken."

I roll my eyes. "No, you're just doing it wrong." I reach across the table, and press his hand down. "Like this."

The details of the moment catch up with me in a rush—my fingers curled around his. Palmer's gray gaze, steady on my face.

"I see," he murmurs.

I yank away and blindly flip through my packet. "So. Just six pictures. That doesn't sound too bad."

"Nope." Palmer is cheerful. Unaffected. "Sounds pretty easy."

When the bell sounds a few minutes later, Palmer tosses his bag over his shoulder. I'm gathering my supplies, fingers lingering on the Wite-Out pen, when he bends close. "Bye, Gabrielle."

And even though I repeat to myself that he only leaned close so others wouldn't hear, my stomach is fluttery and my heart insists on racing.

I'm still trampling the butterflies in my stomach when I emerge from the classroom and find Chase waiting in his usual spot, leaning against the stucco wall. Seeing him there, his black hair gleaming from his morning shower, makes my heart beat even faster. Out of relief.

My hand wants the reassurance of touching him, but I stuff it in my pocket. "You made it."

His smile hangs sheepish. "Yeah. Head's killing me, though."

"And whose fault is that?"

Chase falls in step with me. "I can always count on you for sympathy, Ellie." Then quietly, almost too quiet to hear, he says, "Thanks for coming to get me."

"Of course. This isn't going to be routine, right?"

Chase gives a vigorous shake of his head, then winces. "I was just mad and acting stupid."

"What were you mad about?" He seemed like his normal self at school yesterday.

"Nothing important enough for you to worry about." Chase hitches his bag higher on his shoulder as we start our climb over the bridge. Once we're on the main campus, he says, "My mom says you're coming over Saturday. You don't have to if you don't want."

"No, it's fine. It was nice of her to ask."

Chase turns to me, his forehead wrinkled with his frown. "Should I have asked about dinner?"

"You were unconscious. I won't judge too harshly."

His frown only deepens with my teasing. "I mean before. You made it clear you didn't want to hang out outside of school . . ."

My smile fades. "Well, it's not that I don't *want* to. But I'd like to minimize how often I lie to my parents."

"And you can't tell them about me." His voice is flat.

I bite my lip as I consider my response. "Not if I want to be able to see you."

Chase stops walking, even though the bell must be close to ringing. "You *want* to be able to see me?"

"You're my friend." I take a couple steps. "And we're gonna be late for Spanish if we don't—"

His large, warm hand cups my elbow and holds me there. "There's something I gotta tell you about my parents, Ellie. They kinda . . . well, they kinda sorta think you're my girlfriend."

My laugh sounds nervous as I tuck imaginary loose strands of hair behind my ears. "Uh, yeah. I figured that out last night."

"But . . . you must not have corrected her . . . ?"

There's a spark of hope in Chase's eyes that makes me queasy. "It's not mine to correct. Just tell her before Saturday, okay?"

Chase studies my face for a few seconds, then tilts his head. "No."

I blink a few times. "What?"

Chase continues to Spanish, easily pulling out of my grasp when I reach for him. "I said 'no.' I'm not telling them."

I scamper alongside him. "But, why?"

He shrugs. "Just don't feel like it."

"It's going to make dinner horribly awkward. Do you realize that?"

"Won't be awkward for me."

"And that's all that matters," I grumble as we enter Spanish. "How *you* feel."

Chase's laugh is humorless. "If *that* were the case, Ellie . . ."

But he leaves his thought unfinished.

Chapter 14

When I get home, I'm not only greeted by James's senior portrait, but also real-life James and a couple of his friends planted in front of the TV with some stupid video game blaring.

James isn't playing, and he glances over his shoulder when I come in. "Hey, sis."

"Hey." I focus on grabbing a snack so I can head to my room.

"We've got popcorn over here. Lots of it."

My stomach growls at the thought, especially as I survey the granola bar options. I'm not thrilled about entering the man-land they've got going on in the living room, but they're so absorbed in their game, I can probably get myself a bowl and be in my room in thirty seconds. I'm itching to write, to get back to medieval Italy where the world makes sense.

The two who are playing don't even glance at me. The third guy—Adam, I think—acknowledges me with a head nod. James, however, seems intent on forcing conversation out of me.

"How was your day?"

I shake some popcorn into my bowl. "Fine. You?"

"I slept until noon. It was great." When I shoot him a look of annoyance, he holds up his hands defensively. "I worked hard all semester long. I deserve a break."

"I worked hard too, and I've already been back at school for a week."

"Well. Them's the breaks, kid."

Adam stretches to refill his popcorn. "Hey, Ellie, do you know when Mark and Francis are up for parole?"

I freeze.

I've got to relax, got to act casual, if I want to get through this without arousing suspicion in James.

"No, I don't know." I take a step backward, ready to make my escape. "Okay, guys, I'll—"

"Why would Ellie know anything about Mark and Francis?" James's gaze is locked on the television screen. "Nice move, Paul."

When Adam glances at me, I give my head a fierce shake.

That he ignores. "Because she's dating Chase Cervantes."

I suck in a breath. Oh, man . . .

James's look skewers me. "You're *what*?"

"I'm not dating Chase." The words come out in a rush. "We're just friends. I swear."

"*Friends*?" James rises to his full six-foot-four height. "If he's anything like his brothers, he doesn't have friends who are girls."

Paul pauses the video game, and the room turns terrifyingly quiet.

"He's not like his brothers." I dart nervous glances at the other guys. "It's not a big deal. Just please don't tell Mom and Dad."

James crosses his arms over his chest. "If it's not a big deal, then why don't Mom and Dad already know?"

Oh, I so set myself up for that one. "Because they'd react just like you are, except they'd ban me from seeing him."

"*I'm* banning you from seeing him."

I've never seen him like this, like the big brother. Of course, he's never needed to be.

I take a few breaths, collect my thoughts. I have to get control of this situation.

"Look, I understand you being concerned. But I never see Chase outside of school, and—"

"Uh . . ."

All of us look to Paul, whose gaze shifts between me and James. "I don't want to get in the middle or anything, but . . ."

"Just say it!" James snaps.

"I saw Ellie last night at a party with Chase."

James turns his gaze back to me. At any moment, I expect steam to billow from his ears.

I have my reasons prepped and ready to go—Chase had been abandoned, and what else could I do but take him home? My reasons were purely mercenary. I might even throw in a WWJD.

"This is totally unacceptable, Ellie. A Thursday night party? Hanging out with a Cervantes? You're the stay at home and study type. This isn't like you at all."

James's words slice deep. The "stay at home and study type"? Does James really see that as my defining quality? And if this isn't like me, why not give me the benefit of the doubt? Why not give me a chance to explain?

I whirl on my heel and march to my room. Why stand there and let James keep flogging me in front of his stupid friends who don't know how to keep their mouths shut? I slam my bedroom door, though I doubt he hears since the video game is back on at full blast.

I sit rigid on my bed and shovel in too-salty popcorn. If I relax, I'll cry. I don't want to cry. It's what "normal" Ellie would do, and I don't want to be me. I don't want to be a type. Unless "unpredictable" counts, and then I'll take that one.

Everybody thinks they know me so well. What a delight it'd be to shock them. If only I could snap my fingers and get my book published. That'd shock them for sure.

"*Ellie* did that?" they would say. "Ellie *Sweet*? Are you sure?"

And maybe it's not such a crazy idea. Bronte thinks my stuff is great. She thinks I'm ready for this. The only thing holding me back is me.

I pace my room as my laptop boots up.

I open the email I drafted at 4 a.m., the email to Emma Miller at Reese that I was too chicken to send. No more. I'm done being too intimidated to take action.

With my heart springing around my chest, I hit send.

There. I did it.

I queried.

With one click, I moved from hobby writer to serious writer.

I email Bronte about my boldness, but then I'm back to just sitting there in my room. Being me.

I resume pacing. I need something else, something immediate. Not like stealing a car or getting bombed at whatever party is surely happening tonight. Just something that's out of the ordinary for me.

And even before the thought is fully formed, I know exactly what I'm going to do.

I snatch my keys off my bed and barrel down the hallway. When I turn the corner into the living room, I crash into James.

"Ellie!"

"Not now." I weave around him, the garage door in my sights.

"I'm sorry I yelled at you." James trails after me. "But you've gotta understand the panic involved in hearing you're with someone like Chase. I'm just looking out for you."

With one hand on the doorknob, I turn to face him. "I'll be home in about fifteen minutes. We can talk about this then."

"Where are you going?" he calls after me, but I don't answer. I just close the door behind me, anxious to get on with it, anxious to make a change.

One that people can't help but notice.

Okay, it's possible this will take longer than fifteen minutes.

I didn't anticipate the sudden case of nerves I'd have once I arrived. I thought it would be simple—seven minutes to drive here, one minute to sign my name, and seven minutes to drive home. But so far, I've stood here for five, staring at the foreign sheet of paper. There's a list of times on the right hand column, and blank lines on the left where I'm supposed to fill in my name. A decent amount of options remain. How do I choose the best?

I look for Palmer. He's got one of the first audition slots—Thursday at 3:30.

I reach for the pen dangling from the clipboard. My hand shakes like I'm about to inflict pain on myself. How stupid. It's an audition. It's not accepting a part, or even doing something humiliating in front of my peers. Won't it just be me and the drama teacher?

I set my jaw and sign my name to one of the final timeslots—Friday at 4:15. I reach into the manila folder hanging next to the clipboard and pull out the audition materials. Just skimming the lines makes my breathing quicken again. I can recite for either "Anne" or "Mrs. Rachel." I make the snap decision to read for Mrs. Rachel—Anne's name is in the title, so obviously she's the main character. I don't want there to be even the slightest chance that I'll be cast as a lead.

"What are you doing here?"

I yelp, then cover my racing heart with my hand at the sight of Chase. "You scared me."

"Yeah, I noticed. Why are you here?" He looks from me to the sign-up sheets posted outside Mr. Freeman's door.

"Why are *you* here?"

"Detention. Again, why are *you* here?"

My instinct is to make up something, but that's stupid. I'm not doing this for some secret love of performing arts. I'm doing this to make a point, a splash, a statement.

I force my head high. "I'm auditioning for *Anne of Green Gables.*"

Chase blinks at me a few times. "You are."

"Yeah."

"*You* are."

I roll my eyes. "How many times will you make me say it?"

"Do you realize you'll be on stage? That people will be able to see you?"

"Well, that's where plays normally happen. On a stage. In front of people."

"And you're okay with that?"

"It's just an audition. *If* they cast me, my guess is they'll give me whatever non-speaking part they can. You headed out to your car?"

"Yeah." Chase strolls alongside me, his hands jammed in his pockets. "I just don't get why you'd want to do it. It's just a stupid school play."

"What makes it stupid? That it's not illegal?"

Chase glances at me, and there's a flash of irritation in his eyes. An awareness zips through me that he's considered by many to be rather dangerous.

I shut my mouth and face forward.

"I just don't get why you want to do it. That's all." Chase kicks a pebble that dared to be in his path. "Doesn't really seem like you."

Everybody thinks they have me so pegged, don't they?

"Maybe you don't know me as well as you think."

"Maybe I don't," Chase says as we reach his car. "Because I never thought you'd do something so stupid just to get Palmer's attention."

I don't realize I've done it until it's over. My hand smarts from slapping Chase. He stares at me with unblinking eyes and his mouth hangs open.

"Please tell your mom thank you for the invitation, but something's come up on Saturday." I march away, holding my body rigid so I won't tremble.

❦ ❦ ❦

When I arrive home, nearly thirty minutes past my predicted return time, James's friends are gone and the house smells of fajitas. It's James's last weekend at home, and Mom has been slipping out of work a few minutes early every day so she can be home in time to prepare James's favorite meals. I don't even want to think about the funk her and dad will be in on Sunday when we take him to the airport.

Mom turns from grating cheese. "Hey, El. Is Marie okay?"

Beyond her, James gives me an intense look and vigorous nod of his head.

I shrug out of my coat. "Yeah, fine. Just . . . girl stuff."

Mom laughs merrily. "That happens, I guess. But you're sticking around here this weekend, right? I want us to enjoy the last of our family time."

James snitches a bite of chopped tomato. "It's not the *last* of our family time, Mom."

Her smile is affectionate. "Of course not. Just for a couple months. I can't believe our luck that your spring breaks coordinate this year. How often do you think that happens? We'll have to all take a trip or something."

"I'll probably just feel like coming home."

Mom pauses her cheese grating as she considers this. "Oh, I guess that's true."

Sure. Let's stay home because James wants to.

Not that I can complain too much. Judging by the fact that Mom's alive and well—not dead of a heart attack—James hasn't blown the whistle on me yet.

Mom turns to the stove and stirs the searing chicken. "Ellie, how was your day?"

"Good. I . . ." I suck in a deep breath. "I signed up to audition for the school play."

Satisfaction warms me as shock registers on their faces, especially James's.

"Like . . . to act?" Mom finally says.

"Yeah, I'm pretty sure that's what they expect out of the cast." I pop an olive in my mouth, hoping I seem nonchalant.

"But . . ." Mom's brow furrows. "Do you know how to do that?"

I have more experience than she might think.

❦ ❦ ❦

That night, when Mom and Dad bid us goodnight and their door clicks shut, James gives me an expectant look. "So."

I pull a blanket off the back of the couch and draw it up over my knees. "I'm not dating Chase."

"But you hang around him enough that people think you are."

"You know how it is. You simply talk to a member of the opposite sex, and all of Redwood thinks you're hooking up."

I can feel James's quizzical stare, but I keep my eyes on the TV.

He clicks through the channels, away from the nightly news we had watched with Mom and Dad. "And that's all you're doing? 'Simply talking'?"

"We have similar classes. It's inevitable that we spend time together."

"Is it?"

"Yeah."

"What do your friends think about him?"

I take a moment to consider my response. "They haven't said much."

James lowers the remote when he lands on SportsCenter. "And what about the party last night?"

I hike the blanket up to just under my chin. "I thought you'd already made up your mind about that. You practically crucified me in front of your friends."

"Well, I'm listening now. What's the deal?"

Finally a question I can answer without wordsmithing. "Chase and all his friends were at Stacey Holbrook's, and he passed out. His friends were all moving on to another party and called me to come get him. This guy who used to date Lucy helped me load Chase in the car, and rode with me to take him home. That's it."

James's frown softens through my explanation, and by the end his mouth is a grim line. "I don't like the idea of my baby sister traipsing around some party . . . but it was nice of you to go get him."

Chase's vulnerable, boyish face from last night comes to mind unbidden. It's not like it was much of a choice.

"Chase really isn't like Francis and Mark." But another image pops into my mind—the harsh look he threw me today on campus. Though I don't think Francis or Mark would have allowed a girl to slap them without retribution. "But I'm still careful. We don't do stuff outside of school. We just eat lunch together sometimes."

Like every day. But at least the rest is true.

James's gaze skims up and down my face. "Okay. So long as you're being careful."

"I am."

"Because when guys like Chase are hanging around a girl like you—"

There it is again—a girl like me. A goody-goody.

"—they're on their best behavior. They *like* that you're good. It's intriguing to them. Chase probably isn't bad at the core, and maybe he has good intentions toward you, but he can only be on his best behavior for so long. Unless he lets God change him on the inside, who he's burying will come out eventually."

I wrap the drawstring of my PJs around my finger, then unwrap it. "But don't you think that's true about everybody? That you can only fake it for so long?"

"Yeah, Ellie." James slants me a look that feels expectant, probing. "I do."

It's as if he thinks I have something to confess to him.

And a few silent minutes later, when I excuse myself to bed, his, "Goodnight, El," lilts in a way that makes me think I've somehow disappointed him.

Chapter 15

I ignore Chase's calls all weekend and throw myself into memorizing my lines. From the block of dialogue they've provided, Mrs. Rachel seems to be an old lady version of Bianca and Marie, a total gossip.

When I arrive at school on Monday, Chase is waiting for me. The Quad is thick with morning fog, and I'm hopeful he won't notice me as I pass him.

But he does. "Ellie!" He easily catches up. "Ellie, come on. At least let me apologize."

"I really don't want to hear it."

"I know I shouldn't have said it. I knew when it was coming out of my mouth that it was wrong. I just . . . I got jealous, okay?"

My heart flip-flops in my chest. I caused Chase to be jealous? *I* did? With my unruly hair, lack of a chest, and bookish ways? I slow my steps, as if it even matters since Chase's strides are nearly twice as long as mine.

Chase jams his hands into his pockets. "You could say something, you know."

Being jealous is awful. I spent most my life envying Lucy, wishing I could be as effortless as her. As popular.

I stop walking and look him in the eye. "You don't need to be jealous. Trying out for the play isn't about . . ." Palmer's name sticks in my throat. "It isn't about what you thought it was. I just wanted to do something different, is all. Wanted to *be* somebody different."

Chase exhales slowly. "But what's wrong with who you are?"

I wish he wouldn't have asked because the list forms automatically, and tears spring to my eyes: I'm too shy, too insecure, too ugly, too rules-oriented, too afraid, too mindful of what people think of me, too obsessed with a guy I shouldn't even like, and too proud to give Chase—who by now has proven he deserves one—a chance.

Chase must notice I'm blinking away tears. "What's going on, Ellie Jane?"

I suck in a breath, ready to tell him nothing is wrong, to chock it up to PMS so there aren't any follow-up questions. But then I catch sight of his face.

Chase watches me with concern. And he's doing that because—and I'm not sure why this is only now impacting me—he likes me. Chase knows me, and he likes me anyway. He doesn't care that I'm a Christian or a bookworm. He doesn't care that I'm shy or wear glasses. He's been hanging around me for four months now because he likes me. ME.

I'm struck with a disoriented feeling, like when you've been on a boat for hours, then step on steady land.

There are a lot of things on that list I can't change right away, but I could change that last one. I could date Chase. I could push up on my toes right now and kiss him. I could tell him I've changed my mind, that I *do* want to be more than friends.

"I'm really sorry I hurt you, okay?" Chase's voice drops low. "And it's not like you didn't tell me from the beginning that this"—he gestures between the two of us—"wasn't going to happen, so it's my own fault. I'll do better. I promise."

I nod dumbly. I can't seem to do anything else.

He examines my face. "We're cool?"

I nod again, and Chase gives me a buddy-buddy clap on the shoulder.

"Then let's head over to Vista. Don't want you to be late. I know how cranky that makes you."

As my feet clunk up the metal bridge, I try to sort out if I just let an opportunity pass me by, or if I saved myself from more scars.

"Gabrielle Sweet?"

I stop my pacing and force a smile at the teacher's aide who's been calling everyone in for their audition. "That's me."

The maze of dark, velvet curtains leaves me feeling lost and small. Mr. Freeman, the drama teacher, is seated at a long table with papers spread before him. I've never been on stage before, though the houselights being on sucks away some of the magic.

As the flop of my shoes against the stage announces my presence, Mr. Freeman looks up and smiles at me. "Hi, there. Who will you be reading for today?"

Is this a trick question?

"Uh . . . myself. Gabrielle Sweet."

His laugh echoes in the auditorium. "No, dear, I mean are you reading Anne's part or Mrs. Rachel's?"

"Oh." What am I doing here? I'm so stupid! I don't even know how to answer the most basic questions. "Mrs. Rachel."

"Begin when ready."

That's it? I just . . . start?

"Um . . ." Air scrapes my suddenly dry throat. After a quick, nervous swallow, I take a deep breath, tell myself this will all be over within a minute, and blurt the lines. "Marilla! Marilla!"

I go through my whole senseless babble about why on earth would I have seen Matthew wearing his good suit in the afternoon of what should be a busy day. "So I thought, I'll just step over to Green Gables after tea and find out from Marilla where he's gone and why."

Okay, that's it.

Do I bow or curtsy or . . . ?

"Nice job." Mr. Freeman strokes his dark, curly beard as he peers at a sheet of paper on his desk. "Very nice, Gabrielle. Now, what productions have you done?"

"Um, none."

Mr. Freeman's eyebrows rise. "None?"

"I just thought this sounded like fun." As if I need to justify being here. I'm screwing this up so badly.

But it's not like it really matters. I don't *need* this. I'm not even sure I remember why I thought auditioning would be a good idea.

My skin is clammy all the same.

"Well, you did very well. Call backs will be posted on Monday and the casting list on Wednesday." Mr. Freeman's smile is dismissive. "Have a nice weekend."

I feel like a kid whose coloring has been fussed over by a group of overeager adults—what nice colors you used! You did such a good job staying in the lines!

I know I'm being coddled, but I smile back. "Thanks, you too."

As I step into the hazy sunshine, I say a quick prayer of thanks for how kind Mr. Freeman was when I clearly had no idea what I was doing. I shiver as I think of the query letter I emailed a week ago—I doubt Emma Miller will respond quite so kindly to my meager attempts.

As I head to my car, my cell chimes with a text message. Good thing that didn't happen *during* my audition.

Karen wants to know how it went. Rather than typing, "I don't know," I call her.

"Why hello, my budding Meryl Streep." Karen's voice is warm, and I envision her stretched out poolside, basking in lemony sunlight, breathing clean, dry air.

"That's something of a stretch. I delivered my lines, he told me when call backs and the cast list would be posted, and then I left pretty sure my name wouldn't be on it."

"I told you that's what it would be like."

"I know." I fumble in my backpack pocket for my car keys. "I just thought there would be something else."

"Like?"

"It's hard to explain. I thought I would feel different afterward, like I had accomplished something. But mostly I just felt awkward."

"It was your first time auditioning. Awkwardness is expected."

"I guess. I thought there would be more adrenaline involved or something."

"Maybe if it was something you *really* wanted, there would be. But it seems like you're not too hung up on what kind of part you get."

"That's true. I mean, if they gave me no part, that'd be just fine."

Karen laughs. "A better way to ensure that would have been to *not* try out."

I unlock my car and chuck my backpack into the passenger seat. "Okay, enough about me. Give me a Karen update. What are you doing this weekend?"

"Working."

"Well, obviously. What else?"

"Uh, laundry? Maybe washing my car?"

"That's what you're doing *every* weekend since you moved." I check traffic before heading for my car door. "You used to always be out with friends and stuff. When you lived here, I mean."

"Well, I don't really have friends in Phoenix yet. I know people at work, but that's all."

I close myself into my car. "No offense, but your life sounds kinda boring since you moved."

Karen sighs. "Adulthood isn't all it's cracked up to be."

The words grate on me. Most days that's what I'm living for—adulthood. Freedom. Finally striking out on my own and becoming the person I'm meant to be. Meeting new people, with whom I don't have to hide my passion for writing.

The question pops into my mind unbidden: What's stopping me from having that now?

Bronte's computer wheezes in the background of our phone call. "I don't know what exactly, but there's something missing. It's making me crazy."

I scroll through the first few pages of her manuscript. "I hated George."

"That's fine. You're supposed to."

"Okay." I lean back in my desk chair. "Well . . . good, then. Cause I really hated him."

There's a pause on the other end of the phone. "Maybe he's too flat. Maybe I need to add some likability to him."

"And while you're doing that, you should consider giving Reagan a flaw." I blink at my dark window. How long ago did the sun go down?

"Reagan has flaws."

I stretch to tug my curtains closed. My muscles protest, yet also seem grateful to be moving. "Like what?"

"Like she's driven to be perfect."

"And she's achieving it. At least in these early chapters."

"That's not true." Bronte's voice has taken on an edge. She's sounding increasingly frazzled. She needs to go to bed instead of staying up talking to me about her WIP.

I love getting to use all the new terms I've learned since joining AFW. Makes me feel all writery to talk about our WIPs and our MCs instead of just our works-in-progress and main characters.

Bronte takes a deep breath. "The story is about Reagan falling from perfection, so she really needs to be perfect in the beginning."

I want to tell her I don't think it's working. I also would like to retain her friendship.

"Could you at least have her think something unkind about Penelope? Maybe eat one more pastry than she should? It would give the reader something to latch on to."

"She'll do those things later."

Sounds like there's no persuading Bronte she's wrong. And maybe she isn't. She's the one represented by Reese Literary and who has a book coming out in June. Maybe her MC is fine as is.

Bronte huffs. "If I hadn't agreed to judge that stupid contest, I would be much further along in my revisions. I do *not* want to be the type of author who asks for an extension."

My breath catches. "What contest did you agree to judge?"

"The Great Debut."

"Oh . . ." She must not have judged my entry. Surely she would have said something. "But I thought you said that contest was stupid."

"Well, I figured if I agreed to judge it would be one less stupid writer judging. And that's why I think it's a waste of money to enter, because you just never know who they're going to stick you with."

My heart is so loud, it seems to pound in my ears. "What genre did you judge?"

"Romantic suspense. It was fine. They sent me fifteen. One was decent." Bronte's laugh sounds like she might be on the verge of tears. "And I guess judging was a nice thing to do, but now I just don't know how I'm going to get this book done in time."

"I think you should get some sleep, Bronte."

"I know. But Tim's out of town and the girls are sleeping, so the house is quiet. I could actually get work done without Dora theme music in the background."

I glance at the clock. "It's eleven there."

"Yeah, I know. I'll go to bed soon."

But as we hang up, I hear clacking keys.

I stare at my empty email with a mix of dread and excitement slithering up my spine. If Bronte turned in her entries, that must mean finalists will be announced soon.

I refresh the screen in vain, sigh, and head to the kitchen for some juice.

Dad sits at the counter, his laptop open, note cards scattered around him.

The writer in me knows I should leave him alone. Knows how hard it can be to jump in and out of a story world.

But my conversation with Bronte only whet my appetite for talking about what I love.

"Are you writing?"

Dad looks up. "Kind of."

I hold up the carton of orange juice. "Juice break?"

"Sure."

Dad closes his laptop as I take the seat next to him. "Sorry to interrupt your work."

He shrugs. "I don't know if it can be called work, really. I was just staring at my blinking cursor."

"I know the feeling. With papers for school, I mean." I finger one of his index cards. On it is scribbled *James throws the peanut butter?* "What do you use the note cards for?"

"Plotting. I know you're thinking my books aren't even five hundred words, how could they possibly require a plot? But I find them very helpful."

I pull another note card toward me. This one is more sure of itself: *James's mom sees the lizard.* "Where'd you get the idea to use note cards?"

"Oh, I read it somewhere." Dad waves his hand. "Probably back when I was still writing short stories. It helps me visualize the plot, what little of it there is."

I give him a look. "Why are you being so condescending about what you do?"

Dad's eyes—sky blue, like mine—widen. "Am I?"

"Yeah. You're acting like because it's short, it's easy. Writing short just means there's no room for wasted words or plot points."

A smile tugs at the corner of Dad's mouth. "Where'd you learn the phrase 'plot points'?"

I shrug. "School, I guess."

He takes a long drink of juice. "Well, I appreciate that, Ellie. I guess I'm feeling a bit down. Every idea I have these days is met with, 'Sorry, try again.'" He sighs. "Kinda makes me long for the days before all this. Before my agent and my editor, back when it was just me having fun with stories I loved."

The turn in the conversation makes something inside me bristle. "But wouldn't you miss seeing your books on the shelf? Or doing all those readings at schools and libraries? Or getting paid?"

Dad snorts. "I don't know about that last one. I would miss the kids, for sure, but I wouldn't miss the anxiety involved in school visits. And my books on the shelf . . . I don't know." He drums his fingertips on the countertop. "I thought it would matter more than it does. Don't get me wrong, it's fun. But . . ."

Dad stares off into his note cards. "It's like that trip we took to Disneyland when you and James were kids. I was excited to take you on your first roller coaster and introduce you to Mickey and all that. But what I *really* remember from that day is the fun we had while waiting in line. We didn't go for the lines, of course, and it wouldn't have been fun had we never ridden anything, but what I thought mattered about the day really didn't. If that makes sense."

Emotion swells in my eyes, and I look away. He can't be right, can he? I've never heard Bronte talk like that, certainly. Who would possibly complain about the gift of being *published*? What more could a writer want?

I tap the edge of one of Dad's cards against the counter as I debate my next words, as I weigh what might result in such a confession. "You know, I've been thinking about maybe doing some writing too."

"Really?" Dad's eyebrows arch. "Like what kind?"

"Well . . . I had this idea for a historical novel set in the royal court back in medieval Italy. Where this girl is forced to marry the prince to save the man she really loves."

Dad's eyes hold . . . amusement? "Are you studying that in school or something?"

"No. It's just the idea I had." I pull my sweater sleeves over my hands. Does he think it's silly?

"Well, sounds interesting. And like a lot of research." Dad claps my back with his hand. "There's plenty of time ahead for all the things you want to do, El. Now's for being young and having fun. Leave the work to us old guys."

With that, he opens his laptop and effectively dismisses me.

Face hot, I slink back to my room and stare at my empty inbox, willing away the tears. Why does he think I have no business doing something to achieve my dream simply because my age starts with a one?

Well, he'll see.

I click over to my Word document, ideas for the new scene suddenly cramping my brain, eager to get down on the page.

He'll see reverberates in my brain as I type. *They'll all see.*

Chapter 16

"Did you see they posted call backs yesterday?"

Palmer's words stiffen my spine. As if I wasn't already on edge being alone in the darkroom with him.

"Uh, no, I didn't."

"I have another audition after school today. I think I'm gonna be Gilbert."

I force my shoulders to relax. Obviously my name wasn't listed. Palmer would definitely have something to say about that.

Why do I feel such a strange sense of disappointment? I guess I had allowed myself this teeny-tiny fantasy of making a splash as the lead and using that as a catalyst to the rest of my adventurous life. But I don't *really* want everything that would come from a big role in the play. All those rehearsals would take up way too much writing time.

"You think I'm cocky, don't you?" Palmer says from the sink. I can't see his face, but I hear amusement in his voice.

"A little, yeah. Brad Carver always gets cast as the lead male."

"Brad will be Matthew."

I roll my eyes, even though he can't see. "How can you say things like that? Like you know what will happen?"

"Because I'm a man who believes in making my own way."

"You're not a man, you're sixteen."

Palmer laughs as he clips his picture on the drying line. "You're hard on a guy's ego, you know that, Gabrielle?"

The room is quiet as I move my picture, a candid of James and my mom in deep conversation, to the developer. It's too dark to tell for sure, but I think the photo is turning out all wrong. As if my bitterness over catching them in that moment, doing something Mom never takes time to do with me anymore, shades everything.

I turn away, eyes burning. How can Palmer think life's that simple? Some things—like appearances or parents' affections—we have little to no control over.

"What did you mean that you believe in making your own way?"

"Exactly what I said. I don't believe in just sitting back and letting life happen. If I want somethin', I go get it. I make it work."

I frown. "That's ridiculous. You can't control everything."

"You can control more that you think." Palmer stands behind me, boxing me into the corner. "Don't you get tired of just reading about everything, Gabrielle?"

My blood pressure spikes. "I *like* reading."

"But you shouldn't make it an excuse for not living."

I think I actually hear something inside me snap. "I do plenty of living, thank you."

"You're a smart girl." His words are a low rumble in my ear. "There's no way you need to study as much as you say you do."

My bangs have fallen between us like a shield, and Palmer brushes them back. His fingertips are a warm whisper against my temple as he tucks my hair behind my ear.

The intensity of my heartbeat can't be healthy.

"Gabrielle . . ."

From my back pocket, my cell phone belts out an old Jack Johnson song and Palmer backs away from me. He angles toward the wall as he packs up his stuff.

I take a shaky breath and stare at the unfamiliar phone number. Should I push the call into voicemail? But if I do that, then it's just me, Palmer, and the awkward silence. Even if it's a wrong number, I can fake a conversation until Palmer leaves. Which shouldn't be long; he shoves his folder into his backpack.

"Hello?"

"Hi!" The voice is female and as distinctly southern as my darkroom partner's. "My name's Rachelle Rea, and I'm with American Fiction Writers. Is Gabrielle Sweet available please?"

I clutch the nearest counter. "This is she."

"Oh, hi! I'm so excited to call and tell you that *Invisibly Yours* is one of five young adult finalists for the Great Debut contest!"

The revolving door swishes with Palmer's exit.

"Oh . . . that's . . ." I can't think of a single interesting thing to say. "That's so . . . exciting."

"Bless your heart!" Rachelle's laugh is warm. "I remember a few years ago when I was a finalist, I thought I was gonna faint."

"Okay, good, then it's not just me." I force a deep breath. A finalist. I'm a finalist. Abbie Ross is going to read my manuscript.

"On the call I made five minutes ago, the finalist screamed. I like this much better. Now I'll be emailing you the feedback from your first round judges. You'll have until Friday to make any changes you want, and then I need you to return the manuscript to me so I can pass it on to the second round judges."

Abbie Ross. She'll be sending my manuscript to Abbie Ross. "Okay." I sound breathless, as if I just crossed the bridge.

"And I'll include all this in an email, so if you don't remember every detail, that's just fine."

Rachelle congratulates me again before we hang up, and then I gaze into the developer where my ruined picture lies.

It finalled. Out of hundreds of entries, *Invisibly Yours* was one of the top five.

The sounding of the bell snaps me from my stupor. I rinse off my picture and chuck it in the trash.

Stepping out of the darkroom and into the morning's thin sunshine feels like being transported back to my real life. In there, I had been Gabrielle, both to Palmer and Rachelle. Out here with the other Redwood High students scurrying to second period, I'm back to being Ellie.

❧❧❧

When I leave Biology, I've missed two phone calls from Bronte, plus I have a text reading YOU FINALLED?!?!

So apparently it's been announced.

Fortunately, it's time for study hall. I seclude myself at a corner table in the library. My inbox is full of congratulations emails from fellow AFW members, but I ignore them when I see the green light by Bronte's name.

My fingers hesitate over the keys. What exactly should I say?

SWEETGIRL: Hey.

I suck in a nervous breath as I await Bronte's response.

BRONTEWRITES: Don't "hey" me! You finalled, Gabrielle! That's awesome!

My relieved sigh is loud enough that a freshman at a nearby table glances at me.

SWEETGIRL: Thanks! I thought you might be mad that I entered without telling you. But you had talked so much about how stupid it was, that I felt like I was somehow betraying you by entering.

BRONTEWRITES: Betraying me? That's ridiculous. I'm so glad you ignored me and entered. You're going to get feedback from Abbie Ross!

I grin and allow myself to dream for a moment, just a moment, of this being my big break. Of winning, of finding an agent, and of revising the boring life of Ellie Sweet into something worth living.

Dear Ms. White,

I'm seeking representation for my 90,000-word YA medieval romance. I know you're not actively recruiting YA writers, but your client, Bronte Harrington, is a mentor of mine. She speaks so highly of you that I can't resist querying.

Invisibly Yours is the story of Lady Gabrielle Moretti, who has been supernaturally gifted with an ability to know and tell the truth. Set in Italy circa 1410, Gabrielle is a member of the court and has been marked as the prince's favorite. But three other ladies, Lucia, Bianca, and Maria, are bent on winning the crown for themselves and set out to sabotage Gabrielle. While they're no match for her, Gabrielle is blindsided by a newcomer, Rafe. He's a drifting artist who makes a living selling pots in the market. He's far below her social status, but Gabrielle can't help but be intrigued. While the two fall in love, Gabrielle knows her future is marriage to the prince. Her heart she's already given to Rafe, but to whom will she give her hand?

Invisibly Yours recently received the honor of being named a Great Debut finalist. Thank you for taking the

time to consider my novel. I have great respect for you
and the writers you represent, particularly Bronte.

Sincerely,
Gabrielle Sweet

As I stare at the email that I've spent the day writing and
revising, there's a pulsing in the nape of my neck and Palmer's words
circle my thoughts like vultures—*"Don't you get tired of just reading
about everything?"*
Yes. I'm tired of reading all the "Made my first sale!"
announcements on the AFW forums, of feeling that jealous bite in my
stomach, yet knowing I've done so little to change my circumstances.
Finalling in the Great Debut is a foothold available to me if I'll be
bold enough to step out in faith.
While my resistance to querying and looking for a home for
Invisibly Yours has invited no rejection, it's also invited very little
hope.
My hand shudders as I rest it over the mouse.
I skim the email one more time, hunting for nonexistent typos,
and then click the button. My query is on her way.
I write ten more emails before the night is over, feeling hope
buoy inside me with every click of the mouse.

Chapter 17

"You lied to me."

I shield my eyes from the glaring sunlight and blink at Palmer, who's interrupted my quiet lunch with Chase. "What? When?"

"You made it."

I made it? Is it possible Palmer knows about the Great Debut? How would he know? Do his parents write? Does *he*?

"Have you not seen the casting list?" There's a hint of impatience in Palmer's words. "I'm talkin' about the play. You're Marilla."

I'm in the play? And whoever I am, I have a name. I'm not School Girl #4 or anything.

Shoot. That means I'll probably have lines and stuff.

"Who's Marilla?" Chase asks me.

"One of the leads," Palmer answers on my behalf. He turns his grin back to me. "Your name's listed just above mine on the cast list. I, as you might have guessed, am playing Gilbert." He bows for his less-than-receptive audience.

Dread squeezes my heart. "I'm one of the leads?"

"Rehearsal starts tomorrow. See you then, sweetheart." Palmer drops my script into my lap. Across the top, someone—Mr. Freeman?—has written GABRIELLE with a black Sharpie.

"Well. Congratulations." Chase's smile and voice are both stretched tight.

"Thanks, I guess."

"You look nervous."

"Because I am."

"They wouldn't have cast you if you hadn't done a good job." That makes sense, right? "Yeah . . ."

"And I bet the lights will be really bright. You probably won't be able to see anyone in the audience at all."

Oh, yikes, the audience. I'd been too busy thinking about having to act in front of Palmer to think of everybody else. "Yeah . . ."

Chase's smile turns soft. "Or you could back out. No one's gonna make you do this, Ellie. And if you're this nervous, maybe you shouldn't."

But as I stare at my name printed across the script, I know that's not an option. Not just because of how embarrassing backing out would be, but because I keep thinking about Palmer's words to me. About hiding behind my books, about using them as an excuse for not living.

I peel back the cover and skim the character descriptions.

MARILLA CUTHBERT: An elderly woman who adopts Anne. Prim and duty-driven to a fault, and initially unwilling to accept Anne because of her wild imagination.

The words prim and duty-driven land heavy on my heart. *This* is who I've been cast to play? Am I so straight-laced, so prudish, it comes through even when I'm acting?

It doesn't matter, really. I'm just doing this for the experience, to try something new.

But as I cram the script into my backpack, there's a tremor in my jaw from holding in tears.

The lucky girl to be cast as Anne is Christine Hart, a sophomore who does nothing but blush and make doe eyes whenever Palmer's around. It's sickening.

I get shaky and vomity when I'm up on stage, which is about 75% of the time right now, but should diminish to about 50% as we practice later acts. We're one week in, and I already have my lines memorized for act one. Having no social life is helpful with tasks like that. But I still bring my book on stage as a pathetic crutch. Looking into the eyes of the others, my fellow actors, still freaks me out. Thankfully I have exactly zero scenes with Palmer.

I watch him up on stage now, even though I should focus on homework. As Christine pantomimes breaking her slate over Palmer's head, he smiles at me. Or at least I think he does. Palmer is different here at rehearsal than he is during school hours. During breaks this last week, he always comes and sits by me. Like we're friends or something.

I intend to open up my English essay, but I have a new email waiting. Rachelle Rea's email address sends a shudder of nerves through me, but it's just a two-line message telling me my manuscript came through just fine and best of luck to me.

So surely it's with Abbie Ross by now, or will be soon. How long until she reads it?

My attention is drawn back to the stage when Palmer leaps off it, unaware that both Christine and Jenna, the girl cast as Diana, watch him. I grunt with disgust at my computer. If I were writing this as a scene in my novel, I'd say they watched him with "appreciative eyes."

I frown. Is appreciative the right word? Admiring?

"Mr. Davis," Mr. Freeman calls after Palmer. "Use the stairs, please. You don't want to be hobbling around on show nights in a cast, do you?"

"No sir," Palmer says with mock graveness. He turns to me and winks. "Whatcha workin' on?"

I click away from email. "English essay. A compare and contrast between—"

"Enough, enough." Palmer plops beside me. "I'm not thinkin' about that stupid thing until Sunday night."

"Why am I not surprised?"

Palmer grins at me, and I find myself holding eye contact with him, yet not feeling like I'm about to pass out. Improvement.

Palmer glances at the stage where Christine and Jenna fumble through the blocking of their scene. "You got time to run lines with me?" He assumes my yes and holds out his script.

"I'm trying to write an essay, you know."

"Fine." Palmer pulls his script back into his lap and gives a loud, fake sniffle. "I see how it is."

I roll my eyes and reach for his script, but he yanks it further away. "I don't need a pity reading, thank you very much."

"Palmer," I say with a laugh, reaching across him.

"Mr. Davis and Miss Sweet." Mr. Freeman's bass voice reverberates in the auditorium. I jump, and my face burns as I see Palmer and I are the focus of everyone in the room. "I don't know if you've noticed, but we have a rehearsal going on. Quiet, please."

"Sorry, Mr. Freeman." Palmer and I say at the same time, only Palmer's voice is loud and clear, and my apology is barely audible.

Mr. Freeman turns back to the stage and asks Christine and Jenna to resume.

I hide behind my laptop, my eyes hot with shame.

"See? You should've just read with me." Palmer's words are low and teasing in my ear.

When I look at him, he's smiling in a reassuring way.

I close my laptop. "Where do you want to start?"

His smile turns triumphant and his fingertips brush mine as he hands me the script. "The bottom of that page, where I'm following Anne."

I clear my throat. "Come, Diana, let's ignore him and he'll go away."

Palmer doesn't say anything, and I look up to find him grinning. "What?"

"Don't tell Christine this"—he leans close to share his secret— "but you're a much better Anne Shirley."

If I wasn't red-faced before, I'm sure I am now. The coconut scent of his hair gel makes me dizzy, or maybe it's the quick, shallow breaths I'm taking. "You're crazy."

"Seriously, you're great." His gaze is intense and strangely reminiscent of how Chase looks at me sometimes when . . .

No. Impossible.

I take a deep breath and recite Anne's line once again. "Come, Diana, let's ignore him and he'll go away."

Palmer's southern accent melts away. "I'm awful sorry I made fun of your hair, Anne. Honest I am."

"Diana, I shall never forgive Gilbert Blythe."

"Don't be mad for keeps, now."

I turn the page, preparing to read Anne's response, when my gaze catches on . . .

I'm hallucinating. I know I am.

I'm not possibly looking at my name—my full name, Gabrielle— printed in Palmer's neat script, then framed with a heart.

"Is there more to my line?" Palmer's voice makes me jump. "Or did I mess it up entirely? This scene makes me crazy because she's talkin' to Diana, so I don't have the line to feed off of."

I'm woozy, as if I stood too fast. "Um, no. You had it right. Sorry." I force myself to look at Anne's response. "And Mr. Phillips spelled my name without an 'e' too."

Palmer doesn't recite his line right away, and I steal a glance at my name, the heart. What does it mean? I tilt the script away from Palmer, as if to conceal it.

"Is somethin' wrong?" His words are softly southern again.

"No, nothing." I close the script and shove it at him. "I just remembered, I'm supposed to meet Ms. Shaw so she can measure me for my costume."

I leap to my feet and scurry across the auditorium as quick as I can without running.

Outside, with the sounds of traffic in my ears and the breeze cold on my cheeks, it's easier to think practically. Guys like Palmer do *not* write a girl's name and draw a heart around it in their play scripts. Especially *my* name.

When the auditorium door opens, I turn away and hurry toward Ms. Shaw's office.

"Gabrielle, wait!" Palmer sounds like he's jogging. "What's going on?"

I don't turn. With a mere glance he'll see how agitated I am. "Nothing, I'll be back in a minute."

"I'm not an idiot. I can tell you're mad at me." He's alongside me now, and I avert my face toward the shrubs along the theater.

"I'm not mad, I'm fine."

"Why else would you be acting like this? Hey, look at me." Palmer grabs my arm, but I keep my head turned.

"I'm not mad at you." My eyes focus on his sneakers, the vacant practice field, anything but him.

"If you're not mad, then what's goin' on?" His fingers shift on my arm, sparking life in my nerves. "I thought we were friends."

I think I'm composed enough to make eye contact.

Bad idea. He's very close.

My cheeks flame. "It's nothing. I saw . . . I saw something on your script that . . . but it's nothing."

"Oh." Palmer's face registers surprise. For some reason his expression reminds me of Palmer-as-Gilbert rather than Palmer-as-himself. "Look, I'm sorry if that upset you. I was thinking about you the other day at rehearsal and . . ."

My heart feels like a taut guitar string that's been strummed. So he really did draw it? I swallow and wrestle for words. "It didn't upset me. I was just surprised."

"Surprised that . . ." Palmer ducks his head in a rare, endearing moment of shyness. I drink in his features—long bronze lashes, his mop of curls, high cheekbones. "That I like you?"

Palmer Davis likes me.

He's looking at me like that because he likes me. *Me.*

I should respond, but the huge, involuntary smile on my face makes it impossible.

Palmer's hand runs down my arm, captures my hand in his. "Does that smile mean you maybe like me too?"

I think I nod, but maybe I just look at my shoes.

"I gotta get back in there." Palmer pushes my long bangs back to their normal spot behind my ears. "But I'll call you tonight, okay?"

I murmur an acknowledgment, then he saunters away, somehow leaving me breathless.

※ ※ ※

Alone in my room, I practice answering my phone with a casual, "Hello?" I do this over and over, to the point where the word sounds weird, and I'm not even sure it's the best way to respond to an incoming call.

Of course, this is assuming my phone actually rings at some point tonight.

I stare at the manuscript on my computer, which has been open for an hour now, ever since I returned to my room from dinner. I've barely written a hundred words. Instead, I've been reliving the events of this afternoon. I'm not embellishing them, right? The idea that I'm hallucinating Palmer liking me seems more plausible than Palmer actually being interested in skinny, boring me.

And say—miracle of miracles—this is all for real. What does Ellie + Palmer really equal? Me hanging out with a bunch of people who've sworn me their enemy for life? Palling around with Bianca and Marie again? And I can only imagine what Lucy will say when she hears—

I jump as my cell phone launches into the familiar Jack Johnson melody. The call is from a local number I don't recognize. This has to be Palmer.

Knock, knock. "Ellie?"

My dad—no!

The doorknob turns, and with a grimace, I push the incoming call into voicemail. "Hey, Dad, what's up?" Instead of casual and friendly, like I had hoped, I sound impatient and irritated.

Dad glances at my phone, which is gripped in my lap. "Sorry, were you on the phone?"

"Nothing important." I startle at the sight of Mom coming in behind him. Both parents? That can't be good. "What's going on?"

Dad perches on the edge of my bed. "I just had a phone call . . ." He glances at Mom, who's leaning against the doorway. "And your mother and I have something to ask you."

Oh no, did Palmer call the house before my cell? I never planned on hiding Palmer from my parents or anything, but I thought *I* would be the one to tell them I have a boyfriend.

"Did you enter the Great Debut contest?"

I blink at my father, who's watching me with a perplexed expression.

Dad takes a deep breath. "My agent just called to ask me if the Gabrielle Sweet who finalled in the Great Debut contest is by any chance related to me."

Agents see those lists? I guess I knew that, I just didn't expect that my *dad's* agent might. "Uh, yeah, that's me."

Rain pelting my window is the only sound in the room.

Mom exhales loudly. "But why didn't you tell us, Ellie? Why would you keep something so wonderful from us? And when did you find time to write a whole novel?"

"I . . ." I rub the hem of my sweater between my fingers. "I don't really need to spend so much time studying."

Dad's face lights with triumph. "I knew she was spending too much time on schoolwork! Didn't I say that to you, Ally? Didn't I?"

Mom shoots him an annoyed look before turning back to me. "But *why* didn't you tell us?"

"I don't know. I really don't. I didn't know if anything was going to come of it, and . . ." It sounds lame, and I know it. "It just felt . . . private."

Mom is still looking at me as if I stomped on her favorite rose bush, but Dad's nodding his head. "I think I get that, Ellie. And . . . well, you tried to talk to me about it, didn't you?"

Mom's eyes blaze at my father. "And you didn't tell me?"

Dad glances at me before shrugging at her. "I honestly forgot until just now. I was working on *James in Moscow* and . . ." He shrugs again.

Mom huffs out a breath. "I'm not sure I'll survive living with two writers." There's a softening in her voice and a hint of smile on her face.

Dad grins at her, then at me. "Well, Ellie. Coffee? Ice cream? This is something to celebrate."

My heart seems to stammer in my chest. "It is? I mean, I know it is. I just didn't . . ."

I just didn't think you guys would know it.

"Of course it is! Your name is out there, Ellie-girl. And that doesn't come easy in this business."

Their reaction should delight me, but instead it makes my stomach clench. What if Mom wants to blab my great news to Jan Shears or Bianca and Marie's moms? Lucy, Bianca, and Marie aren't the brightest, but surely even they would recognize themselves under the thin disguise of medieval Italy.

And what if—my throat goes dry—Palmer recognizes himself as Rafe?

"I don't want to share this with anybody yet." My voice bleeds with panic. "I don't, um . . . I just . . . I'm not ready."

Mom and Dad exchange looks, then Dad nods at me. "That can be your choice, Ellie. But what won't be your decision to make is this—you're going to the American Fiction Writers conference this year. Because I want you sitting in the awards banquet when they call your name."

Chapter 18

Because Dad insists that we must have ice cream *and* coffee to celebrate, I don't get home until after 11. I'm shrugging out of my coat when Palmer calls for the fourth time that evening.

"Hi!" My voice is abuzz with sugar and caffeine.

"Well. *You* are a hard girl to get ahold of."

"I know, sorry. I had a . . . a thing come up tonight."

"A thing, hmm? That's rather vague." Palmer sounds . . . irritated?

"I was with my parents for a family event of sorts."

"Ah."

Yes. Definitely irritated. As if my nerves weren't tight enough, they seem to pull even tauter. "If I could have taken your phone call, I would have. We seriously just got home. I was about to call *you*, actually."

Palmer's exhale reaches me through the phone. "Okay. I thought you maybe changed your mind or something."

Is he crazy? In what universe would *I* change my mind about *him*? "You think me so flippant?"

"No, not at all. Just . . ." There's a heavy sigh on Palmer's end. "This is not how I imagined this conversation going."

The idea of him imagining our conversations sends a zip all the way down to my toes. I pace my room, fueled by caffeine, sugar, and hormones.

"Then let's make it go a different way." I pivot on the heel of my foot. "Did Christine and Jenna ever get their blocking figured out?"

Palmer hesitates, seeming thrown by the abrupt subject change. "Uh, not really. Were you listening during my scene with Christine?

She stumbled over every line. I swear you should've been cast as Anne."

I frown at my reflection in the dark window. "Be nice. She's nervous, that's all."

"I don't get why, though. It's just the cast, not even a real audience."

When I pivot this time, it's slower. "Do you really not know . . . or is this false modesty?"

"Do I seem capable of false modesty?"

"So you really don't know?"

"Don't know what?"

"That Christine's nervous because she has a huge crush on you."

A pause. "Did she tell you that?"

"Of course not." Even as a sophomore, Christine is *way* cooler than me. We talk on stage as Anne and Marilla, and that's it.

"Then how do you know?"

"I have eyes, don't I?"

Why did I bring up Christine? Like I need to be pointing out to Palmer all the other girls he could be dating.

His chuckle is warm in my ear. "Well, if you're right, that's too bad for her. Because I'm interested in somebody else."

My pacing halts. "Yeah?" Other than being a touch too breathy, I sound pretty casual.

"Yeah. She's great. Funny. Smart. Shy, though. It's been tough for me to get much of a read on how she feels about me."

I catch sight of my reflection in the window again. Of my T-shirt printed with the word Adorkable, my glasses, the strands of hair loose from their knot. *This* is who Palmer likes?

I turn my back on the image. "Maybe she just needs time to adjust."

"Adjust to what?"

"The idea of you liking her."

"But why should that be an adjustment? I've liked her for a long time."

I sink to the floor and hug my legs tight to my chest. "I don't think she realized that."

"Really? I thought I was being pretty obvious."

With my eyes pressed closed, moments from the last weeks slide by as if on a roll of film—the intense way he teased me about Chase, as if he somehow posed a threat. Palmer with my Wite-Out pen, goading me into touching him. The darkroom, his fingertips against my temple.

"Maybe you were obvious, but she just couldn't comprehend that you might like her."

"Are you insulting her? You better not be insulting her."

"I'm just stating facts." A rush of light-headedness comes over me. Oh, right—*breathing.* "You know . . ." I pick at a ball of fuzz on my sock. Should I say it? One of us has to. "Your friends won't be too happy about this. About . . . us."

"Well." Palmer clears his throat. "I don't feel the need to tell my friends every detail about my life. Do you?"

There's a wobble in his confidence, which makes this crystal clear.

Yes, he likes me. Yes, he wants us to be together. But this conversation—this relationship—is private.

If I agree.

And how can I not? It's Palmer Davis. This is what I've wanted, what I've *written* about. Rafe and Gabrielle had to keep their relationship a secret too . . . so really, it's kinda romantic in a way.

I inhale deeply. "Why does it need to be anybody's business but ours?"

As I tie back my hair the following morning, I study my reflection in search of evidence that I'm not simply Ellie anymore, but that I'm Gabrielle, Palmer's girlfriend. The only change I see is that I look more haggard. That's to be expected since I only got about three hours of sleep.

Around 2 a.m., after spending hours obsessing, I thought it might help if I wrote everything down, from finalling in the Great Debut to every word Palmer and I had exchanged at play practice and on the phone. Maybe helping the events escape from the cramped space in my brain would help.

At some point after 3 a.m., I apparently conked out. When I awoke this morning, my alarm had been sounding for fifteen minutes, and my open notebook was squished beneath my face.

I lean close to the mirror. Good. The spiral imprint has faded significantly.

I agonize in front of my closet before pulling on a pair of Karen's discarded skinny jeans and a top she said made my eyes look bluer. The neckline scoops a bit more than my normal T-shirts, but after a moment's debate, I leave it on. Smart move—as it is, I dash into first period to the sound of the bell.

Palmer—it's okay for me to notice him now, right?—sits in the middle of the class, looking like he always does: good.

As I slide into my usual seat up front, questions race through my mind. Is he looking at me? Should I look at him? Exactly how far are we carrying this "secret relationship" thing?

As Mr. Dolcer takes roll, I risk a glance over my shoulder. Palmer must sense me looking at him because he grins back, then winks.

And I have the freedom to smile back.

I turn back to the front of the class, buzzing from no sleep and Palmer's smile. So it's not some story I'm telling myself. Palmer really is my boyfriend.

Chapter 19

When I exit photography class, Chase stands in his normal spot, but he's frowning at me. "Where were you this morning?"

"I overslept."

"Oh." He scrutinizes me a moment longer. "You look . . . happy."

I grin. "That's allowed, right?"

His mouth twitches into a half smile, then he pushes off the wall and walks beside me to the bridge. He's silent the whole way to main campus, which is rare, even for Chase.

I glance at him and find his forehead knotted, as if deep in thought. "You okay?"

Chase's coffee-colored gaze meets mine. "You want to come to dinner next Wednesday? Like the tenth?"

I hope I don't look as surprised and reluctant as I feel. "At your house?"

"Yeah. No big deal if you can't, but it's kinda my birthday. My mom's making a special dinner and asked if I wanted to invite someone. So . . ." He shrugs and jams his hands deep in his pockets.

But not before I note the tremor in them.

Something catches in my throat. It's his birthday; how can I not go? Palmer won't like it, of course, but it's just dinner with my friend Chase's family. It's no different, really, than eating dinner at Lucy's.

Well, except for the whole Chase having a crush on me thing.

"Sure, it sounds like fun."

Chase's dimples pop. "Okay. I'll tell my mom."

"And I'll tell my parents . . . something. That I'm going to Bianca's or Marie's, I guess."

They won't be any trouble, but Palmer? What on earth am I going to tell him?

Chase shakes his head. "I can't believe your parents really believe you're still friends with those girls."

"I bet if they stopped to think about it, they'd realize Bianca and Marie never call the house, come over, or invite me for sleepovers. But so far they haven't bothered to pay attention. James has been in town, after all."

In my back pocket, my phone vibrates with a text message. I'm with Chase, so it must be Karen.

No—Palmer. MISS YOU.

My face heats as I try to figure out what to say back. Miss you too? See you soon?

"What's Karen want?"

I stuff my phone in my pocket, message unanswered. "Just saying hi."

Odd. I always thought if Palmer confessed feelings for me, I'd want to shout it out to the world. Instead, I have no desire to tell Chase my secret.

Last night on the phone, Palmer said he wanted some time to figure out "us" without all the attention from everybody. Which I think is really smart. A couple like us, so mismatched, will be big news. I don't want all that pressure right away. Just like Palmer, I want time to ease into this.

Really, I couldn't be happier about our arrangement.

"That sucks. I'm so sorry."

"No worries. They fight like this all the time." Palmer sounds so casual. If my parents were throwing stuff at one in the morning, I'd freak out. "They're just one of those couples, you know? They love each other, but they also drive each other crazy."

"That sounds horrible." I snuggle deeper under the covers. "Do you have brothers or sisters?"

"One of each."

"What do they think about all the fighting?"

"They don't hear it anymore. Paxton is still in Kentucky, and Paisley's at school in Florida."

"Paxton, Paisley, and Palmer?"

"Cute, huh?" Palmer snorts. "Wanna know my parents' names?"

"Do I?"

"Paul and Patricia."

"That's too much."

"Yeah, I agree."

I pluck at the lace hem of my duvet. "At least your parents intentionally named you. You know it wasn't some accident."

"What do you mean?"

I tell him about Mom saying I never looked like a Gabrielle, how she already had towels monogrammed with my name and didn't want to waste them. "And so they decided to call me Ellie instead."

Palmer takes a deep breath. "I promise to never ever call you Ellie again."

"It's fine." I roll a strand of hair around my finger. "I'm used to it."

"I meant to call you Gabrielle ever since you told me you liked it better, but . . ." Palmer clears his throat.

"Lucy, right?" It feels good to bring her up, as if we've been intentionally avoiding her during the first week of our relationship.

"No. Well, kinda, I guess. Cause I was with Lucy, but then . . . then I was having these feelings for you, and . . ."

"You started avoiding me." The words come out as an unintentional whisper.

"I thought maybe they would disappear if I stayed away from you. But they never did."

I could ask about his motivations for ignoring his feelings, but why torture myself? Why make him say something he doesn't want to? We run with different crowds. I'm not exactly a prize of a girlfriend. Not like Lucy, who has a gravitational pull built into her personality.

Instead I ask the question that matters. "Why'd you change your mind?"

"Other than deciding I couldn't live without you?"

"Yeah." I'm impressed by how airy my tone sounds despite my heart feeling like it might beat right out of my chest. "Other than the obvious."

Palmer chuckles. "It was Chase, actually. I saw you taking care of him at the party, and it drove me crazy."

Seconds tick by, and still he doesn't elaborate. I'm about to say something about it being late, that we should get some sleep, when he speaks again.

"I had convinced myself that you'd never want to be with me because I party and stuff. I know you disapprove. Then I saw you taking care of Chase after he'd passed out, and it made me realize . . . Originally I said it in jest because of your last name, but you truly are a sweetheart, Gabrielle."

Tears leak from the corners of my eyes and dribble into my hairline.

Palmer's chuckle is husky. "I shoulda known that'd make you quiet. You don't like compliments much, do you?"

I swipe away the tears with the palm of my hand. "I don't know how to handle them very well, no."

"You need more practice. Let's see. Your eyes are like the fathomless blue of the Caribbean Seas—"

"Okay, that's enough."

"I'm not finished. And you skin has the softness of—"

"Seriously." I strain to suppress my nervous laughter. How would I ever explain a 1 a.m. phone call to my parents? "Enough."

"We'll ease you into it. Now, while we're on the subject—Chase. While it may be his birthday, I don't—"

"Were we talking about Chase? I thought we were talking about my inability to accept compliments."

"At some point we talked about him tonight, and I'm thinking, Chase has served his purpose, he got us together, and now it's time for him to make his exit."

In a novel, it can work like that—the character of convenience, Bronte calls it.

But real life is different. I can't cut people. Especially not Chase.

"Palmer." I try to make my voice warm but authoritative. "He's my friend."

"Gabrielle." His matter-of-fact tone mimics mine. "He's your friend who's in love with you."

"But—"

"Whose parents think you're dating."

"Well, yeah, but—"

"And who most the school thinks you're dating, by the way."

I sigh. "Is it my turn to talk yet?"

"Sure."

I blink into the blurry darkness of my bedroom, crafting my response. "Your friends hate me, and I don't like them either. But I'm not asking you to give up anyone."

"They don't hate you, Gabrielle. And I'd give up Troy if you asked. You want me to give up Troy?"

I laugh, remembering the smoky bathroom on prom night, trying to rinse Troy's vomit from the skirt of my dress without taking it off. "No, Troy is all yours. As is Diego, Bianca, Marie, and whomever else you want."

"Which is very nice, but I'd still like you to give Chase the heave-ho."

My stomach twists with nerves, but what else can I do? This is non-negotiable. "That's not going to happen."

There's a pause. Or did he hang up?

"What about those other girls in that group? Bambi and Bimbo, or whatever. Couldn't you hang out with them a little bit more?"

"Chase is my friend. He's my only friend, and I'm not getting rid of him." My voice wavers a bit more than I would like.

"You have me now, Gabrielle."

A whisper of a laugh escapes. "Not at lunch time, I don't."

There's a brief, wounded silence. "Is that what this is about? You're mad because I'm not ready to tell people yet? If it's that important to you, I'll tell them tomorrow. Or I'll start making phone calls right now."

But would he?

"I'm not mad, Palmer. I'm just not giving up Chase."

"I know he'd be hurt at first, but maybe it'd be better for him in the long run. Have you thought about that?"

"I have, but Chase says he's fine. That he can handle it."

"So, you and Chase have talked about this?"

"A little." My stomach squirms as guilt surges through me. Because if I were a good friend, I *would* push Chase away regardless of him insisting he can handle it. "He knows I don't feel the same way."

Palmer is quiet, working up another argument, I assume.

"Okay." He sounds resigned. "So long as that line doesn't get blurry for *you*. He's your friend. I'm your boyfriend."

The words send a thrill running through me. "Believe me. That line is clear as can be."

Chapter 20

"Extended play practice," is the excuse I invent for why I won't be home until late on Wednesday.

Mom had frowned at the schedule stuck to the fridge. "Did Mr. Freeman adjust something?"

"Well, the leads decided to stay late to make sure we really have act one down, and Mr. Freeman said he'd order us pizza."

So I'm relieved to see Mrs. Cervantes pulling two homemade pizzas from the oven. Now if Mom or Dad ask how the pizza was, I can answer without lying. Sorta.

I inhale deeply. "Those smell great."

She points to one. "This has spicy sausage. But my Chase says you do not like spicy things, so I made a vegetarian one for you and me."

Her eyes regard me with warmth that makes my conscious tickle. She's going to all this effort to make me feel welcome because she thinks I'm dating her son. What will she do when she finds out the truth? "Thank you. That's very kind."

Mrs. Cervantes turns off the oven and rummages through a drawer. "Chase, get our guest something to drink."

"Oh no, I can get it." I say to Chase's retreating figure. "It's your birthday."

"It's fine." Chase opens the refrigerator and raises an inquisitive eyebrow at me. It's stocked with multiple soda options. I nod, and he grabs me a Coke.

As I crack open the can, Mrs. Cervantes turns from the pizzas to observe. "Did you ask her or just assume?"

"Ellie likes Coke."

"We have glasses and ice." Mrs. Cervantes seems flustered, as if Chase somehow embarrassed her. "Ellie, would you like—"

"She only likes Coke with ice when it's out of the fountain."

I blink up at Chase. "How do you know that?"

He shrugs and offers me a smile that seems bashful, which makes my heart feel like Chase just draped a warm blanket around it.

An inner voice of reason screams *Palmer*!

I break eye contact, but I can't do anything to hide my heat-stained cheeks.

I sip my Coke. "I didn't know you could make pizza at home. Other than frozen, I mean."

"When we first move here, we live next door to wonderful Italian family. She taught me."

I jump when a hand rests on the small of my back. Chase's gaze is on his mother, his expression attentive. As if he doesn't even realize he's touching me.

Oh, sure. Real likely.

I inch away as Mr. Cervantes ducks into the kitchen. "Ready for the table yet, Marietta?"

She nods, and from the corner of the eat-in kitchen, Mr. Cervantes drags a rickety Formica table. Donnie finagles four chairs around it, and I do my best to stay out of the way. How would we all fit if Francis and Mark were here too?

Much to my surprise, when we sit to eat, Mr. Cervantes bows his head and gives thanks for our food. It sounds almost exactly like my father's normal dinner prayer—"Dear Lord, thank you for this food. Bless it to our bodies. In Jesus' name, Amen."

As Mrs. Cervantes scoops pizza onto my plate, Chase's leg leans against mine. I yank away, causing my knee to knock into Donnie.

"Ouch!"

I know my face flames red. "Sorry."

Mrs. Cervantes chuckles, but it sounds higher than her normal laugh. "It is tight squeeze in here, Ellie. My apologies."

Oh, great. Now I've made my hostess feel bad. "No, it's fine. This all looks so amazing. Thank you for inviting me."

"Of course. It wouldn't feel like Chase's birthday celebration without his lovely girlfriend."

I freeze under the warm gaze of Chase's mother, then turn to him. *Please correct her.*

Instead he grins at me. "That's true." Laughter laces his words, and a dare glints in his eyes as his leg once again settles against mine.

I grit my teeth. It's his birthday dinner! How can I tell his family now that he's been lying to them?

As I cut into my pizza, Mr. and Mrs. Cervantes ask all the questions I expect with adults—what kind of classes I'm in, what my parents do, if I know so-and-so who attends my church. Later, thankfully, the attention shifts off me. They talk about visiting Francis or Mark this weekend, same as my parents might James. They ask Donnie about a test he took at school today. Mrs. Cervantes relates an anecdote about a three-year-old she watches who told her his full name was, "Hayden Michael No."

After dinner, I attempt to help Mrs. Cervantes with dishes, but she shoos me out of the kitchen. "No, no, no. You two enjoy time together. I will get this cleaned up, then we will have cake and open presents."

I hover until Chase takes my hand and tugs me out of the kitchen. Though I follow him, I keep my hand limp in his. His dad and brother are camped out in the living room watching a basketball game, but instead of joining them, Chase leads me toward the narrow hallway.

"Door open, son," Mr. Cervantes calls after us.

At any second, I'm going to spontaneously combust from embarrassment.

Inside Chase's room, I yank my hand free and fix him with a glare. "I can't believe you didn't tell them that we aren't . . . aren't what they think we are."

Chase nudges the door until it's only open about the width of a fingertip, then turns a dimpled grin my way. "I notice you didn't rush to correct them. And why's that Ellie Jane?"

When my back bumps into the wall, I realize I had been taking steps backward. "How could I? It's your birthday, Chase."

At the mention, determination lights his eyes, and I instinctively press close to the wall.

But all Chase says is, "You didn't say anything about my room."

I glance about. "It's nice. Very . . ." Basic. Shabby. "Clean."

Chase rolls his eyes and plops on the edge of his bed. "Mom seemed to think you wouldn't want to hang out with me anymore if you knew I was a slob."

My insides have felt twisted up like a wrung dishtowel, but with the mention of his mom, the pressure loosens. "I like your mom."

"She's very impressed with you. Says you're mature."

I keep my gaze on the walls of his room and try not to seem too pleased by the compliment. There are no posters of bikini-clad girls, just cars. That's something.

My eye catches on the corkboard above his desk. "Hey, that's a picture of me."

Chase gives me a mockingly impressed look. "Gold star, Einstein."

I take a few steps closer. It's my school picture from this year. Not a fabulous shot, but not horrible either. "Where did you get that? And why do you have it up?"

Chase doesn't answer, but I hear the creak of the bed and sense him standing close behind me. "Because I like looking at you."

He grips my arms and turns me until I'm facing him. The only word my brain seems capable of producing is *Palmer!* but it won't come out, so I just stare up at him and wish I had worn my glasses instead of my contacts tonight. I have nothing to hide behind.

"Did you know"—Chase's words are quiet but gruff with emotion—"that I've liked you since seventh grade?"

The edge of his desk bites into my back. "Uh, no I didn't."

"I used to think you were snotty like those other girls. But you gave half your lunch money to Nina Huerta every day until she moved."

He knew? "How do you know that?"

Chase and Nina were once an "item" as my mother would call it, but I didn't expect her to share *that*.

"Nina told me. I was"—Chase swallows, endearingly embarrassed—"making fun of you, and she told me you weren't like Lucy and them. And then I started to notice you."

No, let's keep talking about Nina. I keep my voice light as I ask, "Do you ever talk to Nina? How is she?"

He shrugs. "We haven't talked since she moved."

"Oh. I hope she's okay."

Nina was always skittish from life with her negligent mother and her mom's abusive boyfriend. The lunch money had been the only thing I offered that she took me up on.

"I'd really like to kiss you."

I blink at Chase, who has obviously not been standing here dwelling on Nina. His arms are on either side of me, his hands braced against the desk. I'm pinned.

And as he bends closer, his intentions clearly marked, it's hard to avoid the thoughts that I'm normally so good at sweeping under the rug. Like how good looking Chase is. How my heart hums in my chest when he looks at me like this. How my toes strain to push up, to push me closer to kissing him.

I shake my head. "We can't. We shouldn't."

"Like you said—it's my birthday." He's teasing . . . but not. "And I think you might like it, Ellie Jane."

How handy it would be to tell Chase that I have a boyfriend. "I don't doubt you're a good kisser, Chase. I just think it'll make things weird with us."

"I'm okay with a little weirdness."

"I know. But . . . but we're just friends." I think of Palmer's words over the weekend, about keeping the line of friend and boyfriend clear. Kissing sounds blurry.

Chase's mouth brushes mine, drawing my thoughts completely to him. "Are we?"

His eyes are closed, his thick lashes fanning on his strong cheekbones. And then he's kissing me. One hand is pressed into my back and the other is tangled in my hair, holding me there as if I'm putting up any kind of fight.

Chase's kiss is filled with longing and . . . and something else that I'm not thinking quite clear enough to label. And just when the name of the emotion seems within my grasp, Chase breaks away.

I have nothing to compare the kiss to, but I have to uncurl my toes and remind myself to breathe. These seem like indicators of a good kiss.

Chase breathes heavily through his nose, then looks at me. My heart thuds in my chest, and I have an inexplicable desire to apologize, though I'm not sure what for.

Chase retracts his hand from my hair, his arm from my back. "It's Palmer, isn't it? You still like him."

There's a tug in my hands. They want to reach out for Chase, comfort him. Instead, I put them behind my back and knot my fingers together. "I'm sorry."

His jaw clenches, and I catch a flash in his eyes as he averts his gaze.

Only then do I realize the other thing his kiss held—anger.

While I've never been in a relationship, I've seen enough movies to know I absolutely have to tell Palmer what happened.

"He *kissed* you?" Palmer interrupts my story later that night. "You *let* him kiss you?"

"It's not like I puckered up, Palmer."

"Couldn't you have moved?"

Shame flames within me. "No, he had me cornered—"

"And you couldn't scream? Couldn't push him? Couldn't kick him in the—"

"I froze, okay?"

"You're lucky all he did was kiss you." Palmer's words are a snarl. "Why would you let yourself be alone with him, Gabrielle? Why?"

"His family was just down the hall, he wouldn't have tried anything more."

Palmer snorts. "Why are you so blinded by him? Why can't you see that guy is nothing but trouble for you?"

"He doesn't know you and I are dating. It's not like he knew he was pressuring another guy's girlfriend to kiss him."

"Oh, it's much better that he thought he was pressuring a single girl. My mistake."

I grit my teeth at his sarcasm. I shouldn't have defended Chase. How would I feel if Bianca had thrown herself at Palmer, but then he defended her to me?

I take a deep breath. "You're right. He shouldn't have done it, and he realized that it didn't have the effect on me he wanted it to."

Or at least, he couldn't tell that it did.

Palmer's silent.

My gaze catches on my computer screen, where I had been registering for the American Fiction Writers conference. There's a scene in *Invisibly Yours* where Lady Gabrielle has been invited to the palace for a masquerade, and Rafe is furious because of it. What does she say to soothe him?

"I understand you being mad, and I won't try to talk you out of that. But I didn't know how to outright refuse him without telling him about us." I wish I could revise the way I have Lady Gabrielle yelling these words at Rafe. These aren't words one yells. "Should I have told him?"

Palmer swears under his breath, just as Rafe does in the book, and my breath hitches as I remember—Rafe leaves soon after. Leaves Lady Gabrielle to her inevitable engagement to the prince. Leaves without saying goodbye.

"Can I come over?"

Once I process Palmer's words, I whirl to look at my computer clock. Eleven. "Now?"

"I know it's late, but I'll meet you out front or something. Please? I don't want to have this conversation over the phone."

"My parents are already asleep . . ."

Mom and Dad will like Palmer fine, I think, but I can't imagine it'll help matters if their introduction to him happens when they find me chatting with him on the front porch after curfew.

"Never mind. It's probably a really stupid idea. Maybe we could talk tomorrow before Photography. Or at rehearsal."

This sounds bad. "Okay . . ."

"Why do you sound like that?"

"Like what?"

"All freaked out."

"Because I *am* freaked out. You're not . . ." I pull my knees up to my chest, like a shield. "We're not breaking up, are we?"

"If I break anything, it'll be Chase's face. But we're not breaking up. Unless . . . you've changed your mind. About your feelings for Chase."

I banish thoughts about how Chase knew my quirky Coke preferences without being told, how he keeps a picture of me up in his room. "No. And he knows it. He knows I like you."

"You told him that?"

"He guessed, actually. He—" I swallow back my embarrassment and make myself say it. "He's known for a while now that I like you."

Palmer doesn't answer. I'm about to ask if he's still there when he says, "What are you doing Sunday?"

"This Sunday?"

"Yeah. Like Valentine's Day."

"Oh." I look at my calendar. Yep, February fourteenth. This Sunday. "Just church in the morning."

"No plans with Chase?" His light-hearted tone seems forced, but the shift in our conversation makes breathing easier.

"Not yet. Why?"

"Well, because I was thinking that we should go out."

"Like . . . on a date?"

"Mm-hmm."

"In public? Where there might be people?"

"Sound too risky for you?"

I'm glad no one's here, and I can smile as big as I want. "Just risky enough."

"Although privacy can be good too."

I think of earlier, that sizzle in my chest as Chase's mouth pressed against mine. And how much better would it be to kiss Palmer?

"Yeah," I say. "Privacy has some definite advantages."

When Chase sees me coming across the Quad, he stands. It calls to mind the forgotten custom of a gentleman rising to his feet when a lady enters a room.

He holds out a cup of coffee. "Hey."

I glance from it to his pleading eyes before taking it. "Thanks."

He stuffs his hands in his pockets and shuffles his sneaker on the grass. "Are you furious?"

"No." I take a sip of coffee as I formulate my response. "But I *am* worried that us hanging out isn't a good idea."

For either of us.

Chase's jaw has a determined set to it. "I'm fine, Ellie, I promise. I just got a little . . . carried away last night."

My cheeks are hot with the reminder, and my brain is so preoccupied with replaying what happened in Chase's room, I can't come up with an intelligent response.

"There you are, sweetheart." Palmer's lazy and convincingly casual drawl pulls me into the present. Where'd he come from? "Mr. Freeman is looking for you. Important play business."

Sure there is. "Okay, thanks."

"He said we should go right away." Palmer grins at Chase as he puts his hand on my back and nudges me along, somehow finding the exact place Chase laid his the night before. "Sorry to interrupt."

Chase's scowl wrenches my heart. "See you after class, Ellie."

"Thanks for the coffee."

His face softens slightly when he nods at me, but when he sees Palmer's hand on my back he looks just like he did a month ago when I slapped him.

I hate to imagine what he'll look like after this Sunday when word gets around that Palmer and I are together.

❦ ❦ ❦

"You can't just send out a few queries and call it good, Gabrielle." Sounds like Bronte just rolled her eyes. "Let's send out more. I'm emailing you a list of possibilities now."

"But shouldn't I wait until after the conference? To find out if I won the Great Debut?"

"You have to consider there are four other finalists in your category." Bronte seems somewhat impatient as she explains this to me. "If you don't final, then you'll be sending out queries that say you *were* a finalist. If you send stuff out now, you're saying you *are* a finalist. Much more intriguing."

"But . . . shouldn't I wait to hear from the other agents before I get too query crazy?"

"It could be months. Heck, you may never hear."

I nod my thanks to the barista who just made my latte. "Seriously?"

She sighs. "Happens to the best of us."

I settle into my seat, feeling very writery. Laptop open, latte in hand, conversing with my writing friend about literary agents. I'm even wearing my glasses and an argyle cardigan.

"If I wait until after the AFW conference, then I can just tell agents and editors, 'I'm the one whose *daddy* was sitting next to her at the awards banquet.'"

Bronte lets loose a laugh. "You won't be the only one. There are usually two or three teens there with a chaperone, but I've never seen *their* names on a finalist list." There's a shriek in the background and Bronte morphs from writer to Mom. "Mackenzie Paige! You give that toy back to her right now . . . I don't want to hear it. She's nine months old, and you have an entire room full of toys."

I scroll through the AFW conference registration form as Bronte argues with her oldest daughter. My eyes blur at the information I've yet to enter—emergency contact name, my local paper, where I heard about AFW—and lock on the amazing classes I'll get to attend. Some of my favorite writers and several of the agents I queried last week are on the faculty list, including Emma Miller. And they just added a class from Erica Chally, a big time YA editor. Even if I *do* have to attend with my dad, this is gonna be epic.

Bronte huffs into the phone. "You know what I get to do this afternoon? Write a glowing review for a sucky book by this writer acquaintance of mine. I get so sick of writing great reviews for books that don't deserve them."

I pop the top off my latte. "Couldn't you write one that's nice, but not great?"

"I guess. I wish I could write a flaming review at least once. I had a dream last week that I had an anonymous blog where I got to blast all the books I hate." Bronte sighs. "It was wonderful."

"At least you're—"

"That's it, Mackenzie Paige! To your room right now!" As a shrill cry sounds in the background, Bronte says to me, "Talking to me is like natural birth control, right?"

I laugh as I resume filling out my registration form. "Because there are so many guys out there trying to steal my virtue."

Bronte chuckles. "I was a late bloomer myself. My first date was junior year of college. Mom told me she'd given up and assumed me a lesbian."

I click to select a class with Bronte's editor. "How are page proofs for *Fire Eyes* going?"

Bronte whimpers. "So slow. Mackenzie's finally back at school, but she gave her cold to Maggie, plus Melody has two teeth coming in. Tim promised he'd watch the kids tonight so I can make progress, but I have my doubts that it'll actually happen. Melody is in such a mommy phase right now."

"I'm sorry. I wish I could do the proofs for you."

"I love my kids, but . . ." Bronte sighs. "I'm sorry. I'm sure it's no fun listening to the complaints of an old woman."

"Twenty-nine isn't old."

"No, I'm old, Gabrielle. I have gray hair and no desire to leave the house on Friday nights."

"Same here. Not the gray hair, but the Friday night thing."

Another wail comes from Bronte's end. "That's my cue. Gotta go, girl. And trust me—send out more queries." As she hangs up, I hear her cooing, "Mellie, it's okay, sweetie."

I smile as I tuck my cell phone into my backpack.

Within minutes, Bronte's email arrives. I scroll through the list of agents. The names are unfamiliar, but chilling nonetheless. I take a deep breath, then pull up the website for—who's first on Bronte's list?—Paula Banks.

As I click around the Banks Literary site, an inconsiderately loud group enters the coffeehouse. Tucked around the corner like this, I can't see them, but I can definitely hear them. How obnoxious. Doesn't it occur to them that there might be busy people in here? People who aren't interested in—

Was that Palmer's laugh I just heard?

I shrink in my seat and pull my laptop closer, like a security blanket. Because, yes, that's Palmer. And that's definitely Bianca and Marie debating the wisdom of ordering a nonfat peppermint latte but with extra whip.

I absently tap a few keys on my laptop, as if there's any chance I could pay attention to writing now.

"Let's sit in back," Marie says.

No!

A groan from . . . Diego? "Girl, I just got comfy. Don't make me move."

I love Diego. I take back every mean thought I've ever had about him.

"You're so lazy." But the scraping of the chair against the floor indicates Marie isn't going to fight for it.

"I totally don't want to go to school tomorrow," Bianca says. "And I bet you're exhausted, Palmer. How much longer do you have play practice?"

"About a month."

"That's *horrible*." Bianca's voice is sticky with sympathy. "You *definitely* need a weekend away. You have to come to Shaver with us."

Yes, hearing my boyfriend get propositioned feels as yucky as I would've imagined. I don't even have the privilege of thinking mean thoughts about Bianca for hitting on a guy who's spoken for.

"I think I'm gonna skip Shaver this time, guys."

My heart gallops at Palmer's words.

"Dude, you can't. It's gonna be all-time." This gem comes from Troy.

"I'm behind on homework," Palmer says smoothly.

I share a smile with my reflection in the computer screen. That's usually my line. Or it was, back when I needed one.

"But you have to come." The pleading of Bianca's voice leaves no mystery about it—she had plans for Palmer this weekend. "It's Valentine's Day."

"Maybe next time," Palmer says.

I can't believe a guy is picking me over shiny, curvy Bianca.

Their conversation turns to its usual minutiae—calories and lame movies—and I return to my queries. If a guy like Palmer is interested enough in me to turn down someone like Bianca Sutton, it doesn't seem so far-fetched that a literary agent might choose me too.

Chapter 21

Sitting in church on Valentine's morning, I realize I can't remember when I last prayed. Normally, I pray at night when I'm lying in bed, but recently I've been on the phone with Palmer until I'm so exhausted my eyes keep closing.

I bow my head and run through a list of things I'm grateful for— my parents, Aunt Karen, AFW and finalling in the Great Debut, the A on my Spanish test, Chase.

An elbow in my ribs jolts me out of my prayer.

"Ellie, wake up." Grandmom speaks much louder than necessary. Several around us chuckle.

I flush. "I was praying."

"Church is not the time for prayer. Church is the time to listen."

While I don't completely agree, this doesn't seem like the best time to argue. I sigh and return my attention to Pastor David. He's a nice enough guy, same as toast is a nice enough breakfast. Maybe it's just because I've been sitting in this pew for sixteen years now, but I can't remember the last fresh, interesting statement he made. My grandparents, however, think Pastor David can do no wrong. He's been at this church as long as they have. And if my parents have an opinion, it's not one they've shared with me.

"And stop your fidgeting," Grandmom hisses. "Feels like an earthquake when you do that."

I slow my bouncing leg to a stop. I can't help being jittery. This afternoon, Palmer and I have our First Date. During which, I'm sure I'll get my First Kiss. Or my first *invited* kiss, anyway.

As Pastor David reiterates his major points, I conjure up a mental image of the outfit I painstakingly chose for this afternoon. I tried to be versatile enough for any restaurant he might take me to—

nice enough that I won't feel ridiculously underdressed if he took me to, oh, the Vintage Press. But not so nice that if we wind up at Chipotle, I look like I expected my boyfriend to take me to the fanciest restaurant in town.

Around me, my family and the rest of the congregation stand. Apparently it's time for the benediction.

I leap to my feet, but instead of listening to Pastor David, I pray *Lord, please don't let me make a fool of myself today.*

"You know," Mom says as I zip up my boots. "Bianca and Marie are welcome here as well. You don't always have to go to their houses."

"Marie's family just got a new TV. We're gonna spend the afternoon watching old movies and bemoaning how chivalry is dead."

The TV thing, at least, is true. I overheard it at the coffeehouse.

"Sounds good to me." Dad cracks open a novel. "Just stay away from those Redwood boys. Pure trouble. Right, honey?"

Mom winks back at him, then returns her attention to me. "Seems like Bianca and Marie don't have much of a hankering for partying now that Lucy's gone."

I smooth my jeans. "Yeah."

Mom shakes her head and clucks. "That Lucy must have been the bad influence. What a shock Jan's in for when she realizes."

Should I defend Lucy? Does she deserve defending?

I throw my purse over my shoulder. "Yeah, well, I gotta go. See you guys later."

"Have a nice time, honey!" Mom calls after me.

I arrive at the school, where Palmer and I agreed to meet and ditch my car, way early. Why didn't I bring a book with me? I almost always have one. And now I'll have to spend the next fifteen minutes just sitting here—

A familiar white Jeep pulls in behind me. He's super early too. That's gotta be a good sign, right?

Feeling hyper-aware of my every move, I climb out of my car, lock it, and smile at Palmer.

"Goin' my way?" he teases in a husky voice that induces goose bumps all over my arms.

Why do Lady Gabrielle's witty responses flow from my fingers when I'm writing, yet fail me in real life? I duck my head and slide into the car, which smells of his hair gel and the vanilla sachet dangling from the rearview mirror.

Palmer effortlessly takes my hand. His curls look damp from a shower, and his steel-colored shirt does something amazing to his eyes. It should be illegal to look so good. "Hi."

I need to look him in the eyes. Lucy would. Lady Gabrielle would. "Hi."

"You look great." When his thumb rubs over my knuckles like that, it's difficult to think clearly.

"You too."

It won't always be this way, right? Where every touch puts me on sensory overload? Where I can hardly form a comprehensive sentence when we're face-to-face?

Palmer's grin turns amused. "You're blushing, Gabrielle."

"I'm a little nervous."

"Why? Chase didn't normally pick you up for dates?"

I swallow. "So, where are we going?"

Best to stay clear of all Chase-related topics. There's an edge in Palmer's voice whenever his name arises.

"Well, if it's cool with you, since it's such a nice day, I thought we could pick up sandwiches and head out to Mooney Grove for a picnic. Sound fun?"

I snap my seat belt into place. "Perfect."

As Palmer pulls away from the curb, I'm nearly dizzy with anticipation. This will by far be the best Valentine's Day I've ever had.

$$\mathscr{B}\mathscr{B}\mathscr{B}$$

It's my fault. It must be.

Palmer squeezes my hand one last time as I climb out of the Jeep. "I'll call you."

I force a smile. "Sounds good. And thank you again."

"Thank you." He flashes his teeth, then I shut the door and head for my car.

A true Southern gentleman, Palmer waits until I've pulled away from the curb before he does the same. Which is a shame, because all I really want to do is sit here and cry.

I drive to Karen's house. It's sold, but the new owners won't arrive for another month or so. And I'm glad, because I don't know where else in town I'd go at a moment like this.

I stretch out on Karen's front porch, where we used to spend summers drinking iced tea and painting each other's toenails. My eyes pool with tears. Karen has always been half-sister, half-aunt to me. A girlfriend, but wise. Protective, but not overbearing. She would know why things went wrong today. She would know what makes me so . . . unkissable.

Maybe I had too high of expectations for my first date with Palmer. Or maybe he doesn't kiss on a first date, though that's a rule like that seems more fitting for me than it does him. And I used to see him hanging all over Lucy at school.

When he took my hand so quickly in the car, I'd thought the afternoon would progress easily and naturally toward our first kiss.

My fingers had seemed "complete when entwined with his." I read that in a book once and liked the sound of it. I never thought I would experience it for myself, but then there I was sitting in the Jeep, holding hands with Palmer. And it felt as natural as if he was the other half of my hand, something that had been missing all these years. And I knew when he kissed me, it would be like something out of a Disney movie.

"What do you like?" Palmer asked as he turned into the parking lot for Port of Subs. "I'll run in and get it."

"The turkey and provolone, but I can come with you."

I unbuckled my seat belt, but he put his hand over mine and smiled. "You wait in the car. Be a lady of leisure."

It sounded so Jane Austen, I instantly warmed to the idea and relaxed in my seat. Or tried to relax anyway.

He emerged a few minutes later, sandwiches and fountain drinks in hand.

I settled the drinks into the cup holders. "That was fast."

"No line at all. Weird for here."

"Well, it's two-thirty on Valentine's Day."

"True." Palmer seemed bashful. "I guess it's not the most romantic choice for food, but it's such a nice day, and I thought—"

"Stop."

He looked at me through his lashes, sending my heart into hyperactivity once again.

I rested my hand on top of his. "This is perfect."

And what followed was the first time I thought he might kiss me. His gaze hovered around my face, and I swear it even lingered on my mouth. And then—just as I expected him to forge the distance between us—he snapped back to his side of the car and turned the ignition. "I'm starving," he said as he backed out.

I looked out my window, hoping he couldn't see my red face. "Yeah, me too."

Even with it being a nice day, Mooney Grove Park was mostly empty. Just a few other couples and their picnic blankets littered the grass. I foresaw a flawless afternoon stretched before us. Hours and hours alone with Palmer. I could stay out until curfew, easy. My parents thought I was watching black and whites and probably didn't expect me home until eleven. I could maybe buy myself even more time if I called around 10:30 and said the movie had another hour, or something. Never in my life had I pushed curfew, and now it would pay off.

Palmer spread an old, ugly afghan on the grass beside the lagoon.

I turned my gaze to the water, which winks in the afternoon sun. "What a perfect spot."

"A perfect spot for a perfect girl." His remark came too quick, too rehearsed, for me to fool myself into thinking I was the only one he'd ever called perfect. Still, I couldn't keep from feeling flattered.

We chatted as we ate our sandwiches. I told him about getting bit by a duck at Mooney Grove when I was three. He told stories about friends back in Louisville, few of whom he still talked to.

"You miss it there?" I asked.

Palmer shrugged and gave me a meaningful look. "Not as much these days."

I smiled and took a thoughtful bite of my sandwich. "It seems strange that you wouldn't miss the place you lived most your life. But of course I won't miss it here when I leave."

"You hate it here that much?"

"Well. Not as much these days."

Palmer grinned and leaned forward slightly . . . or did I imagine that? Because as I reciprocated by leaning forward as well, Palmer declared, "This is the best meatball sub ever," and shoved a quarter of his sandwich in his mouth.

At the time, I thought I must have misunderstood. But now, with the advantage of hindsight, I'm not so sure. I couldn't have imagined *all* the near-kiss incidents, could I? My imagination isn't *that* powerful.

After we finished our sandwiches, Palmer pulled from his pocket a small box wrapped in red paper. "Happy Valentine's Day, Gabrielle."

I clasped a hand over my mouth. Why had I never thought to get him a gift? What an idiot! "I didn't get you anything. I'm so sorry. I just never—"

He waved me away. "Valentine's Day is about spoiling your girl. You didn't need to get me anything." He pressed the box in my hand.

Stephanie Morrill

From the weight and size, I knew it was jewelry even before I opened it. "Palmer . . ."

He nudged me with his shoulder. "Just open it."

At the sight of the delicate silver bracelet, I sucked in a sharp breath.

"You like it?" He seemed nervous, which filled me with a strange sense of power.

"It's perfect." Just a wisp of a band, beautiful and simple.

"I know you don't wear much jewelry, but I thought this one looked like you. Here, let me help." His fingertips brushed against the tender part of my wrist while he worked the clasp. Bracelet secured, he looked up and swallowed.

This was it. He was going to kiss me.

"Thank you." My words emerged as an unintended whisper.

His hand smoothed my hair, which I'd tied back in a more careful version of its usual knot. "You're very special, Gabrielle. Someone worth . . ."

I leaned forward. Someone worth *what*?

"Protecting."

His word choice sent warmth surging through me. I liked the idea of Palmer protecting me.

He leaned forward, and I did too, my eyes closing on their own free will.

When I opened them, I found Palmer no longer hovered near, but had sprawled on his back. His arms were crossed under his head, and his stormy eyes trained on the blue sky above.

"What great weather, huh?"

Despite the bracelet wreathing my wrist, despite Palmer choosing to spend the day with me instead of going to Shaver, he suddenly seemed as far out of reach as a million-dollar book contract.

Palmer squinted in the thin winter sunlight, and though he smiled, it seemed strained. "Come here. Relax a little."

I leaned against him, conscious of every bone in my body that might cause him discomfort. Maybe if I stopped obsessing over every tilt of his head, every teeny-tiny indicator that he might be about to kiss me, I could actually enjoy myself. After all, we'd only been together a few weeks. And this was our first date. There was no rush on the kissing thing.

Though as we packed up our picnic supplies and strolled around the park, I couldn't keep from dwelling on how Lady Gabrielle would have known how to make him kiss her. And I knew Palmer hadn't held back with Lucy. What was her trick? Of course if you looked like Lucy Shears, you probably didn't have to trick guys into kissing you. It just happened.

As we walked, clouds formed on the horizon and eventually obscured the sun. I shivered and cursed myself for forgetting a jacket. I was just about to suggest we go see a movie in a nice warm theater when Palmer draped an arm around me and pulled me close.

"Sorry you're cold. I have to get home, anyway. My mom is militant about Sunday night being family time."

"Oh . . . no big deal. I should probably get home too."

Chase would have recognized the disappointment in my voice, but Palmer didn't know those things about me yet.

He apologized again as he dropped me off at my car. "We'll go out again soon. A real date. Tablecloths. Waiters. The whole nine yards."

"I thought today was great." And I did. It just would be *more* great if he'd kiss me already.

"Well, happy Valentine's Day."

"You too. And thanks again for my bracelet. I love it."

"You're welcome."

He had leaned closer, and I realized I had reciprocated. Oh. *This* was it. *This* was the moment of the big kiss.

"See you tomorrow," he murmured as he leaned the last couple inches and . . .

Kissed my forehead.

My forehead! Same as James did when he boarded his flight back to D.C.

As I got out of the car, Palmer said, "I'll call you tonight."

I forced myself to smile at his dazzling grin, all the while my brain echoing that there was something wrong with me. That I was defective. That this was my fault.

"What is it, God?" I whisper on Karen's porch. I twist my beautiful bracelet around and around as I rack my brain for the answer. "What did I do wrong?"

But no response comes. Or if it does, I miss it.

$$\mathscr{L}\mathscr{L}\mathscr{L}$$

Sometimes Gabrielle didn't understand Rafe one bit. He claimed to like her—claimed to love her—but then when she served him the perfect opportunity to kiss her, he did nothing about it.

"Now, why would you do that, Rafe?" I mutter to the screen.

Oh. Right.

With a sigh, I poise my fingers above the keyboard and type the obvious explanation:

Of course, there was the prince to consider. Her betrothed.

Another sigh leaks out. So Gabrielle and Rafe have no wisdom to share in this situation, as I have no fiancé to be mindful of. Or any other type of guy. Except my dad and James, that is.

And Chase.

I tilt my head at the computer screen in consideration.

No. Surely Palmer, my boyfriend, wouldn't hold back because of Chase, my friend. Dumb idea. Time to focus on Gabrielle and Rafe.

Gabrielle knew she bordered on being petty, but she couldn't refrain from throwing down the gauntlet. "I thought you weren't afraid of anything."

Rafe met her eyes. "All men fear something, Lady Gabrielle."

Palmer had once told me that while we talked about Chase, but what does Palmer fear? Besides his friends finding out about us.

I shake my thoughts away from my personal life and dive into my manuscript, forcing myself to get lost in medieval Italy. So lost that when I wind down for the night, I blink at the clock several times before believing the time—12:34. I worked for four hours without taking a break?

Was I so focused I missed Palmer's nightly call?

But my cell phone says I didn't miss anything. I bite my lip, willing myself not to be one of those girls who cries just because her boyfriend didn't call. Why would he, really, when we spent the afternoon together? He doesn't *have* to call me every night.

The good thing is it's now February 15. Maybe that'll help keep my expectations in check.

Chapter 22

After gym, I glance at my phone. Two new emails. Neither of which are responses from literary agents.

I chuck my phone onto my backpack and tug at my jeans. With fifteen unanswered queries floating around in the world, I would be fine sitting and staring at my inbox all day.

And obsessing about literary agents seems a good alternative to obsessing about Palmer.

My email notification sounds as I pull my sweater over my head, and my heart leaps as if this might finally be the email I've waited for. Even though after weeks of this, my heart should know better than to hope. It's always just a newsletter from a store or an update from one of the writing blogs I follow.

I need to meet Chase so we can head to lunch, he's probably waiting for me. I shouldn't stop to check.

But it'll just take a couple seconds . . .

When I pull open my email, I almost can't believe what I'm seeing—an unopened email, not even a minute old, from Paula@BanksLitAgency.com

A form rejection, most likely. It won't be anything more than a form rejection. But a tiny part of me won't stop screaming, "It could be a request!" And I can't seem to shut it up.

I suck in a fortifying breath and click.

It's short—a bad sign.

"Dear Ms. Sweet, I've recently signed several new clients and am not looking for any more at the moment. Best of luck to you. Paula Banks."

The part of me that had bellowed "it could be a request" was apparently much larger than I'd thought. Disappointment wraps around my chest and squeezes.

A real writer wouldn't cry. This isn't a big deal. She didn't even read my manuscript. And how many rejections, after all, did proven writers like Stephen King or J. K. Rowling get before their first book sold? And did they cry? Of course not! Suck it up, Ellie.

I take a wobbly breath, then another. But the burn in my eyes only increases.

No. I'm not going to cry about this. I'm going to be a professional.

You're only sixteen.

There are still fourteen other queries out there . . .

They'll all say no.

. . . and it's just a matter of time before I find the right agent. These things take time.

It'll never happen for you.

I brush away the tear that leaks through and leap to my feet. I can't just sit here in the locker room. I need to get moving, need to forge on. Need to binge on cinnamon twists and Dr Pepper.

Even though I'm late, Chase stands at the usual spot in the Quad, waiting.

I jog the last few steps, huffing out, "I'm so sorry. Did the others already leave?"

"Yeah, they're getting a table." Chase frowns. "What's wrong?"

I avert my face to the street. "Nothing."

"You don't look good. Your face is all pinched. Like you've been crying."

I force a laugh as I walk past him. "Enough, Casanova. You're sweeping me off my feet."

Chase falls into step alongside me. "Who was Casanova, anyway?"

"An Italian womanizer from the fourteenth century."

"I knew you would know. You know everything."

"That's completely untrue."

I don't know how to get my boyfriend to kiss me. Or what to say in a query letter to make an agent take notice.

"Is that new?"

Palmer's bracelet has snuck out from under my sleeve and flashes in the sunlight. "Yeah. From my parents. For Valentine's Day."

Chase zips his coat against the frigid wind. Yesterday's good weather vanished overnight. "My parents never get me nothing for V-day. Must be a daughter thing."

"Must be." My parents usually give me candy, but Lucy always got new perfume or earrings for Valentine's Day and Easter.

"So." Chase ducks his head closer to mine and lowers his volume. "Francis is up for parole today."

Chase has never talked to me about his brothers. As far as I can tell, he never talks to anybody about them.

I've never been in a "so-and-so might make parole" conversation. Do I say congratulations? I clear my throat and say the only semi-intelligent thing I can come up with. "Just Francis? Not Mark?"

He shakes his head. "Mark did the shooting. It'll be a while."

Chase has yet to give me his side of the story, but according to the papers, Mark and Francis Cervantes attempted to rob a convenience store on a less-than-reputable side of town. Shots were fired, both by the owner of the store and Mark, but no one got hurt.

I shudder—not a conversation I find particularly enjoyable.

"You cold?" Without waiting for an answer, Chase throws an arm over my shoulders.

"Thanks." It's easier than telling him I shuddered from the reminder of who his family is.

I glance up in time to see Palmer and crew sauntering past us on the sidewalk. When Palmer and I cross paths at school, we usually ignore each other. Especially if he's with his friends.

But today he looks at Chase, looks at his arm around me, and then makes searing eye contact.

$$\text{\textonehalf}\text{\textonehalf}\text{\textonehalf}$$

"You sure you're okay?"

"I said yes, didn't I?"

Palmer has asked me this about fifty times since rehearsal started. How many times does he need me to say I'm fine? Regardless of the fact that it's not true.

Palmer sighs. "Would you stop messing with those stupid props and look at me?"

I do what he asks. His face is a mixture of frustration and . . . sadness?

"Please just stop being such a girl and tell me what I did." He touches my arm, and I instinctively recoil. "Great. Chase can put his arm around you for all of Redwood to see, but I can't even touch you when no one's lookin'. Nice, Gabrielle. That's real nice."

He deserves the glare I give him. "As if you even want to touch me."

Palmer looks like I just said my hair is made of peanut butter. "What? Gabrielle, how can you—"

"Palmer, you back here?" Christine's sing-song voice reaches us here in the tiny prop closet.

He closes his eyes for a second before answering. "Yeah."

She bounces into the prop room and beams a bright smile at me. "Oh, Kelly, you're back here too. Good! Mr. Freeman wants you out front. I guess we're starting act three today."

"Her name's *Ellie*," Palmer snaps.

Christine flushes. "I'm sorry, Ellie."

"Not the first time it's happened." I shoot Palmer a look as I brush past him.

I exhale a breath of relief at the unexpected escape route. Obviously, Palmer was about to say that I was being crazy. What else can he say? I'm sure it'd be just as awkward for him to say he doesn't want to kiss me as it would be for me to *hear* it.

Fortunately, we don't have another chance to talk. After rehearsal, Mr. Freeman holds back those in a schoolroom scene. I don't look over my shoulder as I scurry out the door.

❦ ❦ ❦

When the phone rings, I've already been asleep for a few hours. I don't even look at my caller's name. Only one person calls me at—a quick glance at my alarm clock—2 a.m. "Hey."

"Were you asleep?" His voice is husky, as if he too is lying in bed.

"Yeah, but it's okay."

"I wanted to call you all night, but I just . . . couldn't. This is really hard."

A breakup. I've never been through one, but this is clearly a lead in. I do a quick calculation. Nineteen days. That's all we had in us. What a horrible disappointment. Perhaps we should've told people. Maybe that would have made it feel more real. The way things are now, it's like Palmer and I are floating, totally disconnected from our real lives.

"You see, Gabrielle. It's not that I don't wanna kiss you. It's just that . . ."

That he thinks of me more like a sister. That I had something in my teeth on Sunday. That he feels disloyal to Lucy. That—

"That you're so perfect."

I blink in the darkness of my room. Uh, what? "That I'm so *perfect*?"

"Yeah."

"But shouldn't that make you *want* to kiss me?"

"I know, right? But every time I tried, I just got so . . . so nervous."

I bite my lip. Okay, what do I do with this? I had prepared myself for being unkissable. Being "perfect" I don't know how to handle.

"It's not like I'm new at this or anything. Kissing, I mean. But I've never dated a girl like you." Palmer's voice quiets. "You're the first girl I've ever dated who I didn't *know* I was going to break up with soon. With others, I could only take so much of them before I burned out. But it feels different with you."

I think about that tug in my heart that I've always felt for Palmer. Even when it made no sense. Even when it seemed outright dumb, something within me has always strained toward him. "I know what you mean."

"And Chase." Palmer growls his name. "Like it's not enough that he gets to walk around school with his arm around you, he basically stole your first kiss from me."

Something within me bristles. Wasn't that the choice Palmer made when he asked me to keep this quiet? "We could tell people, you know."

"I know, I know. And I want to soon. First I want a couple weeks of peace."

"Which is fine, but you don't get to grumble about Chase in the meantime."

"How would you feel if you saw me with Bianca or somethin'? If she was making a move, and I did nothing to stop her?"

My stomach squirms as I think of that afternoon at the coffeehouse, when I heard the lure in her voice as she asked him about coming to the lake. "I'd feel bad. But I'm not the one who's scared to tell my friends."

"It's not like that."

But we both know it is.

$$\mathcal{\&}\mathcal{\&}\mathcal{\&}$$

"Karen claims she likes it down there, but I just don't know how it's possible," Grandmom says as she saws through her dried-out chicken. "She has five hundred square feet of living space, works crazy hours, has no friends, and she hasn't found a church yet. Mark my words, as soon as she's done with this little"—Grandmom waves her fork—"rebellion, she'll be right back here where she belongs. And she won't have money for another house because of how stupidly expensive it is to live in Scottsdale. She'll have to rent again. Foolishness."

"She sounded very happy when I last talked to her." Mom seems hesitant to contradict her mother.

"It's an act." Grandmom scowls at her plate. "Mark my words."

I poke at my food. I'm not in a mood tolerant of tasteless cuisine or narrow-minded drivel. Two more rejections came today. I've barely gotten over thinking about the first one with every intake of breath, and now I have two more to stomach. One read similar to the first—just took on several new clients, not looking for any more. Thanks, but no thanks.

But the other . . .

"Your premise does not appeal to me."

For the rest of my life, I'll remember those words. When I'm in a nursing home and too senile to remember if underwear goes outside of pants or inside, they can say to me, "What did Greenwillow say in their rejection of *Invisibly Yours*?" And I will promptly reply, "Your premise does not appeal to me."

Bronte keeps telling me I'll get used to it, that every rejection won't feel like a drive-by shooting. I don't know how that's possible.

Mom sighs. "Why don't we talk about something nicer?"

"I talked to Marge today. That horrible Cervantes kid is out on parole."

I snap to attention. Francis?

"I said something nicer, Mom. *Nicer*."

I catch Mom rolling her eyes at Dad. Wow, bold. Normally my mom is much better at hiding her frustrations.

"Jails are overcrowded," Granddad mutters into his roll. "They're forced to turn criminals out on the street."

"Well, you can't lock up someone like Francis forever." Did I just say that? Everyone seems as surprised as I do that I've spoken. I poke at my lima beans. "I mean, eventually you have to trust the system, you know?"

This comment seems to please my father, who admits he can be an idealist. The other three give me blank looks.

"System's broken," Granddad mutters.

"I don't know what this town's turning into. Hoodlums running free." Grandmom shakes her head. "Maybe Karen's got the right idea. Maybe this isn't a good place for raising kids anymore."

She gives me a wistful look, as if measuring how I've turned out. She shakes her head. Clearly, I've fallen short. A sentiment I'm used to.

"I think you're too hard on yourself," Palmer says as we exit the auditorium. "You were great."

I hitch my backpack higher on my shoulders. "You've repeated that so much, I don't believe you anymore."

He rolls his eyes. "Yeah, that's logical."

I laugh and he laughs too. As we cross campus together in the warm sunshine, my heart feels like an inflating balloon. School's been out for hours, and no one's around, but it still feels like a public declaration of sorts.

"Let's go do something." The words bubble out. "Let's go get coffee. My treat."

"Oh, I wish I could. I've got homework."

The balloon of happiness within me shrivels as I recall him saying the same thing to Bianca over a week ago when he wanted to get out of going to Shaver. Of how many times I've used that excuse.

I choose my words carefully. "No time for even a cup of coffee, huh?"

"Afraid not. My homework has really slipped since we started rehearsals." He tugs playfully on my hair. "Not all of us can be as on top of things as you, Gabrielle."

"I still manage to make time for the things that are important to me."

Palmer catches me by the arm and pierces me with his gaze. "If you've got somethin' to say, just come right out and say it."

"Fine." I plant my feet and cross my arms over my chest. "We've been dating for three weeks, and we've been out once."

"We're both busy." Palmer runs a hand through his curls, like he does during tests. "After the play's over, we'll have more time."

"Oh, okay. After the play's over, you'll be able to afford spending fifteen minutes getting coffee with me?"

"I didn't know it was about coffee. I thought you'd want to sit there and talk and stuff."

"Which would be torturous."

Palmer presses his fingertips to his temples and squeezes his eyes shut. "Come on, Gabrielle. Don't sink to this. You know I love talking to you. I'm bettin' we'll spend several hours on the phone tonight when we should be asleep."

The words are angry bubbles, rising up and bursting before I can stop them. "When it's safe. When no one can see us."

Palmer rolls his eyes. "This again? Really? This is an old fight, Gabrielle. We both—"

"An old fight? How can it be an old fight? We've been together for three weeks."

He takes a deep breath. "We *both* agreed to keep this relationship to ourselves. Just until we understand it better."

"What are we waiting to understand?"

And then it hits me.

My laugh rings hollow. Lucy said it best—for a smart girl, I can sure be dumb sometimes. "We're not waiting for understanding, are we? We're waiting for you to get tired of me. Like the other girls you've dated."

"I can't believe you just said that." Palmer looks genuinely hurt. "It's not like that at all."

"I think it is. And I don't think you're willing to do anything to prove me wrong."

Palmer's eyes flash with anger. "I don't have to prove anything." He stalks away from me, toward his car.

I shift my weight from foot to foot as I watch. Part of me itches to chase after him. The other part says *I'm* the girl. If anyone in this relationship should be chased, it's me.

But that seems an increasingly silly sentiment as the evening ticks by, then Saturday, then Sunday morning, and still there's been no phone call.

❦ ❦ ❦

By Sunday afternoon, I've had it with staring at the walls of my room, with trying to draw words out of my distracted brain. My anger with Palmer is seriously bad for where I am in the story. Gabrielle is wishing Rafe away, wishing he would leave her alone once and for all. Meanwhile all I want is for Palmer to call me, to make amends.

I grab my coat and keys and head to Barnes and Noble, which has always felt like a place of happiness and hope. This is where, I've always imagined, I'll see my dream coming true. Where I'll first see *Invisibly Yours* on a shelf, where I'll hold my first book signing.

Only today, I don't feel any of that.

Today, when I step through those double doors, all I see are the books. Rows and rows of them. An impossible amount. They surround me, mock me.

What makes me think I have anything to say that hasn't already been said in one of these volumes? What makes my thoughts special? Does simply thinking them, writing them down, weaving them into characters entitle me to shelf space?

I take about five steps in before I turn and flee.

I'm crying so hard I can barely see to get my car door open. Shut inside, I try to take deep breaths, try to calm myself, but the doubt is suffocating.

Who do you think you are? You think you pound out a few words on your computer, and it's good enough for people to spend money on? You think you'll ever be the caliber of writer that a publishing house demands?

Or the caliber of girl that Palmer demands?

I try to sweet talk my fears away—God values me, and that means something. My manuscript isn't perfect, but it has potential.

I fumble in my purse for my phone and call my writer version of 9-1-1—Bronte.

"Oh, Gabrielle, everyone goes through this." It's the same tone I've heard her use when trying to comfort the baby. "All writers have had those thoughts. Especially after their first real rejection."

The panic wells within me as I picture Abbie Ross, my dream editor, reading my manuscript. Has she read it by now? We're only a month out from the conference, the awards banquet. "How will I bear it when I get Abbie's feedback?"

"You get used to it, I promise. I know it doesn't feel like it now, but you really will."

In my head, I see Abbie's red pen slashing the pages. "I should have worked harder to sell that twist in act three. The way it is now, Abbie will never buy that Rafe might have royal blood in him."

"You didn't change that?" Bronte's voice dips with concern.

"I didn't have time! I barely got my revisions in on time as it was!"

There's a brief pause on Bronte's end. "You're young, Gabrielle, okay? Not winning the Great Debut will hardly be the end of your career. It's just impressive that you finaled."

Within a few minutes, I can breathe easier and some of the panic has melted away. Until I realize she never once assured me that I have a chance of winning.

Chapter 23

Monday morning, as Chase and I cross the bridge to Vista, I overhear Marie squeal, "He *kissed* you?"

My heart seizes in my chest. I'm unsure of how I know, but I'm confident they're talking about Palmer.

"How did this happen? *When* did this happen?" Marie has Bianca by the arm and shakes her like she shook me the morning Chase brought me coffee. They're oblivious that I'm behind them, though even if they realized, they wouldn't know to be sensitive.

"It was so out of the blue." Bianca's brassy voice seems even louder than normal. "Last night, we were just standing there—"

"Where?"

"Diego's porch. He was just getting ready to leave and we were chatting."

Okay, that pronoun usage makes it sound more like she kissed Diego. Though why would Diego be leaving his own house?

Marie gives an overeager bob of her head. "What were you talking about?"

"I barely even remember." But Bianca's airiness seems fake to me. "Something unimportant, like what I order at Port of Subs. I said that I like the turkey and provolone and then out of nowhere, Palmer was kissing me."

Breath whooshes out of me at the sound of his name. *No . . .*

Marie presses her hand to her heart, as if this is the most romantic story ever. "Are you guys dating now?"

"I don't know. Maybe." Bianca shrugs, like it's irrelevant. But I know her better than that.

I feel Chase looking at me, and I realize that I too have a hand clutching my chest where my heart throbs within.

"I'm so happy for you!" Marie squeezes Bianca close with a side hug. "And I'm so glad Palmer's getting on with his life. He took Lucy's move so hard."

"Oh, I know, poor guy." Bianca's attempts at sympathy fall flat.

"I mean, he's been a monk since she left. Like on Valentine's Day, when we all went up to the lake and he stayed home? I assumed he stayed here pining over Lucy." Marie bumps Bianca with her hip. "But apparently he was planning how to make the move on *you*."

We've reached the base of the stairs, and my former friends, girls who I once pinkie swore my allegiance to forever, split off from us.

I didn't know my heart was capable of aching like this. Like an overused, exhausted muscle.

I jump when Chase's warm hand presses against the base of my neck, and I look into his dark eyes, his solemn face. "Sorry, Ellie Jane."

And to his credit, he seems sincere.

My fake smile wobbles. "No big deal."

I can't cry. I absolutely cannot cry. I must focus on something else, must engage my brain fully. I conjugate a Spanish verb. *Lloro, lloras, llora, lloramos . . .*

"You wanna ditch? Go see a movie or something?" Chase asks as we arrived at his classroom. "Doesn't matter to me."

"No, really, I'm fine." I force another smile as the bell rings. "I'll see you after class."

I wave and rush away, trying to look like I'm *not* rushing. There's a bathroom close by. Keep it together, Ellie. No crying until you get there. *Lloráis, lloran—*

"Is it just me, or does Chase have a serious problem keeping his hands off you?"

I look up to find Palmer walking alongside me, though he's left a generous berth between us. There's an angry glint in his eyes, like he has any right to be angry with me.

Hot tears pool in my eyes. Not much longer, and I'll be free. *Lloraré, llorarás, llorará.* I can see the bathroom door. A few girls filter out, on their way to first period. Hopefully I'll be alone.

"Gabrielle, are you okay?" There's a shift in Palmer's tone.

"Go away."

"Hey, what's going on?" He grabs for my arm, but I wrench away and plow into the bathroom.

Empty, praise God.

Yet even with the cloud of fresh cigarette smoke burning my eyes, I can't *lloro*. Instead, the tears dam as I glare at my reflection, hypnotized by all the reasons I'm not good enough for Palmer. My glasses. My hair, thick, wild, and unwilling to lay flat. My pale skin, which looks downright sickly in this lighting.

"Gabrielle?"

I jump at Palmer's voice echoing in the girls' bathroom. His head pokes through the barely-open door.

I back against the sink. "What are you doing?"

"Are you alone?"

"You shouldn't be in here!"

"Are you alone?"

"Yeah, but—"

Palmer closes the door behind him, then slides the lock into place. "I'm worried about you. What's going on?"

I turn away from him as tears threaten. He's watching me; I can see it in the mirror. There it is—visible proof that Palmer and I are together. That we're real.

But we're not, are we? We're no more real than Lady Gabrielle, Rafe, Lucia, or any of the other characters in my novels. Despite his hands resting on my waist, his image reflecting in the mirror, our relationship has been imaginary.

I bite my lip and battle away the tears. "You should leave. We'll get in trouble if someone finds us here."

"Forget the rules for one blasted second, Gabrielle, and tell me what's going on."

In the mirror, I catch sight of the angry snarl on my face as I whirl to face him. "How was Diego's party?"

Palmer's cheeks grow pink. "Look, I can only imagine what you must think of me, but—"

"You had a girlfriend to kiss, you know. It's not like I've been pushing you away!"

"I know, I know." His fingers are in his hair, curled into fists. "You're just so . . . so intimidating, Gabrielle. So perfect, I—"

"Yeah, I'm *perfect*." The word tastes like burned coffee. "That's why you hide me from your friends. That's why you won't even walk into a sandwich shop with me."

"We can tell people, okay? Will that make you happy? Will that fix this?"

"No, it's way too late for that." The blunt edge of the sink presses into my back, and I suck in a breath. I can't believe what I'm about to say. "I'm done. *We're* done."

He doesn't react, just stares at me blankly. "What do you mean?"

"I mean we're over."

More blank staring. Great. He's not even going to answer? Rafe would answer. Rafe would find a way to fix everything.

But of course, Palmer's not Rafe.

I push past him, but Palmer grabs my arm.

"Wait." He yanks me into an embrace.

Other than the intense smell of cinnamon air freshener, kissing Palmer is everything I once dreamed it would be. Tingles. Chills. Curled toes.

The same side effects Bianca likely experienced last night.

Palmer releases me, his eyes pleading sorrow and regret.

I step away from him. "You're too late."

Palmer doesn't chase after me, and I don't realize until I'm halfway to class that I hoped he would.

Clichés are clichés for a reason. Like I totally get the whole "when it rains it pours," thing.

I suppose I should be grateful to Emma Miller for getting back to me today of all days. Might as well get the mourning done and over with.

I click the email.

Dear Ms. Sweet,
Thank you for sending me your query for INVISIBLY
YOURS. Unfortunately—

Yep, just like I thought. What vague reason will I receive this time?

—at this time I'm not interested in seeing projects from a
writer with no visibility. While your premise sounds
interesting enough, it's very challenging to find a
publisher willing to take a risk on a debut author. I
suggest you work on building an audience for yourself.

Best of luck to you in your writing endeavors,
Emma Miller

I stare at the email until my eyes go fuzzy. With each tick of the clock, hope drains further from me.

I don't know a single thing about building "visibility." All I want to do is write. It's what I love, what I'm good at.

Right? Or is writing like everything else in my life, where I don't quite measure up?

Loved, but not quite the Gabrielle they had in mind.

Fine for hanging out and talking with, but not cool enough to include in plans.

"Perfect," yet not someone to be seen with.

Why did I think writing would be any different?

I close the email and snuff out those fantastical ideas I once had of seeing my book on store shelves. I'm a girl destined for average. A girl who will never possess, achieve, or acquire anything out of the ordinary.

Chapter 24

My body hums with nerves as I wait backstage. I just want to get tonight—opening night of *Anne of Green Gables*—and the rest of the weekend done with. Then it'll be over. No more long, torturous afternoons and evenings trapped in the same space as Palmer. No more gray wigs and uncomfortable dresses. No more pretending like this stupid play even matters to me.

"I'm so nervous!" Jenna, the freshman who plays Diana, squeezes my hands. "Why am I so nervous?"

"You'll do great." My words sound empty, as they have for the weeks since the one-two punch of breaking up with Palmer and being informed by my dream agency that I'm not publishable.

Jenna giggles as she fluffs her dark ponytail. "Don't tell anyone, but Christine just threw up, she's so nervous."

"Is she okay?"

"She's hunting down mouthwash because she's afraid of grossing out Palmer during their scenes together. Do you have any? We thought you'd be the most likely."

Great. My *grandmother* is the only person I know who carries mouthwash with her. "No. But Brad always has gum."

"Oh! Good idea. Thanks." Jenna rushes off in search of Brad, and I return to wringing my hands, running my lines through my head once again.

"Don't worry. You'll knock 'em dead."

The voice comes from behind me. I stop pacing and close my eyes. "Thank you."

"Can I talk to you for a second?"

Of course. Three-plus weeks of the silent treatment, and *now* he wants to talk. "The show is starting."

"And you're not on for another five. This'll be quick, I promise."

His hand curls around my arm, but I stand firm. I refuse to behave like I so stupidly did when I agreed to keep our relationship a secret. I refuse to be a gullible, naive puppy, lured by gentle words and a dog biscuit.

Palmer glances around, then whispers in my ear, "This is crazy. We're obviously both miserable."

Every time I've seen him since our breakup, he's been laughing and joking with his friends, same as always. "Leave me alone."

He groans. "Why, Gabrielle? I know you still care about me. And you know I'm crazy about you."

And there's the dog biscuit.

I turn and look him full in the face. He could be mine again if I just say the word. But I know by now it's an illusion. Palmer doesn't want to be mine; he just wants *me* to be *his*.

"I'm not interested, okay? What I used to feel for you is gone. And whatever it is you think you feel for me will go away soon too."

I attempt to jerk my arm from his grasp, but he holds tight. "You think you have it all figured out, don't you? That you're so smart." His face is close, his gaze penetrating.

I swallow. "Not about you."

He releases his crushing grip on my arm. "Have it your way, sweetheart."

Odd how the nickname sounds like an insult.

Palmer stalks away as the stage director rushes up. "Ellie, it's almost time."

I blink at her a moment as I try to grasp what's going on around me. I'm backstage, waiting to go on, aren't I? I just had that conversation with Palmer while wearing my gray-bun wig and awful maroon lipstick. And . . . my lines! What are my lines?!

"I don't know my lines!" I struggle to keep my voice at a whisper as the stage director nudges me toward the curtain.

"'Good evening, Rachel. This is a real fine night, isn't it?'" The steel in her voice tells me she thinks I'm just some newbie actress, paralyzed by stage-fright.

As I wait at the edge of the curtain, fingers fidgeting with my stiff skirts, I wish I really was Marilla Cuthbert. I wish I was old and sure of myself, my days of silly boys behind me. There'd been heartbreak, sure, but it was long ago. The pain was fuzzy at most.

I wish this again at the end of the night, when Palmer leaves with an arm draped around Bianca's shoulders.

"I still just can't believe it." Karen grins at me over her steaming cup of tea. "You had such presence up there."

I bite back a yawn. It's nearly midnight, and, after performing five shows in three days, I'm exhausted. The smart thing would be to rest up for school tomorrow, but I want to enjoy my last opportunity for a late night chat with Karen before she heads back to Scottsdale. Mom and Dad went to bed hours ago, but Karen just put on a fresh pot of her new favorite tea for us. Which I find way more enjoyable than getting loaded at the cast party tonight.

I tuck my legs underneath me. "I think you're biased."

"I'm serious. You were golden up there. You sparkled. You shimmered."

I give Karen a look. "Then I played my part all wrong. Marilla Cuthbert doesn't sparkle or shimmer."

Karen grins. "I'll have you know that I'm an *Anne of Green Gables* expert, and when acted correctly, Marilla both sparkles *and* shimmers."

"Okay, new subject."

Karen chuckles and drops her voice. "So was that your Palmer playing Gilbert Blythe? I noticed his name in the playbill."

I force a laugh that sounds pretty natural. "I think he'd be surprised to hear you call him 'my Palmer.'"

"You were right. Very cute. I'll forgive that he has light hair. Gilbert's should be dark. But at least he had curls. Gilbert should have curls, don't you think?"

"Sure." I take a sip of tea and pray the conversation turns away from Palmer.

"So. Has anything ever happened with him?"

I hate lying to my aunt. "No. But I'm fine with it."

"Yeah?"

"Yeah."

"Because of another fella?"

I smile into my mug. "No. Just . . . I don't think Palmer's really my type."

As the words come out, I'm struck by their truth. I'd never felt like Palmer was the type of guy I should be with. So why am I letting it hit me so hard that it didn't work out?

"Sounds like you have a healthy attitude about it."

I feel oddly lightheaded from my revelation, like a weight has shifted. "I'm getting there."

Chapter 25

"Whatcha doing?"

I close the lid of my laptop as Chase's shadow falls over me. "Just some email."

"Looked like you had a flight schedule pulled up." Chase's face is silhouetted in the sun, but his voice has a suspicious edge in it. Of course I've been reading suspicion into everything he says lately. Paranoia.

"Dad and I are talking about a trip to Minneapolis."

"What's in Minneapolis?"

"Some writing thing." I shrug as if the writing thing in Minneapolis isn't the biggest thing that'll happen to me all year. In six days, I will board a flight with my father to Minneapolis for the AFW conference. In eight days, I'll attend the awards dinner and find out if *Invisibly Yours* won the Great Debut.

Chase sits beside me. "You're not leaving anytime soon, though?"

I open my mouth, only to be cut off by giggling that I would recognize anywhere, and a loud, "Hey, Marilla!"

Bianca is the one who said it, but my gaze catches on Palmer. His face is a blank mask, but his eyes flash with fear.

Bianca feigns shock. "Oh, it's *you*, Ellie. I could have sworn it really was Marilla sitting there. My compliments to whoever casted the play." She laughs through her final insult, unable to hold together the act any longer. "You're the spitting image."

Marie giggles behind her hand. Troy seems confused, a slightly wistful look on his face. Stoned, most likely. And Palmer looks away, the slight pink of his cheeks and the set of his jaw the only indication that he feels anything at all.

My eyes are hot with tears and my mouth full of angry words, ones that don't bear the Sunday school stamp of approval.

"Bianca, Bianca." Chase's tone is falsely soothing. "No need to run Ellie down just because your boyfriend has a thing for her."

Palmer snaps to attention, his eyes blazing. The look he gives me is clear—*you told him?*

Bianca's laugh is loud yet angry. "Now *that's* a good one."

She stalks away in a stiff version of the hip-swishing way she once practiced at a slumber party our freshman year. She says something that involves the word incarcerated, but she's smart enough to not make herself clear.

I have the odd sensation that I just got slapped across the face. First by Bianca with those Marilla comments, then Palmer and his averted gaze. He doesn't even value me enough to say *something* to quiet Bianca?

Chase's deep breath shivers with contained anger. "That girl has issues. You okay?"

His hand is warm on my neck, but I duck away. "Fine." But I don't sound fine at all. "Why'd you say anything? It just makes it worse."

Chase huffs a humorless laugh. "You gotta be kidding me, El. You're mad at *me*?"

"*Don't* call me El."

"Yes, forgive me *Gabrielle*." Cruel and mocking. "Forgive me for speaking up when I know you like your guys to keep silent."

Chase's glare makes the fight within me wither, makes my harsh words die in my throat. As he stalks away, I swear he mutters, "Enjoy Minneapolis."

❀❀❀

Writing is a blessed escape again.

It's nearly midnight, but Rafe and Gabrielle are galloping toward misery, and I can't slow down now. Plus it's the first night of spring break, so no one my age is asleep yet anyway. The party at Stacey's tonight is probably still ramping up.

Her choice was made, Gabrielle kept telling herself. And each time she repeated it, she felt better. Tonight she would become Princess Gabrielle Ferrero. Rafe could move on. Maybe he finally would now that she belonged to another man.

What kind of life might she have had with Rafe, anyway? Yes, there'd have been excitement and romance, but for how long? As strong as their love felt now, wasn't it possible he would turn back to his dark ways? Wasn't it possible her good influence would fail? At least with the prince, she knew what to expect. Men who wore crowns were not faithful—everybody knew that. She would find a way to cope, for the security of the title to be enough.

With Rafe, there would've been—

My email pings, but I finish my thought before peeking. Bronte sometimes emails me at this hour. It's 3 a.m. where she is, and if her kids wake her up, she has problems going back to sleep.

Yep, Bronte. I'm skimming her note when my gaze catches on the gap between my bedroom wall and the blinds. There's a strange car parked in the street.

Though it's not a strange car. The Jeep is familiar, just not in my neighborhood.

I assumed Palmer would be at the party, or packing for his Mexican cruise, which I overheard him telling Diego about during Algebra. But apparently not. Apparently he's loitering in my cul-de-sac.

It's been nearly six weeks since we split, and our only conversation has been his pathetic efforts to get back together. After what happened today with Bianca, I should definitely just ignore him.

But curiosity wins. I slide my feet into flip-flops and redo the knot in my hair.

The light's on in the living room. Not Mom and Dad, right? I peek around the corner and relief washes over me. Just James, watching TV. There's only a fraction of time that I'll be visible—I bet I can sneak past him. Getting back in the house might be tricky, but maybe he'll have gone to bed by then.

And if he catches me and wants to tattle, it's not like I don't have plenty of dirt I could tell Mom and Dad about him. They think he's so perfect? Just wait until I tell them how drunk he got after graduation.

I take one step and cringe. I'd forgotten my shoes squeak on the tile.

What's wrong with me? I can't even properly sneak out of the house. I'm like the worst teenager ever.

"And where are you going, missy?"

I wince and turn, finding James's beefy arms crossed over his chest and a grin on his face.

"Um, well. Bianca called and needs me to come over for—"

"Save it." James shoos me with a hand gesture. "Go on out there. Talk to whatever guy is parked in front of the Shears' house. Just don't go anywhere, don't wake up Mom or Dad, and as far as I'm concerned, we never had this conversation."

I hesitate. Is this some kind of prank? Is James going to call Mom and Dad out here the second I walk out the door?

James frowns. "It's not Chase, right?"

"No."

"Then go, little sis. It's about time you broke a few rules, don't you think?"

Hearing it phrased that way makes me uneasy. I hear people say rules were meant to be broken, but it's never been a sentiment I've shared.

James sighs and turns back to the TV.

I glance out the front door. Palmer's Jeep is still there. I suck in a deep breath and head into the dry night air.

There's something surreal about being out this time of night, with the moon high in the sky, the breeze cutting through my thin PJ pants, and my shoes flapping against the blacktop.

I wrench open the passenger door. "Just out for a drive?"

He doesn't smile back, just looks at me with round eyes. "I thought you'd be sleeping."

"Nope. So, let's hear it." I slide into the seat and pull the door shut. "What'd you come here for?"

"Nothing." The dim street lamp reveals a tick in Palmer's tense jaw.

I sigh. "Palmer, it's midnight. I'd like to go to bed. Can you please just tell me whatever it is you came here hoping to say?"

He trains his gaze on something out the window.

I reach for the door handle but stop when Palmer touches my arm. How I loathe the jolt it gives me.

He says something but not loud enough for me to hear.

"What?"

"I'm sorry I kissed Bianca." His gaze skitters my way. "And I'm sorry you didn't hear it from me. And that when you confronted me about it, I just made excuses."

I don't know what I expected when I came out here; but his apologies leave me reeling. I guess I thought he had come to try and explain away the events of today, to smooth over his actions with his charm. I didn't expect him to look broken, close to tears. It tugs down whatever fragile defenses I'd built against him.

"It's okay. I was stupid to think it could work out between us."

"Please don't say that." Palmer sounds wounded.

"I don't mean just because of you. Because of me too. It would've ended soon, whether or not you kissed her."

He holds eye contact for a moment, then reverts to gazing out the window. "I'm sorry about the stuff Bianca said today. She shouldn't have done that."

"Why are you even dating her? You don't like her." My mouth runs on, leaving my brain behind. "She's one of those girls you know you'll burn out on. And that's the only time you're comfortable in a relationship—when you're in charge."

Palmer's teeth grind. "Can we please not do this, Gabrielle? I didn't come here to fight. I came here to make sure you're okay."

"You don't *get* to be concerned about that anymore, okay?"

"I know you're still hurting, but—"

"It was three weeks of my life, Palmer. We've been broken up *twice* as long as we were together. And with each day that passes, I feel a little more confused about why I dated you in the first place."

Why did I say that? He'll think I'm bitter.

And maybe I am. Maybe I'm not as "over it" as I thought.

Palmer shoots me a look. "I liked you better when you were nice."

"Well, we're even." I yank the door handle and kick it open. "Because I liked you better when I didn't know you." I slam the door and march toward my house.

"Gabrielle!"

I stop and turn, but he doesn't say anything.

I should've just kept walking. Made him follow me for once. "What, Palmer?"

"Just . . . please don't date Chase. Okay?"

"It's none of your business who I date. And frankly—"

"Just *please* don't date him." Palmer's voice is strained. "This isn't about me. Or us. This is about you. And you deserve much better than him."

"I'll date whomever I want," I say. "And you can do the same."

Then I turn on my heel and walk away. He gives me the last word, but there's no satisfaction in it.

Chapter 26

I awake to a soft knock on the door and sunshine filling my bedroom. "You awake, Ellie?"

I groan.

"Great," Mom chirps. "Breakfast will be ready pretty soon."

Mom always makes big breakfasts on Saturday mornings—food is her love language—and my empty stomach urges me out of bed.

I rub my eyes, stretch, and grapple for my bearings. My mind is a mangled mush of wisps of dreams, Lady Gabrielle and Prince Domenico, and my conversation with Palmer last night.

My phone launches into its jingle and yanks me into the present. Chase. He's awake early.

I sit up and pull my blanket to my chest, as if it's somehow indecent to talk to him while wearing my ratty sleep shirt. "Hey."

There's a long pause, followed by, "Ellie?"

A female voice. Not really what I expected. "Uh, yeah?"

"This is Marietta Cervantes. Chase's mother."

"Oh. Hi." I stand and arch my back. "How are you?"

"Were you at the party?" Her words are low and tight, as if she's restraining tears.

"You mean Stacey's? No."

She sighs. "I thought so. Donnie still said I should call you."

My stomach knots, and my hand freezes in smoothing my sheets. "Did something happen to Chase?"

She sighs again. "Chase got a DUI last night."

"A DUI." I press my eyes closed. He'd been so good recently. What happened?

"I wondered if you maybe broke up. Maybe my Chase was sad. Maybe that's why he did this."

Thank you oh-so-much, Chase, for leaving me to enlighten your sweet mom.

I sink onto my partially made bed. "Mrs. Cervantes, I don't know why Chase did what he did last night, but it wasn't because we broke up. Because the truth is we're just friends. We've always been just friends, but I didn't want to embarrass him in front of you guys by saying anything. I thought he should be the one to tell you. I'm sorry."

Mrs. Cervantes is silent, but I can hear kitchen sounds behind her—breakfast dishes? When her voice comes, it's venomous. "You led him on."

"I . . ." I swallow. "That's not fair. We were friends, and—"

"Where I come from, boys and girls are not friends. Only trash girls flirt with boys who are not their boyfriend."

"It's not like that, Mrs. Cervantes. And I never flirted with Chase. I—"

"You did! I saw! I saw how you looked at him!"

The words are a lump in my throat—*how did I look at him*? I force them back down.

There's a gentle knock on my bedroom door, then Mom's head pokes in. "You coming in for breakfast, sunshine?"

I cover the mouthpiece with my hand and aim a bright smile at Mom. "Be right there."

Meanwhile, Mrs. Cervantes continues to verbally flog me. "You even went to his bedroom alone! What kind of girl does that but a trash girl?"

"You're wrapping up your conversation, right?" Mom nods, as if hinting what my answer is. "Dad and James are already at the table."

"And my Chase, he tells me about all the things you do together! Dinners and movies! You think my Chase is made of money?"

I nod at Mom. "I just need thirty seconds."

"Okay, sweetie." The door gives a gentle click as she leaves.

"I made such big mistake. I thought you were a nice girl. I thought you were helping my Chase—"

"Mrs. Cervantes, listen to me, please. I care about your son. A lot. He's"—my voice hitches—"my best friend. However, seeing as I wasn't at the party last night, encouraging him to do keg stands or whatever, you can hardly blame me for what happened."

Silence. No breakfast dishes or anything.

"Mrs. Cervantes?"

I pull away my phone and see that, yes, at some point during my spiel, she hung up. Excellent.

I clutch my phone wishing I had asked how and where he is before being hung up on. Do you go to jail for DUIs?

"Ellie!" There's an impatient edge in Mom's voice.

I smell buttermilk biscuits and sage sausage long before I reach the dining room. Mom's gone to extra work for James, of course. There's a cloth on the table, a pitcher of orange juice, and all three of them are seated, blinking at me as I enter.

"Well, sit down." Mom sounds as though she has only a thread of patience.

Dad prays over our food, and my mind flitters to Mr. Cervantes, to the familiar way he blessed dinner on Chase's birthday. Did he pray over their breakfast this morning? In their tiny nook of an eating space, with Chase in his bedroom sleeping off last night?

Or maybe he's sleeping it off in a cell.

"Ellie?"

I raise my head and find myself under scrutiny. Apparently we've finished praying.

Dad's forehead etches with concern. "You okay, pumpkin?"

"Yeah, fine." I reach for the bowl of fruit salad and heap some on my plate. "Looks good, Mom."

Her cheeks match the rosy tablecloth. "Thank you."

Despite the formal setting, normal conversation ensues. James entertains us with stories from college. Mom and Dad laugh along with him and relive their days at Fresno State. I have little to contribute to the conversation, but that works out fine because I'm the only one who gets to eat the cheesy eggs while they're still hot.

As the conversation winds down, I catch Mom and Dad exchanging a look I don't recognize. What are they—

"Kids, we have something we'd like to talk to you about," Dad says. "A surprise of sorts."

"Disneyland?" James asks with a wry smile.

"A dog?"

"No, I . . . I mean, we . . ." He smiles at Mom, kind of dopey like.

My mouth goes dry. "You're having a baby."

Mom erupts into laughter. "What on earth would give you that idea?"

"I don't know. You're being all moony and hesitant."

"I'm not pregnant." Mom's cheeks are stained red.

Dad covers her hand with his. "We're excited because there's been interest at Nickelodeon for making a TV show based on *James*. Nothing is final, of course. But there have been a couple meetings about it, and they've ordered a pilot episode for audience testing."

"That's amazing!" My heart hums as I think about what that must feel like, about what a miracle it would seem like if *Invisibly Yours* were ever adapted for TV. "You must be elated."

"Nothing's for sure. I wouldn't even say it's promising or anything. I'm sure they look at and reject pilots all the time." Dad's words say one thing, but his smile another.

"I can't believe I might wind up on TV," James says. "Cow-me, anyway."

I fork another sausage patty onto my plate. "When will they make a decision?"

"The pilot's being made now, but I have no idea when or if we'll get to see it. Maybe never. Nothing's for sure."

Mom moves her hand on top of Dad's. "You've said that about ten times now, Stu. Give the kids some credit."

"You're right, Ally. I'm just trying to not get my hopes up too much, I guess."

"But even if nothing develops with Nickelodeon, this will help move things along with your editor. Right?"

Dad grins. "Yes. I talked to Ron yesterday. He said Becky is reconsidering the Russia idea, and that I should get together a few more concepts. So I'll be putting that together on our flight to Minneapolis, I would guess."

"Oh, Ellie, that reminds me." Mom smiles at me over her coffee cup. "You had a letter from Lucy yesterday. It got stuck in one of my magazines."

A letter from Lucy? Why on earth would she be sending me a letter?

James laughs as he reaches for the creamer. "Mom, how does that have anything to do with what Dad said?"

"Jan is from Minneapolis, so it made sense in my head." She shrugs. "It's on the kitchen counter, El."

As I approach the kitchen, I feel as if I'm walking into a place of unknown dangers. Lucy is *not* the letter writing type. What could she possibly say that wouldn't fit in a text message?

The first thing I pull out of the envelope, however, is not a letter but a picture. An unfamiliar black and white photograph of Palmer and me at school. We're talking to each other. I look nervous, but he's just Palmer. Perfect Palmer. When did Lucy . . . ?

Then I remember—right after she found out about San Diego.

"You're supposed to tell people before you take their picture," I had said.

And she'd rolled her eyes. "Not when it's for your 'candid' photography assignment."

Lucy has never been prolific, so I'm surprised to find the letter takes up the front and back of her "From the desk of Lucy Grace Shears" stationery.

Dear Ellie,
I wonder who of us is more surprised by this letter, me or you. I had every intention of never talking to you again after your attempts to ruin our overnight at Shaver, but here I am. Writing.

I'm writing because of this picture. Do you remember me taking it? It was right after Palmer and I got together, and I came across you guys chatting. I took it so I could slyly take a picture of him, but I got a lot more than I bargained for.

Even as I developed it, I noticed the way Palmer was looking at you.

I yank the picture close. What's she talking about? I mean, yeah, he's looking at me, but I don't see anything remarkable about it. Lucy's crazy.

Knowing you, you'll think I'm talking crazy.

So Lucy does know me. At least a little.

For a while, I convinced myself I was seeing things. But then when Mr. Dolcer graded the photo, he left me a note saying I "captured the emotions well." And then my mom saw it and asked who that cute boy was looking at you with "moony eyes."

Bianca called and told me her and Palmer are together now. I can't imagine it'll work out. Not if he still feels the way about you that I now realize he did when he and I were together. I thought it was all an act, the "sweetheart" thing. And when he got all ogreish about Chase, I thought he was just being protective of you because you were my best friend. But actually I think he felt something very real for you.

I'm writing to say it's okay with me if you guys date. Palmer's a good guy. He's got some problems, like we all

*do, but the fact that he saw through your wall and fell
for you means there's hope for him.*

*Sorry it took me so long to give this (the picture) to you. I
held on to it, to be perfectly honest, because I didn't want
you to know. Now that I've made some good friends here
and have this really great boyfriend you'd totally
disapprove of (ha ha), I don't mind so much. Though it
might not matter. Bianca says you and Chase are fused
at the hip. Good for you.*

*Love,
Lucy*

I stare at the picture for a long time trying to decide if it matters
that Palmer cared enough that others noticed.

"Everything okay, Ellie?" Dad calls from the other room.

I stuff the letter and photograph back into the envelope. "Yeah,
fine."

I can't decide if I'm lying or not.

Chapter 27

Tuesday morning, I emerge from my room bleary eyed and jumpy from a night of restless sleep. I kept dreaming that I was at the AFW awards banquet, only instead of wearing a dress, I had on my pajamas and kept trying to fall asleep on the dinner table. But Bronte was telling me I couldn't fall asleep, that I needed to stay awake and find out if I won. Only when they announced the finalists for the YA category of the Great Debut, *Invisibly Yours* wasn't on the list.

This morning, I checked the list again. Just to be sure.

I expect to find myself alone—James has been hanging with friends all week—but Mom is sitting at the counter, grocery ads spread before her. She beams at me. "Hi!"

I blink at her enthusiasm. "Hey. Why are you home?"

She shrugs. Somehow jauntily. "I thought it'd be fun to take off work and spend some time with you before your big trip. We can go get what you need for your conference. Is that okay? Do you have plans? I guess I should've asked."

I pull Grape-Nuts from the cabinet. "No, I don't. But I don't really need anything other than a nice dress for Saturday night."

"Oh, you need more than that, Ellie! I'm thinking we should have a girl's day. Shopping, makeovers, the whole package."

My distaste must be obvious because Mom instantly says, "Oh, honey, it'll be fun, I promise! I've been working on our schedule, and here's what I think we should do."

She goes through the list so rapidly I can hardly keep up. Mom has a hair appointment at ten, and apparently she talked to Julia (*who???*) and they just hired on a new girl who's supposed to be fabulous, but has openings today because she's still building her client list.

After hair, shopping. Lots of shopping.

"You need new clothes," Mom says as I join her at the counter with my bowl of cereal. "Yours are looking all raggedy."

I glance at my black T-shirt—which, okay, has seen better days—and my favorite jeans. "My clothes are fine. I mean, maybe not *this* shirt, but if it makes you feel better, I don't intend to wear it at the conference."

Mom sighs, then gives me a look. A Mom-look.

I'm about to lose.

"At the start of the school year, I wanted to buy you new clothes, and you told me no over and over. Do you remember what I said to you?"

I wince. "That I owed you a shopping trip."

"Bingo. And so you know what today is?"

"Payback?"

She grins. "Precisely."

$$\mathcal{B}\mathcal{B}\mathcal{B}$$

But at the salon, with my head warm and sudsy in Erin's shampoo sink, payback feels pretty sweet. I suppose a haircut isn't the worst idea before I go to my conference. Although it's not like I can ever get my hair to do anything but fuzz when I try to style it.

Erin's fingertips massage my scalp as she peppers me with questions. Where do you go to school? Are you in sports? What kind of movies do you like? She looks to be in her early twenties, has a tiny nose that flips up at the end, and a head full of blond curls. If only my hair could do *that*.

The shampoo sink experience is over far too quickly and we return to Erin's chair. My mom, freshly trimmed and looking beautiful, asks, "How's it going, girls?"

"Great!" Erin whips a cape over my shirt and snaps it in the back. "I just love Ellie's hair. She has so much natural curl!"

"She does?"

"I do?"

Erin looks between Mom and me like she thinks we might be joking. "Oh, yeah. Look at this." She scrunches my hair with the towel for a second, then releases and holds out several waved strands for us to see. "This is the same thing my hair does when it's wet."

I gaze once again at Erin's golden ringlets. "My hair could look like yours?"

Erin nods. "With the right cut to get rid of these dried-out ends and loosen up the curls. Plus some good gel and a little technique."

I press my back into the chair. "Let's get started."

I try to calm my hopeful heart. Erin's a new hairdresser. It's possible she can't tell the difference between a frizzy mess and curls when hair is wet.

After a period of snipping and small talk, Erin spins me toward her and studies my hair. "Just making sure I got the layers right. The right layers will help release your curls. Without them, your hair will just hang."

Apparently satisfied, she unsnaps the cape. "Let's go back to the shampoo sink for a second, okay? I want to show you how to style this."

After rewetting my hair, Erin props me up. "Now what you want to do is squash your hair with a towel or T-shirt. Don't brush it—then it'll fuzz rather than curl. Why don't you try bending at the waist and drying it upside down? It's easier to get all the hair that way."

I take the towel from Erin and do as instructed, feeling self-conscious in the crowded salon. But when I look in the mirror, I forget about everyone around me. I have a head full of dark, loose waves.

"Amazing." Mom's hand hovers above my hair, as if afraid to touch it. "This is why we've never been able to get your hair to do a single thing, El. It's curly."

"The curls will get tighter as they dry. To make them shiny, I use this." Erin hands me a pot of thick gel. She shows me how to rub it between my hands and scrunch it through my curls, handling them as little as possible. "When it dries, you won't believe how good it looks."

Mom scribbles an amount on a check. "Erin, you're a genius."

Erin waves away the compliment. "You girls have a good day." Then she moves on to greeting her next client. It's just a normal day for her.

On the patio of my mom's favorite French café, beneath the warmth of the sun, my hair dries into the shiny curls Erin promised. Mom keeps looking at my hair with a dazed expression.

"I suppose this is what I get for always having Karen cut your hair." Mom sighs as if thoroughly disappointed in herself.

I try to not think about my curls too much, as if paying attention to my good hair day might make it run off and disappear, never to return again. Though it's hard to completely forget about it when curls keep tickling my ears.

"Where do you want to go shopping?" Mom asks as we walk back out to the car. "There's the mall, of course. Or we could drive to Fresno if you want—"

"Mall sounds great."

If I let Mom get too carried away, she'll be whisking me down to Los Angeles for a mega shopping spree.

"That'll be a good place to start, anyway."

"All I need is a nice dress for the banquet, Mom."

"And a few nice outfits for the days. You don't want to go in to meet an editor dressed like that, do you, Ellie?"

I roll my eyes. "I'm not planning on wearing *this*, Mom. I'll wear something nice, I promise."

"You don't need something *nice*, you need something professional." Mom's gaze sweeps across my face. "And you could use some new makeup as well."

Not surprising, considering the only makeup I own is the tube of lip gloss Mom put in my stocking this Christmas.

At Macy's, I head for the rack of solid-colored shirts and pull out a few that will match skirts I already have and that can also be worn with jeans.

"What do you think?" Mom holds up an outfit for my approval. The skirt is brown and billowy, the shirt lacy and feminine.

I would never have picked them out, and they don't match a thing in my closet, but Mom's eager expression keeps me from saying any of this. What's the harm in trying them on?

"Yeah, sure." I hang a black shirt over my arm. "I'll try it on."

The problem with this is that my mom starts pulling out similar outfits—pretty spring dresses in bright colors, pants with glittery, feminine details, and shirts cut in ways to make it clear I'm a girl.

When I close myself into the dressing room, my mom settles on a bench just outside, making it clear she expects to see me in all of them. I give the pile of clothes a resigned look. We're going to be here all day.

On the plus side, we may not make it to the makeup counters.

As I fuss with a complicated tie on the flowing skirt Mom first showed me, my teeth grind together. This is just way too feminine. I bet I look stupid. I bet Mom laughs when I walk out there. I bet—

I catch sight of myself in the mirror.

I look . . . good.

Nothing along the lines of Lucy Shears of course, but somehow with my new hair, the girly, modern-hippie style suits me.

"How's it going, Ellie?" Mom's voice is bright but tinged with nerves. Like she knows she's pushing me.

"Not too bad." I turn and marvel my profile. "Pretty good, actually."

$$\mathscr{B}\mathscr{B}\mathscr{B}$$

Mom buys everything I try on. *Everything.*
And she does it again at the next store.
I nervously eye the amount due. "Are you sure this is okay?"
"Ellie, I don't want you giving it a second thought. Your father and I already discussed it, so stop your worrying."
"But—"
Mom gives me a look, and I shut my mouth. Then she drags me down to the makeup counter, where she sends the makeup lady into a tizzy with the word "makeover."
"Ellie has really beautiful, clear skin." The makeup lady buzzes around the counter, pulling out shadows, brushes, and pencils of all types. "I think less is more with her. We should do a very natural look, lots of browns and peaches . . ."
The little brushes tickle my face, but in a good way. They're relaxing, kind of like Erin's shampoo sink. While my mom nods at every trinket of makeup wisdom the woman shares, I focus on not sneezing when I accidentally breathe in some of the powder.
"Well, I hate to admit it, but that wasn't so bad," I say as we head for Dairy Queen in the food court.
"Really?" Mom looks pleased, but like she doesn't want to seem *too* pleased.
"Yeah. I mean, I don't know when I'll ever use bronzer, but the other stuff . . ." I tug at the skirt of my new dress. Mom and the makeup lady had insisted I change so they had a better idea of what to "work from," and I should have thought to change back before we left the department store.
"Where should we go next?" Mom asks as we settle into a table. "Maybe we should take a quick gander and see if anyone is having a great sale, and then we could drive up to Fresno."
I lick Oreo Blast from my spoon. "I don't need anything else."
"You know what that brown skirt could use is cute sandals. I wonder if anyone is having a shoe sale."
"Let's look for new shoes for you, okay? I'm set for a couple lifetimes, I think."
Mom's mouth quirks into an amused smile. "Just let me do this for you, Ellie, okay? I'm having a great time."

I grin and duck my head. What a childish thing, to be so delighted by my mom spending time with me.

When I look up again, she's admiring my hair. "I just can't get over it. Curls. And the funny thing is, you look different . . . but somehow, you just look more like you." Mom shakes her head. "That sounded stupid, didn't it? Your father's the one who's good with words."

I don't think it sounds so stupid, but maybe that's because I like the idea, that somehow my curls are a piece of the puzzle of who I'm meant to be.

As I ponder this, my gaze catches on a pair of dark eyes. Chase.

He's wearing the drab, button-down shirt and pants of his janitor's uniform, and wipes off a table several over from us. Or he *was*. He seems to be frozen in place as he stares at me. In my sleeveless dress, I feel silly and exposed.

I tuck my hair behind my ears before remembering I'm not supposed to touch it. "I need to go to the bathroom."

Mom is scrolling through her work email on her phone and doesn't seem to notice the strain in my voice. "Okay, sweetie."

I weave through the tables, hurrying toward the bathroom. Though what do I plan to do once I get there? It's not like Chase has anywhere else he needs to—

"Ellie, wait."

I pivot. Chase still holds the damp rag in one hand. His other hand clutches the radio clipped to his belt.

"Hi!" My voice is bright, as if I hadn't just been dashing away from him. "How's it going?"

His eyes linger on my legs. I want to pull my jeans back on and curl into a ball.

"I've never seen you so . . ." His gaze travels up my dress, along my made-up face, my thick curls. "Your hair's down."

"Yeah."

"I didn't know it was curly."

"Me neither, actually."

"And the dress . . ." Chase clears his throat and looks me in the eyes. "You look good. Pretty."

"Thanks." I shift my weight from foot to foot. I haven't been this uncomfortable since a certain announcement was made during Algebra class.

A long silence ensues. When I look at Chase, he's again looking not-at-my-face. Time to get some conversation going. "So. Had an interesting talk with your mom Saturday morning."

That snaps Chase out of looking at me like some tricked-out sports car. "Oh, right."

"How are you?"

He rubs the back of his neck. "I'm . . . I don't know how I am, honestly. How's that for an answer?"

"Uh, confusing." I pull my arms tighter over my chest. "She seemed angry."

"She was. I woke up with a killer headache and her yelling at me for lying to them." He flicks his gaze to me, then away again. "About us, I mean."

"I'm sorry. I just didn't know how else to answer her questions."

"It's my fault. I should have told them a long time ago."

"Maybe then your mother wouldn't have called me a 'trash girl.'"

Chase groans and scuffs his work boot along the linoleum. "Sorry."

"Believe it or not, that's not a reputation that's been applied to me before."

Chase exhales slow and loud through his nose. "I really blew it."

"At least they know."

"Right."

There's another long silence. I need to get back to my table before Mom comes looking for me. "I should go," I say as Chase says, "I've gotta tell you something."

His voice quivers, and one look at his face tells me I won't like what he has to say. He inhales deeply. "So . . . you know Harper?"

I blink a few times. "Yeah. Of course."

"Well. We kinda . . . fooled around a little."

I fight for control over my facial muscles, to keep from displaying how my heart throbs. With *Harper*? How could he? I had always thought Harper too flirtatious for her own good, but I just can't believe Chase would be dumb enough to fall for her or do this to one of his best friends.

I take a long deep breath and exhale before allowing myself to speak. "What about Jose? Does he know yet?"

Chase stares at me as if he didn't hear my question.

"Chase?"

A jaw muscle ticks, but otherwise he seems void of emotion. "I guess I shouldn't be surprised. I figured you'd say that."

"Well, I think it's a pretty natural thing to say. I mean, she and Jose have been together for a few months, and he's one of your closest friends, so—"

"Stop. This isn't about Jose. It's not even about Harper."

I massage my temples. "Okay, then what's it about?"

"How can you not know?"

"Well, I don't, okay? And I really need you to start connecting some dots for me."

"It's about you." His words are flat, measured.

"I wasn't even there! I can't be your guardian angel, Chase. I know your mom would like that, but I can't force you to be good."

"That's not what I meant," he says through gritted teeth.

"Okay, why are *you* frustrated with *me*? I didn't do anything."

"Because I knew you'd react this way."

"How else should I have acted? Should I have told you it was no big deal? I mean, you and Jose—"

"Because I knew you wouldn't care!"

I've heard Chase yell before, just never at me. Even though we're in a public place, even though Chase has never been anything but gentle with me, his snarl forces me back a couple steps.

He squeezes his eyes closed and rubs the back of his neck. "That was the worst part." His words are so low, I have to lean forward to hear. "Knowing that when you found out, you'd scold me for what I did with my friend's girl, and for driving when I could barely remember where I was in town." He opens his eyes and sears me with his intense gaze. "But I knew you wouldn't feel a single ounce of jealousy."

I swallow as Chase labels the feeling that engulfed my chest at the mention of Harper. Jealous. Of course. I'm jealous.

"Chase, I'm so—"

"I don't want to hear that you're sorry."

I clamp my mouth shut.

"Did you . . . feel anything at all?" His voice bleeds desperation.

My eyes burn with tears. I can't seem to speak. What do I do with this mess of feelings going on inside me? Yes, I'm jealous, but does it matter? What kind of a relationship could Chase and I possibly have?

He huffs a disgruntled noise at my silence, then, "See ya, Ellie."

I swallow, try to say bye, but it doesn't matter. He's stalked out of hearing range.

"Hey, El, you ready?"

I jump at the sound of Mom's voice behind me. She smiles brightly, so it's clear she didn't see me with Chase.

"Yeah, sure."

"Great. I'll just use the restroom, then we can go hunt down some cute shoes. And you know what we should do on our way home? Rent a movie. Something girly that Dad and James will hate."

I pull my mouth up into a smile. "Sounds perfect."

Her hazel eyes, the ones she and James share, spark with delight, and for the first time I feel like I'm the daughter she hoped for when she named me Gabrielle.

Chapter 28

"Don't look now," Bronte murmurs to me, "but Kelly McCormick is about to walk by."

I clutch my conference agenda booklet to my chest and battle the temptation to turn my head. "No way."

Bronte's green gaze tracks something beyond me. "She'll be the one with the long dark hair, wearing the aubergine blazer."

"Wait, wearing what?"

"Aubergine." Bronte gives me a look. "Like dark purple. Are you a historical writer or aren't you, Gabrielle?"

"We don't call dark purple 'aubergine' in medieval Italy, and can I turn around yet?"

Bronte chuckles. "Yes, sorry. Over by the registration desk. She's talking to Angela Putnam right now."

I scan the crowd around the registration desk in the foyer of the hotel. If I had held off just two minutes, I would have been standing in line with *Kelly McCormick* to pick up my conference packet. "Angela Putnam . . . I know that name, don't I?"

"She's the AFW publicity officer. She's wearing black—"

"Not helpful." A roomful of writers, I learned upon arrival, means a lot of black clothes.

"She has the blond waves and cute bangs?"

"Who are we spying on, girls?" The voice comes from behind us. It makes me jump, but it causes Bronte to laugh and throw her arms around the woman's neck.

"Betsy Ann Daniels, you bad girl! What are you doing sneaking up on people?"

"You two were obviously up to no good." Betsy Ann flips her sleek brown hair. She looks to be in her mid-twenties and is the closest to my age that I've seen yet. Most of the other attendees are at least in their thirties, like Bronte, but the majority are middle-aged.

When she sees me, Betsy Ann covers her mouth with a manicured hand. "Oh, gosh, I didn't realize I don't know you yet! How embarrassing!"

"This is Gabrielle Sweet." Bronte seems to stand a bit taller as she introduces me. "You may recognize her name from the finalists of the Great Debut."

"Oh, congratulations!" Betsy Ann pulls me into a hug as if we're already friends. "That's so wonderful!"

"It is." Bronte nods like a proud mother. "It really is. Especially because she's so young. You'd never know it from her book, though. It's breathtaking. I've been mentoring her."

My cheeks heat from Bronte's praise.

"Are you still in school, Gabrielle?" Betsy Ann asks. "And don't you just have the most darling hair? I've always wanted curls."

"Gabrielle, I'm sure you've heard of Betsy Ann." More and more Bronte makes me feel like I'm at my mother's office Christmas party, where she shuffles me around and reintroduces me to all her coworkers. "She won the Great Debut two years ago in the historical romance category."

Betsy Ann laughs heartily. "I'm sure she *hasn't* heard of me. I've finally given up on that manuscript." She sticks out her lip to me in an exaggerated pout. "I won, but everyone passed on the story. With historical romance, it seems houses either want really gritty or really light, and mine is right in the middle. Got my picture in the local paper, though."

"Someone's bound to want it." Bronte scans the crowd, appearing to have checked out of the conversation.

"That's what Rose tells me," Betsy says. "She says we just have to keep at it, but honestly, I think she's discouraged too."

"I see someone, I'll be right back." Bronte strides away.

I grapple for a way to continue the conversation. "And Rose is?"

"My agent. Rose White."

"Oh." I'm so startled to recognize an industry name, I laugh. "That's Bronte's agent too."

Betsy Ann rubs a chandelier earring between her fingers. "She was a bit smarter when she signed Bronte. She didn't win that year, but her manuscript obviously was more suited to the market."

So . . . ? "Bronte entered the Great Debut?"

"Yep. Hard to find an AFWer who hasn't, really. It's a real honor to be a finalist, Gabrielle. Congratulations." Betsy Ann squeezes my arm. "Now, do you want me to introduce you to Kelly McCormick, or do you just want to stalk her all weekend?"

"And then Betsy Ann took me right over to meet Kelly McCormick! It was amazing! And I tried not to gush to Kelly *too* much about how much I loved *And Today We Die* but she was so friendly that it was hard not to."

Bronte's smile seems stiffly polite as she sips at her coffee. We came to the hotel coffee bar to get a little quiet before general session and so Bronte could get a signal to call home. "Yeah, isn't Kelly nice? We haven't talked a ton, but she does seem friendly. Onto more important things. Who are your appointments with?"

I gasp. "I totally forgot to check!" I rip open my packet and spread the contents on the round table. "How could I have forgotten?"

"It's the yellow one," Bronte says in a calm, amused voice.

I yank out the yellow sheet and skim the lines. When you register for the conference, you're given two appointment slots that you can use for either agents or editors. It's first come, first serve, and since I didn't register early—

My excitement over meeting Kelly McCormick morphs into nervous jitters when I see the name. "Not Abbie. It's Erica Chally, the young adult editor at—"

"I know who she is."

I groan. "And Emma Miller, who of course already rejected me because I have no audience yet."

"Well." Bronte drums her fingers on the formica table. "It could be worse. I once had to pitch to an editor who hates historicals. At least Erica Chally is a young adult editor."

"I can't go in there and pitch to her." I knead my temples with my fingertips. "I'll just skip it."

"No." Bronte sets down her cup and gives me a severe look. "This is an opportunity, Gabrielle. Erica Chally is an editor that you would never have access to had you not paid to come to this conference. You're gonna march in there and pitch."

I roll my lower lip over my bottom teeth. "What if I keep the appointment, but just, like, ask questions about publishing and such."

"No." Bronte's severity increases. "You won't. You'll *pitch*. You'll pitch your butt off or you'll totally regret it."

"Hello, ladies," Dad says as he approaches our table. He catches sight of my face. "Ellie, what's wrong?"

"They didn't give me Abbie. They gave me Erica Chally instead. I'm terrified."

Dad frowns. "But isn't Abbie with Blue Door? I think they're every bit as big and prestigious as Open Flame."

But Blue Door acquires warm, fun reads. Everything I've read from Erica's authors has been full of symbolism I don't understand and has dark, often morbid endings.

"This is ideal, Gabrielle. Really." Bronte shuffles my papers together and hands them to me. "You'll be getting Abbie's feedback from Great Debut and meeting with Erica, which exposes you to two houses who churn out a phenomenal amount of young adult books."

Dad claps a fatherly hand on my shoulder that in a stronger moment, I would brush off. "You just go in and be yourself, Ellie. She'll love you."

Oh, yeah. I'm a teen writer with no visibility and no clue of how to develop any. I'm sure I'll really wow her.

"I feel horrible about abandoning you tonight," Bronte whispers. "But when your editor asks you to go out to dinner, you just *can't* say no."

I keep my eyes trained on the instructor as he wraps up his talk about effective story structure. "It's fine."

"If I could bring you with me, I would, but it's not one of those types of things. It's just for their authors."

"Can we talk about this after class?" I try to not be *too* annoyed that I missed what he said about an effective *dénoument*.

Bronte turns her attention back up front as the instructor says, "We have a few minutes left. Can I answer any questions?"

Which Bronte seems to take as her cue to start talking to me again. "I assume my editor is paying for dinner, but of course I'll order on the safe side, just in case."

Maybe if I don't acknowledge her, she'll get the hint that this goody-goody is trying to pay attention to the class her parents paid a lot for her to attend.

A writer in the front row raises her hand. "How many words is it, typically, before you reach the inciting incident?"

Bronte pops a peppermint in her mouth and rolls her eyes at me. Apparently, she finds this a stupid question.

I take a deep breath. I'm sure she's taken a class or two like this before, but has she completely forgotten what it's like to not know these things? Isn't this an ideal time for new writers to ask?

When class ends, Bronte immediately starts in with, "Tomorrow night I have *another* conflict, but it's just a dessert reception my publishing house is putting on after the banquet, so I won't be gone the whole night. Still. I remember my first year when I didn't know anybody, so I hate to abandon you at a table by yourself. Especially when you'll either be celebrating or crying over contest results." She follows this with a quick smile. "Of course you'll mostly likely be celebrating. Your book is going to be a smashing success."

I push my laptop into the red leather briefcase Mom bought for me on our girls' day and try to brush away my annoyance with Bronte. All day it's been almost nonstop chatter about all the big deal author stuff she has going on. "It's really important for you to have time to bond with your editor. I'll hang out with Dad. Or I'll text Betsy Ann."

"Good idea." Bronte fluffs her straight, dark hair. "She probably doesn't have anything going on tonight."

I pull my schedule out. "Next I have Finding Your Character's Inner Strength. What about you?"

"Same."

I glance at my cell phone. The rubbery chicken I ate for lunch threatens to come up. "I'll have to leave fifteen minutes into class for my appointment with Emma Miller."

"Maybe we should just skip the class then." Bronte shrugs.

"You're a bad influence, Bronte Harrington."

She laughs. "I've always been way too jittery to focus if I have an appointment soon. I'm so glad that Rose gave me permission not to pitch, because I hate doing it."

"Betsy Ann seems to love pitching." I tuck my schedule into my bag. "I think she's crazy."

Bronte waves to a group of writers passing the other way in the wide hall. "She may love it, but she must not be much good at it. She's been doing it for years and still no contract."

While that may be true, it doesn't seem like a very nice thing to say.

Bronte drops her volume. "She's always bragging about how she won Great Debut that year and acts like she's so well connected. It's just because she spends so much of her time doing stuff for AFW. She's been an officer, a forum moderator, a contest coordinator, and who knows what else. Honestly, when does she even find time to write?"

I'm sure I'm looking at Bronte with shock. When they hugged yesterday in the lobby, I thought for sure she and Betsy Ann were close. "She doesn't have three little kids. That must make it a lot easier to volunteer *and* write."

Bronte scans the bustle of the hallway. "We used to be friends. Until she started thinking she was such a big deal."

I've only spent about thirty minutes with Betsy Ann between yesterday and this morning, but not once has she come across to me that way. Time for a new topic. "So. Have you talked to Tim? How have things been there?"

As Bronte details for me which of her girls cried on the phone that morning, and who isn't napping because Mommy isn't there, my mind wanders to the appointment room, to the desk I'll soon be sitting at with Emma Miller. And if I'm this nervous for my appointment with her, how will I ever survive the one after it with Erica Chally?

🦋🦋🦋

From the hallway, I catch glimpses of the small meeting room. There are four folding tables, and at each one sits an editor or agent on one side and a very nervous writer on the other.

The hall is full of anxious writers, lined up outside various doors. The man in front of me keeps switching his folder from hand to hand. The woman behind me mutters prayers or her pitch or a combination of both.

"Hey!"

I jump when Betsy Ann materializes beside me.

She giggles and presses a hand to her mouth. "Sorry. I'm a time keeper for a room down the hall. Just wanted to say good luck. I better get back. Need to give the two-minute warning." She gives my arm a squeeze, then strides down the hall, the bracelets on her arm jangling.

As the time keeper for our room gives the two-minute warning, I remind myself that there's no need to feel anxious. Emma already rejected me, so there's nothing for me to lose.

Despite the pep talk, blood pounds in my ears when I'm waved into the room, and I sigh with relief when I make it to the seat across from Emma without collapsing.

Emma smiles, weary yet warm, over the offered bowl of Hershey's Kisses. "Chocolate?"

"Uh, sure, thank you."

She leans back in her chair and unwraps a Kiss. "I recognize your name, Gabrielle Sweet. I just can't place it."

On the table is a list of times and names, and I spot mine at the 2:20 slot.

"Oh, um. You recently rejected a query of mine."

Did that sound accusatory? Bitter?

If it does, Emma doesn't seem to care. She snaps her fingers. "That's right. The medieval Italy book. An intriguing idea. Kind of *The Princess Bride* meets YA fiction. I was quite tempted to ask to see more, but . . . well, I'm just starting with Reese Literary. I have to minimize my risk, as I said in my note to you. I did say that, right?"

I smile, hoping I seem professional and confident. "Yes, you did. You encouraged me to work on becoming more visible."

"Yes. You'll hear others refer to it as a platform or marketability, but really what we're talking about is a number. How many people will buy your book? How many people know who you are?"

The question plucks at something in my heart. Because, really, who *does* know who I am? My life is so segmented—Bronte knows about writing, Lucy knows about my childhood, Palmer about our relationship, and Chase . . . well, Chase probably comes closest to seeing me for who I am, and yet I've withheld so much from him.

But now certainly isn't the time for introspection—the clock is ticking.

I wind the paper tail of the Kiss around my finger. "But how do you build visibility when you don't have anything to build it around? If that makes sense."

"It does, and it's a question new writers often ask. We have lots of articles on our agency website that have suggestions. Being here at something like this—" she holds out her hands, as if gesturing the conference. "—is a great start. And sometimes publishers get really excited about a book and take on a debut author even if the visibility isn't there yet, but it's increasingly rare."

"I see." I had a whole list of questions that I could ask if we hit a lull in the conversation, but now I can't think of any.

"Of course, if you meet with an editor here, it's possible they'll ask for a proposal and eventually offer a contract. If you already have an offer, it's much easier to find representation."

"Okay." Why can't I think of any of my questions?

Emma blinks at me, as if waiting.

"Well. Thank you for your time." I stick out my hand. "And the chocolate."

"Wonderful to meet you, Gabrielle." Her hand is warm in mine, and I realize for the first time how suffocatingly hot this room is.

Or maybe it's the tears clogging my throat that make breathing feel impossible.

The other writers—all older than me and surely smarter and with more "visibility"—are still in conversations with editors and agents as I slip out of the room.

And the worst of it is that I know I have to be back here in thirty minutes for my appointment with Erica Chally. If I could hardly make conversation with Emma Miller, how much worse will it be with Erica?

The answer is *much* worse. So much worse.

There isn't even chocolate on Erica's table, just her looking at me from under a fringe of severe bangs. I've already introduced myself, now what? Do I just start in with my pitch?

"Well . . . I've written a . . . a historical, medieval, fiction novel for teens."

Did I just say fiction novel? I swallow a gulp of air and try to force out the first words of my rehearsed pitch.

Before I can get out a word, Erica says, "Do you have representation?"

I blink a few times. "Like a literary agent?"

Erica nods, a smile pasted on her face.

"Um, no. But, I *am* a Great Debut finalist."

"Ah." Erica's smile stays in place, but she doesn't sound particularly interested or impressed.

There's a piece of me wanting to say *Stu Sweet is my father* but I hold the words in. I vowed to myself in the beginning that if I pursued writing, I was only going to take what I could earn *myself*.

"Well, my book is about Lady Gabrielle, who is a marked favorite of the prince . . ."

Erica's eyes take on a vacant expression, so I look away and force the rest of my rehearsed words out of my mouth.

" . . . which makes a rival out of the other ladies of the court. Gabrielle has resigned herself to a life with a faithless husband and no close friends, when a handsome merchant, Rafe, rolls into town. Socially, he's everything that's wrong for her, and yet he sees her in a way that no one else does. She must figure out if she can survive giving her hand to the prince when she's already given her heart to Rafe."

Erica blinks unseeing eyes at me.

"And . . ." I clear my throat. "That's what it's about."

"Well." She leans back in her chair. "Well, you would want to make it a challenge, your main character winning the prince. You would want to build in conflict and not make it too easy."

Okay, she definitely was *not* listening. My smile is huge and fake, my voice far too loud and cheery. "Yes, that's true. Thank you."

She smiles back, as if pleased with herself for offering me such a valuable nugget of information. "I would suggest you search for a literary agent first. Best of luck to you." She sticks out a hand, dismissing me.

Luck, indeed. Emma Miller tells me it'll take a publishing contract to make me appealing to literary agents. Erica Chally tells me I need an agent to get a publisher. And where does that leave me?

In need of a good cry and some chocolate.

Chapter 29

I rip a tissue from the box and blow my nose with an unladylike honk. "I just thought it was going to mean something that I had finalled in this contest. I thought it would matter."

"Oh, Ellie, it *does* matter." Dad rests a hand on my knee and squeezes. His eyes are wet as well, or maybe it's just because I'm looking at him through blurred vision. "No matter what that agent and editor said, it matters."

"Not if it doesn't get me where I'm trying to go. Betsy Ann finalled three years ago and still hasn't sold her manuscript. She said nobody wanted it." The fears that have dominated my thoughts since I left my meeting with Erica now come out of my mouth: "What if I worked so hard on this book, and nothing ever happens with it?"

Dad bites his lower lip, same as I do when I'm debating what to say next. "Ellie, as your dad, I wish I could tell you that won't happen. But the writer in me knows better. Hard work without the promise of public payoff is a reality of the biz, honey. It's why ultimately you'll have to decide if it's worth it to write regardless. Because we get no promises of success."

I reach into the bag of dark chocolate M&Ms Dad bought me from the hotel gift shop. As I crunch away on a handful, I turn his words over in my head. "I really love my book. It's not perfect, and maybe it's not even publishable. But it meant something to me to write it."

Like survival when my friends decided they were too cool for me.

"Then don't you think it was worth writing it? Even if it doesn't win tomorrow night? Even if it never gets published?"

"Yeah, I guess so." I offer the bag of M&Ms to Dad, but he shakes his head.

"You need them more than I do."

I grin and pour more into my palm. "Thanks for coming with me, Dad. It means a lot."

"It's my pleasure. Your mom and I believe in you, kiddo. That's why we got this for you."

From his pocket, Dad pulls a small, cinched velvet bag. "This is to remind you, Ellie Jane, that you are a writer no matter what happens."

I loosen the braided cord, and into my hand falls a charm. It's a black typewriter key with a G on it.

Dad's voice is thick with emotion. "It's not dependent on if you win tomorrow or if your book gets published or anything the world tells you. You're a writer simply because you write, and no one can take that away from you."

Tears burn my eyes, but they're a different type than I've been crying this afternoon. "Thanks," I whisper as I rub the G of the charm between my fingers. I undo the clasp of Palmer's bracelet and slip it on.

"Perfect," Dad says when I hold my wrist out for him to see. His gaze hangs on me for a long moment. "You know, I would be happy to ask Ron to take a look at your book."

I pour a couple M&Ms into my hand as I consider the offer. "Thanks. But this is something I want to earn on my own."

"Yeah, I figured that's what you'd say." Dad's smile holds affection, and I realize that even though I always knew I would turn down the offer, the little girl in me needed him to make it, needed to know he believed in me.

❀ ❀ ❀

"I wish I wrote contemporaries," I murmur to Betsy Ann as the winner of the Great Debut for Contemporary Fiction takes the stage. She's crying audibly and stumbles on the stairs. "Then it would be done and over with, and I could get on with feeling depressed."

Betsy Ann continues clapping, but gives me a look, part chastisement, part sympathy. "You can't lose, girl. It's already great exposure to be a finalist."

Not good enough, apparently.

My dad elbows me in the ribs. "Try to stop worrying. This can be a fun moment, Gabrielle, but you have to let go."

I blink at my father. "You just called me Gabrielle."

"Did I?" He laughs. "That *is* your name, you know."

I know. I wasn't so sure he and Mom did.

The writer on stage gushes out an acceptance speech between sobs. Mine is clutched in my palm, so damp it probably won't be readable if I have to go up there. I smooth the skirt of my black dress, fighting away panic about static cling and walking on my high heels through the crowded ballroom to the stage.

The contest coordinator for contemporary romance takes the stage. He announces the names of the three finalists as their photographs are displayed on the screen, finally declaring "Tonya LaCourse!" as the winner.

Panic twists deep in my gut as I watch her accept the flowers, the certificate. She gives a speech that I don't hear because my mind whirls so. I stare at the untouched cheesecake in front of me, my eyes going out of focus as I dwell on what I want my face to look like when Rachelle Rea *doesn't* call my name.

I'm jolted back to the banquet by the proclamation of "Nick Page!" being the winner of the historical fiction category. Then, minutes later, "Clare Kolenda!" for historical romance. Betsy Ann jumps to her feet and whoops. Apparently she's a friend of Clare's, though that's no surprise.

I glimpse Bronte sitting several tables away with her editor. She notices and gives me an encouraging smile and wave. I wave back, but I'm sure I look like I'm about to pee my pants.

Actually, I *do* need to go to the bathroom . . .

"Allison Perdue!" wins for something. I've lost of track of what we're on.

I take a gulp of water to ease my dry throat. Why didn't I go to the bathroom before they started the awards? There are only a couple categories now until YA.

At least needing to pee gives me something else to think about. I completely miss the romantic suspense winner announcement because I'm rethinking the best route to the stage.

As the speculative fiction winner gives her speech, Dad whispers, "Take a bite of that cake instead of just poking it to death, would ya?"

I attempt a smile. My throat is so tight that I'm sure I wouldn't be able to swallow.

A petite lady with big, dark curls steps behind the microphone. I know with her first, "Hey, y'all," that this is Rachelle Rea. "In the YA category, our finalists are . . ." She waits for the slide. A lady in her thirties wearing a cowgirl hat materializes on the screen. "Bethany Baldwin with *Always a Cowgirl.*"

The screen flicks to a head shot of a cute twenty-something with brown hair and a saucy smile. "Katelyn Whitley with *My Secret Teenage Life*."

The screen flicks once more, and it's me up there, a snapshot from our last trip to Bodega Beach. "And Gabrielle Sweet with *Invisibly Yours*."

Dad and Betsy Ann clap and a "Whoop-whoop!" comes from the general direction of Bronte.

Tears pool in my eyes—is that a side effect of nerves?

"And the winner is . . ." Rachelle tugs open the envelope—this banquet desperately wants to be the Oscars. "Gabrielle Sweet!"

I hear Bronte's cry of excitement and see her leap to her feet. Betsy Ann jumps up as well, clapping and screaming. I gaze up at her, having this odd sensation that I too should stand, if only I remembered how.

Dad pulls me up out of my chair, and nudges me forward with his broad hand.

The other writers are a mere blur of glittery skirts and suit coats as I weave my way up to the stage. I find myself in front of Rachelle's beaming smile. She hands me roses—the first flowers I've ever been given—and my winner's certificate, then guides me up to the microphone.

The blinding stage lights make it impossible to see anyone beyond the front tables, and when I open my mouth, I realize—

"Oh! My speech is on the table!"

There are loud laughs around the room, and Betsy Ann jogs—though I'm not sure how since she's wearing three inch heels—to the stage.

With a trembling hand, I unfold the scrap of paper and stare at the speech that I wrote one bored day in study hall.

"I found writing while I was in a dark and desperate place. It somehow both rescued me from my ordinary existence, providing a place of escape, and helped me to tune-in more, to soak up the emotions of life. I feel extremely honored and humbled to have won the Great Debut, and my thanks go to AFW and everyone involved in the contest. Thank you to my mentor, Bronte Harrington, who was the first person to tell me I could do this. And to my parents who believed so deeply that this would happen, they made it a priority for me to be here. Thank you."

Rachelle guides me off the stage, apparently prepared for my dazed state. "Stop here for a picture." She angles my body toward a photographer, who I can barely make out because of the spots in my vision from the ferocious stage lights. "Hold up your certificate and the flowers."

I do as I'm told, and after the flash fires, my feet somehow find their way back toward my table. I'm detained briefly by a fierce hug from Bronte and a, "You did it, Gabrielle!"

I plop into my seat and find my limbs shaking from gripping my certificate and flowers so tightly.

Dad beams a proud smile my way. "Maybe now you can eat your cheesecake."

I press a hand to my fluttering stomach. "Somehow I don't think so."

The screen of my silenced phone lights with an incoming message. My mom.

A bubble of laughter escapes. "You already called Mom?"

"No, she's watching the live feed on the website." Dad tugs my cheesecake toward him. "If you're not going to eat your cheesecake, can I have it? I hardly ate a bite of my dinner, I was so nervous."

"The banquet is being broadcast on-line?"

My question is punctuated with my phone lighting once more. CONGRATULATIONS, GABRIELLE SWEET.

But this one is from Chase.

Chapter 30

After the banquet, as the other winners and I are herded from photo to photo by Angela Putnam, the words of Chase's text pound in my ears. *Congratulations, Gabrielle Sweet*. What was the tone? Had he snarled the phrase? Cheered it? The lack of exclamation point suggests he didn't, but of course I'm much more particular about those kinds of things.

"Writers, let's shuffle to the left just a bit." Angela flicks her wrist, beckoning us. "Let's get that AFW logo in the background."

A few people loiter behind the photographer, waiting for us to finish. Betsy Ann and my father chat amicably, while Bronte stands nearby and checks her watch frequently. She's worried about missing her dessert reception, I'm sure.

"Okay, Great Debut winners, you're released. Nora winners, would you stay for one more shot, please?" Angela points to me. "Except for you, Gabrielle. Do you have a second?"

I get the prickly sensation of being called to the principal's office in the middle of class. Did I do something wrong? Was there a mix up? Am I not really the winner?

"Uh, sure."

Angela beckons me closer with a crooked finger, her smile wide and gleaming red. How is her lipstick still on after so many hours? "Congratulations, Gabrielle. What an accomplishment."

"Thank you."

"One of your judges wanted to talk to you. She's over there." Angela points toward a table in the ballroom. It's been cleared of plates and cutlery but is still dressed in the glitter black tablecloth from dinner. A woman with hair the color of pennies sits there, reading glasses perched low on her nose as she leafs through a stack of papers. "I promised her I would get you out of here early."

"Okay . . ." I don't recognize her. At least not from here. "So, I just go over there?"

Angela grins. "Nothing to be afraid of, Gabrielle. Editors are people too."

Editor?

As I wind through the banquet staff breaking down tables, I feel increasingly ridiculous about the flowers and certificate clutched in my arms. Like wearing a homecoming dress long after you've left the streamers and punch.

When the lady sees me approaching, she pushes her reading glasses on top of her head and stands. She's wearing a simple black dress, and her heels have been discarded beside the chair.

"I borrowed them from my sister." Her grin is wide and friendly, as if we're already on good terms. "She assured me they were comfortable, but we clearly have different standards."

"You were smart to take yours off. I'm pretty sure I have a blister."

Her grin widens even further. "Well, please, have a seat." She gestures to a chair with a dramatic swoop, then sinks into the one she had already occupied. "I'm Abbie Ross, by the way. I'm the YA editor at Blue Door, and I was one of your judges for the Great Debut."

It's all I can do not to say *I know—you're the reason I entered.* "Nice to meet you." I offer my hand, and she shakes it.

"I loved *Invisibly Yours.* Absolutely loved it. That Rafe." Abbie presses a hand to her heart "So handsome, but so infuriating. In a charming way, of course."

The scent of roses is strong in my nose, and I realize I'm pressing my flowers to my chest. "Thank you."

I feel like I should say more, do more, but if I open my mouth now, I'll likely shriek with delight. Hardly a professional response.

"I really want Blue Door to publish this book, Gabrielle. Several of the other editors are reading it now, and assuming they like it, I intend to take it to the next pub-board meeting. Do you think you could have a proposal put together for me by then?"

Is this actually happening? Or did I pass out from nerves during dinner and am now enjoying the best dream ever?

"Absolutely," I hear myself say. As if I put together book proposals all the time. As if it's routine to have my manuscripts go to the pub-board.

Abbie reaches into her bag and magically extracts a business card. "Here's my email address. You or your agent can email the proposal here."

"Okay, great."

"I'm *so* glad we had a chance to meet." Abbie beams at me as she shuffles her stack of papers into her bag. "I hoped to have an appointment with you, but this worked out even better."

"I registered late. You were my first choice, but I guess you filled up fast."

Abbie shrugs, as if used to this. With one hand she picks up her shoes by the back strap, and the other she holds out to me. "I'm going to do the best I can for you at the meeting," she says as we shake. "I really believe in your book, Gabrielle. And I think teenage girls would love reading something written by someone as young as yourself. You'll be very marketable—my sales guys will love that."

I'm marketable?

The typewriter charm on my bracelet dances as I shake her hand. "Thanks for judging the contest."

"I look forward to seeing your proposal." Abbie smiles a farewell, then pads barefoot out of the ballroom, shoes dangling at her side.

As the ballroom doors glide to a close, Dad, Bronte, and Betsy Ann materialize at the table.

"Was that what I think it was about?" Dad's voice is hushed, as if in reverence of the moment.

I turn Abbie's thick business card over in my fingers. "Yes." I rub my thumb over the Blue Door logo. "Yes, it was."

Chapter 31

Many return from spring break bronze and glowing, Palmer included. His skin is golden once again, like when we first met back in September. Bianca, who hangs off his arm like the proudest trophy of a girlfriend you've ever seen, sports a tan as well. Though hers is tinted orange.

I turn away from the two of them, feeling a strange mix of amusement, disgust, and another emotion that I don't care to explore too closely. I continue toward the bridge for Photography. I'll be super early, but I brought my laptop so I could keep working on my proposal for Abbie. And if I avoid the Quad, I won't run into—

Chase is seated on a stone bench, legs spread apart and elbows propped on his knees. With his earbuds and scowl, he has a serious "Don't talk to me, don't even *look* at me," kind of vibe going on.

But before I can turn away, he glances at me.

I expect a rebuff, for him to duck his head. After all, I never responded to his congratulatory text message.

Instead, he nods, and my feet stop walking.

Back in October, I wanted to rip this guy apart for humiliating me. And now I'm standing here with Jell-O for knees. Like when Lady Gabrielle sees Rafe for the first time since he vanished. Usually in my real life, Rafe equals Palmer, but when I wasn't paying attention, Chase wiggled his way into my heart.

"Your hair's up."

I touch the knot on the back of my head. "Yeah . . ."

And while I'm wearing a little makeup and a new shirt, I stuck with my glasses and jeans this morning. Mom just sighed at me when I came downstairs wearing them. I don't know how to explain it to her, but at the moment, it's enough to know I *could* be different, if I wanted. Embracing the new look feels too scary. Too much, too soon.

I scuff my foot along the grass. Do I thank him for texting me? Do I acknowledge that I've had this big secret this whole time?

I glance at him—and gasp. "What happened to your eye?"

"You can still tell?" He presses his fingertips around his bruised right eye. "I didn't think it looked so bad anymore."

"What happened?" I sit so I can see better. "It looks painful."

"It's not anymore. Just forget about it, Ellie."

"Who did that to you?"

"I said forget about it."

I bite my lip. "Was it Jose?"

"Is that forgetting about it?"

"I can't just forget about it, Chase. I care about you. I . . ." Words sit garbled in my brain. I know I could say all this better in a letter. I close my eyes. *Dear Chase, I know I've always said that I didn't like you in 'that way' but . . .* "I hate how things are now. With us."

"It's fine, Ellie. You warned me from the start, and I had no right to expect anything of you. I shouldn't have yelled at you at the mall."

I swallow. "I've made mistakes too, obviously. But I've had a lot of time to think these last couple days. And the thing is . . ."

The words stick in my throat. They're too embarrassing, too . . . honest.

"The thing is?"

"The thing is, I hate the thought of losing you." I say it so quietly, I'm surprised he hears.

"I don't like it either, but it can't be like this anymore. I don't like getting mad at you for something you can't control. And I don't like fooling myself into thinking we're friends, that I matter to you, and then finding out . . ." Chase swallows. "Then finding out you have this whole other life you never even told me about."

"Chase, about that, I'm so sorry—"

He waves away my apology. "You don't need to apologize, Ellie. I get it. We weren't friends, we weren't anything."

"Stop saying that. Because we were friends. We *are* friends. I should've told you about writing and . . . and everything."

Chase's gaze skewers me. "What do you mean 'everything.' What else is there?"

A pair of gray eyes flashes in my mind. I swallow. "I meant everything that goes along with writing. That I was entering this contest. That I was going to Minneapolis for the conference."

Chase's mouth curls into a smirk. "Oh, I see. So we're friends, but you're still not planning on telling me about Palmer."

Oh.

I knit my fingers together in my lap and draw in a shaky breath. "How long have you known?"

"Since the day you broke up." Chase's knee bounces, sending a tremor through the whole bench. "You took off after we heard about him and Bianca. I was gonna go after you, but then . . ." He shakes his head. "I saw him follow you, and I waited until he went into the bathroom before I followed too. I overheard enough to know you were together, but it was tough to hear too much. I didn't want to stand there with my ear pressed against the girls' bathroom door."

A sparrow hops along the sidewalk near us. I watch it peck at the ground, waiting for the threat of tears to ebb before I open my mouth.

"I'm sorry I didn't tell you." The words emerge as a whisper. "I couldn't."

"Were you actually together, or just . . . ?"

"Just what?"

The bob of his Adam's apple is enough of an answer.

"You really think I would do that?"

His eyes appraise me. "Not usually. But with Palmer your judgment's always been kinda fuzzy."

I can't argue that. "You're right. But, no. It wasn't like that. We were just sorta secretly together."

Chase's laugh is harsh. "What does that mean? Like you drove to Fresno to see movies?"

"No, like he didn't tell his friends, I didn't tell mine." I sigh. "It was stupid. I wish I hadn't done it. I wish instead I had . . ."

Again the words feel stuck. On paper I find it so easy to be honest, to be vulnerable. In real life I seem to have lost the ability.

Chase's gaze is heavy. "You wish what, Ellie?"

I close my eyes as the emotions grip me. This is just like when I was seven, when I tried to jump off the high-dive at swimming lessons. The way my knees wanted to collapse, the way the board bobbed beneath me, how I knew I *should* jump, that others had before me and they'd survived, but the fear paralyzed me. Even with my coach shouting encouragement, shushing the kids who laughed, I couldn't do it. Ultimately, I had to crawl back down the ladder. It had been the last year of swimming lessons.

I look in Chase's eyes, which hold a glint of anger at the moment, but which I know are also accepting. Caring. Perhaps even loving.

I squeeze mine shut, take a deep breath, and jump.

"I wish I had admitted to myself that I like you. I wish I had said yes when you kept asking me out. And I wish, when you kissed me, that I had known how to be honest."

I take a deep breath and peek.

His face is a stone wall. "Really." Doubt.

"Yes! I mean, I still don't know what a relationship would look like for us . . . or if I'd be able to tell my parents . . . but I think I'd still like to try." I swallow. "Dating, I mean."

Chase snorts. "You're really sweeping me off my feet, here, Ellie."

My face burns. That's what I get? A snort, then an insult? "I'm trying to be honest, Chase."

"That'd be new for you."

Something within me bristles at the jab, but I know I deserve it. "If it makes you feel any better, I hadn't told anyone about writing. Not even my parents knew until recently."

"And what about him?" Chase nods across the Quad, where Palmer yaks with Troy, oblivious.

"No. I never told him either."

"Why not?"

"Because our relationship was at best a horrible idea and at worst, toxic. I regret it. I can't even express how deeply I regret it."

Chase rubs at the scruff of his chin. "So then you must get why I'm not jumping into the same thing with you."

What? That's so not . . .

My heart thuds—convicted—as my words come back to me. *I don't really know what a relationship would look like for us . . . or if I'd be able to tell my parents . . . but I think I'd still like to try.*

I really did just suggest the same thing to Chase that Palmer did to me. "Palmer was ashamed of me. I'm not ashamed of you, Chase. I just don't know how to explain you to my parents."

"Well, stop worrying about it 'cause you won't have to."

My bruised feelings morph into angry words. "Great. So I try to be honest, and this is what I get?"

"I don't need some pity relationship from you just because you like being buddies."

"That's not it at all!"

"Oh, really? Then why don't you take another stab at asking me to be your boyfriend? And this time try to be a bit more of a snob when you ask. I'd like to see if it's possible."

The gleam in his eyes is cruel. He's never looked at me like that, intending to hurt me. Even when he *was* hurting me, like in Algebra class, it didn't look intentional. Just . . . what?

"You never told me why you did it, why you embarrassed me in front of everybody. Why you told them about my crush on Palmer."

Chase turns his attention back to his hands. "It wasn't planned. I gave it maybe ten seconds of thought. I just . . ." He shakes his head. "Imagine feeling what you do for Palmer—"

"Did."

"Whatever. Imagine feeling that for years, and him never even looking at you. That was me. And it was okay when you weren't interested in anyone else, but then Palmer showed up." He looks at me with kicked-puppy eyes. "He's the worst kind of guy, Ellie Jane. Because he made you feel like less. Like you didn't deserve him. But you liked him. And you were so obvious about it, and I just . . . I don't know. It just came out."

My face burns at the memory. I had never wanted to like Palmer. I knew as soon as we met that if anything ever happened between us, it would lead to my heart being broken.

I can deal with it damaging me—it was my stupid crush, after all. But Chase getting hurt is different.

He rubs at his forehead, looking tired. "I'm sorry I hurt you."

I chuckle drily. "I think that's my line."

His dimples make a swift entrance and exit.

"I didn't express it well at all, but I *do* like you." I sit on my hands so they'll stop trembling. "A lot."

He doesn't look tired anymore, but dazed. "Really?"

I turn away. "Yes."

Chase scuffs the ground with a sneaker. "So. What now?"

I bite my lip. "We can't just be friends."

Chase shakes his head so vehemently, I see it in my peripherals.

"But we also can't ignore that you and I have . . . issues to work through."

"Like your parents."

"Yeah. And our lifestyles. I'm not a party girl, Chase."

"I know."

"And I'm guessing you don't want to just sit around and read with me."

"Nope."

"And then . . . there's the God thing."

Chase sighs. "I believe in God, Ellie. I just don't live quite the same as you." His hand warms my knee. "You want to be accepted for who you are, right? Well, I want the same thing."

He leaves me there on the bench, wondering about the balance of loving someone for who they are, but not wanting them to settle for anything less than who they could become.

It's nice, really, that I'm not exactly talking to anybody at the moment. It means I have plenty of time to work on my book proposal for Abbie Ross. And since I'm having to do it without Bronte's help, I need *lots* of time.

In the darkroom, I watch Bronte's face appear in the tub of developer. I took the photo at the banquet, when she was decked out in her 1920s garb, but I hadn't realized it was my last chance to capture her smiling.

Bronte turned frigid after the banquet when she heard the news about Abbie. And the next morning, when Angela tracked me down in the coffee bar and interviewed me for the AFW newsletter, Bronte had scowled at her phone for the entire ten minutes. And after Betsy Ann joined us at the table, it was like the warmer Betsy Ann got, the more she gushed over the excitement of it all, the darker Bronte's face grew.

When the airport shuttle came to pick up Bronte, our goodbye hug felt stiff. Completely different from that hug on Thursday, when we met in person for the first time.

"I'm gonna need your help on this proposal." I thought maybe that was it. Maybe she thought I was already too big-headed, that I wouldn't recognize how I still needed her, still had much to learn.

Bronte's laugh was all air and no emotion. "I'm afraid I won't have time. I don't know if you've noticed, but *Fire Eyes* hits shelves in two month's time. I had already been planning on telling you that I needed to step back from our mentorship. So this comes at the perfect time."

"Of course." I forced myself to smile as if her words hadn't felt like a slap in the face. "*Fire Eyes* is the priority. Obviously."

And then she charged through the revolving door and climbed onto the blue shuttle bus, leaving me confused and wounded in the hotel lobby.

I shift my photograph into the stop solution, wishing I could so easily shift my thoughts. No matter how much I think about this, I come back to the same befuddling question: Why would she work so hard to help me get to this place, only to abandon me when I need her more than ever?

"I've noticed—" Palmer pauses to clear his throat, which is froggy from passing the last forty or so minutes in silence. "You and Chase haven't been talking."

I rinse my picture and say in what I hope is a calm, detached voice, "I really don't see how that's any of your business."

Since our breakup, Palmer and I have managed to trade out days with other classmates to avoid being locked in this tiny closet of a room together. Until today. We have a photo due on Monday and apparently neither of us planned ahead.

I hear him fussing with a spool of negatives but don't turn to look. Not that I could see much if I did.

"Do you remember when I showed up at your house before spring break?"

As if that's a memory I could somehow lose. "Yeah."

"I came because I was at a party and saw Chase flirting with the girl who used to be Jose's girlfriend. I can't think of her name."

"Harper."

"Right. As I watched them flirting, I got madder and madder. I mean, here he'd been after you, he seemed so close, and he was going to blow it just for a bit of action."

Talking about Chase, Harper, and "action" causes a painful twist in my heart. I take several deep breaths. "I don't want to talk about this."

"I got somethin' to say to you, Gabrielle."

"Maybe it's not something I want to hear."

Palmer moves behind me, so close that if I shift at all, I'll be touching him. "As I watched Chase and Harper, as I grew angrier by the second, I realized I was actually mad at myself. For blowing things with you." His nervous swallow is loud in my ear. "You deserved better. I could *be* better for you this time, Gabrielle."

I abandon my pretense of working and face him. "I'm not interested in getting back together."

Something flashes on Palmer's face, but in the gray, I can't quite make it out. "Because of Chase?"

"No. Because you're not good for me. I've spent my entire life in someone's shadow. At home, it was James. At school, it was Lucy. And then the unthinkable happened and you noticed me, *chose* me. But then what did you do? Kept me a secret. Practically told me I belonged in those shadows."

"Gabrielle, it's not like—"

I hold up a hand. "You said you had stuff to say, well so do I. It's all so clear now, why you made the choices you did. Like why you had me stay in the car on Valentine's Day. You were afraid of people seeing us together, weren't you? You were ashamed."

"You don't understand." But he exerts no effort to explain himself. As if he hoped I'd cut him off again.

A long silence stretches between us. Finally I say, "I understand, Palmer. Because I'm ashamed of me too, of who I was. I'm ashamed that I was the type of person who let you get away with keeping me hidden." I brush past him and clip my finished photo to the drying line. At the door, I pause. "You were right that I deserved better. But so did you."

Chapter 32

I bet the other Great Debut winners don't have to run basketball drills today.

When the bell sounds, I breathe an exhausted sigh of relief. I never really *like* gym, but being forced to train for a game I loathe, then being left with the choice of "Take a shower or eat lunch" makes me even crankier.

"Hey, Ellie, come here a second." Coach Taylor's summon echoes in the gymnasium.

I groan under my breath. Does he know I exaggerated that leg cramp to keep from running the last sprint?

I know I shouldn't have done that, but I was feeling exhausted and desperate for a break. I hardly slept last night because of trying to finish my book proposal. I was so close too, but at one o'clock decided to just go to bed and finish it up today after school. I stopped trusting my judgment when I spent twenty minutes drafting an email to Bronte, begging her to please tell me what I did to make her angry, and to please have mercy on me and look at the attached proposal.

Fortunately I caught myself before I sent it. I didn't even shut out of email, just closed my laptop and crawled into bed.

Coach Taylor tucks his pencil into his clipboard and smiles at me. "Just wanted to congratulate you on the write-up in the paper. I know what a huge accomplishment that is because I tried for years to get my novel published."

AFW churns the newsletter out three days after the conference? Why haven't I received mine yet? "You're an AFW member?"

Coach Taylor blinks a few times. "No. I'm talking about in the *Times Delta*. The write-up. Didn't you see it?"

I shake my head. The *Visalia Times Delta*? But how did . . . ?

It comes back in a rush—stating the name of my newspaper when I registered for the contest, Betsy Ann's comment about being featured in her local paper, sitting for coffee with Angela Sunday morning. I had just assumed it was for the AFW newsletter.

"Here. I brought my copy, thinking you might want an extra or two." Coach Taylor grins and hands the folded paper to me.

TEENAGE DAUGHTER OF LOCAL AUTHOR STU SWEET WINS PRESTIGIOUS WRITING CONTEST

No.

I skim the article, fear squeezing my heart with every word. Yes, this is definitely a piece put together by Angela. It has everything we talked about—my age, the inspiration for the title, the typewriter key charm my parents gave me. There's even a quote from Abbie about how excited she is about my project and what a great addition she thinks *Invisibly Yours* could be at Blue Door.

But there's nothing so specific to get me in trouble, nothing like—

There it is. The back cover copy I submitted when I entered the contest.

" . . . the story of Lady Gabrielle Moretti, who has been supernaturally gifted with an ability to know and tell the truth. Set in Italy circa 1410, Gabrielle is a member of the court and has been marked as the prince's favorite. But Ladies Lucia, Bianca, and Maria . . ."

As the words whirl around my head, I close my eyes.

I am so dead.

Many of the girls are dressed and leaving the locker room as I charge through the door, the newspaper secured under my arm. Maybe this isn't as big of a deal as I think it is. I mean, this is the first I've heard about it, so Bianca and Marie must not know. They would break their pact of silence for *this*, right?

But what are the odds that they'll see this, really? Hardly anyone takes the paper anymore. Other than my family. And my grandparents. And Coach Taylor, apparently.

I yank my gym shirt, sticky with sweat from stupid basketball drills, over my head and reach to open my locker.

The unhinged padlock hangs ominously crooked.

I open the door and instantly close my eyes. Yep, it's all gone. My clothes, my backpack, my flip-flops.

Instead I'm looking at the article Mr. Taylor just showed me. Scribbled over the photograph of me accepting my award, in red Sharpie, are the words ENJOY THE SWIM.

I've never actually strolled the banks of Mill Creek, though I've seen a few others do so during my years as a Redwood Ranger. Until now, the creek has always seemed like a charming twist on our campus. But as I scour the water for my clothes and backpack, I don't feel quite as enchanted.

And even though walking around campus in my sweaty gym clothes doesn't *feel* like a lucky turn of events, I'm counting my blessings that my backpack holds only homework. My ringing cell phone was confiscated this morning in Spanish, and I left my laptop with the librarian, knowing I would be back for lunch.

"Oh, there she is. The *writer*." The cold edge of Bianca's voice makes me shiver.

I look up from the creek bed. Bianca stands about twenty feet ahead of me, up on a footbridge over the creek. I've often thought of Bianca as being classically beautiful, with her blond waves and blue eyes. At the moment, it's hard to see past the scowl on her face.

She's flanked by Marie, who looks vicious as well, and Palmer, who grips the high, chain-link fence with white knuckles. His face blanches as I look at him. Diego and Troy linger too, but they only seem semi-interested.

"Where's Rafe when you really need him, huh, *Lady Gabrielle*?" Marie cackles at her own joke.

I grit my teeth as one of my sneakers sinks into the mud. I'm not going to engage in conversation. I'll just find my stuff and drive home.

"Talk about the thinnest veil I've ever seen." Bianca's nose is in the air. "How's your little crush on my boyfriend going, Ellie?"

I glance at her boyfriend, who looks away. How could I have ever conceived of Palmer being white knight material? No person of character would hold his tongue at a moment like this. Did he help take my clothes? Help plant them in the muckiest spot he could find?

My blurred eyes make me stumble in the reedy grass, and the laughter from above feels harder to shrug off. Where's Chase when I need him? Despite our rift, he'd eviscerate them, I know it.

"You always thought you were so much better than me and Bianca," Marie snarls. "You thought it made you special to be Lucy's best friend, but really it just made her stupid."

I blink up at Marie, at the anger distorting her features. "I've never thought that."

"Haven't you?" Bianca says. "Isn't that why you wrote the book?"

I catch a flash of red in the water. Karen's sweater.

"I wish *my* dad were a published author." Troy's lazy voice floats down to me. "Then maybe *I'd* get me a book deal."

"Your dad's the principal, and you can barely pass your classes." I bend to untie my already muddy sneakers. "Somehow I don't think he could wrangle a book deal for you."

Troy scowls and flips me the bird.

I shoot a glare at Palmer, who's still looking miserable and cowardly.

"D'you see the look she gave you?" Bianca laughs and turns her voice high and breathy. "Oh, Rafe, come save me!"

Palmer mutters something to her that I can't make out.

No matter. I pull off my socks and stand, brushing grass off my butt. Mud squishes between my toes.

Up on the footbridge, Bianca makes a production of unfolding something that looks eerily like the *Times Delta*. Apparently they didn't put their only copy in my gym locker.

She clears her throat. "*Invisibly Yours* is the story of Lady Gabrielle Moretti, who has been supernaturally gifted with an ability to know and tell the truth." Her high, mocking tone and Marie's giggles set my face ablaze. "Set in Italy circa fourteen ten, Gabrielle is a member of the court and has been marked as the prince's favorite." A bark of laughter comes from Marie on this one. "But Ladies Lucia, Bianca, and Maria—" Marie bows to mock applause from Diego and Troy. "—are bent on winning the crown for themselves and set out to sabotage Gabrielle. While they're no match for her, Gabrielle is blindsided by a newcomer, Rafe."

Diego and Troy give Palmer good-humored shoves, and in my peripherals I see Bianca plant a kiss on his cheek. I resist the temptation to look and instead keep my focus locked on the middle of the creek, where they appear to have sunk my clothes and backpack with rocks.

"He's far below her social status—" Bianca pauses to smack her own knee with laughter. I hoist my backpack from the mud, feeling swampy water splatter on my legs. "But Gabrielle can't help but be intrigued. While the two fall in love, Gabrielle knows her future is marriage to the prince."

My backpack feels heavier than it did when I carried it to the locker room. Perhaps it's just the water and the mud. Or maybe . . .

I yank open the zipper. On the bridge, they're laughing and guffawing, and my world spins as I watch them.

"Her heart she's already given to Rafe, but to whom will she give her hand?" Bianca, with her one-woman show behind her, looks down at me and smirks. "Oh, yeah. I told Ms. Hatfield you had to go home sick. She thought it was so sweet of me to come pick up your laptop."

I'm vaguely aware that I'm sitting in the mud, that the water is up to my chest. How could I have been so stupid to not save a back-up of my book proposal on a thumb drive? I had been so focused on getting it done that I hadn't bothered with details like saving a copy elsewhere. I hadn't imagined I'd need it.

Tears pulse behind my eyes. I'm sitting in the creek in my gym clothes, with a ruined backpack and computer, being laughed at by two girls who used to be my best friends, who I thought would always be there. I'm too tired, too heartbroken, too humiliated to push the tears away.

I drag myself up from the bed of the creek. My muddy clothes suction to my body and my fingers fumble with the zipper of the small pocket on my backpack, where I keep my car keys.

"Oh, Ellie. There's one thing we didn't throw in there."

I squeeze my eyes shut. Oh, gosh, my phone. They have my phone.

But when I turn, I find Bianca dangling my car keys—my quick escape—over the creek.

"Bianca." For the first time, Palmer's voice is clear enough for me to hear. "What are you possibly going to do with her car keys?"

Bianca shrugs, but his chastising tone seems to have unsteadied her. "I don't know. Why?"

"I just . . . I don't think you should." Palmer's hands are in his curls, tugging. "Let's just give Ellie her keys before a teacher comes along and sees us."

Bianca blinks rapidly, like she does when she's furious. "She wrote *you* into her stupid book too. Don't you care about that?"

Palmer glances at me, then returns his gaze to Bianca. "Maybe Rafe isn't me. Maybe he's Chase."

"No, *you* are Rafe. And it's disgusting. And you can't let her get away with it."

Palmer studies Bianca for a moment, then takes the keys from Bianca's hand. He looks at them in his palm, as if weighing them. "Actually, I don't find it disgusting at all." Palmer's gaze pierces me. "Because Ellie used to be my girlfriend."

I don't think I've ever been more aware of how I look than at this moment. With all their eyes on me, I acutely feel the mud caked on my feet, the splatters on my glasses, the tear tracks on my cheeks, my gym shorts plastered to my skinny legs, and how my knot of hair has come loose in a fuzzy, lumpy mess.

I can't seem to look away from Palmer, who watches me with . . . with . . . what is that expression on his face, exactly? Pity? Heartbreak?

"What you said in the darkroom was true. About Port of Subs." Palmer steps away from the group, toward the sidewalk that parallels the creek.

"Palmer?" Panic edges Bianca's voice.

If he hears her, he shows no signs. He keeps his gaze on me, his footsteps moving my direction. "And you were right about why I didn't want to tell people, and that I thought . . . I thought . . ." Palmer swallows hard. "I thought I would just be able to get over you."

He stands only a few feet from me now, though we're still separated by the chain-link fence. "Ever since October, when we had that moment by your car, I've been afraid of you."

"Afraid of me?" The idea would always seem ridiculous, but it's especially hard to believe when I'm up to my ankles in mud.

"I was so scared to tell you I liked you that I couldn't even say it. Finally, I drew the heart in my script and asked you to read lines with me." He kicks at a pebble. "Lame."

I chew on my lower lip, which tastes of Mill Creek mud. "I just don't understand. Didn't you know I liked you? What'd you think was going to happen?"

He hooks a hand on the fence and says in a low voice. "I can't control you. I can't even predict you most the time. And that's terrifying." Palmer's gaze hangs on me for a moment, then he stretches a hand over the fence. "C'mon. I'll help you over."

Ever mindful of our audience on the bridge, I hand him my dripping backpack and clothes before I climb over the fence. Palmer reaches to steady me.

"Don't. I'll get you muddy."

He grabs hold of my waist. "I don't care, Gabrielle." When I turn and face him, he pushes a strand of dripping hair off my cheek. "I'm sorry about all this. Please believe me—I had no idea they were doing it."

"I believe you."

Palmer's mouth quirks into a slight smile, and he drops my car keys into my open hand. "Your quick escape, m'lady. Let me help you to your car."

I stare at the keys, considering, and exhale through my nose. "You know . . . I think I'll pay a visit to the school office before I go home and change."

His mouth curls into a full smile now. "Why don't I come with you?" In one hand, he takes my soggy backpack, in the other my sweaty gym shoes.

As we walk away from the creek, toward the front office, I try not to look, but I can't help it. The guys wear expressions of confusion, but Bianca and Marie practically glow red with anger.

"Somehow I don't think this is the end with them." I try to sound flippant, but a shudder of fear courses through me as I consider the possibilities.

Palmer looks past me, to our old group. "It'll keep things interesting." Then he hangs an arm around my shoulder as we head for the school office. Which, at the moment, feels like riding into the proverbial sunset.

Chapter 33

When my doorbell rings that afternoon, Harper is the last person I expect to find on the other side. I didn't even know she knew where I lived.

Her hair, usually styled straight and sleek, hangs in careless, fluffy waves. Without her typical getup of mascara, liquid liner, and frosty shadow, her eyes seem small and tired.

"I heard what happened. You okay?" She looks me up and down, as if examining for mud.

"Yep, I'm fine. My stuff isn't so great, but of course neither are Bianca, Marie, Troy, or Diego's school records at the moment, so that kinda makes it worth it."

Palmer and I had been at the office for over two hours while the parents were all called and the mess got sorted out. To the credit of Principal Lewis, he showed no hesitation in suspending his son and the others.

But Harper's smile at the news of justice seems weak.

I lean against the doorway. "Are *you* okay? Why'd you drop by?"

Harper jams her hands into the pocket of her oversized hoodie. "Figured you'd just hang up if I called."

"Why? I'm not mad at you, Harper."

"Well." She blows strings of bangs from her eyes. "That makes one, then. Everybody else hates me. Because of what I did with Chase."

My stomach squirms with the mention. "They don't all hate you."

"Yeah they do. Even Chase."

"Why would Chase hate you? He's just as much to blame."

"Him and Jose have said their fill and smacked each other around, so now they're cool." She sags against the post on my patio. "Now it's just me everyone has a problem with."

Well, that explains Chase's shiner. "I don't get guys."

"Me neither." Her gaze, which had been jumping all over, steadies on me. "You're really not mad?"

I shake my head.

Tears brim her eyes, and she wipes her nose with the sleeve of her sweatshirt. "I'm sorry anyhow. Official or not, Chase was yours."

I sigh. "Chase is his and nobody else's."

"You know what I mean. His heart is yours. I don't know how you've withstood him all these months. He turned those big, beautiful eyes on me, and I was doomed."

Okay, that was a definite twinge of jealousy. More like a stab, really.

I fuss with the hem of my T-shirt. "It's never really been that way with me and Chase."

Harper's forehead pinches with a frown. "What do you mean, 'that way'?"

"I mean, like he's never tried to . . . woo me."

"Woo?"

"I knew he liked me, but he never tried to win me over, really."

Harper's laugh is hoarse, as if she's out of practice. "Typical. Flirt with the girl who doesn't matter"—she jabs at herself—"and not with the girl who does."

"You matter. What Chase did was wrong."

"There were two of us there, Ellie. Don't blame him just because you're hurting."

"I'm not hurting." Ugh. I've *got* to work on that honesty thing. "Or I am, but . . . he's not my boyfriend."

Harper shrugs. "A formality."

"Well, an important one. If he'd actually cheated, that'd be one thing."

Harper's quiet for a moment. "I heard about the article in the paper. I think it's really great. And I wasn't surprised at all. You're so smart."

I scrunch my damp curls with one hand. "If I were really smart, I would have backed up my hard drive *before* it went for a dip in Mill."

Lines form on Harper's forehead. "Did you lose your book?"

"No, just my book proposal. But I was hoping to have it to this editor by the end of the week in case she has changes she wants me to make. And I was really close." My stomach lurches with disgust. It would have taken me maybe ten seconds to save the file on a thumb drive. How basic is that?

"Well, that sucks." And Harper really sounds like she means it.

"The computer was off when they threw it in, so there's a chance that after it dries out, it might still work." I shrug. "I have it on rice, anyway. I'll still need to redo the proposal, but at least there's a chance I'll get my computer back. What's really maddening is that normally I would've sent it to my friend Bronte, but . . ."

A fuzzy memory floats through my thoughts. That 1 a.m. desperate plea I drafted to Bronte. "But did I attach it? If I attached it, it'd be in my email, right?"

"What?" Harper follows me down the hall to where my brother's old computer, the one Mom and Dad replaced when he graduated, sits in its bulky, dead-battery state.

Five minutes later, full of cord-hunting, pacing, and cursing myself for forgetting to retrieve my phone from Señora Lopez's desk, where I could have checked in about fifteen seconds, my email pulls up.

I actually scream when I see the attachment. I whoop and cheer and Harper throws an arm around my shoulders and whoops and cheers as well.

Which is how my dad finds us when he comes home from work moments later.

After changing into pajamas, I seek out Mom and Dad in the living room. Dad's on the couch, notepad on his lap, sketching. Somebody else illustrates for *James*, but Dad's always said that drawing scenes helps him get the creative juices going. At dinner tonight, Dad said I've been a real inspiration to him, that he's had a "batch" of new ideas bouncing around his head.

Maybe cow-James will get himself a baby sister sometime soon. I wave from the hall. "Good night, guys."

Mom pauses her crossword puzzle and holds out a hand to me, beckoning me closer. "Oh, honey, I'm sure proud of you. You handled yourself real well at school today."

A mix of pleasure and discomfort tangles in my stomach. Falling short of the mark, I'm used to. Approval will take some adjustment. "Thanks again for asking Harper to stay for dinner."

"Sure. I'm glad she could join us."

"Yeah, me too."

"So, Harper. She's a . . . new friend?"

"Kinda. We've known each other since December."

"I see. How'd you meet?"

Chase's handsome face fills my mind. I really want to call and talk to him about today. "Just . . . you know. Through school. Mutual friends."

"She seems . . ." Mom ticks her head from side to side. "Different than your other friends. Which, given what your other friends turned out like, is probably a very good thing."

I grin. "Well said."

"And having friends from different walks of life is a plus, I think."

"Harper had a rough upbringing. Her dad left when she was little." Why am I justifying who Harper is?

"Poor girl." Mom smoothes her crossword puzzle on her lap. "I'm glad you're friends with her. She needs a good influence."

Why do I keep getting pushed into that role? I just want to be Harper's friend. I don't want to need her to change.

"Good night," I say again, then return to my room, where James's computer wheezes on my desk.

After verifying that there's no email from Betsy Ann—she agreed to proofread my proposal for me and offer suggestions—I shut it down. As long as I turn it in to Abbie by Friday so I can enjoy my weekend with Karen, I'll be fine.

Out of habit, I reach for my nightstand to turn off my phone, only to be reminded yet again that it's in Señora Lopez's desk. Has Chase tried calling me tonight? I'm sure he's heard what happened. Half the school probably heard Bianca's father chewing her out, informing her that she would be replacing everything of mine that she ruined.

How did she think she'd get away with it? Or did she think I would do nothing, just play the victim? If so, she should have considered that I was the girl who didn't just get mad, but who wrote a novel.

I'm sure Chase hears me calling after him, so why isn't he stopping?

Finally, right before the bridge to Vista, I grab him by the arm. "Hey, are you, deaf? I've been calling for you."

Chase pulls out of my grip under the pretense of adjusting his backpack. "What's up?" His gaze darts from his shoes, to the water tower, to the hazy sky. Basically anywhere that isn't me.

"Did I do something to make you mad?"

"Nope."

"Because you're acting mad."

"I'm not."

Anger thrums in my chest. "Well, I'm a bit peeved, to be honest. You're not even going to ask me about yesterday?"

Something in Chase's armor breaks and his dimples deepen. "I can't believe you just said peeved, Ellie Jane. My *grandmother* says peeved."

His grin evaporates just before I hear a chipper, "Hey!" behind me.

Palmer.

I turn and find Palmer sauntering toward us, looking preppy and perfect as always. "Thought we could walk to Photography together." Before I can answer, Palmer nods at Chase, still smiling. "Hey, man."

Chase pivots on his heel and mounts the steps two at a time.

"Chase, wait! We'll walk with you."

But he doesn't even slow.

Palmer watches Chase's retreating figure as well. "I'm sorry. I didn't think he'd be thrilled to see me, but I also didn't think he'd just leave."

"It's not your fault. If he would open his stubborn mouth and talk to me, then maybe we could actually work it out. I don't know what he's mad about this time."

"Haven't you figured out by now that guys will do anything to avoid having to talk?" Palmer makes a swooping gesture with his arm, indicating I should go up the stairs first.

We hoof it over the bridge before continuing our conversation.

"There's all kinds of crazy rumors flying around about yesterday." Palmer huffs out. "Who knows what he heard?"

"Well, he could get some facts from me if he'd just *listen* for two seconds."

But Chase seems to have no interest in listening to me. He doesn't wait for me after Photography, he's quick to partner with someone else during Spanish, and he ducks in and out of classes so quickly, I can't get out anything beyond, "Chase, wait!" before he vanishes.

Karen takes a long drag of her lemonade, then tips her head toward me. "I think it's obvious she's jealous."

I draw my knees up to my chest and stare at my reflection in Karen's movie star-esque sunglasses. "Really?"

"Definitely. Bronte liked being your mentor, but now you've rapidly and unexpectedly moved to a new place. A place where you don't need her as much."

"But that's not true at all! There's still so much I don't know, so much I need her for. And I know it was unexpected, but I still thought she'd be happy for me."

"Maybe she is. It's not like emotions are always cut and dry, you know? She could be happy for you, but also jealous that it's happening so quickly and paranoid that you'll be more successful. She doesn't have to be just one thing. Take me for example." Karen rattles the ice in her cup. "I'm very excited for you, yet also kinda hurt that you never told me about your interest in writing."

The sun's rays, which had felt warm and inviting, now feel hot with accusation. I fuss my damp curls off my neck. "I know, I'm sorry."

She takes another drink of lemonade. "I thought you told me everything, Ellie. And then to learn something this huge . . . I don't know. Makes me wonder what else I don't know."

And why *had* I never told her about it? Years of experience indicated she would have been supportive and encouraging, that she wouldn't have pushed me for details I wasn't ready to share.

"I don't know why I didn't tell you." I wrap my arms tight around my knees and stare at my childhood handprint pressed into the hot concrete of our back patio. "It's hard for me to share things with people."

Karen glances over her shoulder, through the sliding glass door where we can see Mom mixing up more lemonade. "Ally's the same way. She'll talk forever about your dad and James and you, but heaven forbid she share a piece of herself. It's why she's never had good friends."

I frown at this assessment. You know . . . that's true. My mom doesn't have friends, really. She has people she talks to at work and church, but she doesn't go out with "the girls" for lunch or anything. Even when Jan lived here, they rarely did much more than chat at the mailbox or plant spring bulbs.

This no-friends thing of mine was supposed to be a phase, a miserable part of my adolescence. What if it's forever?

I glance at my mom, then back to Karen. "But is it so wrong that it's hard for me to share stuff? It's just who I am."

"Well, it depends on why it's hard. Why didn't you want to tell me about your writing?"

I bite my lip. "I don't know. Because it was new, and I didn't really know yet what I was doing. Or how it was going to go."

"You were worried about your image."

"No. Just about . . . I don't know." I poke at my ice with my straw. "Not about my image per se, just about how awkward it could be if I decided writing wasn't for me after all. Or if I tried, but it went nowhere."

Karen snorts a laugh. "Sweetie, I'm not the writer in the room, but all those excuses sounded like a euphemism for 'I was worried about my image.'" She gulps the last of her drink. "I've got many more years under my belt than you, so listen up because this is some darn good advice. Do you know what worrying about your image, worrying about what everybody's saying and thinking will get you?"

I get the feeling her question is rhetorical, but I shake my head anyway.

"It'll get you stuck." Karen pushes her sunglasses up on her head and makes intense eye contact. "You'll wake up one day and find you're almost forty, and you haven't done any of the things you wanted. That you let in so many voices when you were trying to make decisions, instead of listening to the One voice that mattered, that you never decided anything at all. That the only guy you ever loved got away because you were too scared, and because your mom disapproved. That you never *did* figure out what you wanted to be when you grew up. That you never left home, because what would people say if it didn't work out?"

Karen pulls her shades back down over her eyes and tips her face toward the sun. "Shake off your image issues as soon as you can, Ellie-girl. You can't control what people are going to say, and paying too much attention to it can cost you your dreams."

The slide of the glass door prevents me from responding. Of course with how my head spins from Karen's warning, I wouldn't know where to begin.

"Now that is one good looking guy."

I look up from my burrito to see Harper eyeing Palmer. He's at Taco Bell too, in line with Brad Carver. Will that be his new group? The theater people? "Yeah, not bad."

"What's going on with the two of you?" Harper pops a chip in her mouth. "It's all over school, you know. That you guys had some kind of secret relationship. That he wants to be together."

I shrug. "That's just a rumor. We're friends, but too much has happened for us to be more."

On the table, my phone buzzes with a new email. Breath whooshes from my lungs when I see it's from Abbie Ross.

Gabrielle,
Thanks for sending this so quickly! I'll look it over and get back to you if I think it needs additions or if I have questions. Can't wait to take it to committee!
—A

I hadn't realized how knotted my neck muscles were until they loosen. Rather than read it to Harper, I hand her my phone. "At least I know she got it."

Harper reads it, then hands my phone back to me. "What does she mean by committee?"

"Abbie has to get approval from other people at the publishing house, like the other editors, marketing people, sales people, money people, you get the idea. They talk about if they think it's a good idea to publish me, and if they think they can make money. If they say yes, I get published. If they don't . . . I don't." I shrug, like there aren't butterflies crashing all over my chest.

"They'll say yes."

I tear at my tortilla, now too nervous to eat. "We don't know that."

"But look how excited this editor is about you! That says something, Ellie."

"The committee's job is to find reasons to say no. That can't be discounted."

I think of Bronte's mantra as I plodded through edits—*don't give them a reason to say no.*

The absence of her has started to feel less like a hole and more like a weight. She was the first to believe in me, and her belief pushed me through my fears of putting myself out there. Of accepting rejection. Well, "accepting" is an overstatement. She taught me that rejection didn't define me.

"I saw Jose with what's-her-face." Harper uses her straw to stab at the ice in her soda. So far she hasn't touched her tostada.

"Bet that was fun."

"Oh, a blast. She gave me a look like I'm a child of Satan." Harper pushes her drink away. "I don't know why this is so hard for me. I knew this was how Jose operated. I came along a couple weeks after Britney. And she came along a week after whoever was before her. I knew he'd move on fast."

"Still. No one likes to be gotten over quickly."

"I notice Chase isn't seeing anyone." She gives me a pointed look.

I shrug.

"Oh, whatever. I know you like him."

I take a deep breath as I think about my conversation with Karen over the weekend. About my image issues. "You're right. I do."

Harper's jaw flops open. "I can't believe you just admitted that. I thought you'd take your crush to the grave."

My attempts to smile fall flat. "Chase already knows. No point in keeping it from you."

"Chase *knows*?"

"Yep."

"You told him?"

"Yep."

"And he's not dancing on the rooftops *why*?"

I wind my discarded straw wrapper around my finger, then unwind it. "Because we're very different people, and I think we both know our differences would eventually pose a problem."

Harper throws her hands in the air. "Who cares? Chase is crazy about you. I mean, I would venture to say he loves you, Ellie. I'm sure he's willing to work at it."

I tear at my tortilla some more. "Are you? Because he hasn't talked to me since last Wednesday."

Harper blows a raspberry. "That's because he thinks things are back on with you and Palmer."

"Well, if he would let me talk to him, I could easily tell him that's not true."

Her thin eyebrows arch. "And then would you somehow explain to him about Rafe too?"

I open my mouth, then snap it shut. Then open it again. "I can't change that I used to like Palmer. Or that I wrote him as the hero in my novel. But I also can't change that I like Chase. So where does that leave me?"

Harper considers a moment. She shrugs.

"Exactly," I mutter.

❀❀❀

Once again, Palmer and I find ourselves in the darkroom together.

I traded my next-week time slot with Chris, who still needed to take shots for the assignment. I had thought it'd be a win-win. I could finish my next assignment early, and I wouldn't have to spend awkward time alone with Palmer in the darkroom.

What I didn't expect was that Chris's darkroom partner, Patrick, apparently also asked to switch. With Palmer.

At least things are basically settled between me and Palmer. We have both acknowledged we made a mistake by dating, we've let go of hard feelings, and I'm sure he's as ready to move on with his life as I am with mine.

Still, an amiable yet awkward relationship is not ideal for the darkroom. If I buckle down, I can hopefully leave early.

There's a distinct *psh-psh* as the darkroom door revolves. Is Palmer leaving?

"Ellie?"

My heart seems to pause, then gallop. "Chase?" As if I could mistake his voice and silhouette.

"Why did you tell Harper you like me?"

Ooookay. I *really* don't want to have this conversation here and now. "Um, could we have this conversation later? Like when we're alone?"

"Hi Chase." Palmer sounds chipper, but . . . edgy somehow.

Chase's laugh is dry. "Figures."

"Go ahead and have your conversation, Gabrielle. No reason why you can't talk in front of me."

"Yeah, I can't think of any reason not to," Chase says. "You're not her boyfriend anymore or anything."

I set aside the negatives I've been working with. "Regardless, I'd like some privacy. Why don't we—"

"Just my two cents, but I think you'd be a darn cute couple." Palmer's drawl is thick with sarcasm. "Why, I remember that night you drank too much at Stacey's party. Remember, when you were depressed because you realized Gabrielle still had a thing for me? The whole time she and I were haulin' you out of there, I thought wouldn't it be sweet if these two wound up together?"

Chase snorts. "I notice she's over you now. Apparently just dating you does the trick."

I clear my throat. "So did you come to talk to me or Palmer? Because—"

"And I notice once Gabrielle and I broke up, things started workin' out real well for you two. Oh wait, I'm thinking about you and your best friend's girl."

I rush to set down my supplies so I can get Chase out of here. "Speaking of Harper, weren't you saying something about her when—"

"Yeah, because you would never cheat like that, would you Palmer? Certainly not if you already had a girlfriend."

"Okay, you two—"

"Gabrielle cheated first."

I whirl to face him. "I, *what?*"

Palmer's voice is sharp, and in the faint amber light, I make out the angry jut of his chin. "You kissed him, didn't you?"

"But it's not like I instigated the kiss with Chase. Nor could I simply say to him, 'I can't, I have a boyfriend.'"

Chase releases a wry laugh. "You were together then? That's hilarious."

"You're a smart girl. You could've gotten out of it." Palmer turns his back to me.

Chase is still chuckling. "Maybe she didn't want to."

I've *got* to put a stop to this conversation. "Maybe 'she' would rather not talk about it with you guys. Chase, if you want to talk, let's step outside. If not, I've got work to do."

"Fine."

Chase goes through the revolving door first.

The morning fog hasn't yet lifted, but I still squint in the light. "You couldn't have figured out *before* you started talking that I wasn't alone in there?"

"I wasn't thinking very clearly. I haven't been since Harper practically attacked me in the Quad this morning about me not 'making a move' on you." He fixes me with a hard look. "Why'd you tell her you like me?"

I look beyond him. "What does it matter?"

"It matters to me."

"She kinda called me on it. And I didn't see any point in denying it when you already know."

He studies my face for a second. "And when you've already decided it won't work out."

"We both decided that. So, yeah. Makes the whole thing a moot point."

"Not to me it doesn't." He paces the width of the sidewalk. "Just . . . what am I supposed to do with this now?"

"What do you mean?"

"You like me. I thought it was impossible, and now . . ." His gaze holds mine. "What if . . . I stop partying and stuff? I could do that. And maybe I could try coming to church with you or something. We could see how the church thing goes."

"I can't be your reason, Chase. That's too much pressure."

Chase jeers at the darkroom door with his thumb. "He doesn't exactly seem like Mr. Choir Boy to me."

"I'm not asking for that. And I'm not asking you to be perfect or to accept my faith blindly. All I'm saying is that it's an issue we can't ignore."

He holds my gaze again. "If I came to church a couple times, if I gave this a try, would you be willing to go on a date? A real one. Where I pick you up at your house and everything."

I knead my lower lip between my teeth. "I don't know that you'll like my church very much. Most Sundays I'm not even sure *I* like it."

"Just let me try."

I imagine the horror that will fill Grandmom's face if she sees Chase Cervantes sitting next to me at church.

I might enjoy that, actually. "Okay."

"Okay . . . ?" Chase's chest rises with a deep inhale. "Like, we'll give this a shot?"

My head clogs with arguments against this. I don't know how my parents will react. Or how I'll deal with learning all those yucky parts of his past—the girls, in particular. And will his mom ever like me again, or am I forever a "trash girl" in her mind?

But I think of Palmer and the way he hid me, the way it scarred my heart. And of Karen's lecture about letting too many voices in, of getting stuck. Of how the only guy she ever loved got away because she was too scared.

I've spent a long time being afraid. Being stuck.

I bite my lip, heart wrenching as I consider the odds of Chase and I ending any way but heartache. "Yes. Let's give it a shot."

I've never seen Chase's smile so big, his dimples so deep.

Oh man, am I ever in trouble.

I feel a dopey smile stretching my face too, and look away. "I've got to get back in there."

Chase glances at the door, then back at me. "No way you can skip?"

"Not without forfeiting my A in Photography."

"Is that so important to you?" His eyes plead with me.

"Nothing's going to happen. He'll make a few snide comments, and in twenty minutes I'll be out of there."

Another glance at the door. "How often are you guys in there together?"

"Rarely. We usually trade so we're *not* together. Apparently today, we wound up trading with people who are also partners."

Chase runs a hand through his hair. "I'm not even gonna ask why Palmer Davis is your darkroom partner."

I consider explaining, but decide against it. "Yeah. Good call."

He smiles at me, warm and familiar. "See you at the bridge." He gives my arm a squeeze and strolls away.

Heading back in, I brace myself for a slew of comments from Palmer. He's probably been cooking up one-liners this whole time. Well, I'll take the high road. Hard for him to spar with me if I won't engage.

Palmer's at the developer when I enter. He's quiet.

Hmm.

I give my eyes a minute to adjust, then return to what I was doing before Chase barged in.

After about five minutes of silence, I relax. Looks like I won't even have to take the high road, because, for once, Palmer's going to keep his mouth shut. What a perfect time for him to start.

The bell sounds as I hang up my photo for drying. Even with the interruption, I still managed to get both pictures developed.

Beside me, Palmer gathers his binder. "See you in bio."

"Yeah, see you there."

He hesitates at the door. "And just so you know, I knew what I was doing when I traded with Patrick."

By the time I piece together that this means he overheard me and Chase, Palmer's out the door.

Chapter 34

"Are you sure you don't want to invite any of your friends out to dinner with us?" Mom asks as she puts in her earrings. Mom and Dad are taking me out for a nice dinner to celebrate that I finished making all Abbie's requested changes, and I'm completely done with the proposal.

I think they're also taking me out just in case they don't get to take me out to celebrate next week. In case the committee turns it down.

"Harper or anyone?"

"No thanks. There's only one other person I'd think of asking, but . . . well . . ."

Mom's eyebrows arch, asking the silent question.

"He's a boy."

Her mouth purses, and I get the impression she's beating back a smile. "An interested editor *and* a boy? My, my, aren't you having quite the week?"

My face heats as Dad comes into the room. "Ellie's got a boy?"

"Apparently." Mom grins at me. "And I'm going to guess it's that handsome Palmer Davis who stayed right by your side at the school office that afternoon."

A nervous laugh sticks in my throat, and I end up coughing.

"I knew it!" Mom claps her hands with triumph. "I could tell by the way you two were looking at each other."

"No, it's not Palmer. He and I are just friends."

"Oh." Mom's clearly disappointed to have guessed wrong. "Well, who is it, then?"

I fiddle with my typewriter charm. "Now, let's try to keep an open mind, okay?"

Dad crosses his arms over his chest. "That's a bad way to start."

"It's"—I take a deep gulp of air—"Chase Cervantes."

They look at me blankly, and I can tell they're spinning their internal Rolodex, waiting for the name to trigger something horrible.

I pull the trigger myself. "His older brothers are Mark and Francis. The guys who robbed that convenience station."

Mom glances at Dad. "Oh, right . . ."

"We've gotten to know each other this year, and he's really not like his brothers. I mean, he's still pretty rough around the edges, but he has a good heart. He's planning on coming to church this Sunday."

They look at me with wide eyes. Mom recovers first. "Are you guys . . . dating?"

I hesitate. "No."

"Really? Because you don't sound so sure." Dad's face is hard.

"We're not dating. We like each other, but he'll have to make some serious changes in his life before anything happens."

"But you *do* like him?"

"Yeah."

Mom wrings her hands. "I don't know what to think about this."

My thumb rubs the typewriter key, as if it'll bring me good luck. "I think you'll like him if you take time to get to know him."

"I can't even express how nervous this makes me, Ellie." Dad seems to grow taller as he glowers at me. "When cute girls are in the picture, guys have a way of behaving however they need to get . . . you know."

I didn't think this conversation could be more uncomfortable, but my dad just managed to ratchet up my mortification level.

"It's not like that with Chase." I take a deep breath. "The thing is, I don't want to have to lie anymore. I want to be honest with you guys about who I am and what I'm doing and who I'm doing it with."

"And we'd love nothing more. But you've got to understand that as your parents, it's our job to guide you down the right path. We're just trying to take care of you, Ellie."

The correction slips out. "Gabrielle."

Mom blinks. "What?"

"I prefer to be called Gabrielle. Whether I look right or not." The steel in my last sentence is unmistakable.

Worry lines form on Mom's forehead. "Who says you don't look right?"

"You."

"I did? When?"

"You always tell people that. You talk about how you wanted a daughter named Gabrielle, but when I came out, I looked all wrong so you called me Ellie instead."

"Oh, honey." Mom laughs like this is some petty issue. "Gabrielle is a rather elegant name for a bald, seven-pound baby. We decided to call you Ellie until you grew into Gabrielle, but then . . ." Mom shrugs. "It was a habit. It seemed weird to switch. Same as if I decided you should start calling me 'Mother' all the time."

This is completely messing with mind. "So, it was a misunderstanding?"

"Apparently."

"Oh."

All my life I've believed that I fell short the moment I popped onto the planet, that I'd been born subpar. How thoroughly have those beliefs colored my choices, my mistakes? Is it why I hung out with Lucy, Bianca, and Marie long after the friendships expired? Why I clung to my pathetic relationship with Palmer? And maybe even why I kept *Invisibly Yours* to myself? So when it fell short, only I would know.

I hate thinking of all the mistakes I might have prevented if I'd just told my parents the truth long ago.

Though, had I not gone through years of putting up with Lucy and crew, I wouldn't have had nearly as much fodder for my writing.

Mom's hand falls on my shoulder. "You look dazed. What are you thinking, honey?"

"Just that I could've been Gabrielle all along. That I didn't really need permission like I thought."

Dad ruffles my curls. "Of course you don't. We love you the most when you're being yourself."

Epilogue

TWO MONTHS LATER

It's later than I normally arrive to school, but I have a good reason.

I rush through the Quad, hunting for Chase, and find him in his usual state—earbuds in, homework that should've been done yesterday balanced on his knees, and coffee waiting for me.

I push the paper in front of his face. "Tell me that's not the coolest thing you've ever seen."

Chase blinks at the image, then takes the paper from me. "You just mailed your contract back Monday. How can this have already come?"

"That's your reaction? Chase! It's my first book cover!"

"Sorry, I'm new at this. I'm just surprised by how fast they're moving."

"I've been fast-tracked, buddy." I take a gulp of coffee, though caffeine is likely a bad idea since already I can't sit still. "They've probably been holding it while my agent negotiated."

My agent. My *agent.* I just love saying that. When I had sent Emma a thank you note for meeting with me at AFW, and when I told her what had happened with Abbie, she offered representation right away. "I hated having to pass on representing you," Emma had said on the phone. "I kept thinking about it, to be honest, wondering if I'd made the right decision."

Chase holds the cover out in front of him. "I like it."

"You *like* it?"

Chase bites the inside of his cheek, studies the cover art once again, then peeks at me over the page. "I don't like it?"

"You can feel however you want, I just hoped for something more descriptive. What do you like about it?"

"This part down here." He taps his finger on my name, big and bold across the bottom.

GABRIELLE SWEET.

I admire the bold font. "It's pretty cool, isn't it?"

"The inside part is good too. That's my other favorite."

"You're reading it?" I'm filled with both dread—what if he hates it?—and warmth. Chase isn't exactly a reader. I had been surprised when he'd asked for a copy.

"Yeah. Though not quickly. Lots of big words." His smile is the embarrassed variety. Now that we're spending more time together out of school, it's easier to detect things like that.

"Thanks. It means a lot."

Chase ducks his head and takes a long drink of his coffee. "Rafe's Palmer, isn't he?"

My teeth press into my lower lip. A month ago, absolutely. But now when I'm working on scenes with Rafe, I'm seeing more and more Chase in his attitudes. "You'll just have to keep reading and see for yourself."

"Well." Chase's shoulder presses against me. "Gabrielle seems strong enough to take him."

I smile and lean in. "Yes, I believe she is."

"So, next March, huh?" He stares at the cover image again. "That's when it starts showing up in bookstores?"

"Can you believe it?" A shiver zips through me. I can't decide if I'm more scared or excited.

When I woke up this morning, there had been a slew of emails in my inbox from the publishing house. The cover had been the exciting one. The others were . . . well, scary. Surveys about what kind of industry contacts I had. What was my marketing plan? What was my local paper, and did I have any contacts there? Did I have any book signings or readings lined up yet?

When I wrote *Invisibly Yours*, I thought of publication as my destination. The ultimate goal. And now, it's like the curtain has been pulled back and I see a long, complicated road ahead of me. One that can't be skirted around, one that I must travel.

And for the most part, I can keep the panic at bay. But every once in a while, it hits me afresh—that I'm sixteen. That I don't know what I'm doing.

"You've gone silent on me." Chase's hand warms my neck. "What's going on?"

"I was thinking about the release date. And wondering if this is all a mistake."

"Why would this be a mistake?" Chase tugs my hand away from my mouth, and I realize I had been gnawing at an already-ratty nail.

"Because I don't know what I'm doing. I kinda feel like . . . I don't know. Like I just accepted a full-time job without realizing it."

Chase rolls his eyes. "What does it matter when it's your dream job? Look at this." He holds the paper in front of my face. "She has brown hair, because *you* said she should. She's wearing that red dress because *you* described it. They've read this book and they love it. That's all that matters."

Beyond Chase, I spot Palmer crossing the Quad. He waves. I wave. He keeps walking.

Palmer can't see it, but Bianca scowls at him from the oak tree where we all hung out ages ago. Now that the four of them have replaced my damaged computer, as worked out by our parents and the school, they've taken to ignoring me again. Which is fine by me. I've experienced the alternative, and I'd rather stay ignored.

Though, if I somehow find myself back on their radar, I guess that could be okay too. I have a sequel to write.

Acknowledgements

Every time I write a book, I'm struck by how impossible it would be to do this on my own. This book especially, since I had a whole crew of teen writers helping me create Ellie's story, *Invisibly Yours*. I have deep gratitude for:

Eliese Callahan and Katie Scheidhauer, who tag-teamed Rafe's name.

Kaitlyn Dalton, Mary Quinn, Courtney Calvert, Jazmine Ortiz, Leah Dymesich, Cherry Hayward, and Emii Krivan who brainstormed the concept of *Invisibly Yours*.

Cina Murray, who showed excellent insight into who Ellie was and what type of book she would be writing.

And Bex Pennefather, who had such a great idea for the book that we just couldn't figure out how to squeeze in. I hope you write it instead, Bex!

And for all the teen writers who hang out with me at GoTeenWriters.com, THANK YOU. You bring so much joy to my life.

I'm also so grateful for my husband, who's known me since I was a teen writer, and who has never failed to encourage me to write. Thank you, Ben, for not giving up on me, and for not letting me give up on my stories. I couldn't do this without you.

Thank you also to my parents, Steve and Beth Hines, and Ann and Bruce Morrill. I'm running out of fresh ways to tell you guys thank you for everything you do, but I continue to be touched by the way you give of your free time to love on my kids so I can escape to pretend worlds for a few hours.

Also, thank you to Chris and Molly Morrill, my favorite brother and sister. Thank you for the unwavering encouragement during the last couple years.

Roseanna White, I would have given up on Ellie years ago if you hadn't pushed me to keep at it. Thank you for believing in this story (in all her variations!), for insisting that we could make this work, and for reading it three times without complaint.

Leah Rutledge, how smart I was to become friends with you in kindergarten! You have gone above and beyond childhood best friend duties as you helped with all the details of life as a Redwood Ranger. Thank you for answering all my crazy questions and for reading the book in its unpolished state. What a blessing you are!

My "allies," Jill Williamson, Nicole O'Dell, Melanie Dickerson, Shellie Neumeier, and Shannon Dittemore. You ladies keep me strong. Thank you.

Thank you Laura Anderson Kurk, Laura L. Smith, Jennifer Murgia, Rajdeep Paulus, and Amanda Luedeke. I love how strong we all are together.

Wendy Chorot, thank you for lending me your editing wisdom and for making Ellie shine.

And finally, Sandra Bishop. Thank you for taking the time to understand my sensitive writer's heart, for empowering me to write the stories that matter, for pushing me to do my absolute best, and for always being on my side.

Here's a sneak peek of

The Unlikely Debut of Ellie Sweet

The sequel to *The Revised Life of Ellie Sweet*, releasing Fall 2013.

Chapter 1

I drove here specifically to buy this book, only now I've stood here for ten minutes asking myself if I should.

"Can I help you find something, miss?"

I turn to the smiling Barnes and Noble employee. "No, thank you."

She shuffles on, and I return to staring at *Fire Eyes* by Bronte Harrington. I lift the book from the shelf and run my thumb over the texture of the title, of Bronte's name. When I flip it over, Bronte smiles up at me. So different than the way she looked on that last morning of the writer's conference, when she stormed out of the hotel lobby.

Someone is behind me again. I turn, prepared to dismiss yet another employee, only to find myself staring at Lucy Shears.

"Oh." Bronte's book makes a muted *thunk* when it falls to the ground. I clutch it to my chest and grapple for a more appropriate greeting for my former best friend. "Uh, hi. What are you doing here?"

Lucy smiles in a cautious way. "I'm visiting my aunt. She's getting her hair done."

"So you came to shop for books?" The only books Lucy has ever shown an interest in are her mother's bodice-rippers.

Lucy shrugs, then nods at the book in my arms. "Is that one good?"

I glance at it. I bent the cover—great. Guess I'll be buying this one. "Yeah, it is. Real good."

Lucy pulls a copy off the shelf and examines the cover, then flips it over. Her skin is a richer tan and her hair longer, but otherwise she looks just like her old self.

I clear my throat. "Thank you for the letter you sent me. Back in the spring."

Lucy arches a well-defined brow at me. "You never responded."

"No. I've been . . . busy."

Lucy smirks, and I don't blame her for doubting me. Surely she remembers me as Ellie Sweet, the girl with no life. The girl who finished all her weekend homework on Friday nights.

"That's what I hear." Lucy shelves Bronte's book. "So I'm Lady Lucia?"

My ability for intelligent thought seems to vanish. When three silent months passed after the newspaper article came out about *Invisibly Yours* winning the Great Debut contest, I assumed the fact that I had written Lucy into my historical novel somehow hadn't reached her in SoCal.

"I . . ." My heart stammers a fierce beat.

"Relax, El. I think it's kinda cool, actually." Lucy shrugs. "I mean, how many people get to be in a book?"

But she won't think so when she reads it. My mind ticks through insulting scenes, like when Rafe calls Lucia an ice princess with a pig snout. And when Domenico refers to her as overrated, and tells Lady Gabrielle that Lucia could never be anything compared to her.

Lucy fusses with her long necklace. "Bianca seemed to take it as some sort of personal attack that you didn't make *her* the main character. But what else would you expect from her?"

"Yeah, she wasn't too pleased with me." I wrap a curly strand around my finger. For a full week after Bianca and Marie chucked my stuff in Mill Creek, I swear my hair reeked of creek water.

"You doing anything now?" Lucy pulls her phone from her back pocket and checks the time. "Want to grab coffee?"

My stomach muscles tighten. Having known Lucy all my life, I shouldn't feel so nervous about spending time together. "Sure, but . . ." I swallow. "James is down there."

"Well in *that* case . . ." Lucy makes a show of withdrawing a tube of lip gloss from her purse as we head toward the coffee bar. "Although with him around, you won't be able to give me the skinny on your boyfriends." Lucy drags the S out like a hissing snake.

My laugh sounds fake—*har har har*. "Not sure who you've been getting your info from, but—"

"Marie."

"Well, Marie doesn't know what she's talking about."

Lucy looks at me over her shoulder as we ride down the escalator. "She told me you and Chase are quasi-dating, and that she often sees you and Palmer together too."

A fairer assessment than I would have thought Marie capable of, given the way she scowls at me whenever we pass each other on campus. "Chase and I are still figuring out what dating looks like for us, and Palmer and I are just friends."

"Oh, puh-lease." Lucy rolls her big, dark eyes. "Palmer Davis doesn't know how to be 'just friends' with a girl."

I rub my thumb along the cut pages of Bronte's book, and the sound sooths me. "We haven't talked about you at all yet. How are your parents? Have you learned how to surf?"

Lucy gives me a *I know what you're up to* kind of look as she steps off the escalator. "Mom and Dad are fine, I guess. They're striving for this to be the 'healthiest divorce possible' so they have all these rules in place about not grumbling about the other to me and Caitlin, or not making us choose between them." She straightens the straps of her tank top, and the store lights glint on her rainbow-colored nails. Lucy's been bored.

As we round a bookshelf, James comes into view. He's exactly where I left him, in one of the coffee shop chairs that's intentionally uncomfortable, hunched over his fat economics textbook.

"Well, it's nice to know there are some things I can count on," Lucy says to me on a sigh. "Like James Sweet being as handsome as ever."

James must hear my snort of laughter because he looks up. Surprise registers on his face as he takes in Lucy. "I thought you were just here to get a book, El."

"That's our Ellie." Lucy links her arm through mine. "Always overachieving."

"We won't disturb you, James. We'll just grab coffee and sit—"

James closes his textbook with a loud *smack*. "No, have a seat. I could use a break."

I purse my lips to hide my grin. "I seem to recall you telling me not to come bother you for at least an hour."

James's laugh registers a touch higher than normal. "Can't you take a joke, Sis?"

Okay, it had most definitely *not* been a joke when James snarled at me that he had to study for his test, and that even if I came back to the coffee area to read, I wasn't to disturb him.

Lucy glides into the chair on one side of James. "So you're in town for the summer?"

"Yeah, how about you?" My brother crosses his arms on the table, and I'm pretty sure it's because he knows it makes him look more muscular.

"Just the week to visit my aunt. It's nice to be back."

James nods. "Isn't it? I like D.C. a lot, but it's not home."

"Exactly." Lucy beams at James as if this was some kind of profound statement. "I feel the same way about San Diego. Great city and all, just not where my heart beats for."

James draws his arms even tighter together. "What a great way to phrase it."

How nice that Lucy and I could log this quality time together.

I clear my throat. "I'm gonna get iced tea. Lucy, you want anything?"

"I'll come with you."

As Lucy and I weave through tables to the register, I glance over my shoulder. James fusses with the collar of his T-shirt, then with his hair that's too short to be mussed. Groan. Do I really have to sit here and watch my brother and childhood BFF flirt with each other? What's wrong with Lucy, anyway? Has she totally forgotten that James used to pick his nose and chase us with his boogies?

I order an iced tea, feeling a pang for my aunt Karen and the pitchers of tea we used to drink on her front porch during the summer.

The barista gestures to me. "Can I ring up that book for you as well?"

"Oh." I draw Bronte's book away from my chest. I had forgotten about it. "Yeah, sure. I thought you could only do coffee here."

"*Fire Eyes*," he reads as he scans the barcode. "Haven't heard of this one."

Do I take the opportunity to talk up Bronte? A few months ago, I definitely would have. But now . . .

"She's an author, you know." Lucy nods at me, then leans against the counter, her dark hair falling fluidly over her shoulder. "Her name's Ellie Sweet."

My face feels as though Lucy just set fire to it.

The barista arches his eyebrows, as if dubious. Probably because with my flat chest, I look like I'm about thirteen. "*You*'re an author?"

"Yeah . . ."

"Like self-published?"

"No, I'm with Blue Door." I tug at the collar of my shirt. Why's it so hot in here?

"Never heard of 'em." He rips off my receipt and hands it to me with my change.

"They do a lot of young adult books. Like for teens."

I look beyond him, to the other barista who's putting together our iced teas. Why's that taking so long?

"So, what's your book about?"

My thirty second explanation that I memorized and pitched to agents and editors just vanished. "Um, well. It's about—"

From my back pocket, my cell phone bursts into song. I've never loved the sound of Jack Johnson's voice quite so much. I leap away from the counter to answer my mom's call.

"Thank God you picked up." Traffic blares in the background, and Mom's breath comes in huffs. "Grandmom broke her hip."

I stare at a package of overpriced biscotti, trying to make sense of her words. "She broke her hip?"

"Getting out of the car, yes. I'm on my way to the hospital now."

"Oh. Should James and I meet you there?"

"There's no urgency. It'll probably be a couple days before she can have replacement surgery, and then she'll go to a rehab facility for a few weeks until she can walk. At least that's what happened when Grandpa Sweet broke his hip." Mom's ignition turns, and talk radio blares for a moment before going silent. "So there's no point in you or James coming to the hospital just yet. Tonight after dinner, a visit might be nice."

My stomach pitches with the thought. I don't know what it is about hospitals, but I always feel so awkward inside their walls. Like I'm going to laugh too loud or accidentally flip some vital, life-giving switch. "Okay."

"I'll call you when I know more."

Mom hangs up without a goodbye. I slide my phone into my back pocket, my gaze still fixed on the biscotti.

A bubble of Lucy's laughter awakens me from my trance. Lucy is back in her seat next to James, her cheeks pink and her smile wide. Both have their elbows on the table, leaning into each other. It's a good thing she lives in San Diego and he in D.C. or I might truly have to be worried about the awkwardness of them dating.

The unexpected sight of Chase's car parked outside the church building makes my heart thump faster. By now, I had assumed he'd never come. For months he's said, "Maybe this Sunday morning," or, "Maybe the next youth group event," only to no-show.

Chase climbs out of his car at the same time as me. For a moment, we just look at each other.

"You came."

Chase shrugs and squints into the late afternoon sunlight. "I like movies."

Our youth group is comprised of three members, me and twin boys from another high school who are living, breathing geek clichés. Because we vote on what to show for movie nights, my suggestion of *Sense and Sensibility* is typically beat out by something with "Star" in the title.

I nudge my door closed. "You don't really seem like a *Star Wars* guy to me."

Chase's mouth ticks with a smile. "Mysterious am I."

Indeed.

I glance at the two other cars in the parking lot. One belongs to the youth pastor, one to the twins. "Well . . . should we go in?"

Chase's nod lacks enthusiasm. "Okay."

"Okay."

I lock my car and pivot toward the church, which—I'm suddenly aware—was built in the 60s and hasn't seen much of an update since. The heat of my face intensifies as I recall bathrooms labeled "Adam" and "Eve," fliers about potlucks, and posters that read *Where Will You Go When You Die?*

"Ellie?"

I look up and find Chase watching me. Apparently I've just been standing here.

"We don't have to go in if you don't want." Chase's words come out so fast it's like they're tripping over each other. "I mean, if you want to just grab something to eat, we can."

And while that *does* sound preferable . . . "I told my parents I was coming to the movie night. And, well, that *was* our bargain. That before we started"—the word *dating* lodges in my throat, and I have to force it out—"dating, you would try."

"I remember." Chase's words are gruff. "It's why I'm here."

I look away and bite my lower lip to hold in an apology. Giving church a try was Chase's suggestion last spring, not mine. I'm not going to apologize for holding him to it.

Inside the church, we find the rest of the meager youth group in the sanctuary. Kevin, the college student who's filled in as youth pastor since my aunt moved last fall, is bent over a tangle of cords, muttering to himself. The Rushford twins have positioned themselves in the front row, along with several friends of theirs who also sport awkward haircuts and pale skin.

Chase looks around as we settle into a middle row. "So. This is church."

"Yep, this is it."

With the dark paneled walls, brown carpet, and wooden beams overhead, I've always thought the architect must have been going for a Noah's ark feel in his design. Karen says her church in Scottsdale meets in an elementary school gymnasium. My grandmother informed her that sounded rather shady.

"It's not too bad." Chase shifts a bit in his chair. "No candles, though."

I frown. "Should we have candles?"

"Ours does." He turns to meet my gaze. "Catholic."

"You are?"

"Yep."

I stare at his face, which resembles a man's more than a boy's. Chase smirks, as if he knows I'm trying to picture him shined up for Sunday mass.

"Ellie, who's your friend?" Kevin leans against a nearby chair and smiles at Chase in the welcoming way they must teach at seminary.

"This is Chase. Chase, Kevin."

Kevin sticks out a hand, and Chase pulls his from his pocket to shake it. "Glad you could join us, Chase. There's cookies and milk on the back table if you want any."

Cookies and milk—great. Like we're in preschool.

I shake it off. Who doesn't love cookies and milk? I'm not going to be embarrassed about it.

Kevin starts the movie rolling, then shuts off the lights. When the title blazes on the screen, the guys in the front row whoop as if Beyonce just strutted onto the stage.

I roll my eyes at Chase, which makes him grin. Something brushes my hand. It's Chase's fingers weaving between mine.

My blood thrums in my veins with the realization that life has changed for me. I'm no longer just, "Lucy's best friend," or, "That girl who sits in the front row." I'm carving out my own place in the world, and I get to choose what it looks like and who I'll bring with me.

Briefly—so briefly that surely it doesn't really matter—Palmer's face flashes in my mind.

I squeeze Chase's hand and tune in to the movie.

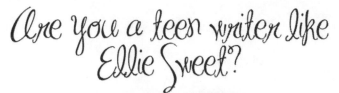

Are you a teen writer like Ellie Sweet?

Stephanie Morrill & Jill Williamson

GO TEEN WRITERS

How to turn your
first draft
into a published book

Written by popular blogging duo, Stephanie Morrill and Jill
Williamson, this book will answer questions like:

How should I deal with people who don't "get" my
writing?

What's the best way to edit my book? How do I know
when I'm done?

Do I need an agent? How do I find one?

Should I self-publish?

Available for purchase at your favorite bookstore or on-line retailer!
For free resources and a community of teen writers,
check out the blog at:

www.GoTeenWriters.com

Stephanie Morrill lives in Overland Park, Kansas with her husband and two kids. Her only talents are reading, writing, and drinking coffee, so career options were somewhat limited. Fortunately she discovered a passion for young adult novels and has been writing them ever since.

Stephanie is the author of The Reinvention of Skylar Hoyt series and *Go Teen Writers: How to Turn Your First Draft into a Published Book*. She enjoys encouraging and teaching teen writers on her blog, www.GoTeenWriters.com.